Copyright © 2019 by Robert Fleming

All rights reserved. No part of this publication may be reproduced, stored or
transmitted in any form or by any means, electronic, mechanical,
photocopying, recording, scanning, or otherwise without written permission
from the publisher. It is illegal to copy this book, post it to a website, or
distribute it by any other means without permission.

First edition

ISBN: 978-1-690-85898-0

Map of the Continent

For a detailed map of the world of The Fall of Erlon, visit
https://roberthfleming.com/home/fantasy-maps/

Prologue

Which is worse? To never know great power and absolute mastery? Or to rise to the pinnacle of the Ascended One himself before collapsing and falling back to ground in a smoldering heap?
The only man on the Continent to know that answer for certain is the Emperor of Imperial Erlon, Gerald Lannes.

Tome of the Emperor
Nelson Wellesley

Nelson

His Royal Highness, King Nelson of Brun, climbed the stairs to the main deck and walked through the sailors hustling about in the wind and spitting rain. His coat swept about him and he moved with precision over the deck as it rolled with the swells of the sea. He went to the starboard and looked out over the shadows of the early evening. The outline of their destination broke the horizon.

Taul.

The island was a cliff jutting from the sea. A fortress rose from the top of the rock and appeared carved directly from the stone by centuries of wind and rain and salt. It was a cold and desolate place, full of old legends and stories of magic within its walls. The remote island was famous and rarely visited.

And it now held the most famous prisoner in all the world.

The ship tacked around the jagged rocks that guarded the island's port. A sweeping shadow passed under the ship, and Nelson shuddered at the visions of monsters roaming the depths of the vast ocean.

The king went below and prepared. He shaved, timing the swipes of his straight razor with the rolls of the ship, and combed his hair before changing into his dress jacket. To look like he'd been sailing for weeks would be rude to the audience that awaited him.

The howling of the wind was cut off by the walls of the port, and Nelson knew they'd successfully navigated the treacherous rocks into port. He was thankful for this crew. He'd chosen well from the royal navy.

The king disembarked first. The crew would unload and bring his things up later. His legs wobbled on the solid stones after being at sea for so long. He smiled at the feeling and nodded respectfully to the sailors and guards who stood at attention by the stairs up to the fortress.

He started the long ascent and shivered under his coat in the stairwell as he climbed. It was damp and the air had a cold bite, even when protected from the wind. Taul was a Brunian territory but sat far to the country's south, and the ocean winds brought clouds and rain and cold up from the arctic lands of Kura.

The prisoner should count himself lucky. Exile was the least of the evils that could've been bestowed on him after his capture.

Though this fortress was quite the choice for a prison.

The Brunian king reached the top of the climb and was greeted by a raging fire in the fortress foyer along with a welcome guard. Nelson shuddered under his coat as the warmth floated over to him.

"Welcome, Your Highness," said the first guard. "Your quarters are this way, at the top of the keep."

More stairs. Grand.

Luckily, Nelson had an excuse to avoid them for now.

"Actually, may I presume the emperor is still awake?"

The guard frowned. "Yes, sir."

"Then I will go and see him now," Nelson said. "My men can oversee my things."

"Yes, sir." The guard gestured towards a shadowy hallway. "This way, sir. The emperor's in his study."

"Have someone make sure the crew below gets a good meal, they've earned it."

"Yes, sir," another guard said.

Nelson turned away and followed the first guard through the entrance hall and into the depths of the keep, where the ceilings were low and lit by torches. The ancient construction of this fortress had not been focused on comfort.

They reached a door and the guard turned the doorknob before bowing to the king. Nelson stepped inside and found a smoky room lined with shelves, each stuffed with books. A desk stood in front of him and held a burning lamp. Opposite the desk was a fireplace with two chairs positioned in front. On one of these chairs sat the former emperor of the entire world.

Nelson stepped forward and shut the door behind him. "Emperor Lannes."

The fire backlit the scene. Smoke from the pipe swirled about the dark figure and his head turned slightly. He reached up and removed the pipe from his mouth.

"Visitors are so few and far between here." The emperor's voice was soft, but carried the length of the room easily. A strength shown through the tone, even in simple conversation. "But when the guards told me it was you that was coming, I became intrigued indeed."

"I hope I'm not a burden or trouble."

"Not at all," Lannes said. "But if you were, would I have a say in the matter?"

"No, I guess you wouldn't."

The emperor stood and stepped forward. His features found the dim light for the first time. A strong jawline on a small head. Only the right side of his mouth turned up in the smile he gave Nelson as they shook hands. "Your Highness, it's a pleasure to meet you."

Lannes was taller than Nelson, but not as broad. His hair and eyes were dark, like most Erlonians, and his face was starting to show the wear of living through many triumphs and defeats. He was still under forty-five, not too much older than Nelson, but his skin was starting to betray more years than it owned.

"Come, sit. I hope my study is comfortable for you," Lannes said. There wasn't a bow. No royal formalities beyond the first "Your Highness."

Nelson followed the imprisoned emperor and took the chair opposite him by the fire. The firelight shone on Lannes's face as he sat, and Nelson saw even more lines of aging. The man was weathered, certainly compared to the regal portraits Nelson had seen years ago, but there was still a spark behind the former emperor's eyes. His mind remained intact despite the loss of his armies and palaces.

The emperor picked up his pipe and puffed on it. New smoke swirled up towards the ceiling. He lifted a second pipe off the table next to his chair and offered it across the gap between them.

Nelson shook his head politely.

The second pipe was set back down next to a thick book. Nelson recognized it immediately and tilted his head in surprise.

"Not religious, are we?" Lannes raised his eyebrows at Nelson's reaction to the book.

"Not particularly." Nelson regained his composure and sat up straight. He shot a grin at Lannes. "Don't tell my subjects."

"I think your secrets are safe with me and this island." Lannes's right-sided grin widened to a full smile. He reached over and brought the book up in front of him. He turned it over and looked at both sides of the thick cover. "I go back to it often. There are a lot of military maxims. Useful in my old line of work."

"I guess that's true. I've never thought of them that way." Nelson rested his chin on one of his hands. His head felt heavy and congested from the long travel. But his thoughts were coming alive. There was too much potential to learn from the man in front of him to get groggy now.

The emperor set the book back on the table and looked into the fire. The chair's back dwarfed his tall frame, making him look like a child sitting on the favorite seat of his father for the first time.

"Is your library to your satisfaction?" Nelson said.

The emperor looked around at all the books.

"Oh, yes. Your volumes are over there." He pointed over Nelson's right shoulder. "Although I've read them many times. Long before I was sent here."

"Thank you for the flattery. It was easy writing them as a prince, before the burdens of the nation were on my shoulders."

Lannes stood and walked to the other side of the desk. His boots clacked on the stones of the floor and echoed in the room. "I enjoy your history of your country's civil war the most, especially the second volume."

"A dreadful part of our history, but one that needed to be recorded." Nelson stayed seated and watched Lannes through the haze in the room.

"The interviews with your country's veteran generals were fascinating." Lannes picked out one book and opened it at random. He walked back to his own chair while flicking through the pages.

Nelson didn't respond. He watched the emperor resume his seat, close the book, and set it on top of the religious tome already on the table.

Lannes looked up at the king. "Which brings us to 'Why?'"

"Why?" Nelson raised his eyebrows.

"The reclusive scholar-king has come to visit the defeated emperor." Lannes's expression remained set. Nelson felt as if the emperor was trying to look straight through him. "Why?"

Nelson tried to keep a grin from forming on his face. Lannes certainly did cut to the chase. The king forced his voice to remain level. "To study you, naturally."

"Me?" Lannes turned his hand to point the pipe stem back at his chest. The shadows threw darkness over one side of his expression.

Nelson nodded. "You conquered the Continent, destroyed numerous dynastic families. Conquered armies and countries thought unconquerable—"

"And then lost it all."

Nelson stopped. A frank answer for a topic so heavy.

The emperor leaned back in his chair and kept his eyes on Nelson.

The king pursed his lips. "And then lost it all, yes. Fascinating material, don't you think?"

The emperor thought for a second before giving a single shrug. He glanced at the fire and back at Nelson. "You don't think it's premature?"

"Premature?"

Lannes held his hands out to either side and gave a smile. "I'm still here. There remains more story to unfold."

"Your life has stories that merit a thousand books. That's enough already, don't you think?"

"True, but there's always more to come. I could return to power, you know."

Nelson stopped again. The emperor was smiling, but the idea of Lannes returning to the Continent and reclaiming the conquering armies of Erlon sent a chill along Nelson's spine.

Lannes leaned forward. "You called me emperor when you came in, you know," he said. "I don't think your subjects would like that."

"It was the Wahrians that removed your titles, not Brun. It's semantics, but respect is given where it's due." Nelson came out of his trance and waved away the emperor's comments. He smiled, hoping it would show Lannes how ridiculous the notion of his return to power was.

Lannes sat back, the chair's back swallowing him once more. "Not much of a title without an army to lead, I suppose. Emperor of Taul is a lot less intimidating."

Nelson allowed the next silence to sit between them. He wanted the emperor to think. Behind the dark eyes the spark was moving about, working, thinking. The chill of fear that moments before had shocked Nelson turned to a thrill.

His thoughts surged. There was a rush of energy despite the late hour. His hand itched to write pages and pages of notes, and his mouth wanted to shout all the questions he had for this man all at once.

Famous historical figures often had this effect on Nelson, even after he'd ascended to his father's throne. But sitting with Lannes was different somehow. The feeling seemed stronger, and the discussion had barely even started.

Nelson now understood what the Erlonian historians had described when they said Lannes had the gift of silence.

The pipe went back to the emperor's mouth. His lips tightened on the wood before opening again. "I'm to be a subject of a book, then?"

"Yes."

A very important book, Nelson thought. *One that could save us all.*

"The Horde is farther north than it's ever been," Emperor Lannes said.

And you've fought them more than anyone, Nelson thought.

"Wahring is reforming, demanding expansion," Lannes said.

And you've defeated them.

"Morada is back to its scheming ways."

And you're the master diplomat.

"Brun is surrounded by dangerous friends, and angry enemies."

And that's why we need a strong ally. The strongest possible.

"And you want to write a book about me? The one who blew everything up?"

The king reached down and pulled a pen and paper pad out of his bag. The emperor didn't object. He stayed motionless in his chair and stared back at Nelson.

Nelson set an ink jar on the side table and looked back up. Lannes seemed larger now, as if the discussion was strengthening him. Nelson had piqued his interest. He couldn't resist Nelson's offer.

"Things aren't over. Many battles are still to come," Lannes said.

Nelson didn't respond. He dipped his pen in the ink, noted the date at the top of a clean sheet of paper, and looked up at the emperor.

Lannes nodded but spoke before Nelson could ask his first question.

"If we discuss my past, I want to discuss the present as well." The emperor pressed his hands together in front of him and leaned forward. "I want to know what's happening with the war on the Continent."

"Certainly." King Nelson set his pen down on the parchment. It made sense the emperor would be starved for information on current events. His empire collapsed, his friends fought the end of the war, and he was far away in exile. "What do you want to know?"

Emperor Lannes turned his head and looked into the fire. His eyes glistened in the firelight, a hint of sadness on an otherwise stoic face.

The emperor spoke softly, the strength of his words from earlier gone completely. He turned and looked the king in the eye. "What news of my daughter in the capital? Is she safe?"

Chapter 1

To his enemies, Emperor Lannes was demon reincarnate. To his family, a source of warmth. To battlefields, a master. And to his friends, he was nothing but loyal.

A Marshal's Memoir
Alexandre Lauriston

Elisa

Elisa Lannes, Princess of Erlon, hauled the dead stag down the road. She'd been dragging it along the dirt for most of the way. Now she bent and hoisted it up on her shoulders and staggered slightly under the weight and moved towards the farmhouse.

Sweat dripped down her forehead even with the fall chill in the afternoon air. The farmer Montholon was on the front porch of the main house when she passed.

"Quite a kill today," he said.

"Only four points, but he's heavy." Elisa dropped the beast back to the ground.

"I can see that," Mon said. "We could've come and helped, you know."

Elisa didn't answer. She wiped the sweat off her face and realized all she was doing was spreading dirt to more places on her cheeks and forehead.

Mon chuckled and took a long pull from his bottle. The man was always drinking, even this early in the morning. Elisa had sneaked a taste from the farmer's bottles when she'd first been brought to the farm. The red liquid had burned her throat on the way down and made her cough. Mon drank it like water.

"How far'd you go to bag him?"

9

"Not far," Elisa said. "Edge of the eastern field."

Mon looked at her over his bottle as if waiting to see if a better truth would appear. After a few beats, he shook his head. "East is fine. But don't go too far. And don't you run off south, even after a buck." Mon pointed off towards the forest south of the farmhouse. "Those cannon shots coming from Plancenoit aren't your father's army practicing."

She was surprised to feel the flush in her cheeks after Mon's comments. She thought she had her emotions well in check. But the mention of Plancenoit and her father had been enough to break some of her barriers.

Erlon was defeated. Elisa's family broken. Her mother gone. Her father exiled half the world away. Her home about to fall to the Kurakin Horde.

And Elisa was stuck on some worthless farm.

Mon took another pull from his bottle. Elisa stooped down and lifted the stag up on her shoulders again. The motion was more to keep her mind off the memories of her father and what was to become of the nearby capital than anything. Her muscles still screamed at her for more rest.

She almost stumbled on the last steps to the barn door. She held strong and let her mind rage with her thoughts as fuel for the final few feet.

What did Mon know of her father? What could this farmer possibly know about the Erlonian royals?

And what did he know of the army? The rumblings of those cannons attacking Elisa's home was the closest he'd ever been to a war.

Elisa knew not to go near the city. She didn't need a drunk farmer to tell her the Kurakin would be looking for her.

The barn door was open and Elisa slipped inside. All she wanted was some quiet to clean the stag in peace. She found more company in the barn instead.

"Elisa, welcome back."

Wonderful. Just wonderful.

Elisa had found three of the farmhands stacking bales of hay on the far end of the barn. These three would be even more talkative than Mon.

"That's a big one today," Artur said.

"Ah, the usual silent treatment," Louis said.

Elisa dropped the stag onto the cleaning table and set to work. The farmhands stopped their work and walked over to join her. They knew better than to ask if Elisa needed help.

"Did you go south to get him?" Gabriel said. He was the closest of the boys to her own age, but still a few years older than her. "See any of the Horde?"

Louis and Artur ran with their own thoughts without giving Elisa a chance to answer.

"This'll be a good dinner, eh?"

"She probably went north, no use risking running into a Kurakin Scythe."

"I heard their wolverines like younger girls." Louis showed off his gap-toothed smile.

"I've heard all the southern animals, soldiers included, like younger girls."

Elisa blocked them out and continued with her work. She sliced at the stag's stomach skin and peeled back the fur. She opened the kill and pulled the innards out, letting the smell fill the barn.

"I heard when they took Beauhar, they lined the women up and took them off for the soldiers to rape."

"Easy, Artur, not in front of virgin ears." Gabriel shot the other farmhand a glare.

"She's old enough."

"How old are you, Elisa, twelve?"

Elisa looked up from her work to scowl at Louis and his stupid grin.

"She's fourteen," Gabriel said. He gave a quick smile in Elisa's direction. "I heard Mon say it once."

"Old enough, see?" Artur shrugged.

"I heard they burned the Citadel of Mere to the ground just for fun." Louis sucked in a breath through the opening in the front of his teeth.

"They like fire, both in war and out."

"Their capital burns." Gabriel folded his arms across his chest. Elisa noticed the sweat glistening on the muscles of his forearms. "Half the city's been on fire for years and their kind just keep on living."

"I don't believe that."

"It's true, I heard a merchant say it in Plancenoit."

"Flames probably keep them warm that far south." Artur shrugged again.

"See? It makes sense."

"And I thought it was their beards that kept them warm."

"It's called fur, actually."

The three men had a chuckle at this last comment. Elisa disposed of the stag's innards and was working on the cuts of meat. She'd become very adept at ignoring the boys and their rambling.

A whistle sounded from outside the barn and saved her from having to block out more of their conversation.

"Off to work then," Gabriel said. "Thanks for shooting us some dinner, Elisa."

"So long," Artur said.

"Don't wander off and get captured today," Louis said.

The three men went out the front door of the barn and left her alone. Mon never made her work the fields, thankfully. The farmhands never questioned it and fully believed Elisa was the farmer's granddaughter. Elisa could've sat around and relaxed and enjoyed the indoors of the farmhouse and no one would've complained. Instead, she spent most of her time out hunting and exploring the forests north of the capital and tried to get her pent-up energy out.

Elisa needed to move. Working the fields could've helped, but she knew she could never stand spending all day with the farmhands. Gabriel was nice to her most of the time, but the other two enjoyed the sound of their own voices too much and didn't have a good thought between them. Their banter, combined with Mon taking pull after pull of his bottle from atop a till, would be too much.

As this war became worse and worse for Erlon, Elisa found a restlessness growing inside of her. It was like her gut was screaming for her to run out into the woods and never return.

When she was younger, her father had been off on campaign in the east often enough, but she'd never had this feeling before. This was different. Her father wasn't coming back this time.

Her father was in exile. Her mother had abandoned them both. Her country now collapsed around her and a barbarian army knocked on her city's gates.

Elisa set her knife down on the table. The stag was fully gutted. She drew out another blade and sliced around some strips of fat and cut out the tenderloin on the first side.

The first rumbles of cannons came in the distance. That would be the start to the day's bombardment at Plancenoit.

Elisa couldn't tell if it was Plancenoit or some other battle, but it didn't matter. She set the hunk of venison on an adjacent table and sighed. The exhaustion from the morning hunt and hauling the kill back to the farm from the south fully hit her. The rumbles of the artillery grew louder. She blocked out the sounds of her country dying and cut back into the stag.

Blood ran from the beast and pooled on the table. It dribbled off and slowly mixed with the dirt and the weeds at her feet.

Lauriston

The group of horses galloped around the corner and cut up the road between the houses. The marshal led them and willed his horse to churn up the dirt faster towards their destination as the world devolved into chaos around them.

A cannonball crashed through the house on their right. Lauriston turned in time to see another bouncing down the street. The horse behind him took the ball in the side of the neck. Blood and flecks of flesh flew through the air as the unfortunate rider tumbled forward.

"Keep moving!" Marshal Lauriston yelled to the others. The fallen aide, if he was still alive, would have to get to cover himself. The others couldn't stop to help him.

The group galloped on through the town of Notain with explosions all around them. Lauriston kept his eyes forward.

He pulled hard on the reins and turned down a side street. The column compressed and slowed behind him in the narrow pathway. More cannonballs screamed overhead. The rumble of artillery roared continuously to their south.

South. Lauriston was slowly catching up to the situation. How was the enemy on the southern flank of the town?

No time for answers yet, there was only the sound of the cannon fire and the galloping horse underneath him. He'd have answers soon enough. He just had to get to the headquarters.

The column turned around another house. To their right, houses burned and cannon craters lined the streets. Erlonian soldiers stumbled about or hid behind cover. There was no organization, no way to fight back.

Marshal Lauriston needed to regain order.

They reached the house and Lauriston jumped off his horse. The men behind him did the same and the officers ducked inside the headquarters.

"We've got to move, sir," someone said.

"We're still in range of their cannons," another voice said.

More men began talking over each other. The noise became louder than even the cannon barrage outside. Lauriston couldn't think clearly.

"Enough." His voice was low, but it had the desired effect. His men knew when to listen to him.

Lauriston looked at the men. There wasn't fear in anyone's eyes. They'd all seen too many battles to feel true fear. But there was confusion. Lauriston knew it was showing on his own face as well.

"How are they attacking from the south?" He did his best to keep his voice calm and controlled.

The men talked all at once again and Lauriston held up a hand to silence them.

"Lodi." He pointed to the Lakmian officer with the long hair at the front of the group.

"They must have gotten through a hole in the lines," Lodi said.

"You think Desaix would've missed artillery moving by his scouts?"

"No," Lodi said. "But how else?"

"I don't know."

The door crashed open and three more men crowded in with the others.

"Sir, the eastern flank needs reinforcing. They have too many cannons," one of the new arrivals said.

"Everywhere needs reinforcements, Murat," Lauriston said.

Murat removed his hat. "Their infantry is pressing in through the forest near Lanzere. They're wearing all black."

"Are you sure?" Lauriston said.

The room grew quiet. Realization swept across the faces of officers and staff all at once. Lauriston wiped his hand across his face and let out a breath.

Black could only mean one thing.

"The Horde?" he heard someone say from the back of the room.

"I saw them myself, sir. It's the Horde," Murat said.

Lauriston looked at Lodi. The Lakmian only raised his eyebrows in reply.

That explained how a force this big could suddenly appear on their rear. It wasn't the Brunians; it was the Kurakin Horde. The other marshals must've been overrun in the south.

Beauhar and Mere would've fallen. And now the Horde was farther north than seemed possible. North of the Broadwater. North of Plancenoit.

The rest of the men had the same thought process as Lauriston.

"Plancenoit?" someone said. Murmurs went through the men.

A cannon ball exploded into a house very close to them and the entire room ducked.

Lauriston had to block out all the questions. He had to push the concerns for the capital back until later. The focus had to be this battle in this town.

"Enough," Lauriston said to quiet the group of officers again. "Murat, are the bridges of Lanzere still up?"

"No."

"Shit."

Lauriston wiped a hand across his face again and pinched the bridge of his nose. He turned and looked at Lodi. The Lakmian was leaning against the wall with his arms crossed, as if bored in a pub.

"How about in the west?" Lauriston said.

"We're still good there. And there's a ford if we need it," Lodi said. He kept his relaxed position, but Lauriston knew him well enough to hear the stress in his voice.

Lauriston looked over the rest of the room and nodded. He had to give the men confidence. "We're strong here in the center. We'll just have to retreat under cannon fire and hope the bridges hold."

"Retreat, sir?" A general who'd remained quiet until now stepped forward. He stood with a straight back, his normally pristine uniform jacket torn on one side during the flight through the town.

"Yes, Quatre," Lauriston said. "We can't match those cannons on the high ground. There's no way to hold this position. Our lines are facing the wrong way."

"We can push against them. Then head south to Plancenoit." Quatre had his fists clenched at his sides.

Lauriston felt the same anger and frustration. He knew the entire room would feel the same way.

But acting on it would be rash. Lauriston would throw the army into a hopeless situation, even more hopeless than their current predicament.

"No. Plancenoit is over twenty miles away. Even if we could turn this battle, that's too far. For all we know, the city is already fallen." Lauriston made sure to meet the eyes of everyone in the room. "We must fall back here, get the men to safety. Then we figure out how to fight the rest of this war."

Marshal Lauriston saw Quatre's fists unclench slightly. The tension of the room didn't disappear, but it lessened enough to be noticed. Quatre's mouth opened but only hung there silent. The general understood, even if he wanted to argue against retreat. There was no time for discussion.

Lauriston continued with his orders for the whole group. "Men, return to your positions and begin withdrawing. I want order. We have houses for cover from the cannons. Two small bridges here in the center. Quatre, put the First and Third on them. No mistakes."

Quatre gave a nod.

"Murat." Lauriston looked to the next general. "You're in danger of getting cut off in Lanzere, you must pull back towards the center, hold that infantry push off as long as you can."

"Yes, sir."

Lauriston hoped Murat would have enough time to pull back, otherwise they'd lose a fourth of the army trapped up against the river.

"Lodi, fall back across your bridge in the same manner. Spike the cannons if you have to. The same goes to everyone else as well. The priority is getting the men to safety."

Lauriston looked around the room. He needed to hold the men together.

"Onward, Erlon." He tried to put force and confidence behind the words. "Onward, Emperor."

"Onward," the officers responded in unison. They nodded and turned to leave.

When the door of the headquarters opened, the sound of the Kurakin barrage filled the room fully once again. The generals filed out and left Lauriston alone with only the din of the battle for company.

What would the emperor do in this situation? How would Lannes pull Erlon to victory? Lauriston had seen too many battlefield miracles to doubt that his friend would find a way.

But Lannes wasn't here. He was trapped on an island far away. Exiled. Lost forever.

There was only the last Marshal of Erlon left and the bare bones of an army to defend his old empire. And this battle was already lost.

"Shit," Lauriston said to the empty room. He turned and began gathering his things to join in the retreat.

Elisa

Elisa woke early the next morning, just as the colors of the sun were spreading from behind the horizon in the east. She gathered her things—her two pistols, a coat for the morning chill, and the hunting musket from downstairs—and headed out the door.

With the buck from yesterday, they wouldn't need more venison for at least a few days, but Elisa felt like killing something.

Hunting was not very befitting for a princess, Elisa knew. Neither were her britches with tears and mud caked on. A princess wouldn't have tangled and knotted hair. But Elisa was no longer royalty.

That part of herself was lost long before she was taken from the city and brought to this farm. She'd stopped being a princess when her mother disappeared. When the Horde defeated the Erlonian army in the south. And when her father was exiled to the far corner of the world by her nation's enemies.

Elisa had been allowed to stay in Plancenoit for a short while, in her dresses and palace gardens and high four-poster beds with plush sheets from Calvaria. But that had changed when the war started going poorly. When the Horde landed at Beauhar, she'd been whisked away without anyone asking what she wanted in all this, how she wanted to be protected, or if she even needed protection at all.

They'd taken her to this farm, not very far from the capital, and set a drunk in charge of watching her while the guard went off to fight a hopeless war. The farmer Montholon took care of her, Elisa thought to herself as she marched through the forest south of the farm, but if it came to protecting her, she doubted the drunk could rise to the occasion.

None of this mattered, though. The enemy Coalition would find her no matter what. There was only the waiting left.

Elisa realized she'd been walking heavily and fast through the forest for quite a while. Any deer in the woods would've spooked away by now. Elisa slowed and tried to focus on the trees instead of the problems swirling around her. The morning sun was fully above the mountains now and Elisa saw landmarks in the woods that told her she was a few miles south of the farmstead.

An idea came to Elisa and she ignored the various trails of her desired game on the forest floor and moved deeper into the woods. The ground rose here and she followed a slope up to a ridgeline she was familiar with. She rounded a corner and came to the top of the ridge.

The trees fell away from the top of the hill and a gap in the forest revealed the land sweeping away to the south. It was a straight-shot view of the capital of the Erlonian Empire, Plancenoit.

The city was white, the walls of the defenses and the houses beyond rising like pieces of chalk stuck in the dirt. The center was dominated by the mound that had led her Erlonian ancestors to settle here, a hill of rock that now served as the foundation for the palace of Erlon, her former home.

It was beautiful from this distance. The light coming in from Elisa's right shone golden on the buildings and the spires of the palace and the Temple of the Ascended One.

But the scene was shattered by the war that was forever breaking Elisa's life in two. Plumes of smoke rose from the walls. Units of enemies moved over the hills to the west of the city. They looked like ants from this distance.

The artillery was still waking up, but Elisa heard the rumbles of the first barrages for the day starting up. She saw parts of the walls taking the brunt of the attacks and too few defenders scrambling about the battlements.

"It'll fall soon."

Elisa spun and drew both her pistols and pointed them at the source of the voice. The click of both flintlock hammers greeted the intruder.

"Woah now," the man said.

Not a man, Elisa realized. A Lakmian. She could see his furry tail hanging between his legs.

The man had long hair, blond and well kept. His face was soft, like all of the Lakmian race, and held no hostility. He was smiling at Elisa.

"There's that Erlonian fire I've heard so much about," the intruder said after a beat of silence. Now that she looked closer, his features were slightly darker than most Lakmians Elisa had seen. The differences were subtle, but they were there.

"What do you want?" Elisa said. Her mind couldn't make sense of why a Lakmian would be this far south. "Are you with the army?"

That would be the only explanation, but there shouldn't be any Erlonian troops anywhere near here except within the now besieged city.

"No," the Lakmian said. "I'm not much of a fighter." His smile grew, as if a funny thought had hit him.

"Who are you, then?" Elisa said.

"I bring a message."

"A message." Elisa took a quick glance at the empty forest around them. She had no idea what was going on.

"Yes. A warning. There's no need for those pistols."

Elisa kept the pistols pointed at the intruder's head.

"They wouldn't hurt me anyway."

Elisa's wits returned to her at this comment. She felt the breeze shift around her in a mysterious way. She felt a chill run up her spine and realization came to her.

"You're a sorcerer?" she said.

She'd felt the same feelings in her spine before, but only around her mother. This man was certainly more dangerous than he was letting on.

"No, but similar. I'm more of a guide. Although your world has long forgotten me."

"A guide?"

"Yes."

"Did my mother send you?"

"No, I don't believe she knows I've returned yet."

A long rumble of an artillery volley reached them and the man glanced south at the city.

"I bring a warning," the man said again. "You must flee this area, Elisa Lannes. You, of all people, should not be this close to the Horde."

Elisa didn't respond. She could only stare at the Lakmian with her mouth open.

"You must flee."

"And go where? I have no family left." The words burst from Elisa's mouth. A dam burst and her anger threated to pour out towards this strange vision.

"North. Fly north. You must run as far away from the Horde as possible."

Elisa wanted to turn and look at the city again, but restrained herself. She kept the pistols aimed at the intruder. Something in her mind was telling her it was okay to trust the Lakmian, but she wasn't sure what to believe.

"You know the farm won't protect you," the Lakmian said. "You must flee and escape this war on your own. Go north, I will appear to you again soon and help you along the way. But you must run, before that army comes over the hills in search of the emperor's daughter."

The Lakmian began to fade before Elisa's eyes. It happened quickly and she barely had time to process her shock before he was gone. Elisa was left standing in the clearing, pointing her pistols at nothing, the guide's last words echoing inside her head.

"You must run, Elisa. You're far too important to this war to be lost at the very beginning."

Chapter 2

The defeat at Riom foretold of future loss coming for Wahring. But no one,
not even King Charles himself, could've predicted what waited for them once
Gerard Lannes fully rose to power. The emperor would destroy the royals of
Wahring and wreck the realm's armies completely on a scale not seen since
the Ascended One.

Tome of the Emperor
Nelson Wellesley

Rapp

"Fire!"

The muskets erupted. Smoke billowed across the open field and into the
Wahrian prince's face. Rapp held his breath and let the black cloud pass
before returning to glare at the rows of musketmen from the city guard.

"Reload!" The regiment's captain yelled the orders down the line.

The unit was too slow. Did these guards ever practice? Did they drill at all
when the king was off at war?

Rapp bore holes into the back of the captain's hat.

The prince shook his head and spat into the mud and continued observing
while he seethed through his teeth. One musketman dropped his ramrod
while attempting to stuff wadding down his barrel. He bent to pick it up from
the mud and his musket toppled into the soldier's next to him and both guns
clattered to the ground.

The captain in front of Rapp took a quick glance at the prince before
continuing his cadence.

"Make ready!"

The muskets came up at different times. A few soldiers were still finishing
the reload.

Enemy Erlonian lines would've gotten off two volleys in this space and overrun these Wahrians by now.

Rapp shook his head and spat again. He turned his back on the line as the second round of shots finally went off and smoke returned to blow across the field.

The Wahrian capital of Citiva, jewel of the eastern realms, stood behind where the army drilled. A grand wall encircled her for defense and the rows of houses and buildings stretched behind.

In the city center, the land shot up like a spear thrust and formed a tall plateau with sheer rock walls. The royal seat of the realm sat on top. Spires of large stone around a palace with marble floors and tall glass windows. Luxury and power and majesty.

Rapp hated it all.

He turned his back on the sight. The guard unit was reloading again. Their captain kept one eye on the prince and the other on his struggling soldiers.

Rapp wanted to be anywhere but here with these second-rate soldiers. Even if it was only the eastern front, along the Lakmian range, with General Neipperg. He would much prefer that than to be stuck here with his mother and the pointless diplomats of the world.

Rapp was a Prince of Wahring. He should be a general. He should be with the soldiers fighting in the great war of their time.

Erlon was about to fall. And Rapp was going to miss everything.

His father fought in the west. The king led a combined army of Brunians and Wahrians for the Coalition and would take the great Erlonian cities from the emperor's marshals. All while Rapp sat in stuffy rooms with foreign dignitaries hundreds of miles away.

There was certainly nothing dignified about it.

The Ascended One praised war. The god wanted to see bravery and valor and brilliant strategy. What could Rapp possibly hope to achieve up on that plateau in the palace at a *peace summit?*

"Captain." Rapp kept his voice stern.

The captain scrambled over to his prince and bowed.

"One more volley only. We shouldn't waste shot until the guard is better at their motions."

The captain nodded and bowed again.

"I'd like us to practice formations again too. Hollow squares."

"Yes, Your Highness."

Rapp could only hope this regiment of city guard would be better at maneuvers than they were at reloading.

He glanced back towards the city and the towering plateau. Movement at the outer wall caught his eye and held it. The city gate was opening.

A caravan proceeded out. Royal guards on horseback in front and a carriage in the middle with more guards behind.

Rapp rolled his eyes. His mother was coming to see him.

Great.

Rapp turned his back on their approach and watched the regiment move about in continued rushed chaos.

The captain called out orders for the last volley and the men fumbled about. Rapp had half a mind to stop the whole proceeding and yell at them. But he was now too focused on the sound of the approaching Royal Guard.

He glanced west. Open fields of flat land that would run all the way to the Lakmian Range and the eastern theater of the war. Rapp could grab his horse right now and ride for the front. He could find Neipperg's Corps and take over the fight with the Lakmians and their stubborn alliance with Erlon.

He could even push farther and enter Erlon and find his father's army marching south on the western front.

He could run away and no one could stop him.

Except for a queen.

"Form up! Make ready!"

The regiment had to stop mid motion and reform to greet the queen. They scrambled into crooked rows as the carriage procession turned on the path through the drill field and pulled to a stop in front of them.

Rapp stepped forward as the doors to the carriage were opened by a servant. His mother stepped down and the regiment saluted.

Rapp's mother was the image of Wahrian beauty. Tall, with flowing golden hair. Fair cheeks and strong posture.

Her eyes were green. They glared at Rapp.

"Mother," Rapp said as he stepped forward. He put on his best smile. "I'm drilling the city guard to strengthen our defenses, I'm so glad you came to view their progress."

"Walk with me," the queen said.

She walked away from her guard and the city regiment. Rapp trudged after her.

"You will return to the plateau with me in my carriage," his mother said once they were out of earshot of the soldiers.

"The city guard needs a lot of work," Rapp said truthfully.

"The delegates have already started to arrive." His mother walked smoothly down the dirt road. But Rapp could feel her anger underneath the words. "The Lainian ambassador has already asked about you. You have a duty to Wahring to ensure this peace summit is successful."

"I have a duty to the army." Rapp held his frustrations in check behind the words. It was all he could do to not yell them back in his mother's face. "I have a duty to ensure victory and glorify the Ascended One."

"You have a duty to lead."

"Yes." Rapp waved an arm back towards the guard regiment. "Lead the army."

"No." Caroline stopped and looked Rapp in the eye. The green was an even harder glare this time. "Your duty is to the realm. And your family."

Rapp looked away. He looked west across the plain again. Neipperg's army would be a few days' march away. What good did a peace summit do? War had the glory, war had the fun.

"War almost ruined our family," Caroline's voice softened. Rapp kept his eyes to the west. "War ruined your childhood. It tore our family from this place."

His mother's eyes flicked back to the plateau and the palace.

War is what brought the family back, Rapp thought.

The Coalition finally defeated and captured the emperor. That's what returned the royals to power. The lifting of the occupation of Citiva was what allowed them to return home. It was what gave his mother back her precious palace.

The queen had done nothing but sit and weep and despair while in exile for years before their fortunes turned. At least King Charles had tried to fight.

His mother had never been religious. She'd never approved of war. Rapp knew it was hard for women to be pious towards the Ascended One without serving in the army.

But the queen should still be able to see what would bring Wahring back to glory.

Rapp's father may have lost the first wars against Emperor Lannes, but that wasn't what turned their family out of power and into the streets.

The sorceress's betrayal had caused that. Wahring and the Coalition would never have lost if Epona hadn't defected from his father's bed to the emperor's.

Rapp shook his head. Bringing up that subject would most certainly make his mother's mood worse.

"You're done sleeping in a tent with the army," Caroline said. The sternness had returned to her tone. "It's time to stay in the palace. You came back to Citiva for a reason."

"I came back because you made me."

Rapp regretted saying the words even before he finished. At least he hadn't said his opinions on his mother's lack of religion or his thoughts on his father and the sorceress out loud.

"Rapp, it's time to forget boyhood fantasies of valor."

Boyhood fantasies? The Ascended One's teaching was a boyhood fantasy? The defense of the realm was a boyhood fantasy?

Caroline turned and walked back towards her carriage. Rapp stayed rooted to the spot.

The citizens of Wahring wanted a strong ruler again. They wanted the royal family to return to their golden age when Rapp's ancestors were the strongest royals on the Continent and all feared their soldiers. The prince glanced at the crooked line of the guard regiment and shook his head.

He let out a grumbling sigh.

His parents had let Wahring's greatness waver even before Lannes and the Erlonians had come from the west. They were the reason the realm had fallen. They were the reason the entire Continent was in the mess with Erlon in the first place.

It would be up to Rapp to change that.

"Rapp, come now." Caroline's voice was soft, but her words somehow had the most bite behind them yet.

Rapp's feet moved on their own accord. It was a reaction built from the years of his childhood under the woman. He hated his legs for responding in such a way.

"I will finish the drills today and join you and my sisters for dinner tonight," Rapp said. He thought that was a good compromise.

"No, you are returning with me now." Caroline reached the carriage door and turned to glare at Rapp. "We have things to discuss before the rest of the delegates get here."

Rapp looked at the Royal Guard around them. The queen wouldn't want a scene in front of them and the other soldiers.

"I have drills to finish with these men. I will see you for dinner tonight, Mother."

Rapp turned away from her and left before she could respond. He looked to the west and thought briefly of running off to the front once again.

He wouldn't go that far, not yet at least. But he relished in the small victory over his mother as he heard her carriage door slam shut.

The city guard truly did need the drilling work. If the queen was going to make Rapp stay in Citiva for the pointless peace summit, the least he could do was improve the standards of the city's defense.

He ordered the captain to resume the drill and stewed on his thoughts about his family. He would let things simmer but not boil over. The Ascended One taught how a general had to be level-headed and Rapp knew he would have to be strong to survive being trapped here.

He could bide his time. His mother's peace summit was pointless. Erlon would be broken up according to who conquered what, not which ambassadors signed what agreement hundreds of miles from the main fighting.

His father would get the glory with the army. But once Rapp became king, he would have his time to fight and win and be praised. His parents would be gone then. Glory would return for Wahring. And Rapp would be able to fight whatever war he wanted in whatever way he saw fit.

Pitt

The armies made camp along the edge of a forest with a stream bed
between them that ran towards Vendome. The Brunians sat in the forest on
one side and the Wahrians camped in the adjacent fields. General Pitt crossed
the bridge to the Wahrian side at a trot. The air was cool and the sun wasn't
too heavy on either the rider or the horse.

Commotion and movement surrounded the Wahrian king's tent. Beyond,
on the main road leading towards the Erlonian city, Pitt could see the Wahrian
cannons being hauled towards the city. The siege was moving quickly.

Pitt rubbed his horse's neck as he tied him to a post. The general paused
before turning towards the tent entrance.

He took a deep breath and tried to settle his thoughts before going in to
meet with the king. He adjusted the cuffs of his jacket and straightened his
collar and said a quick prayer to the Ascended One for the army.

A guard pulled the tent flap open and motioned for Pitt to enter. The
general ran a hand through his brown hair and hoped it would fall back into a
neat enough position after his ride. He ducked into the king's tent.

The cabal of Wahrian generals were strewn about the inside and King
Charles Franz of the Wahrian Realm sat in the middle of them.

"Ah, Pitt, welcome." The king lounged in a chair and gnawed on a greasy
chicken leg. "Please join us."

Pitt bowed to the king and walked forward. He politely refused the glass of
wine offered by a servant.

"Artillery should be in place by tonight." One of the Wahrian generals
leaned across a map on a table and shifted markers around. The Coalition
army was in the north of the former empire, with the major rivers still to cross
and plenty of dense forest between it and the Erlonian capital to the south.

"Good, good," King Charles said between the last bites of the chicken leg.

The generals around the king wore the normal black and yellow jackets of
the Wahrian army. A flowing silk bedroom robe hung off the king, striped in
the same bright yellow of his realm. Pitt's red Brunian uniform clashed badly
with the others in the tent.

The Wahrian generals slouched where Pitt stood straight and tall. He kept
his hands locked together behind his back and held his chin up, the formal
stance ingrained into him since his schoolboy days back in Brun.

The Wahrian culture was significantly more lax when it came to manners and formality, even in the military. To Pitt, the present scene in this tent only highlighted the strange nature of their alliance against Erlon even more.

The king turned towards Pitt and pointed the greasy chicken bone at him. "Pitt, do you think the garrison will surrender?"

"No, Your Highness."

Wahrian heads turned towards Pitt, surprise strewn across their faces.

"Why not?" the king said.

"These Erlonians won't surrender a city easily, it's not in their nature."

"We outnumber them ten to one," a tall general said.

"They don't have long cannons," another said.

"If I were them, I'd give up and save some lives." Charles checked to make sure he'd gotten all the chicken meat off the bone before tossing it over his shoulder.

"They'll fight, sir." Pitt took a step closer to the map table and looked at the positions of attack. "I'll state again that we don't need this city, sir. We could push farther south and let our rear guard besiege these walls."

"No, Vendome is important. It's the gateway to the north," Charles said.

And we're moving south, Pitt wanted to say.

He looked around the room. He'd made that argument before. There would be no changing the king's mind.

Charles looked around for more food and waved a servant over. "When will your artillery be in position around the south, Pitt?"

"It's already in position, sir."

"Good. You can bombard from the south. Our main attack will be from the north through General Lukas."

The tall general standing to the right of the king's chair nodded. "The men are ready, Your Highness," the general said.

Charles received his next piece of chicken. This breast piece proved much messier for the king's evening jacket than the leg.

Pitt looked from General Lukas to the king and the rest of the room. He wanted to tell them again how pointless this attack would be, how many men would be lost against the high walls of the non-strategic city.

He passed a hand back through his hair and chewed the side of his mouth. Charles had final say over this two-nation army and he wanted the city. His generals would do or say anything to please him.

The king wanted glory. Even if that glory was pointless.

Pitt left the meeting in a foul mood. He remounted his horse and moved back through the Wahrian camp. He splashed back over the stream and reached his own camp in what felt like no time at all as his mind swirled with thoughts and helplessness.

They'd take the city. There weren't enough Erlonian defenders to hold an attack for long. But they'd lose many men in the process. And they'd lose very precious time for this campaign.

Reports were already putting the Kurakin at Plancenoit. The southern part of the Coalition was going to take the capital. They were going to be seated in the palace and ruling over the larger part of Erlon. All while the Wahrian king threw men at the wall of a pointless northern city.

Pitt ducked under a low branch on his path and continued towards the flicking lights of fires in the Brunian camp. He nudged his horse into a slightly faster trot.

Pitt understood what King Charles was doing. He'd been humiliated by the emperor. He'd been thoroughly outsmarted in multiple wars and lost his throne. Charles had overseen the first Wahrian capital to be occupied in centuries, and he'd done it in embarrassing fashion.

But now Charles was back. And there was an opening to take a city Emperor Lannes was famous for taking during the Erlonian consolidation. Charles could take the city and then say he conquered the same city as the infamous Lannes. He could finally say he was equal with the emperor.

The king was saving face where it didn't matter.

Pitt shook his head and muttered something under his breath he wouldn't want the king to overhear.

Pitt's horse came out of the trees and moved along the edge of his Brunian camp. Some of the Brunian soldiers were sitting outside their tents. They stood up as their general passed by them and saluted and Pitt nodded and touched the tip of his hat in return.

Pitt's tent was in the center of camp near a fire pit. It was the same size as the others and a far cry from the giant pavilion of the Wahrian king on the other side of the forest.

Pitt found a group of his officers waiting for him.

"Sir," Win said, taking off his plumed cavalry hat. The other officers stepped up behind him.

Pitt let out a heavy breath before beginning. "The attack will move forward. There's no swaying the Wahrians."

He saw one of the officers spit into the mud at his own feet but let it pass.

"We're to barrage from the south. Luckily, the Wahrians will be the ones attacking. Our side will be a decoy."

A few of the officers nodded their heads at this.

"I still want us to be ready. If we're needed as reserve, I want us to be quick."

Nods came from the circle of men.

"General Smith, I want pickets out in full force in front of your cannons. No sallying force will get through our side. Understand?"

"Yes, sir," the artillery officer said.

"My men are scouting the forest paths as well, sir," Win, the cavalry officer, said.

General Win was a stiff man. The bright colors and flamboyant decorations of the cavalry uniform seemed to wear him instead of the other way around. But he was dependable and a great fighter.

"Good." Pitt looked around at the group again. He was the commanding general of this army but felt like he controlled nothing. Everything depended on the Wahrian king lounging and feasting in his tent on the other side of the army. "Gentlemen, you are responsible for your own pickets. The attack begins tomorrow, be sure your lines aren't compromised in the night. You're dismissed. General Win, wait a moment, we need to speak in private."

Win nodded. The other officers left and walked off into the camp.

"Sir." Win stood at attention, the white plume from his hat swaying in the nighttime breeze.

"The forest is dense south of here," Pitt said. "This attack will slow us down, but I want us ready to move once the city is taken."

"Yes, sir." As usual, Win knew the orders before they were fully given.

"Find us the best path south. I want us Brunians to be the van once the city is taken. I mean to move as far south as possible. We'll be the ones who find the remaining Erlonian armies."

"Yes, sir."

Win was dismissed and rode into the night with his men. Pitt was left alone. The sounds of the camp slowed as the soldiers found sleep. The next day would bring the rumble of battle and Pitt knew he needed rest. It would be hard to come by, but he forced himself into bed and let his thoughts and worries rage at the back of his eyelids until slumber finally took him deep into the night.

Chapter 3

Nothing will get accomplished when two or more diplomats are gathered in the same place. If the diplomatic number rises above ten, progress will prove extremely elusive.

Maxims of State, Entry Three
Emperor Gerald Lannes

Elisa

Elisa felt the cool breeze moving between the trees of the forest. It felt nice against the thickness of her coat. It threatened to calm her and would've succeeded if not for the persistent raging of her thoughts.

Midday was fast approaching. She'd bagged two rabbits in the early hours and seen nothing else. It was as if the forest animals knew an army of evil was close by and the land was now dangerous.

The animals had vacated their normal homes. Elisa wondered if she should do the same.

She continued her walk back towards the farm, her eyes at the ground and her mind lost in thought. She knew this forest by heart now, every tall pine and wide oak and thick bush full of thorns.

She could turn and run from it all. This was on the northern side of Mon's land and she could just as easily turn around and flee. The rabbits hanging from her belt bumping against her legs would serve for her first few meals out on her own. She could hunt and kill more food.

She could survive.

A few days ago, the Lakmian vision on the hilltop overlooking Plancenoit had made it sound like such a simple task. Elisa looked around at the woods and wished the Lakmian would appear again.

The farm was still about a mile away through the low hills. This was plenty of space for her mind to roam. Her thoughts often behaved the same as Elisa's body and wandered in random directions.

Today, Elisa's focus was on the god who'd appeared to her. He'd told her to flee. He'd said the farm wasn't safe. And that the Kurakin were looking for her.

As if in answer to her thoughts, a low rumble echoed from the west.

Plancenoit. Her home. Still under siege and soon to fall.

But even when it fell, would the Horde find her here? The vision had said they would, but should she trust a strange Lakmian who could appear out of thin air to her in the woods?

Elisa knew what her mother would say. Epona had told Elisa to never trust visions and dreams. Even if the Ascended One himself spoke from the heavens, it should be met with caution.

The princess had never had reason to consider that advice until now.

But her mother wasn't here. The sorceress had abandoned Elisa. She hadn't returned from the campaign in the south. The stories and rumors said she'd not returned to her father either and had betrayed the empire. Some said her disappearance led directly to her father's capture and exile.

Elisa didn't want to believe it. Something must've happened to her mother. She wouldn't abandon her family.

But sorceresses made their own rules. History had shown that time and time again, most recently through Elisa's Aunt Thirona's actions against the Erlonians at the Battle of Three Bridges.

Elisa also knew of her mother's history before coming to Erlon to marry her father. The stories were unavoidable and scandalous. Her time with the Wahrian king in the east...

Elisa didn't want to think on it. Her thoughts wanted to wander to dark places and she wouldn't let them.

She crested a low rise and dropped down into a creek bed. The trickle of water in the ditch would lead her back to Mon's field.

She reached down and adjusted her belt and made sure the rabbits were still tied on tight before continuing beside the water. Her hand brushed the silver of one of her pistols. It was cold from the morning air, but Elisa felt a peace run up her arm.

The weapons had been a gift from her father. A pair of silver pistols engraved with the Erlonian imperial seal. Forged using her mother's magic.

Elisa moved her hand away from the pistol. She reached for her sword and drew it instead. The weapon felt light in her hand and took her mind away from her mother.

The pistol's peace had been fleeting. Practicing with the sword would do a better job of easing her thoughts.

She spun the blade vertically to the right of her body and pivoted her feet in the creek bed's clay. The steps of her exercises from the palace's sword master came back to her easily enough. She spun and thrust and parried with an invisible enemy.

Her mind went numb and focused on the movements and nothing else. It was a great escape from her worries.

She completed the training combination with a thrust forward and her blade almost hummed in the air.

More rumbling came from the west. It was deep and felt like it was underneath the ground at her feet.

Elisa sheathed her sword and continued down the creek bed towards the farm.

The questions came back to her mind immediately.

Should she follow the Lakmian vision's advice and flee the farm? Should she leave Mon and the farmhands and go?

Or was she crazy and only seeing visions in the forest?

Even if she was going insane, what was her reason for staying on the farm?

The palace guard had told her to come here and she followed their orders. But the palace was about to fall and Elisa's home was about to be destroyed. The farmer Mon was in charge, but Elisa didn't much trust him, especially after a bottle or two of his wine.

She should leave.

That was her most persistent thought now. She should run.

More cannon fire echoed from the horizon, but this time farther north. Were there more battles north of Plancenoit? Were the other armies of the enemy Coalition encircling central Erlon?

More and more questions appeared any time Elisa thought she made a decision. If she ran north now, she might be running directly into more enemies.

She continued south towards the farm and fingered the imperial seal pressed into the silver and fell deeper into her thoughts. Gabriel might talk to her about this, he might help. But she'd have to explain her real identity to him.

Gabriel had been nice to her and was one of the main reasons she'd tolerated being on the farm for so long. Even with her identity a secret, though, Elisa still wasn't allowed to have these common-girl hopes and dreams. She wasn't allowed to fall for a farmhand. Especially with a war raging across her country.

She should run.

She should stay; the Horde wouldn't find her here.

No answers came to Elisa as the creek bed died and the forest fell away to farmland.

Elisa didn't stop walking south. Montholon worked hard despite his drinking and did provide for her. There was never a shortage of food on the farm despite the rations from the war.

The first field she came to was winter wheat that had only just been planted. She found the path around the side of the field and moved towards the sound of work from the far end.

Mon and the farmhands were starting on the tilling of the next field. Elisa tightened the belt knot holding the rabbits as she moved towards them.

Gabriel was the first to notice her approach. He stood from his work and smiled at her. "Only two then?"

The other farmhands laughed.

"Hard to hunt with cannons nearby." Mon pulled the ox to a stop and hopped off the tiller and gave Elisa a smile before throwing a glare at the farmhands.

"Hard to harvest wheat, too," Gabriel said.

Mon had sweat on his brow despite the coolness of the fall morning. He wiped it on his sleeve and pulled a flask from his pocket for a drink. He chose to ignore Gabriel's comment but pointed for the farmhand to take control of the ox-driven tiller.

"See anything unusual in the forest?"

Elisa froze for the briefest of moments and thought Mon meant another vision. But she quickly realized he meant in regards the Horde army.

"No, nothing," Elisa said. "Most of the animals have cleared out."

"Makes sense. War does that to a forest. It's a shame, really." Mon wiped his brow again and turned to look at the farmhands at work with the dirt.

Elisa watched the light wind blow through tops of the trees on the edge of the clearing and didn't say anything.

"At least you got two." Mon took another pull from the flask.

Elisa nodded. "I'll clean them and put the pelts with the others."

Mon nodded but didn't return to his work. Elisa stayed put and waited for the farmer to say something else.

"Plancenoit won't last much longer," the old farmer said.

The low rumbling was now constant in the distance. Mon stared at the far side of the clearing in the west. Elisa didn't have a response to his statement.

Mon's smile was gone. "If you want to talk about anything, let me know."

Elisa was taken aback by the kindness in Mon's eyes. There was the usual drunken shakiness, but that now gave way slightly to an emotion Elisa hadn't seen in Mon before.

Maybe she should open up to him more. Maybe it would be good for her to talk through her emotions from all that had happened to her family and country instead of hiking and hunting alone in the woods.

Maybe that was a decent idea.

Instead, Elisa only nodded. "Okay."

She wasn't sure talking with a farmer would make her feel much better. She longed for her friends back at court in the palace. But the rumbling from the siege told her they would be far away from here or trapped on the wrong side of the battle.

She wanted to talk to her father. He would be much better than a drunk farmer. He was clear on the other side of the world, though, with a cold sea in between them as well.

Elisa was stuck here.

Mon looked away from her and drank one last time from his flask before returning it to his pocket. "Those rabbit pelts will be good come winter."

Elisa didn't respond. She watched him move back across the dirt and resume his place on top of the tiller.

She was about to continue on to the farmhouse but stopped when she heard the sounds of a horse. The men in the field heard it too and the ox was hauled to a stop.

Galloping.

Mon shielded his eyes against the sun in the direction of the noise. The rider came around the corner on the path and made straight for their location at a frantic pace.

"A rider," Mon said. "From the village."

The rider reined his mount to a halt but didn't dismount. He was out of breath when he spoke.

"The Horde have breached the wall. Plancenoit will fall."

Mon dropped from the tiller again. "Are you sure?"

"News came this morning, they're in the city."

Elisa knew it had to be true no matter how much she wished it wasn't. There had barely been any soldiers left in the city when she'd left for Mon's farm months ago. She was surprised the city had lasted this long.

"Thank you." Mon pulled his flask out again.

The rider nodded and rode off.

Mon looked towards Elisa. "Let's hope he's right," he said. His voice was low and didn't inspire confidence.

Elisa met his eye and felt the questions of the moment run through her again. This would be her time to flee before the Kurakin realized she wasn't in the palace. This was the time to take the Lakmian vision's advice.

But she shouldn't trust visions.

Her mother's voice echoed in her head. The voice of the same mother who'd abandoned her and her father.

Mon turned to the farmhands. "We're done for the day. We'll need to hide some of our stores in case the Horde comes through here."

The men nodded and began gathering up their things. Elisa couldn't help but notice the quick glance Mon gave towards her at the mention of the Horde coming to the farm.

Her thoughts raced and she felt overwhelmed. She didn't know what she wanted to do, what she needed to do.

There was still rumbling in the distance as the final cannon shots were fired at her old home.

Elisa walked back to the farm with the group. No one said much and Elisa's mind wandered in all directions.

There were multiple paths in front of her.

And she didn't know which she wanted to take.

Rapp

The great leaders of the Coalition against the Erlonian Empire descended on the capital of Wahring and gathered atop the heights of the royal plateau to decide the fate of the Continent.

Ambassadors from Morada and Brun and Vith and Laine and all the other factions arrived to much fanfare. Brun brought their sorceress Thirona. The Tribune of the Ascended One's Legion arrived a day before the summit began. Even the Kurakin sent a representative that spoke the northern language and seemed familiar with northern customs.

Queen Caroline pulled out all the best finery to decorate the palace. Rapp's childhood home, the palace of his great ancestors, looked absolutely wonderful.

Prince Rapp still hated it.

Every day he had to leave his military uniform hanging in the closet and instead stuff himself into the formal jackets and puffy shirts that modern fashion demanded of a royal diplomat. The women looked the same and were allowed to wear their normal dresses, but the men looked like birds with their breast feathers puffed out and they waddled around in the jacket tails and spoke in entirely too formal sentences.

It had only been three days and Rapp was already prepared to take drastic measures and flee to the front against his mother's orders.

"The trade rights of a sovereign Laine are vital to the survival of this great alliance."

The Lainian ambassador, a small man with only wisps of white hair remaining on his head, had been talking for almost an hour. Even the diplomats surrounding Rapp were starting to lose interest.

"I urge you all to focus on trade during the coming summit meetings. We are all here to represent our own countries, that much can't be denied. But we are also here for the larger good on the Continent. This Coalition is to ensure peace lasts on this great land."

"Thank you, Ambassador." The queen's voice cut through the brief break between the Lainian's sentences. It appeared like the ambassador wanted to continue his speech, but Queen Caroline stood up from her seat in the center of the room. "We'll keep your wise words in mind as we move forward with this summit."

The ambassador bowed and resumed his seat. Queen Caroline smiled at him and surveyed the table on either side of her.

"Now, next on the agenda I believe we have an update from the Erlonian front of our war effort. Is that correct?"

Rapp sat up. His mind ripped itself out of the haze of a daydream and turned to face the end of the table where the Kurakin Ambassador sat.

Instead of the darkly bearded Kurakin standing to speak, Ambassador Leberecht rose from the middle of the Moradan delegation next to the Kurakin.

"Yes, Your Highness, that's correct."

Anyone who saw Leberecht would instantly guess at his immense love of food. The Moradan purple jacket he'd chosen for today's meeting barely contained his gut as it erupted from his front.

The large man looked up and down the table and gave a quick wink when his eyes passed over Rapp.

The prince had grown up with Leberecht around in the Moradan courts. The ambassador was born in Wahring, but now served as the chief advisor to the Moradan king. When the Erlonian Empire had defeated Rapp's father and occupied Citiva and sent the royal family into exile, they'd fled to the coast and been welcomed with open arms by Leberecht and the Moradans.

While Rapp's father was off at war, Leberecht had become a father figure of sorts during the prince's formative years. Rapp often called him "uncle" despite Leberecht being very far from related to him nor even highborn. It was a strange relationship, but seeing the large man and hearing his voice brought back fond memories for Rapp from his childhood.

"I will relay the updates coming in from General Duroc that were sent to Ambassador Mikhail." Leberecht turned and nodded to the bearded Kurakin. Ambassador Mikhail smiled back up at Leberecht and Rapp thought he saw the diplomat shiver slightly at the sight of Mikhail's row of filed Kurakin teeth.

Leberecht recovered quickly and gave a dramatic pause while looking down the table at the rest of the gathering.

"General Duroc marches on Plancenoit. It will fall within the week, if it hasn't already."

Gasps came from up and down the long table. The murmurs among the delegation members from all the countries grew and Rapp saw the shock on Thirona's face across the table as she whispered with the Brunian delegation.

"Is he confident he can take the city alone, Ambassador?" Queen Caroline stayed seated next to Rapp. Her voice carried over the din of the diplomats around them.

Rapp saw the Kurakin diplomat chuckle at the question as Leberecht answered with a nod.

"Yes. Marshal Lauriston is north of the city somewhere. It appears the Erlonians didn't think the Kurakin would move so quickly through their southern defenses."

"I think we're all surprised by how quickly the Kurakin are moving. They are much farther north than planned, but this is wonderful news."

Rapp felt his mother stiffen at this new voice. It came from directly across from the queen and seemed to have a soft power over the room. The murmuring of the diplomats ceased and all heads turned towards the Sorceress Thirona from Brun.

She was a tall and lean woman who moved very similar to the memories Rapp had of her sister Epona back when she was part of the Wahrian court during Rapp's early childhood. Thirona's hair had a brighter glimmer of red to it, though, and she wore long dresses the color of flames.

Queen Caroline's chair creaked from her tight grip on its arms as Thirona continued her question.

"Is there news of my niece, the Princess Elisa, from Duroc?"

Leberecht turned back to Mikhail and the Kurakin gave a shake of his head to Leberecht.

"No, Sorceress, there's been no news of the princess," Leberecht said. "But we still believe she's in the palace and Duroc assures Mikhail that the girl's safety is of utmost priority when the army breaks through the walls."

"Do be sure to reiterate the importance of the girl to him, Ambassador." Queen Caroline's voice was level and calm, but Rapp knew the words came out too quick. She wanted to be sure to keep Thirona from taking over the conversation.

Leberecht nodded in reply and so did the Kurakin ambassador.

"I have another concern, if I may." Thirona stood up this time and smiled sweetly across the table to the Wahrian queen. All the eyes of the table, especially those belonging to the male diplomats, were now fully focused on the long form of the Brunian sorceress. Rapp could see his mother's knuckles turning white on top of the arm of her chair.

"What concern is that, Sorceress?" Leberecht said. He remained standing and smiled down the table at Thirona.

"When the Horde takes the city, what flag will fly over the walls and the palace?"

The Kurakin Ambassador leaned forward and tilted his head in confusion up at Leberecht. Rapp noticed the hilt of a dagger protruding out of the Kurakin's jacket at his hip for the first time. Leberecht turned from the Kurakin and faced Thirona. He seemed to not comprehend the question either.

"I'm sorry, Sorceress, I don't fully understand your question," Leberecht said.

Rapp was finally getting interested in the summit's conversation. Not only were they discussing the actual war strategy of the western front, but Thirona's words were making his mother visibly upset. It was too good of an opportunity not to enjoy.

Maybe Rapp should stay at this summit a little longer and see how long it took his mother to explode?

"I'm merely concerned about the optics of the matter." Thirona continued to smile down the table at Leberecht, and even though the charm wasn't directed at Rapp, he felt the sudden urge to tell a joke and make the sorceress laugh.

"Duroc is taking the capital of the empire," Thirona continued. "If the black of the Kurakin flies over the city, I worry what the common people will think. This war is a joint effort from everyone in the Coalition."

"That's true," Leberecht said. He bowed his head towards the sorceress. "I'm sure General Duroc already plans to fly the white of the Coalition, but we'll write to ensure that he acquiesces to this summit's wishes."

Ambassador Mikhail nodded his agreement to Leberecht's statement. Thirona resumed her seat.

"Thank you for bringing that up, Sorceress," Leberecht said. "Very good point."

Leberecht rubbed his hands together in front of his large gut. "Another grand step towards our pacification of the former empire. When our Kurakin allies take Plancenoit, they will fly the white flag of the Coalition about the walls to signal our victory."

Chapter 4

Even the most hardened northern veterans waver when faced with the
fanged teeth and charging wolverines of the Kurakin Horde.

Military History of the Continent
Richard Shaw

Andrei

Scythe Commander Andrei looked back to the south and saw the black flag
of Kura raised over the top of the Erlonian palace in the distance. The Scythe
leader pulled his eyes away from the sight and focused on the path in front of
him.

His wolverine grunted and sniffed at the ground of the path. Andrei placed a
hand on the right shoulder of the beast to keep it on the intended route. He
felt the animal's shoulders shift underneath him.

The forest was quiet. There was no rumbling from the Kurakin cannons
behind them. Plancenoit had fallen. The war would soon be over.

But Andrei still had a job to do. He was a key cog in Duroc's grand plan.
Some idea to push the Kurakin farther and higher than they'd ever been.
Something about resurrecting old gods and memories. And it all started with
toppling this great northern empire.

Andrei didn't care about the grand plans of the world leaders. He cared
about getting home, back to the chill air of the south. To do that, he had to
obey orders and accomplish things quickly. He had to take things one step at a
time.

Today's task was easy enough. Find a girl. Bring her to Duroc.

"Dismount here." Andrei gave the order and heard it passed down the line
of his Scythes.

Andrei swung his leg off his wolverine and led the beast over to the nearest tree. He scratched the brown-gray hair on its head and commanded the animal to stay. No ties were ever needed for a Scythe's wolverine.

The beast snarled in reply and showed its white fanged teeth, giving Andrei a final sniff before lying down next to the tree.

Andrei turned and walked back to his Scythe warriors. The men checked their blades and pistols, counted napthas on their belts, and re-buckled boot straps. All had thick beards and long, dark hair. All were ready for a fight.

The Scythes were always ready for a fight. They were the elite of the elite in the Kurakin military and Andrei knew they would be up to this task.

"We'll go stealth from here," Andrei said.

"How far?" Jerkal asked.

"Not far. And there shouldn't be many men, but be careful. We've taken the city, no need for a casualty now." Andrei blinked and saw a flash through the connection with his hawk. The farm was just through the forest to their north.

"An easy day, then." Jerkal smiled at the Scythes around him. His teeth were pointed fangs all the way across the front of his mouth. The other Scythes responded with smiles of their own. All of them bared their pointed teeth to show off the most menacing aspect of their race, the reason the northerners had feared their people over the centuries.

"Maybe." Andrei nodded at his soldiers. "But for a Scythe? No easy day."

"No easy day," the men repeated in unison.

Andrei returned their grins. There never was an easy day as a Scythe.

The group moved off into the woods. They spread into a wedge formation with Andrei at the point. He scratched at fleas in his beard and moved his shoulders about. The fleas had an amazing intuition around settling in places on his back that couldn't be reached.

The farmhouse appeared quickly. It was right where his *sakk*, his hawk, had shown him. Andrei looked up through the canopy of the trees but couldn't see his bird. He silently thanked the hawk and went back to focusing on the farmhouse in front of him.

Andrei gave a nod and the Scythes spread out even farther. They encircled the farm complex in complete silence.

Andrei moved up the road and used a field of tall crops as cover. He knelt at the end of the last plot and looked at the house. There was a porch with plenty of cover and windows facing south. The barn door was open. That could be a trap.

Andrei was about to step forward and move to the porch when the first shot blasted out of the front of the house.

He saw the puff of smoke from the bottom-floor window as the musket ball passed over his head. Andrei ran forward as the next two shots went off in the adjacent windows.

His men moved forward from all around the house. Andrei altered his plan and went across the face of the house, drawing the eyes of the defender. He reached a tree stump and crouched behind it after firing off a wild round from his own musket at the windows.

Jerkal was behind the house. Andrei only had to give him time.

Andrei stayed behind the log and heard the next volley go off. It wasn't aimed at him, it was aimed at the other men. They'd taken Andrei's lead and moved through the fields in front of the house.

Jerkal caught Andrei's eye and winked. The Scythe second-in-command already had a naptha lit. Andrei saw the coloring was a lighter brown. A smoke naptha.

Jerkal climbed up on the porch from the side and waited for the naptha's fuse to cook down. One more shot came from the house and cracked against a nearby wagon some of the Scythes crouched behind. Jerkal threw the bomb into the windows where the latest shot originated.

A muffled bang. Followed by a yell. Smoke began to billow from the windows.

"Forward!" Andrei followed his own order immediately and let his men push up around him. Jerkal remained on the porch with a pistol drawn. The Scythes spread out on the lawn of the farmhouse and kept their eyes on the doors.

"Watch for the girl!" Duroc wanted the girl alive but didn't care about anyone else.

Black smoke continued to billow out of the windows. Coughing came from the house. Andrei and the Scythes waited. His musket grew heavy held up with his arms, but he stayed still.

Finally a shadow moved. A body pushed out of the front door and staggered on the porch.

A man.

Jerkal's pistol shot took him in the head and dropped him.

Another man came out the door behind the first, this one coughing and sputtering as he fell to all fours. A musket shot from one of the Scythes on the lawn took him in the chest when he tried to rise.

Andrei shifted forward. "Watch the back," he called to the Scythes on the other side of the house. He glanced to his right and saw the barn still standing open. "Check the barn."

Two Scythes in the front broke off and moved towards the other building.

Andrei turned his attention back to the main house. Jerkal quickly wrapped a cloth around his mouth and nose and ducked through the black smoke that hung in the doorway. The other Scythes pushed up to below the front porch. Andrei kept his eyes on the windows.

A yell came from the house. It was quickly followed by a bang.

Seconds passed and Andrei felt like it was an eternity before Jerkal yelled, "Clear!"

Andrei let out a breath and lowered his musket. He looked towards the barn and saw one of his men in the doorway shake his head.

The farm was clear.

"Three men, sir," Jerkal said when the smoke had cleared and Andrei stepped into the house.

"No girl?"

"No."

"Upstairs?"

"No one."

Andrei felt a pit form in his stomach. This wasn't going to be an easy day. "Is there a cellar?"

"Not that I've seen." Jerkal stood over the last of his kills in the middle of the kitchen. The boy was on his stomach with a great pool of blood around him.

"Maybe the barn, then." Andrei was surprised. He'd assumed the girl would be hiding upstairs. Had she somehow slipped away while the Scythes advanced on the farm?

Andrei moved back to the porch and looked towards the barn, but could already feel that the men would find nothing there. The three men from the main house had been alone. The girl was gone. This wouldn't be a simple task after all.

Andrei sighed and thought on his hawk. His vision morphed to show the bird's view of the forest north of here as it stretched into the hills. They would track the girl down and find her easily enough. It might just take longer than originally thought.

Elisa

Elisa worked to gather wood for her fire. The chill of the approaching winter hung in the air and the warmth from the fast-disappearing sun would soon abandon her. She wasn't going to freeze to death on her first night on her own.

The galloping horseman and his message about her former home had plagued Elisa's sleep the night before. She'd woken up in the middle of the night and knew what she had to do. There was no more pushing the problems of the world away from her. She had to act.

She'd packed up her things and left early the next morning.

No real plan, but she'd left Mon and Gabriel and the farm forever without a goodbye.

Plancenoit had fallen. The Horde would come for her. Elisa decided to take the risk on her own and strike out north like the Lakmian had suggested. The danger was now greater on the farm than the unknown state of the war in the north. Elisa would rather be in control than sitting idle, anyway.

She'd traveled north before, of course, but always in a carriage as part of a caravan with her father and mother. There'd been soldiers to protect her then. Old guardsmen armed to the teeth and cavalry on tall horses all around.

Now she was alone. The dark of the evening closed in around her. But she was a Lannes, daughter of the Emperor of Imperial Erlon, and she would not be afraid simply from darkness falling.

Her footfalls crunched through the dirt of the forest floor and created the only noise in the forest. There was the occasional bird call through the evening air, but no other sound.

The forest pressed in around her and she had a persistent urge to look over her shoulder. Like there was someone or something watching her.

Maybe her Lakmian guide was out there right now. Or maybe it was something else. Something the guide wanted her to avoid.

She stooped and gathered up kindling and longer sticks and broke the longest branches into pieces and returned to where she'd laid her pack. The darkness was coming fast. She bent down and leaned sticks against each other. The final shape made her think of the paintings of the ancient pyramids across the northeastern sea.

The fire started easily enough. She'd stolen matches from the farmhouse and the forest floor was full of dry leaves. Elisa blew on the infant flames like her father had taught her and felt the warmth as her creation grew. She fed it slowly and basked in her accomplishment.

She could handle herself alone. She could survive, she didn't need anyone else, not even her family. She would be just fine on her own.

A crack came through the trees behind her and her thoughts turned to fear.

Elisa reacted, rising from her seated position into a crouch. She saw nothing but blackness through the trees in the direction of the sound.

What was out there?

Maybe lighting the fire had been a mistake.

Elisa moved around her fire to where her pack leaned against a tree. She drew out one of her pistols. He fingers found the silver engravings on the side as well as the trigger and flintlock.

She could hear nothing over the crackle of her own fire.

Her heart pounded in her ears. The dark closed in around her. She was suddenly far less confident in her ability to make this trip alone.

Elisa moved back away from the firelight. It was more out of instinct than anything. Her mind wasn't working.

Maybe it was only a rabbit. Or a bird.

She prayed for it to be something harmless.

Elisa backed away and reached a large tree trunk. She moved behind it and looked back towards her camp. The fire cast shadows everywhere and made the dark of the surrounding forest even darker. Elisa could see nothing but the flicker of the flames.

She waited. There was no other sound for a long time. Her breathing was loud and she tried to control it. Her heart wouldn't slow and her mind wouldn't think.

Movement. Was it just a flicker of a shadow? No. It was more. There was something there.

Elisa sucked in her breath and held it. A white blur formed from the darkness. It came closer and its edges formed into a person. Elisa shifted farther behind her tree but kept her eyes on the figure.

The blur stumbled into the full firelight. A large man, gray hair, out of breath from carrying a heavy pack.

Montholon the farmer.

Elisa let out her breath. It must've been loud, because Mon looked directly towards her position.

"Elisa!" he called out.

She stood and moved towards him. He saw her and let out a sigh of his own. A sigh of relief.

"I could've shot you." Elisa's fingers still hadn't left her father's silver seal.

"That would've been unfortunate." Mon had a smile on his face as he let the pack down off his back. "Nice fire. A bit dangerous this close to the city, but it's warm."

Mon didn't move to douse the flames. Elisa stepped into the camp circle. "I don't want to go back to the farm." Elisa crossed her arms across her chest, holding the pistol upright against a shoulder.

"I'm not here to take you back."

Elisa blinked. That wasn't the answer she was expecting.

"You've made your choice. And I'll go with you," Mon said. "Although I don't know where you think you're going." Mon reached into his pack and pulled out a bottle of wine. He crouched down and sat with his back against a tree, facing Elisa.

"Where are Gabriel and the other hands?" Elisa sat down opposite Mon and stared at his outline over the fire.

"Back at the farm," Mon said.

Elisa looked at him and saw the hint of sadness in his eyes from over the fire. She understood. She'd forced Mon to abandon his home. The farmhands had stayed to protect a farm against an enemy that was notorious for being unkind occupiers.

She swallowed her sadness and pushed it deep inside of her. She was a Lannes of Erlon; she didn't have time for girlish feelings about a farmhand who smiled at her a few times. She couldn't be slowed down by such things now.

But the feelings were hard to keep down.

Elisa dwelt about Gabriel and the farmhands alone on the farm and surrounded by the Horde now. She didn't know what would happen to them. But now she felt even more alone than before Mon had arrived.

* * *

Mon hadn't talked much more after Elisa's question about the farmhands and the farm. He'd drunk his wine and fallen asleep. Elisa had tried to sleep as well but had found it difficult, and when it finally came, it was fitful at best.

"Where do you propose we go?"

It was now the next morning and they were packing things up. Elisa rolled her sleeping bag up as tight as she could before stuffing it into her bag. The fire was still sending wisps of smoke towards the tops of the trees.

"North." Mon's voice was gruff. More like a grunt than any normal language.

Elisa reached up and attempted to rub the sleep from both her eyes. She'd gotten her tears out in the long hours of the night before. Now it was time to focus on running to safety. "That was my direction, but where in the north? Where do we go?"

"We'll figure that out when we get there."

That wasn't a reassuring answer, but Elisa finished packing up her things and kept quiet. Mon led them into the trees towards the northern hills. Elisa did her best to keep up with his quick pace.

The farmer was dressed in gear she'd never seen before. It was an old jacket that had seen a lot of use. It was well lined and looked warm. It had buttoned pockets on the front and sides. His pack was the same kind issued to the military that Elisa had seen on the soldiers of her father's guard.

And he had a musket.

The weapon was long and freshly polished. A sparkling bayonet jutted from the top as Mon rested the barrel on his shoulder while walking.

Elisa only quietly observed for most of the morning until she couldn't keep the question inside any longer.

"Where'd you get your musket?"

The old man didn't respond. He kept walking at a brisk pace.

"Your musket," Elisa repeated. "Where'd you get it? I never saw it around the farm."

"It was in the attic."

"Was it yours? Did you fight in my father's wars?"

Elisa knew the answer to her question even if Mon wouldn't say it out loud.

"You did. Which campaign, though?" Elisa was thinking out loud. She filled the silence from Mon with thoughts of her own. "Were you at Ice Fields? Maybe you fought earlier. Were you at Riom? Were you a general? A marshal, even? No, you'd have a silver pistol."

Elisa touched the two pistols on her own belt. She thought she saw the faintest of twitches in Mon's shoulder as he walked.

Her eyes locked on his shoulders.

On both jacket shoulders there were scars where old patches had been ripped off. In the Erlonian army, the stripes for rank went on the shoulder.

And the shadows of the removed patches covered most of Mon's shoulder.

An officer? That didn't make sense. Mon drank too much to survive as an officer in her father's military.

The silence hung between them for a long while. Elisa's mind raced with the possibilities of Mon's history as they hiked.

They stopped for a quick bite to eat around midday. Mon stood against a tree and looked at the ground.

"You knew my father too, you were close even." Elisa stared at the farmer. She'd never thought to ask about his past because she thought it was only farming. Now the reasons why she'd been sent from the palace to hide on Mon's farm made more sense. "You wouldn't have come to get me in the city if you didn't know him. He told you to take me into hiding, didn't he?"

"Don't talk so loud, we're still close enough to the city to run into Kurakin scouts. Scythes, even."

Elisa wanted to ask more, but the mention of the Horde stopped her. Mon straightened up from the tree and picked his musket back up. He resumed the hike without another word.

They walked on without conversation for the rest of the afternoon and Elisa allowed her thoughts to run wild with Mon's past.

She'd find out more about him. She'd discover his history with her father and the imperial army.

Despite what she'd told herself the night before, about being confident being alone and trekking north by herself, she was glad to have Mon's company.

He wasn't the best conversationalist, but he would do as a guide. Elisa's mouth turned into a smile and she lengthened her strides to keep up with Mon's pace. They hiked through the forest towards the wide-open north and moved away from the dangers of Plancenoit.

Andrei

The search around the farm took the rest of the morning. Nothing was found and Andrei confirmed the farm was abandoned. The girl was gone.

His hawk came back and rested in a pine tree nearby. She hadn't seen anything of the girl, either. The forest was too thick north of the farm.

Andrei walked alone towards the open doors of the barn and thought through their next steps. His men were completing a sweep around the western side of the farm, some in the corn fields, others going through the store houses and the woods.

"Already given up the search?"

Andrei drew his pistol and knife at the same time and leveled the gun at the source of the voice. It was a man sitting on a bale of hay. His legs were crossed underneath his body in the style of the Lakmians.

"Who are you?" Andrei kept his gun on the man but returned his knife to its holster. The Lakmian's posture wasn't threatening.

"A sibling of your own general's guide," the Lakmian said. He rolled off the hay bale and dropped to Andrei's level.

Andrei got a full look at the man and confirmed he was Lakmian. A tail swung between his legs. His skin was tan and smooth and his hair was a bright blond.

"Sibling? That's a strong word." This was a new voice, but it was more familiar to Andrei. He'd been expecting this vision to show up.

"Is it incorrect?" The Lakmian turned to face the new apparition to Andrei's right. He didn't seem surprised at the appearance either.

Andrei would recognize Duroc's god voice anywhere. It sent a chill up his spine every time.

"In a sense, no." The god stepped closer to the Lakmian.

His dark hair hung back in waves from his head. The pointed teeth could be seen clearly when he talked behind his clean-shaven face.

"You're playing into his hand, Brother," the Lakmian said. Andrei still had a pistol pointed at him.

"Where is she? Where are you leading her?" The Kurakin god took another step forward.

Andrei stayed still. His gun arm was steady.

"You'll find her," the Lakmian said. "You've got the best on it, don't you?" He gave a smile in Andrei's direction.

The Kurakin god didn't respond. Andrei watched as the Lakmian faded away as if he was smoke from a campfire. Before Andrei could even think to fire his pistol, the vision was gone.

"Come." The Kurakin god beckoned Andrei to follow him. He didn't seem concerned that the Lakmian vision had gotten away. He acted as if all that was happening was part of a normal day.

Andrei holstered his pistol and followed the god out the door. They walked across the farm's front yard to the house and entered the wreckage of the front room. The god stood over one of the bodies.

Andrei's mind was numb and thoughtless. He was used to the Kurakin god appearing around Duroc. It'd been happening since before the war. But the Lakmian appearance was something new entirely.

The god lifted his eyes from the body and nodded at Andrei. "North. As you suspected. She'll have one man with her, you should be able to track them easily. Follow the eastern road from this plot and then cut north."

Andrei stared at the god. What had just happened? Andrei looked down at the dead boy on the ground and back up at the god. How had he discovered that from a dead body?

Andrei knew better than to ask questions. He only nodded and turned to gather his men.

"Scythe."

Andrei stopped and turned back to face the god.

"I must have her alive. She's very important."

The god faded away to smoke before Andrei could respond. Andrei took his first breath in what felt like forever.

"Gods." He shook his head. They had work to do; he couldn't spend time questioning orders from a higher being or wondering what that Lakmian vision was. Andrei turned and walked out the door to begin readying his men.

Elisa

The crack of the musket ripped through the silence of morning. Elisa's view was blurred by smoke and she lost sight of the target. When everything cleared and the woods went back to quiet, the deer was gone.

"Did you miss?" Mon scanned the forest from beside her.

"No," she said.

Mon pushed up to a kneeling position and looked off through the trees. Elisa checked the sights on the old musket. She was positive she'd hit the deer.

"Grab your things," Mon said. "We'll look for blood, but we won't linger."

Elisa noticed Mon made frequent glances south in a nervous manner. He seemed to expect the Kurakin army to burst through the brush at any moment.

Mon had pushed them hard the previous day and Elisa's legs were tired. The farmer had taken the watch at night. Elisa was at least thankful for that. But this morning he'd roused her early and told her a deer was walking through the creek bed nearby.

Elisa had smelled the wine on the man's breath, but his speech was steady. She'd rubbed her eyes and brought her mind fully awake and they'd walked to the creek. Elisa had insisted on taking the shot.

"You sure you hit him?" Mon pulled himself to his feet.

"Yes."

"Your father teach you to shoot?"

"Yes. And others."

"Let me guess, Junot?"

"Yes." How did Mon know that?

"I see." Mon shook his head while scavenging the ground for tracks or blood.

"What? You don't approve of him?"

"He's reserve. A home guard." Mon almost spat the words.

They reached the spot where the deer had been standing and began looking for drops of blood. Elisa made a wide circle to the west. "What's wrong with a home guard?"

"They don't fight." Mon moved east at a slow walk with his head down.

"They're fighting now."

"As a last line. And I think they've already been overrun."

Elisa felt a pang of sadness for her old home. Mon was correct. Plancenoit was now ruled by the Horde.

"I say we move on." Mon turned back and looked at her. "We've got plenty of food."

"Spread a little wider. I hit him." Elisa walked out farther and kept her head down on the brush at her feet. They would find the blood. She didn't miss. Mon did the same in the opposite direction and they were soon out of sight of each other.

The breeze that had been dead all morning suddenly woke up around her and she felt a crawling sensation up the top of her spine. Elisa recognized the feeling.

"Hello." Elisa turned around and saw a surprised look on the Lakmian vision's face.

"I was trying not to startle you," he said.

"You didn't." Elisa took a step towards the guide. "I thought you'd already abandoned me."

"No. Just waiting for you to follow my advice."

"To flee north."

"Yes. And just in time, too. The Horde has already attacked your old home."

Elisa knew better than to ask about Gabriel and the other farmhands. She didn't want the answer spoken out loud anyway. "Where do we go from here, then?"

"North."

An exasperated noise escaped Elisa's mouth. "You and Mon are the same. Vague guidance and nothing more."

Elisa's frustration with this vision was getting dangerously close to becoming distrust. What did she know about this Lakmian? Why should she trust him?

Her mother's advice about visions came back to her once again.

"Your path will appear soon, we must be patient." The Lakmian stood rigid and still.

"Are you saying you don't know my path yet?"

"Not completely." The guide shrugged. His tail flicked lazily behind him. "There are other powers at play here, powers that haven't revealed themselves."

Mon's call interrupted Elisa before she could ask another question. "Elisa!"

"Here!" Elisa yelled back.

"I found blood!"

"Oh, good," Elisa said.

"You must go." The Lakmian nodded at her. "I will return soon. Fly north as fast as you can."

Elisa made to move back towards Mon but stopped and turned to the god again. "What do I call you? What is your name?"

The god stared at her for a second. "I have no name in this world. I'm only a guide for you."

"A guide?"

"Yes," the guide said. "Hurry north. You have dangerous enemies chasing you, Princess. And I know your father and mother would hate to lose you now, after all that's been done to protect you."

The guide faded away and his shadow was carried off on a breeze through the trees.

Elisa sighed and moved towards Mon to help track down the deer from the trail of blood it'd left behind.

Chapter 5

In stark contrast to the stern military mastermind that conquered the Continent, Lannes was a doting father to his only child, Princess Elisa.

Tome of the Emperor
Nelson Wellesley

Nelson

King Nelson found Emperor Lannes standing on the second level of the western wall of Taul Fortress. The emperor braced against the howling wind and his cloak whipped around him as he stared out over the sea towards the horizon.

Nelson stopped on the wall walkway below and watched Lannes.

Nelson's lower position was shielded from the elements by the high wall built into the rocky cliffs of the island, making it almost comfortable and quiet to be outside for once. The wind was only a low whistle above his head, while the sun beat down to warm the top of his shoulders.

Lannes sensed the king's presence eventually and turned and smiled down at Nelson. The king nodded up to him and Lannes moved to climb down the steps to the first level.

"I don't think I could stand being up there in the wind for very long." Nelson smiled at Lannes when he stepped off the final step.

"I'm used to it now." Lannes waved his hand back up towards the second level as if it was nothing.

Nelson felt a short pang of guilt at Lannes's words. It was his own country and their allies that had sent the emperor here to this cold island of salt and wind and rock and nothing else.

Lannes fell in next to Nelson and the pair walked side by side towards the northern wall along the eastern walkway. The longer Nelson spent with the emperor, the more the guilt grew.

He found himself liking the man. It seemed strange now, after spending only a little more than a week talking with him, that Nelson had lived his entire adult life fighting Lannes and his empire.

The pair spent most of their days discussing famous battles from the Continent's histories or debating modern theories on government or discussing a passage from the Ascended One's Tome. It amazed Nelson how easy Lannes was to talk to. If someone had told a young Nelson a decade ago, when he was still only a prince, that he would one day walk along the top of the Fortress of Taul and have an enjoyable intellectual conversation with Emperor Lannes of Erlon, he would've assumed that person insane.

And yet, here was King Nelson, strolling along and conversing with Brun's greatest enemy.

"I'm sorry there's not more news of your daughter." Nelson ran his hand along the stones of the wall to his left as they walked. They were warm from the sun and scraped against the tips of his fingers.

"Or much news about anything."

Nelson turned and saw Lannes was smiling behind his jest. Nelson chuckled. "I'm sorry about that as well." The king withdrew his hand from the wall.

"No news may be a good thing," Lannes said.

"True." Nelson shrugged.

The pair turned the corner of the walkway and continued along towards the eastern side. The octave of the wind's whistle changed above them with their new direction.

"Marshal Lauriston was last reported seen at Notain with the central army," Nelson continued. "He seems to have evaded the Kurakin vanguard so far."

"He'll keep the army safe." Lannes looked down at the stone walkway and held his hands clasped behind his back as they walked.

"He's lucky the northern Coalition army moves so slowly."

Lannes chuckled. "King Charles was never one for timeliness."

Nelson shook his head. "No, he's not."

The pair walked along in silence for a while. There was nothing but the whistle of the wind above their heads until Lannes spoke next.

"Lar will evade them too when they cross the Branch. He'll find a way to win this war."

Nelson had to smile at the Erlonian confidence. It never wavered, even now. Decades of victory under Lannes would do that to a people, especially when they were an already confident and strong culture beforehand.

The pair reached the northeastern corner of the fortress and Lannes turned up a flight of stairs. Nelson followed him without a question. The wall on the second level here was shielded from the wind by the main keep rising above them.

"Lar will keep Elisa safe too."

Nelson raised his eyebrows at this. "She's with his army?"

Lannes shrugged and stepped up to the edge of the wall. He looked down at the waves crashing into the spiked rocks far below. "I'm not sure, but she might be. Lar promised to keep her safe."

"I see." Nelson stayed back away from the edge and the view of the drop down towards the sea. It made his head spin and his legs feel weak. "So she could be with him or she could have been in Plancenoit and fled when the Horde arrived?"

Lannes nodded but then shrugged again. "Is this the true reason why you came here, to find out where I've hidden my daughter? Next you'll want to know what I did with Epona."

"No." Nelson was taken aback by the sudden change in Lannes's tone. "No. Not at all. I—"

Lannes turned away from the edge and smiled at Nelson. That settled the king's mind down a bit, but part of Lannes's question still raged.

Why was Nelson here? Why was he not back in Brun, leading the war effort or attending the Coalition summit in Citiva?

As much as Nelson reminded himself of his plan, some days it was hard to rationalize sticking to it, no matter how much he enjoyed talking with Lannes.

"Lar will keep his promise, that I'm sure of." Lannes turned and walked along the top of the wall. The emperor seemed oblivious to the questions now pounding in Nelson's mind.

The large stones of the keep wall towered above the pair as they walked. "He's the greatest warrior we have," Lannes said. "He will always fight. Protecting Elisa or defending Erlon, he and his generals will do their job."

Lauriston

Marshal Lauriston had a decision to make. The army could escape. There was a path east, into the deep hills of the Dune Forest, but he had a promise to keep.

It was a commitment to an old friend. Words that seemed like a lifetime ago that wouldn't leave him now.

It did no good to dwell on Lauriston's old friend, but he found himself thinking on Emperor Lannes more and more as the war dragged on. The marshal thought on the last conversation he'd had with Lannes, the last words they'd spoken to each other.

Fleeing north. Retreating with an army that had finally seen defeat after so many years of victory. The Kurakin were still in the south, but the Coalition forces had finally come out of hiding and now raged all around the retreating Erlonians trapped in the middle of the Continent.

They'd been too far east. Too far away from home.

It'd been Lauriston's idea to split up and for Emperor Lannes to sneak into the north. It'd been his idea that allowed Lannes to be captured in Laine. If that hadn't happened, maybe Erlon would be winning this war. Maybe Erlon would survive.

The marshal hung his head and wished he wouldn't dwell on such questions. But he couldn't help it.

Emperor Lannes had known his end was coming somehow. When he split from Lauriston and the main army, he'd made Lauriston promise to keep the imperial family safe.

His daughter. The princess. That was his focus.

Lauriston had done that well so far, given the circumstances. He'd placed her with a trusted friend. But the Horde had moved too quickly through the south. With Plancenoit fallen, was she still safe?

Lauriston's thoughts wouldn't leave the subject even as he needed to focus on the army's retreat. He stood with two of his generals in a field, watching the army move into the dense woods of the eastern hills.

"If the Kurakin are already this far north, they've taken Plancenoit," Quatre said.

"Means the farm as well," Lodi said.

Quatre's uniform was still ripped and his shoulders were low and tired. Lodi's Lakmian tail drifted back and forth between his legs and he leaned heavily on his spear.

"You think they've already been captured?" Lauriston looked between his generals.

"I would hope not, but seems likely." Quatre shrugged and twisted up his mouth.

Lauriston looked at Lodi. The Lakmian's face was blank, but Lauriston could tell he agreed.

"But we don't know for sure." Lauriston didn't want to believe the most likely scenario. He couldn't have another failure on his hands. Certainly not one of this magnitude involving his friend's family.

"Desaix can ride south and check," Quatre said. "If they're still there and alive, he can bring them here."

"And I would lead the army east and hide in the trees?" Lauriston shook his head. "I'd leave my duty to Lannes to someone else once again?"

"You have a duty to your men as well, sir." Quatre's eyes were hard. His statement was true, but it didn't make the decision any easier.

"I'll go get her," Lodi said. "With Desaix."

"Thank you, Lodi. And you too, Quatre, for the advice. I have a lot of thinking to do on this." Lauriston needed to change the subject and give himself space. He turned back towards the retreating army. "How much longer until we're clear?"

"Not long. The men will be in by nightfall. It'll be hard to track us in these woods," Quatre said.

"Good."

That was all Lauriston could say. His thoughts were far away again. Back to a different era when Erlon was the ruler of the Continent and Lauriston a marshal in the grandest army since the Ascended One's time.

He thought on his promise to the emperor. He'd kept it while leading the army. He'd done well with it, all things considered. But the war was a losing one. And now he had to choose.

The emperor had asked only one thing of Lauriston. Nothing to do with the men or the country. Only a task for the royal family. Only protecting Lannes's princess.

Quatre and Lodi walked off to organize their own units and oversee the men coming over the bridge. Lauriston was alone now. He wandered along the marching men and the officers huddling in groups and organizing the camp for the night.

Cheers came from some of the men as their commanding marshal passed. They were distant in his head, like hymns at a funeral. Lauriston barely heard them, but still went through the motions of nodding acknowledgement to the soldiers.

His mind was in another place. He knew what his decision had to be. He just didn't like it.

"Shit," Lauriston said to himself as he walked. He received a startled look from a horse boy scrubbing buckets nearby, but no one else heard him.

This was his lot. The lot of a marshal. He'd have to fight through it somehow. There had to be a way to keep both his promises.

Lauriston stopped as he reached the edge of the field. The grass here was tall and unkept. It swayed gently in the breeze. The marshal watched his soldiers moving about.

The forest would hide them. Allow them a safer retreat east and some room to plan out the next phase of the war they were losing. The cheers of the men showed Lauriston the army was still confident. They still wanted to fight.

That was good.

Lauriston watched the wind ripple over the grass again and again and thought on his options and his promises to old friends.

His decision came to him.

Lauriston called for an aide. "Call a meeting, all generals," Lauriston said when an aide arrived.

"Yes, sir." The boy ran off.

Lauriston would have to stick with his decision now. Two promises. One had to be broken. He'd made his choice.

Elisa

The cut of venison sizzled on the bone as it was turned over the fire. Elisa's stomach grumbled. Her eyes watched a line of grease form and drip down onto the coals as she made her mind think on other things besides the farm she'd abandoned.

They'd found the deer. Mon had let Elisa clean it and carry the cuts back to their camp while he packed up their campsite. The old man had not allowed them to cook any of the deer for breakfast, instead forcing them to keep moving north at a quick pace. The hard trail biscuits hadn't satisfied Elisa's stomach in the slightest.

Mon now sat across their evening fire, measuring out powder for cartridges. A half-empty bottle of wine sat next to his hip and he stopped to take a pull between each completed cartridge.

Even with the drink, Elisa saw that the old man's hands were deft with the tiny paper pouches and the powder horn. She watched him to keep her mind off the slowly cooking meat and her rumbling stomach, but also because she was now curious about the man's history.

He'd been a soldier in the Erlonian army. That much was clear from his old uniform. But how long ago did he retire? Had he even fought with her father or was he gone before the emperor rose to power?

Which campaigns had he fought in and how did he end up on the farm outside Plancenoit?

She looked at Mon over the fire and decided to voice some of her questions. "Who told you to come get me from the palace? Why did the palace guards allow that?"

Mon paused and looked at her for only a second before resuming with the cartridges.

That wasn't the response Elisa wanted.

"So the plan was to hide me in plain sight." Elisa was thinking fast and she talked to keep things organized in her head. If Mon wasn't going to converse with her, she could at least talk through things on her own. "And with that spectacular plan failing, what are we doing now? Running north? Sounds great to me, right into the Brunian and Wahrian armies. At least there should be miles of wilderness between us and them, right?"

"We'll go north, yes." Mon took a long pull from the bottle and continued measuring powder. Elisa raised her eyebrows at him, imploring him to continue. "Marshal Lauriston is still up there with an army. We'll find him, safest place for you right now, I think."

"With an army that's going to be surrounded soon if it's not already. Great."

"If you have another plan, I'm all ears." Mon set a completed cartridge aside but didn't complete the ritual by drinking from the bottle. His hands settled and he looked at Elisa, ready to listen.

"Just give up and go surrender to the Kurakin in Plancenoit? Maybe they'll let me go live with my father on Taul." Elisa regretted thinking about that option. She wanted to see her father again more than anything, but not in exile on a cold eastern island surrounded by Brunian guards.

"I don't think that's what the Coalition would do with you. I think you're a political piece for them. They'd use you to keep the people in line and pacify the country."

Elisa couldn't argue with that prediction. It seemed logical. And maybe not the worst fate in the world for her?

Elisa shivered and pulled her jacket closer around her. That wasn't a good thought. Her father wouldn't approve of her considering giving up.

Mon set down his powder horn and left his bottle on the dirt. "Do you know what's chasing us? Do you know what was coming to the farm shortly after I left?"

Elisa didn't know. She stayed quiet. Maybe her fate as a political pawn wouldn't be so simple.

"I fought with your father, yes. But I retired from the army before he decided to march south. You've heard the stories of his battles with the Kurakin and Duroc, I know. But you don't know the details. I've heard them from men who were there. Brutal fighting in the cold against the Kurakin elite." Mon took a breath. His eyes bore into Elisa and shimmered in the flickering light of the campfire. "The Scythes are their most brutal. Trackers who can follow any trail, fighting with powder bombs and long swords. They ride beasts the likes of which you've never seen. Like the wolverines you find near Beauhar, but as large as horses."

The last description hung in the air over the fire. Elisa felt her heartbeat pick up as she stared at Mon. She tried to keep her mind from picturing the beasts, but the images came anyway.

"You think that's what's chasing us?" she said.

Mon gave a slight nod and went back to measuring out powder. "They're after the heir to the Erlonian throne. I think they'd send their worst."

Elisa understood now why Mon had pushed them so hard during the day. She took an unconscious glance behind her into the dark outside the camp circle.

"Don't burn the meat." Mon nodded at the fire.

Elisa removed the venison and cut a bite off with her knife. It was ready and the pair shared the meat and ate a good meal. The meat was hot on Elisa's tongue and tasted full of juice and fat, though the meal didn't fully keep her mind off the idea of Kurakin warriors on wolverines rushing towards them through the dark.

"Finish it, you'll need the energy tomorrow," Mon said. Elisa realized she'd been staring at the last few bites of venison in front of her as her mind raced full of nightmares.

Mon doused the fire and Elisa prepared her sleeping pad, wondering if she'd be able to sleep at all.

"I'll watch first. You rest up, we'll be moving fast tomorrow." Mon stepped away from the fire circle into the trees.

Elisa had too many thoughts in her mind. She lay down and tried to calm her thoughts, but nothing worked. There were only visions of bloodthirsty Kurakin beasts for her to see when she closed her eyes.

She rolled over and looked across the dark campsite. Mon was by a tree, standing to ward off sleep. He stared out into the woods. The trees were silent. Not a sound came through the blackness towards them. Elisa shivered in her sleeping bag and stared into the deep darkness and heard the echoes of enemy beasts roaring as they pursued her.

Chapter 6

The event known as the Abandonment is the most perplexing issue of the Continent. Why would the Ascended One, at the height of his power, leave this land and abandon his followers? And, perhaps more importantly, where did he go?

Musings on Ascension, Volume 1
Davout IV, Fifth Tribune to the Ascended One

Andrei

The Kurakin marched with an efficiency the northerners could never hope to match. Andrei stood next to his wolverine in the shadows of trees by the road and watched the black uniforms heading north.

General Duroc rode a tall horse. He towered over the other cavalrymen behind him. The leader of Kura broke from the ranks and moved into the trees. He ducked under the low branches and headed directly for Andrei's position.

The general's dark hair hung down in messy locks and only the darkness of his eyes betrayed emotion, if any at all. His battle ax was strapped to the side of his horse along with a line of black obsidian pistols.

"General." Andrei bowed and stepped forward as Duroc reached him and dismounted.

"Master Scythe." Duroc handed the reins of his horse to a nearby servant. "Do we have the girl's trail?"

"We do, sir. There's someone else with her; we believe it's someone from the farm," Andrei said.

"Where are they heading?"

"North, along the edge of the hill country, sir."

"Good." Duroc stood straight and still. "The army will keep our planned course. We go along the Broadwater north. You go after the girl in parallel to us."

Andrei did his best to match the posture and meet the general's eye. "Where's the Erlonian army?"

"Hiding in the eastern hills, but they can't go far. The rest of the Coalition moves slowly south from Vendome."

"You'll encircle them," Andrei said.

"Yes. But you need not worry about that. Find the girl before she can reach the other Erlonians."

Andrei nodded.

"Go." Duroc looked back towards his marching men. "Keep me informed as we move north. Find the girl."

Andrei nodded again and walked off into the forest as Duroc returned to his army.

Andrei's wolverine was resting on a boulder a hundred paces into the woods. The beast gave him a growl for a welcome and stepped down off the rock to allow Andrei to mount.

The pair traveled northeast and easily found the rest of his Scythes as they tracked the princess north.

Andrei's wolverine fell in at the front of the group with his nose to the ground. Another growl let Andrei know that his beast was on the scent. Growls echoed along the line behind him.

They had the girl. Andrei would push the wolverines at full speed to catch her. He wouldn't take any chances; they'd ride day and night. There'd be no escape for the wolverine's prey this time.

Rapp

The prince grumbled under his breath as he walked. The words were nothingness, pent-up anger and frustration that he needed to let out.

His boots echoed up to the ceiling of the entrance hall of the palace as he moved towards the front entrance. The guards hauled the tall doors open and he stepped out into the crisp air of the morning.

Rapp kept moving down the palace steps and turned to the right to head down the plateau's main street down the center of the rock. There was another summit meeting this morning, a committee on maritime trade regulation, if Rapp remembered the schedule correctly. The only way Rapp would ever attend a discussion like that was if the Ascended One himself was attending.

The main street running away from the main palace building was lined with houses that normally served as quarters for the palace's many servants, but during the summit, the rooms had been cleared for the attendees from the various foreign nations. Flags hung over the fronts of the houses to denote the various countries attending the summit.

The red of Brun, black of Kura, purple of Morada, and so on stretched down the line all the way to the Temple of the Ascended One at the end of the street.

Rapp kept his eyes on the temple. It sat on the southern end of the plateau and faced the backside of the royal palace. It didn't predate the palace, but the building was one of the largest religious structures on the Continent. Its cornerstone was said to mark the location of the war god's ascension to the heavens centuries ago.

The temple loomed larger and larger as Rapp approached and did nothing to quell his worries and thoughts. Rapp had hoped his frustration and annoyance at his family and the state of the country would dissipate as he approached the temple, but it only got worse. His mind wouldn't stop dwelling on the war he was missing and the recent history of his father and the Wahrian army.

They were going to win this war. Erlon was going to fall. But it was the Kurakin who got the glory, not Wahring.

And what was going to happen to the Continent next?

The Coalition held a grand peace summit. Was a group of nations who worshiped war really going to let peace reign for decades simply because the big bad Erlonian Empire was no more?

Rapp climbed the steps of the temple and pushed into the worship chamber. The vaulted ceilings of the temple glowed blue from the morning light pouring in through the tall stained-glass windows on the eastern wall. Rows of pews sat under the temple's heights and stretched all the way to the foot of the great statue to the Ascended One at the front.

The stone god stood over seventeen feet tall and raised his sword even higher. His head was large enough for Rapp to see all the features of the god's face from the back of the hall. He had a strong jaw, curly waves of hair that fell down the side of his face, and wide white eyes that stared down at the prince.

Fight in battle and win glory. Seek out the strongest opponents and defeat them and win praise from the heavens.

The Ascended One preached that all men must seek glory on the battlefield. Rapp felt ashamed at his own history on campaign. Looking up at the statue of the great god only made it worse.

What had Rapp done? What had he ever won?

He'd led a few small battles during the Erlonian campaigns against Morada in the swamps along the border with Laine. He'd been in the north with his father's army when the emperor was defeated at Klostern. And he'd been in exile for the rest of the wars, hiding in a foreign country with his mother and sisters like he was a scared prince too, instead of a man who would one day need to be a great warrior king.

Rapp wanted to cry out and ask for forgiveness from the god that towered over him now. He wanted to plead with the Ascended One, explain that it wasn't his fault that his family was weak. He needed another chance. He would prove himself worthy of the throne if allowed to fight.

Rapp stumbled down the aisle between the pews. He averted his eyes from the statue but knew the god's gaze still followed him.

Rapp walked around the stone base and the massive feet of the god and let out a heavy breath upon reaching the alcove at the front of the worship area. He would pray to the god later. Right now, he didn't feel worthy enough to ask for anything from the great warrior.

The Tribune's dais rose in steps to form various platforms. The right side held the pulpit for the Tribune to preach from and a throne sat in the middle for the king when he was present for worship. On the wall above the royal chair hung Wahring's most prized possession.

The ancient sword of the Ascended One.

It was strapped over a great shield and was short and wide and sharp, appropriate for the fighting styles of the Ascended One's own time on the Continent. Its steel always shone bright, even in low light.

Rapp's father had brought him here when he was a young boy, before the Erlonians had sacked the city and pushed the family to exile. The Tribune had taken the sword down and let Rapp hold it for a moment. It'd been too heavy for his little hands and he'd felt ashamed at almost dropping it.

The memories caused the prince to fall to a knee and he closed his eyes before the sword and tried to block out the depressing thoughts. He didn't pray yet, he didn't attempt to speak with the Ascended One.

His mind went to the present war. His father was far off in the west and marching slowly south. The Horde was about to take the capital, if they hadn't done it already. The eastern theater, along the Lakmian Range, was a stalemate, but would end shortly after the full collapse of Erlon in the west.

Rapp had missed it all. He didn't see how he could serve the war god anymore. He didn't see how he could win glory for the realm and become a great prince who would be an even greater king.

What would the people say about this war when Rapp rose to the throne? Rapp hadn't fought in it. He'd missed every major battle.

A king shouldn't be viewed as a coward who attended a peace summit instead of fighting with his soldiers.

Rapp's mind settled and the right path forward became clear.

He'd chosen to stay in Citiva on the request of his mother and father. But what did a prince care about the whims of others, even if they were the king and queen?

Rapp would leave that afternoon. He would pack up and march off with an honor guard of soldiers from the city guard and he would ride to the front in the east to take part in the final battles of this war. There was no sense in waiting for the rest of the delegation to arrive, no sense in attending the summit instead of fighting.

Rapp would run away, he would—

The foundation of the temple shuddered under Rapp's knees. For a full second his mind was terrified that the entire plateau was cracking and the temple and the palace and everything would tumble down on top of the city below.

But the shaking felt focused. It was only the stone directly under Rapp's knee that shook.

The prince's fear abated quickly. He didn't quite understand what he felt, but there was somehow a calm coming from the movement.

" *Warrior Prince.*"

The voice shook the pillars of the temple and almost knocked Rapp to the floor. His eyes locked on the sword hanging above him and Rapp knew immediately who was speaking. It seemed impossible, but he knew it was the truth.

This was the stuff of legends.

"*Warrior Prince,*" the voice of the Ascended One said. "*A task is laid before you.*"

"Your soldier is at your command, Ascendant General." Rapp couldn't get his voice to speak above a whisper. The shuddering of the world had stopped, but the prince's head spun with every new word from the god.

This only happened in the stories. The voice of the Ascended One only came to the greatest warriors throughout history and guided them on a quest to prove their worthiness and defeat evil.

"*A traitor stands among your united nations. The empire falls, but a new evil rises.*"

"What evil, great Ascended One? The Erlonians? Lakmia? The Kurakin Horde?" Rapp felt the stone under his knee shudder once more at the mention of the Horde, but the sensation was gone just as quickly as it began.

"*The traitor is in the shadows now, he remains hidden from even me.*"

Rapp kept his eyes on the gleaming steel of the sword and didn't respond. His heart was beating in time with the god's words.

"*You will find this person and burn him out. Stay at the summit of nations and protect it. Should it fall, a war you can't win will engulf your people.*"

The pressure within the temple released.

"How do I find the traitor? How do I burn him out?" Rapp said.

The voice didn't respond again. Rapp collapsed all the way to the floor and lay with his arms spread out and looked up at the high ceiling in disbelief and silence.

The Ascended One had chosen him. The warrior god had visited Prince Rapp and given him a task, a mission to prove his greatness.

The task was vague, but Rapp knew he would not fail. He couldn't fail. This was his path to glory.

The prince scrambled to his feet and moved back towards the temple doors. All thoughts of the fleeing to the front were forgotten. He had a new war to wage at this summit.

Rapp stopped halfway and turned to bow at the stone god's head high above him. He ran out the door and into the bright light of the morning and his mind raced with the thoughts on the god's words.

Pitt

Pitt wanted a fight. Vendome had been nothing, a quick sacking with the loss of Wahrian lives due to their king's incompetence.

Now the joint army marched farther south at the extremely slow pace chosen by King Charles. There were bands of Erlonians still out there. Pitt could feel them. He wanted to find them and direct his grand battle before the war ended. But orders held him back. Charles held him back.

Pitt felt sick. He got up and left his tent and went to the central fire of the camp. His staff stood, but he waved them back down to their seats.

"No word from Charles?" Pitt said to the communications officer as he poured himself some tea from the man's kettle.

"Nothing, sir."

Pitt sat down near the fire and held his cup in both hands in front of his face. The army had pushed into the forest south of Vendome and found no sign of any Erlonian force. There were the typical bandits or small groups of militias. But Pitt knew there were more out there farther south.

Pitt felt the pressure in his mind growing daily. He needed glory. He needed victory on the field and stories to be told back home across the island of Brun.

His family depended on it.

Brun was a naval power, there was no glory in the army. The Marines were seen as honorable and a vital part of the Brunian maritime-based military, but Pitt's army had always been an afterthought.

Pitt, as the youngest of four sons, had broken away from his family's tradition of raising naval officers. At Oxtow, he'd joined the land warfare track in order to differentiate from his older brothers.

That decision had kept him alive where his brothers perished.

Their father had fallen blockading the Meridien Straight before Three Bridges. His oldest brother drowned during the Moradan campaigns in the straights of Alcalas. The other two sank as part of the same armada just before the emperor was captured and the war fully turned for Brun.

Pitt's mother and sisters now sat alone back in Brun and depended solely on his general's salary.

His sisters' marriage prospects were greatly diminished now that their mother was a widow and their only brother fought on land and not at sea.

But the end of this war would be fought on land by the army. If Pitt could win glory in the last stages of this war, he could return a hero and turn his family's fortunes around.

Pitt shook his head. His hopes fell away and his thoughts returned to the present and he remembered his hopeless situation. The Wahrian king would keep this joint army from glory through his slow marching. The Kurakin would defeat the last of Erlon's soldiers before Pitt even crossed into the central parts of the empire.

Pitt looked at the maps daily. There was a river called the Branch south of their current position that fed the great Broadwater in the west. Below that were forested hills that the Erlonians called the Dune Forest and even farther south of that would be the ultimate prize at the end of this war.

The Erlonian capital of Plancenoit.

The Wahrian king kept the army from that prize. The king wanted to lead the main force. The Brunians under Pitt were the van, but were only allowed to push out so far. The king wanted to keep his flanks consolidated against the threat of an attack that wasn't ever going to come.

Now Pitt's men would spend their second day in a row sitting in the same spot. The soldiers would only grow more restless waiting for the foreign king to catch up. All while the Horde got the glory of the Erlonian capital and capturing the last marshal.

"Sir, message from General Win." The aide's words pulled Pitt out of his thoughts.

A messenger was brought forward. Pitt offered him some tea but was politely refused.

"General Win's men haven't had any contact in the south, sir. He says the roads are clear and good for marching."

Pitt nodded. A lot of good those clear roads would do them right now with the king still lagging behind.

"Another message, sir." Another boy arrived next to the first and saluted.

"Go on, private."

"The rearguard have made contact with the Wahrians."

Pitt stood up immediately. "Finally." The word escaped his mouth before he could stop it.

"King Charles should arrive at our position this evening, is what they said, sir."

"Thank you, sir. Take a message back to Win to have him keep up the scouting. We should be on his trail soon after the king arrives. Hopefully in the morning."

* * *

King Charles did arrive later that evening, only far later than expected. The main Wahrian army settled in a field to the north of the Brunian position. They were still establishing a camp when Pitt rode up to meet with the Wahrians.

The king's tent had been set up first; the rest of the soldiers worked on the others around its position. Pitt was called into the tent and found the king lounging in a chair with a cup filled with wine.

"General." King Charles raised his cup in greeting.

"Your Highness." Pitt gave only the slightest of bows. "My men are ready to march when you give the order, sir."

"Good, good. Have a seat. Wine!"

The yelled order startled Pitt. Servants came in and poured him a drink and topped the king off.

"I'm finished with this." Charles turned his hand down and flicked his fingers over a platter filled with crumbs at his side. The servants gathered up the remains of the meal in a rush.

The king belched and drank some more wine before addressing Pitt again. "News from the east is that the summit has kicked off. Everyone is praising our conquests and ready to set a lasting peace."

"Good, sir."

"It's a great feeling to win a war, don't you think?" Charles leaned back in his chair and tilted his head side to side to stretch his neck. "And to defeat the armies of Emperor Lannes himself. We should be quite proud."

Pitt didn't correct the king on the fact that the emperor was in exile and had not been opposite them on any of the battles in the current invasion. In fact, Charles had never beaten Lannes in pitched combat before.

"Sir, my men are ready to move farther south in the morning. We'll leave at first light." Pitt had already given the orders for the men to be ready before sunrise tomorrow morning.

"What's the rush?" the king said. He shifted around in his chair. The squeaking of cushion fabric filled the tent.

"Excuse me, sir?" Pitt said.

"Where are we off to? There's nowhere for the Erlonians to go. We have them surrounded. The war is already won."

"Sir, this is a vast forested region, and not all the Erlonian units have surrendered."

"They will," Charles said. "You're just like my son, always wanting to talk war and find the next fight. Let us just enjoy the wine and a nice evening for once, shall we?"

Pitt couldn't believe what he was hearing. "Your Majesty, we've been camped for two days. My men are ready to move."

The king belched again. "And mine need rest. We have all the time in the world. You Brunians are so uptight while on campaign."

Pitt couldn't argue with the man. The Coalition had agreed the Wahrians would lead this part of the campaign and Charles commanded the joint army. Pitt was still as trapped as ever.

The king rambled on about other topics. Pitt drank his cup politely and listened. It was a long time before Pitt had an opening to excuse himself. He walked out of the tent and rode back towards the Brunian camp filled with frustration.

He'd missed the war. The Horde would take Plancenoit and find the last bits of the Erlonian army. They would have the victory spoils. Pitt would have nothing. No chance to win the glory he desired.

Back home, his sisters would be forced into low marriages and their lives would be ruined. His family's stature would continue to fall.

All because their only remaining son was a lowly land general who couldn't win glory in a war full of it.

Pitt's greatest accomplishment would be observing King Charles's eating habits and the type of wine he favored in the evening. Pitt sighed and walked on through the cold night and felt hopeless as the stars spun above him.

Chapter 7

A battle is won many days before the first shot is fired.

Maxims of War, Entry Three
Emperor Gerald Lannes

Rapp

The cliff edge crumbled and fell away with a crack to tumble to the pits below. Rapp stood on the execution platform on the lawn of the palace and watched the workers dangling off the edge of the rock in front of him.

The plateau had been shrinking for centuries. Bit by bit the edge fell away and tumbled down into the pits at the bottom of the rock. The cliff's edge slowly approached the foundation of the royal palace year after year.

Rapp hated metaphors.

The prince turned and stared up at the great spires and the gargoyle-adorned roof of the palace. Back during his teenage years, when the family was in exile and Erlon dominated the Continent, Rapp had always assumed he would feel joy upon returning to this place. He had fond childhood memories here and the palace was vast and comfortable and filled with everything a royal could want.

He'd been close to running, to fleeing his mother and her summit and joining the eastern front along the Lakmian Range. But now he had a divine mission. The Ascended One had chosen Rapp.

The Tome taught that the war god only visited those he deemed worthy and even then only in times of great need. The Continent was approaching peace after decades of war between the empire and Coalition. Why would the Ascended One approach Rapp now?

There had to be an evil lurking in the shadows that no one had seen yet. Rapp would find out. It'd been three days since the voice had come to him in the temple. He'd made no progress yet, but Rapp wouldn't fail the Ascended One.

"Falling away!"

The cries of the workers behind Rapp stole his attention back to the cliff. He turned in time to see another section of the rock crack and break away, this time very close to the wooden lift structure that brought the royals and their guests down to the city and back.

Beyond the crumbling cliff, the city bustled below the royal seat of the realm. The morning market was in full swing in the main square. Smoke drifted up from chimneys and the city guard moved about the walls.

Another bit of the cliffside shifted under the engineers near Rapp as they worked. It didn't break completely free, but the workers gave the spot a wide berth.

The prince shook his head and walked away from the workers. Some said the engineers from Erlon, brought by the foreign emperor when occupying the city, had been able to fix parts of the erosion and stabilize the cliff. Most Wahrians believed that to be lies spread by the emperor's political advisors.

Rapp's mother had spent the months after their return to Citiva sending men in harnesses over the cliff to investigate the supports put in by the Erlonians, but none of the experts had been able to discern how the contraptions worked, or if they provided any benefit at all. It was just another way that Rapp's family was outsmarted by Erlon, while their ancestral home literally crumbled around them.

Erlon's supremacy was finally coming to an end, though. Plancenoit had fallen, the war was almost won. Rapp had just missed it all.

Though he still had a chance at glory. It wasn't through war, but the Ascended One had chosen Rapp to find the traitor in the summit. This was the way for Rapp to make up for all the battles he'd missed while his family wallowed in exile. This was his last opportunity.

Rapp was due to attend another summit meeting, something to do with mining rights on the Erlonian side of the Antres Range. It was pointless and Rapp didn't feel like attending. He had too much else to think about.

He stepped off the execution platform and walked along the perimeter of the cliffside. He stepped around the engineers as they worked and kept well away from the barrier ropes they'd strung along the weakened parts of the edge.

How would Rapp find the traitor within the Coalition? That question pounded inside his head and drowned out his other thoughts as he walked.

He'd spent the first full day after the god's visit observing the diplomats from the various countries while in meetings. He watched the reactions to various bits of news from the war fronts or a turn in the debate over parts of a treaty or agreement. It would've been extremely boring for the prince if he wasn't on a divine mission.

Some of the dignitaries he was able to cross off immediately. The Lainian ambassador was small-minded and weak. He talked of nothing but trade for his peaceful nation and Rapp could never see him being clever enough to come up with a scheme big enough to warrant the attention of the Ascended One.

Moradan Ambassador Leberecht wasn't a good candidate either. While Leberecht was certainly intelligent enough to scheme behind the scenes of the summit, he'd always been jolly and friendly with the Wahrians and a staunch supporter of the Coalition. It was true in his younger days the ambassador had been a supporter of republics, including the Erlonians' revolution when the people overthrew and executed their own king long before they promoted Lannes to Emperor, but now Leberecht worked with and supported the Moradan monarchy. Rapp didn't suspect him in the slightest.

The rest of the Moradan delegation were the same in Rapp's mind as Leberecht, as were the representatives from Wavre and Vith and the countries of the Southern Confederacy.

Rapp approached the southwestern edge of the plateau and turned up the path that led back to the main street in the center of the plateau. The temple to the Ascended One towered above him and only made the pressure of his task worse in his mind.

Rapp's main suspects were the Brunians and, as much as it pained him to say it, the Wahrians.

His mother would be horrified to think that a traitor could come from her own advisors, but Rapp didn't trust a handful of them. The biggest suspect was a slender man named Ambassador Trier.

Rapp had never liked the soft-spoken but extremely wealthy merchant. He spoke to the royals like he knew better than them, even Rapp's mother, and he'd never served in the Wahrian military. This last point was a mark of shame Rapp could never get over and he vowed to watch Trier's every move.

Rapp turned up the main street and headed back towards the palace. The flags of the various countries fluttered in the wind over the doors of the diplomatic housing on either side of him. He didn't have a direction or destination in mind, he only walked to give his mind space to ramble on about the potential traitors.

The other big suspect came from Brun. The Sorceress Thirona, when Rapp looked past the sparkling dress and shiny hair, was the exact kind of representative to have ulterior motives and goals for the summit. The Brunians had always been schemers against Wahrian interests, even in times of peace. On top of that, Brunian King Nelson had chosen not to attend the Coalition's gathering in person. Rapp could easily see Thirona running a larger Brunian scheme to weaken Wahring and take control of the Continent after the war was over.

There were other suspects, of course. The possibilities were endless with this many diplomats in one place, but Rapp's thoughts always returned to Ambassador Trier and the Sorceress as the two main candidates.

Rapp stopped at the end of the street before reaching the palace lawn again and the cliff engineers. He needed to take action. He needed to be decisive.

If he were on the march with his army, he wouldn't sit quietly and think. He would talk with advisors and come up with a plan.

To catch the traitor and save the summit, Rapp needed help. He needed an advisor. He decided on the person easily enough. He wouldn't go to his mother; she would either not believe him or she would set the entire palace staff on the Coalition members to draw out the traitor.

No, Rapp needed an ally that was more subtle and used to moving in the background. He turned his head slightly and saw the purple of the Moradan flag hanging over the door of the second house from the palace.

Rapp nodded to himself. He needed help from Ambassador Leberecht.

Rapp smiled as he settled on his course of action. Leberecht would know how to handle this situation. He would know more about the other dignitaries than anyone and would have a plan to find out their true allegiances.

Together, they would find the traitor in no time at all. Rapp would save the summit and the Ascended One would praise him as a worthy follower and send glory down from the heavens.

Elisa

Elisa's daily view was nothing but Mon's pack and the musket slung over his shoulder. They walked all day and made camp late at night and ate cold bits of meat or some trail biscuits Mon had brought from the farm. The princess's stomach growled at her continuously and her legs ached and stiffened up every night.

On the fifth day after shooting the deer, Elisa found herself in the same position. The forest didn't change, the trail stayed the same. The farm seemed to be hundreds of miles away now, but Elisa knew they still had a long way to go before they found the Erlonian army.

And Elisa could still feel the terrible foreign soldiers that chased her behind them.

She dropped a hand and brushed one of her silver pistols with her fingertips. They would be her defense against anything that attacked them in these woods, her pistols and Mon's musket and whatever fighting experience the old farmer had from his mysterious past.

If Elisa's time on the farm already seemed like a lifetime ago, then her time as a young princess in the Plancenoit palace seemed like another life entirely. The pistols had been a gift from her father when she'd expressed interested in learning how to shoot. The palace smiths forged them and her mother helped with a little magic to improve the design.

Elisa had seen the pistols given to her father's marshals and Epona's magic had made Elisa's smaller and lighter and more smooth. Elisa loved the feel of the cold metal and how the weight felt in her hand when she held them out to aim.

She wondered if her father ever envisioned Elisa would be put in a situation to use them against Kurakin Scythes. When he'd watched her unwrap them and learn to shoot all those years ago, had he even considered this current situation as a possibility?

Not a chance. Elisa didn't think anyone in the palace or Plancenoit or anywhere in Erlon could've predicted what would happen when the emperor marched off from the capital for the final time. No one had seen the fall coming at all.

Mon crested a hill in front of her and Elisa thought about asking for a quick break but decided against it. Mon would refuse and push them on even faster if she asked now.

More memories flooded forward in Elisa's mind as they started down the slope on the far side of the hill. The images of her father leaving the palace for the final time pressed to the front. Her mother rode next him and the army marched out of the city in a long column. Elisa had watched from the top of the palace and tried to count the standards above each section as the army moved towards the northern horizon into the very forest she now walked.

Her childhood had been filled throughout with similar goodbyes with her father. This last goodbye had felt no different.

She remembered going to the barracks and taking shooting practice right after the last of the soldiers disappeared from view into the distant woods. She'd thought she'd see her father again after the campaign season.

He'd always returned victorious. Always.

Even after Three Bridges and the Moradan campaigns, where the army had suffered some of its worst casualty rates, her farther had found a way to strengthen the empire and return home. But his campaign against the Southern Confederacy and eventually General Duroc and the Kurakin proved different.

Elisa knew she shouldn't dwell on these things, but the questions came too quickly and answers never followed.

Where had her mother gone during that campaign? Why had she abandoned her father?

The Kurakin had been too strong on their own ice fields for the mighty Erlonian army. Her father had retreated north and fought the Coalition once again and the army's power slowly diminished. To hear the stories from those final battles, her father would've still made it safely back to the north along the eastern edge of the Antres and Lakmian Ranges had he not been captured.

But the emperor had been betrayed again and sent into exile.

Did the same fate await Elisa at the end of the fall of Erlon? Or, with the Kurakin Scythes chasing her and Mon, was there a worse ending coming for her?

Mon was afraid of what would happen to them if the Kurakin caught up to them. He was afraid of the Scythes.

The old farmer ducked under a branch as they walked. Elisa walked cleanly under its height without moving her head.

Elisa decided to use the farmer as an excuse to stop dwelling on the questions surrounding her parents and the failures that had led to her current situation. Mon had fought in her father's wars. When had he left the army? Which of the famous campaigns of the past two decades had he marched in?

Elisa had tried to ask him directly a few more times on the trail or as they made camp at night, but the farmer never told her anything. He avoided the questions and changed the subject to something else or ordered Elisa to help gather firewood.

Maybe none of the questions around Mon's past mattered anymore. Maybe Elisa wasn't long for this world. It certainly seemed like it, given what chased them and the enemy armies that marched all around them.

How could she possibly survive the end of this war?

The voice of the strange guide that had appeared to her twice now cut through her thoughts as Mon led her up another densely wooded hill.

The first time he'd appeared, on the hill overlooking Plancenoit as it fell, he'd told her to run north. Then he'd said something else, something strange that Elisa was only just now remembering.

"You're far too important to this war to be lost *at the very beginning.*"

At the very beginning? This war was already over, there was only the final part of the fall of the empire to deal with.

What could the guide possibly mean by that?

Elisa's fingertips brushed over the imperial seal protruding from the silver of her pistols as she thought on the questions. Mon stopped at the top of the next hill and moved off the path. Elisa let out a sigh and let her pack drop to the ground as Mon leaned his musket against a tree.

"Time for a short break," Mon said.

Elisa couldn't be more thankful. She collapsed against another tree and leaned back against it, stretching her legs out and working on the tight and cramping muscles.

This break wouldn't be long; none of them ever were. Mon pulled out his canteen and Elisa wondered briefly whether it was full of water or wine before her thoughts went back to the questions surrounding her family and the mysterious vision and the war and her destroyed home.

The question that broke through to the fore again was regarding the guide's statement. He must have misspoken. How could the war only just be beginning?

Elisa took a long drink of water from her canteen and tried to rest while she waited for Mon to start back on the trail and the questions and worries and fears swirled inside her head.

Andrei

Andrei rode in the middle of the line of wolverines. Standard Scythe hunting procedure had Jerkal, Andrei's second-in-command, leading the way in the front to allow Andrei to focus on his hawk scouting above them.

The air was cold and the wind picked up far above the forest. Andrei could feel everything through his hawk's feathers and saw the forest stretch north before him and turn into rolling hills. The sparkle of a large river came from the western horizon. Massive peaks rose white and gray in the east.

And there was no sign of the Scythe's prey.

Yet.

No sign of the prey yet, Andrei had to remind himself. His eyes opened back on the ground and he returned to focusing on the trail. The forest looked the same as before, as if the group hadn't moved at all during his time in the hawk's eyes above.

Andrei let out a soft sigh that wasn't loud enough to be heard by the others around him. The prey had to be close. Andrei could feel the end of this latest mission coming. He was ready for it.

He was ready for the end of the war.

Thoughts of his home came involuntarily and flooded his mind. The images were blurry. He'd been away for too long, fighting wars against the north with Duroc and the Horde.

He could see the details slipping away the farther he marched north, the farther he marched from his home. He'd lost the memories of his wife's face long ago. His children's gap-toothed smiles and bright eyes were long gone as well. All Andrei could see now was his house up on a windswept and snowy hill in the distance.

But even in Andrei's dreams he couldn't get any closer.

He could see his wife on the doorstep, a tiny figure with hair billowing in the wind. He could see the children running around and around the house. But he couldn't approach. He couldn't find a path home.

Another Scythe's wolverine growled behind him while Andrei's own mount sniffed at a bush they passed on the side of the trail. He wondered if the other Scythes and soldiers in Duroc's army were as tired of war as he was. The Kurakin didn't worship war like the northerners did, but they still praised glory and success on the battlefield. Everyone served, everyone wanted to fight and ⁓t Kura.

Duroc certainly didn't tire of war, but the general was driven by his guide and their grand plans for the Continent. Andrei didn't care for the plans of greater men.

He only wanted—

A feeling crept around the back of Andrei's brain. He heard a faint caw through the canopy above and his drifting thoughts stopped immediately.

"Halt," he commanded in a low voice.

The order was carried up to the line for Jerkal in front to stop the group as Andrei closed his eyes and felt himself soaring again. The Scythes would wait on the ground until he came back, hopefully with good news this time.

Andrei knew it would be good, as his hawk wouldn't have bothered him otherwise. The bird had seen something.

The wind howled in his ears and the forest ripped by far below him. The bird banked and the wind's whistling changed as they whipped around to pass back over a spot of trees a few miles in front of the Scythes.

Andrei saw the flash as the bird cawed again. A bit of color passed between the gap in the canopy of the forest. The bird floated over the spot and Andrei waited for it again.

The bird's eyes focused just north of where the first flash had occurred. Andrei waited as the bird floated on the air and held position against the wind.

The flash came again.

It was unmistakable this time, blue against the dark green of the trees and a flash of white right after.

His hawk had found them. And very close to the Scythes, too.

Andrei fell back to earth and opened his eyes. The Scythes were all watching him. Andrei smiled through his beard.

"We ride," he said.

His wolverine let out a growl and Andrei kicked the mount off the path to move up to the front of the group.

They'd spotted the prey and his wolverine would soon have the scent. Andrei nodded to a grinning Jerkal at the front of the line and pressed on into the woods. His Scythes fell in behind him and they moved off towards the girl running from them in the forest.

Chapter 8

A Kurakin Scythe's usefulness as a scout and in battle is almost unparalleled on the Continent.

A Marshal's Memoir
Alexandre Lauriston

Elisa

Elisa reached as high as she could for the final branch of the climb. The tree was tall and would hopefully provide a commanding view of the terrain to the north. The branches thinned at the top and made the going tough.

With a grunt, Elisa hoisted herself up onto the top. The canopy of the forest was below her now and the land stretched down from her position and ran away to the north along the border of the rolling forested hills in the east. Far to the east were the blue and hazy hints of mountains with the rolling hills of the Dune Forest in between.

She took a glance behind her and instantly regretted it. They were still close enough to her old home to see the smoke from Plancenoit. It was small but unmistakable. A dark plume on an otherwise clear horizon to mark the sacking of the Erlonian capital.

Elisa pulled her eyes back to the north. That was what Mon wanted her to scout. She didn't need to look backwards.

There were only a few clouds in the sky. A single hawk drifted lazily over the eastern side of the shallow valley. The forest was dense and Elisa could see nothing but trees and a single cut of what could be a river on the far northern end.

Elisa climbed down without another look back towards the destruction of Plancenoit. The trip down was easier than climbing up and she made good time back to the forest floor.

"How's the path look?" Mon stood up from his resting place against a tree when Elisa reached him.

"Dense forest. Hemmed in on the east by hills."

Mon nodded as if that's what he expected.

"The hills are lower in front of us. I could see the mountains far off. Looks like there might be a river at the end of the valley due north." Elisa tried to remember if there was anything else she'd seen of note.

"That'll be a creek, I think." Mon picked up his pack and slung it over his shoulder. "There shouldn't be a river until we hit the Branch."

Elisa strapped her pistol belt back around her waist and picked up her pack.

"We'll try to stay towards the eastern side. I don't want us up against the hills if the Scythes get to us, but they'll be coming from the west. We don't have much of a choice."

Elisa took an involuntary glance behind her. The now familiar feeling on the back of her neck that something was watching her returned. No matter how fast they moved, it always felt like some beast was in the trees and about to pounce out and take her.

But the forest was peaceful and calm behind them as the pair started north once again. That didn't make the chased feeling in the back of Elisa's mind go away, though.

She couldn't stop thinking about a wolverine with blood-covered jaws hurtling through the forest at them. She shivered as she tried to keep up with Mon and felt shame come to her.

She was afraid.

What would her father say if he knew she was trembling at the mere thought of danger and despair?

Elisa stared at the back of Mon's pack and tried to push the fear away. She thought on the beautiful sky she'd seen while above the canopy. The forest hid the sky from them now, but when she'd been at the top of the tree, it had been a gorgeous day, with clear skies for miles around and the lush forest below.

"Strange." Elisa's mind stuck on one detail that she'd forgotten until just now.

"What?" Mon's word was more of a grunt. He didn't slow down his pace along the trail.

"There weren't many birds out." Elisa thought back on her view over the valley. There'd only been that one hawk drifting lazily. "It's still early fall. There should've been more flying over the forest. More hawks and crows. I only saw that one."

Mon stopped. Elisa almost ran into his back.

"Only one?" Mon looked at her and Elisa saw the concern in his eye. Worry lines creased on his forehead.

"Yeah." Elisa didn't know what was wrong, but her fear came back in full force.

Mon looked back to the south. His eyes darted up to the sky, but the forest canopy hid their view.

"What?" Elisa said.

"We need to move," Mon said. He slung his musket off his shoulders and held it in front of him. He took off down the same path at a jog and Elisa struggled to keep up.

They reached the bottom of the hill's slope and moved off over flat terrain. Elisa heard Mon's breathing grow heavy, but the old farmer didn't slow down.

"Are your pistols loaded?" Mon said without turning back towards her. "Powder dry?"

"Yes. Mon, what is going on?" Elisa couldn't hide the strain in her voice. She felt more shame come to her, but it was quickly drowned out by an overwhelming fear of what had upset Mon.

"You know the Scythes ride wolverines, but what else do you know?" Mon kept pushing them across the forest floor. They found a rocky creek bed where the trees were a bit farther apart and moved along it.

Elisa tried to remember other things she'd read about the Kurakin and the Scythes. Her mind wouldn't work. It was full of adrenaline and fear.

"I don't know."

"Their commanders, the leaders, they have a connection with hawks."

A connection? The adrenaline pumping through Elisa's body wasn't helping her to understand what Mon was talking about anymore.

Mon jumped over a rotting log on their path and kept moving. Elisa almost fell when the toe of her boot caught the obstacle, but she regained her footing and stumbled after the farmer.

"You only saw one hawk in the sky. In the west, you said?" Mon glanced back at her.

"Yes, but close."

Mon didn't say anything else. Elisa could feel a stitch forming in her side from their running.

They pushed on. The only sound in Elisa's ears was the branches moving past her head as they ran.

The ground rose again and Mon climbed faster. Elisa had already lost her sense of direction from the tree she'd climbed earlier. She could only hope Mon knew where to lead them.

A sound broke through their flight. A single cry came down from the sky.

The screech of the hawk hit them and Mon pulled up to a stop. Elisa skidded in behind him and struggled to catch her breath. Mon cocked his head and listened, but the sound didn't come again.

Elisa knew only one thing could've made the call, though. And she didn't want to think about what it meant.

"We need to keep moving," Mon said.

He didn't turn to look at Elisa or wait any longer for them to rest. He ran deeper into the forest with his musket ready in both hands. Elisa took a final deep breath and ran after him, forcing herself to not glance behind her at the still forest that hid the beasts that chased her.

Andrei

Andrei heard the call come down from his *sakk* again. He felt the bird's excitement pick up and his own feelings matched it. The prey was running now. Things would be over soon.

Tracking in this landscape of trees and dirt and rocks was much easier for the Scythes than the tundra of the southern plains back home. There was an abundance of trails and nothing was covered in snow or ice or blown away in the wind.

"Keep formation until we get closer," Andrei said to the men around him.

"Keep formation," Jerkal repeated to his side of the line.

"Break when I call break." The nose on Andrei's wolverine was working along the ground as it moved. Andrei could feel the breathing change in the lungs underneath him. The beast could smell prey close at hand. It could sense their target in front of them.

"Quicken up now," Andrei called out.

The pace of the formation picked up in unison. Andrei looked up and found his hawk again. Another caw hadn't sounded, but they were still on the right track.

"Break."

The formation broke apart at a full gallop on Andrei's order. He felt wind whipping by his ears as they flew down the trail. His wolverine snapped at the air and gave a rumbling growl that Andrei felt in the beast's chest between his legs.

His men would spread out through the forest. Andrei wanted to make sure they encircled the girl and gave her no avenue for escape. That would mean sacrificing their strength in numbers, but that shouldn't matter. They were only hunting two people.

A single Scythe could take them if needed.

Andrei hoped it wouldn't come to that. Once a wolverine found the pair, they would all converge quickly enough. They just needed to find exactly where the girl was in front of them.

She couldn't hide from Andrei's hawk. And she now couldn't run from the wolverines on the ground.

They would shut off the flat lands to the west and force them towards the hills in the east. Then it would only be a matter of time before they were found and trapped.

Escape would be difficult for Andrei's prey now.

Elisa

Elisa heard the wolverines. Growls hurtled through the trees behind them. She stole a look behind but still saw nothing.

"They'll come from the sides," Mon called over his shoulder.

They pushed on at a full run. The ground became rockier. Boulders jutted from the ground between trees.

Elisa saw her first wolverine out of the corner of her left eye.

It ran parallel to them. The beast was low to the ground, with blackish-brown fur and a white strip on the top of its head. The rider was all in black with his head turned directly at Elisa.

The wolverine roared and leapt over a boulder in its path, churning up dirt towards them.

"On our left." Elisa pushed extra effort through her legs and gained on Mon in front of her. She drew one of her pistols.

Mon sped up as well. "Keep going." He broke off their path away from the Scythe and Elisa followed. They moved up a slight incline through the trees on their right, heading east.

Even through the adrenaline of the flight, Elisa had questions in her mind. The wolverines had found them now. How could they outrun them? What was Mon's plan to get out of these woods to safety? Weren't they heading towards the hills they wanted to avoid?

Maybe there wasn't a plan. Maybe there wasn't a way to escape. Maybe they just needed to pray.

There were other wolverines nearby. Elisa heard a growl to their right and turned to see a new Scythe leaping down from a large rock formation not fifty feet away. Another growl came from the first wolverine that still charged them from behind.

Mon changed direction again to get away from the new Scythe. He broke left and pushed on, but Elisa could hear the wolverines gaining on them every second.

The farmer realized the same thing.

Mon threw his pack off his shoulder and slowed next to a boulder big enough for both of them to crouch behind.

Mon pushed Elisa down and stood back up with his musket raised over the barrier. He fired. Elisa looked over the edge of the boulder, but the smoke from the shot blocked her view. She heard the thump of something hitting the forest floor and a gurgled yell.

The sounds of galloping wolverines continued.

Elisa rose and drew her other pistol and leveled both weapons in the direction of the sound. Her hands were shaking.

The wolverine's outline formed through the haze of Mon's gun smoke. It roared and Elisa saw the rows of teeth clearly. She fired both pistols.

Smoke poured out but was blown away quickly. Elisa's ears rang from the shots. She'd hit the wolverine with both shots. Two splashes of blood burst from its white chest.

The beast didn't slow down.

Mon leveled his own pistol over Elisa's head and fired at the charging animal. This final pistol shot finally did it.

The bullet cracked into the beast's face. It stumbled with a growl and crashed into the forest floor and slid forward, dying only a handful of steps away from them.

There was no time to marvel at this small victory. Another growl took the dead wolverine's place.

The second Scythe tore towards them on their right. Elisa ducked behind the boulder and started to reload. Her hands were numb and clumsy. The metal of the pistols felt foreign on her fingertips. She fumbled the first ball she tried to get in the barrel.

Mon stayed upright and faced the charging Scythe. He reloaded his pistol while keeping an eye on the enemy. His hands were deft. He didn't fumble.

The Scythe rider pulled out his own pistol and fired towards them. The ball cracked against the boulder right in front of Mon. The old farmer didn't flinch.

Mon finished with his own pistol and pointed it at the enemy.

The crack sounded far away to Elisa. She fumbled another ball and scrambled to find it in the dirt. She stole a glance up and saw the Scythe rider gripping his neck and falling backwards off his mount.

The wolverine only charged faster. Its eyes glared red within its dark face.

Mon dropped his pistol and drew his sword. The beast was too close for him to reload again. Elisa wasn't going to make it in time, either.

The wolverine only had a few more bounds left to close the distance.

Mon stepped out from behind the boulder and between the monster and Elisa. She continued to reload but felt the hopelessness taking her already. The wolverine roared and Elisa felt the now familiar shame of fear hit her.

The wolverine took one final bound. Mon pointed his sword out in front of him. The wolverine snarled and opened its jaws.

A flash of movement came from behind Elisa.

A spear.

It streaked through the air in a blur and caught the wolverine in the shoulder. The weapon buried itself deep and stopped the beast in its tracks.

The wolverine fell and slid across the dirt. Mon stepped aside and let it smash into the boulder.

Feeling and noise came back to Elisa. Confused relief flooded her.

Her legs were shaking.

But it wasn't from fear. The ground was actually shaking under her feet. Behind her, horses galloped towards them. A Lakmian with long hair led the group. The soldiers were wearing blue uniforms.

The Lakmian frontrunner passed her and ripped his spear from the dead wolverine without slowing his horse. The other horsemen followed and spread out around Elisa's position.

Mon bent and picked up his things. He motioned for Elisa to grab her own pack.

There was a new roar off in the forest. It was answered by multiple gunshots.

One of the horsemen reined his horse up next to the boulder. "Mon." He touched the tip of his cap towards the farmer and grinned down at them.

The man's uniform had the Erlonian imperial seal with swords crossed sewn onto the left breast. Short white feathers ran along the top of his bicorne.

Elisa couldn't believe it. This was one of her father's marshals.

"Lauriston." Mon saluted and then nodded towards the Lakmian horseman. "Lodi's still got his spear arm, I see."

Both men smiled. The marshal nodded and winked at Elisa as well.

Marshal Lauriston. Elisa knew that name. The memories were far away now, though. She felt a heavy fatigue threaten to take her and she struggled to stay standing.

"How many were after you?" Lauriston said.

"Not sure." Mon looked towards the horses on their perimeter. "Only saw two, but there must be more."

"They were spread out. Making sure you couldn't slip away from them. But they didn't expect us to be here." Lauriston smiled, but his eyes were focused on his men around them. "Come, we'll get away from here."

"They have a hawk, Lar," Mon said.

"I know, we shot it down."

"Shot it down?"

"Yes, just winged it, I think, but he'll be down a while."

Lauriston whistled and the horses returned to formation. Elisa was pulled up behind a soldier who smelled of gunpowder. Elisa heard a few more distant musket shots behind her as they pushed up the hill to the east.

Her adrenaline was gone. Her eyelids felt heavy.

She was saved. Somehow she was saved by one of her father's marshals and his soldiers.

Elisa let out a long breath and held on tight to the soldier, letting her new escort carry them off into the woods and away from the horrible beasts and the enemy chasing her.

Chapter 9

The marshals of Erlon were the top generals under Emperor Lannes. Of these select few, the greatest was Alexandre Lauriston, Lannes's most trusted commander.

Tome of the Emperor
Nelson Wellesley

Nelson

"You created the rank of marshal soon after taking power." Nelson flipped open his notebook and dipped his quill in ink. The firelight of the emperor's study flicked over the pages.

"Yes." Lannes looked up and met Nelson's eyes across the hearth.

"Why?"

"To give the men something higher to strive for. Even the generals. I wanted them to be mythic, I wanted stories told about the rank to rival the Ascended One."

"I'd say they succeeded in that."

"Most of them." Lannes shrugged.

"Lauriston especially," Nelson said.

Lannes nodded.

They'd made a routine of their talks about history and the news coming from the present war. Most mornings after breakfast they would walk along the outer walls of the keep and discuss various topics. Nelson would take a break for lunch and meet with his aides and the handful of advisors who'd accompanied him to Taul and then he would resume talks with the emperor in the afternoon.

They were slowly progressing through the emperor's past, starting with his rise to power. Nelson had taken to jotting down notes from their talks. The emperor's life would make a fascinating history tome someday if Nelson survived this war.

Their discussions were enjoyable and the conversations were light. Nelson could tell Lannes enjoyed it too, but they hadn't reached the harder parts of his reign yet. They would eventually need to discuss Three Bridges and the southern campaigns and the slow decline of the empire.

Today, a gale had blown in from the south and frigid rain lashed the outside of the keep as thunder rolled overhead. There would be no outside strolls this morning.

"Like I've said before, Lauriston was the best of them." Lannes shifted in his seat and returned to staring at the flames within the hearth. The seat back still dwarfed him and made the once great man look frail. "Is there official news on any of the others? I'd imagine they haven't fared well against this invasion."

Nelson nodded to confirm the emperor's assumption. "I'm afraid they haven't."

He took a breath and thought through what he remembered from the reports over the last few months.

"Jerome Levou fell in the south, with Beauhar. He's reported to have been in a Kurakin prisoner camp ever since." Nelson noted that this appeared to be new information for the emperor. "Moreau and Beaumont were captured early in the north. They are in a Brunian camp near Vendome, the last I heard. Yalstoy—"

"I know what happened to Yalstoy," Lannes said quickly.

Nelson looked up, taken aback by the emperor's tone. It was a rare betrayal of emotion from the stoic man. But Nelson could understand, given the stories of Yalstoy's defeat while protecting the retreat of the main army in the north at the beginning of the invasion.

"Durand was killed at Clermont," Nelson continued. "Mercier hasn't been confirmed killed but has been missing since the siege of Mere."

"I see," Lannes said.

Nelson let the emperor think through the information. Silence seemed good for the conversation at this moment. He tried to imagine about how he would feel if his own country were falling.

His mind went back to the lead up to Three Bridges. To the despair felt among the people at the threat of the emperor invading the island of Brun.

The Brunians had been close to the current Erlonian fate. Nelson had only been a prince then, but he'd tasted part of what the emperor was going through now along with his people. It had felt like the world was ending.

"We have other leaders besides the marshals," Lannes said. He picked up his pipe from his side table and set about lighting it.

"You do. Which generals would Lauriston have with him in the central region?"

Lannes puffed on the pipe to stoke the small flame within the bowl and blew smoke up towards the ceiling. "Men who would've been marshals eventually had I stayed in power. They still could reach the rank, if they somehow save Erlon."

"Lauriston would promote them?"

"Or my daughter."

Nelson nodded and watched the haze grow around Lannes's head. "Which generals exactly?"

Lannes thought for a second. "I would guess he has Lodi with him."

"The Lakmian master."

Lannes pointed his pipe stem at Nelson and nodded. "Him, along with Desaix for cavalry, and Quatre probably too." Lannes paused and looked up in thought. "Murat as well, if Lar didn't split his forces at any time."

"I see." Nelson knew the names. "All veterans."

"I wish I could make them marshals. Wish I could be fighting with them now." Lannes put his pipe back in his mouth and looked back to the fire.

The thought of Emperor Lannes returning to a battlefield on the Continent sent a brief tremor of terror along Nelson's spine. He shook off the brief feeling quickly.

"But Lauriston still fights on. It doesn't matter where I am, he'll do his duty." Lannes spoke out of the side of his mouth around the pipe stem.

"Which duty is that?" Nelson said.

Emperor Lannes's eyes closed. "He won't be captured. He'll find some way to keep on fighting. He'll die for the country. He'll give his last breath trying to free her and protect the people. He won't be exiled or put in prison. He'll fight for Erlon until the very end."

Elisa

"Princess, sit if you want." Lauriston held out his hand to an open seat on a log.

Elisa looked at the gesture. The scene around her felt like one of her dreams. There was a small fire in the middle of a makeshift camp, with the soldiers who'd saved her moving about between their tents.

Saved.

Elisa got stuck on that word. It didn't seem possible. She and Mon had been finished. The wolverines had been right on top of them.

But this famous marshal from her father's army had appeared and turned the Scythes away.

And Mon knew the marshal.

"We winged the hawk, but it'll be back up." Marshal Lauriston still had his arm outstretched towards the proposed seat, but he now addressed Mon. "You were lucky only a few of the Scythes were able to converge once they spotted you."

"I know." Mon sat on the far side of the fire with his brow in shadows. He took a pull from a new bottle of wine the soldiers had given him.

"They'll be slowed down, but only for a few days." Lauriston dropped his arm and stared into the fire. He still had his marshal's jacket on and held his hat in one hand. His hair was cut short and was a deep and dark brown. Two silver pistols not unlike Elisa's hung from the belt around his waist.

Elisa finally took the seat offered her. Her legs were starting to shake and her head spun. Resting on the log would be better.

She glanced around at the camp in twilight. She counted the soldiers again. Fifteen plus Lauriston and now Mon and herself. The others were setting up tents or on watch duty or tending to the horses on the outskirts of the group's space.

"Elisa, do you need anything? Water?"

It took Elisa a second to realize Lauriston was speaking to her again.

The informal address from the marshal didn't bother her. This was her father's best friend. The man she'd seen with him around the palace the most, especially during wartime. Lauriston was the general he'd fought with for over a decade at the height of the empire and the man he trusted the most.

Elisa shook her head at his question. "No, sir. Thank you."

"She's tough, Lar." Mon's voice was gruff and weary from the shadows on the other side of the fire.

"I know. Surviving a Scythe attack is no small feat." Lauriston smiled at Elisa and took his own seat on another log and stretched out his legs. "But we could tell you had a fire in you even as a toddler, Elisa. Your father was proud of that. Thought you were just like him. We'd be in the middle of a campaign planning meeting and he'd stop and go off on a tangent about your latest adventure as a child."

The marshal stared into the fire. Elisa felt a swell of pride that appeared in her gut any time her father was mentioned, especially if the story involved his thoughts on her.

Lauriston didn't say anything else. The camp and the soldiers shifted around them and Mon's face was a shadow over the bright flames opposite Elisa. He gripped his bottle tightly with both fists.

Most of the other soldiers continued about their tasks outside the fire circle, but some of them broke off and joined Elisa's group one by one. The first few who joined the circle had general stripes sewn on their shoulders. One of them clapped Mon on the shoulder and the old farmer gave a smile and nod in return.

"Our army is north of here." Lauriston looked at Elisa while the rest of his men gathered. "We're going to have a meeting here in a second. My generals are going to discuss what we do next."

Elisa nodded to show she understood.

Lauriston smiled at her. "I want your opinion on that as well."

"Okay." The discussion would help keep Elisa's mind off her memories of the Scythe attack, although she didn't know what Lauriston hoped for Elisa to contribute to a military discussion.

Lauriston turned and pointed at the man who'd clapped Mon on the shoulder earlier. "This is General Desaix of the First Cavalry."

"Evening, Princess." Desaix removed his cavalry hat and bowed low. "We met a long time ago, but you were just a girl."

Elisa nodded in reply. She vaguely remembered the man. He'd often been a part of the cavalry guard that escorted her and her family north for holidays at Papelotte.

The Lakmian who'd thrown the spear during the fight with the Scythes was next to arrive. He took a seat on the same log as Mon and shook the farmer's hand and nodded at everyone else. Elisa received a wink over the fire.

"This is Master Lodi, of the Lakmian regiments," Lauriston said.

"How are the crops?" Lodi turned to Mon.

"Probably burned or in the belly of the enemy now."

Lodi shrugged. "Probably true."

Lauriston pointed to the final figure to arrive at the fire. "Our late arriver is General Quatre. He's the reliable one, if you couldn't tell."

"Thank you, Lauriston, that's the nicest thing you've ever said to me." Quatre took a seat next to Lodi. "I was finishing up a particularly important game of bisset, if you must know."

Lauriston ignored the last comment and moved to start the meeting. He pointed at Elisa and she felt the eyes of the circle swing back to her.

"Everyone knows our princess, our reason for this slight detour. Now the question becomes, what is our direction from here?"

Lauriston looked at his men and Elisa followed the gaze and took in the new faces, but a question jumped from the back of Elisa's mind. She knew of Lauriston. He'd introduced the other generals, but he'd left one important detail out.

"What's Mon's title?" she said.

The heads of the generals rotated from Elisa over to Mon. The old farmer finished his latest pull from his bottle and set it back down between his feet. He didn't offer an answer.

Lauriston raised his eyebrows. "General. Previously General of the Imperial Guard. Although I would hazard to say he's been pressed back into service from retirement."

A general? Elisa couldn't believe it. The old drunken farmer she'd lived with for months was one of her father's generals?

And of the Imperial Guard?

Impossible.

Elisa looked at Lauriston and didn't see a hint of a joke. No one else around the circle laughed or contradicted him

"Looks like I'm back, I guess." Mon raised his bottle in a toast motion and drank again.

"Welcome back, Mon." Lodi reached over and slapped Mon on the back, causing wine to spill down his chin.

"Any other questions, Elisa?" Lauriston looked at her and she saw the surprise behind his eyes at her lack of knowledge about Mon's title.

Elisa shook her head and Lauriston turned back to his men. "Now, to my original question." The group quieted down immediately. All eyes were on the marshal. "I know we're happy to be reunited, but we have a long way to go before we're safe. Those were Scythes out there today, in case anyone missed the wolverines." There were some chuckles from the crowd. "They'll fall back and regroup but then come back at us hard. We hit their hawk, but it'll be back up in the air soon enough. We must put as much ground between us and them as we can before that happens."

"Back to the army?" Quatre asked.

"Yes, we'll have to find them in the Dune Forest."

"We can do that," the cavalryman Desaix said.

"I hope we can." Lauriston's eyes moved to each of the generals as he talked. "We'll go back on the path we came down and then press east and try to catch them. The Dune Forest should make it easy for us to hide from the Scythes. The army will move northeast through the forest, towards Lake Brodeur. Hopefully we'll find them before then, but it may be hard."

The men around the circle nodded. Elisa thought on her knowledge of this part of Erlon. Lake Brodeau was a small lake just south of the Branch. It was well south of Vendome and on the northern outskirts of the forest. It seemed an incredibly long way from their current location.

"Desaix, we'll need some good eyes out there. We must move fast, but we can't go blindly through the woods."

Desaix nodded.

"Quatre, keep the men focused on the trail. We should be ready for a fight at all times."

Quatre nodded as well.

Lauriston paused and looked around at his officers. "Onward," he said in a soft voice that somehow carried over the group.

"Onward." The men responded and the word echoed out to the rest of the camp. Elisa heard a few more responses from the soldiers on watch in the trees as well.

"Lodi." Lauriston turned to the Lakmian. "Do we have a tent for the princess? Help her set it up, please."

Lodi nodded. The meeting ended and the soldiers got up and broke off into separate conversations. Lodi came over to Elisa.

"Come, Princess, I'll show you your tent."

The men had already cleared a space in the middle of their own tents for Elisa. The horses were tethered and being fed off in the thicker trees to her right. Crackles from the fire came behind her, along with the drone of various conversations among the men all around.

Elisa felt like she could barely lift her arms and was grateful for Lodi's help with her things. Her mind felt overwhelmed, but she feared sleep would still be hard to find after this day.

Too much had happened. Too much had changed.

She thought on Lauriston's words. This company of her father's soldiers had come south to save her. There was more of the Erlonian army out there and the marshal's goal was now to get her to it.

All while the Kurakin Scythes still chased her.

Elisa let out a sigh and looked at the men around the camp while Lodi stuck stakes in the ground for the tent. Most sat on logs around fires and talked with each other. Some were already asleep where others were on watch duty.

Elisa recognized the names that'd been introduced to her from stories and legends of her father's conquests. For the other soldiers, she recognized the uniforms of their units.

There were a handful of Lakmian Jinetes that would be under Lodi's command. These soldiers all carried the famous spears of the Lakmians and wore coats of a dark green that would blend in well with the forest.

The Erlonian units she recognized as well. There were a few cavalry guard soldiers now sitting with the one introduced as Desaix and two sharpshooters talking with Quatre.

And then there was Montholon.

Elisa's eyes found him still sitting by the fire with a few soldiers wearing the uniform of the Imperial Guard. A few days ago, Mon had been only a drunk farmer. Now he was a general in her father's army.

He wasn't just a normal general, leading a division of regular infantry. Montholon, with his weathered skin and shaking hands and ever-present bottle, was the former commander of the Imperial Guard. The elite of her father's army.

Elisa watched the three guardsmen that now sat with Mon. They were talking easily, no laughter or jokes, but calm and comfortable looks on their faces. They seemed happy to be reunited as longtime friends.

The Imperial Guard was famous for many reasons. They carried two bayoneted muskets each, strapped across their backs like the Lakmian spears. They trained with the weapons in the mountains east of Plancenoit at the famous Guard Academy. Only the most decorated and brave soldiers gained acceptance.

Her father had established the unit early on in his reign, promoting the best soldiers and giving the rest of the army a perfection to strive towards. The guardsmen with Mon now were not large men, but they clearly had a lean strength found only in experienced fighters. They all crouched on their logs and looked ready to spring forward for a fight in any direction if needed.

And Mon was one of them. Mon had led them.

Had he marched with the guard in the Moradan campaigns? Had he pressed the attack at Three Bridges?

The questions made her head spin. It was too much to believe. But here it was, right in front of her, and he'd never told her anything about it.

She'd never asked.

Fatigue came back to drape itself over Elisa. It was all she could do to crawl inside her tent before collapsing into sleep. Lodi had just finished and didn't say a word as Elisa disappeared.

The questions and observations of only a second ago vanished as Elisa's mind drifted off into a dream. She was safe and surrounded by her father's most loyal soldiers. She felt a calming peace that she knew couldn't last, but for this night, with General Montholon and his soldiers nearby, she could rest easy and float through a dream without worry.

Andrei

Andrei's heart boomed like musket volleys in the midst of battle. He ran through the trees. His wolverine was left back where the remains of the Scythes gathered.

The only thing on his mind was his *sakk*, his hawk.

The Scythes had been so close to a successful chase. They'd had the girl cornered. Andrei had been certain of it.

But just after the girl had been spotted, Andrei felt a pain sear down from the sky.

He knew instantly what it meant. Part of a Scythe commander's training involved the appropriate responses to injuries to *sakks* in the field and Andrei had experienced the pain and shock before, but it still scared him.

He'd felt the musket ball pierce his bird's wing. As he ran through the forest now, his hand involuntarily went to the bright red circle still burned under his own right arm that mirrored the bird's injury.

His *sakk* had been surprised at the bite of the bullet and the sudden loss of control.

And it only got worse.

Andrei's focus had immediately shifted from the ground to the sky and he'd felt the terror of plummeting down from an unthinkable height to the forest below along with the bird. The wind rushed past him. The wall of green approached too fast.

The slam through the canopy to the rocks and dirt below had thrown Andrei back to his own mind, and any time he thought back on the bird, he saw nothing but blackness.

It terrified him.

Andrei ran on through the woods and picked up his pace. He didn't feel the branches and thorns of the underbrush that hooked his clothes and scratched his skin. He only focused on the pain and sadness and cries of help that echoed in his thoughts.

A screech came from Andrei's left. She was weak but felt his proximity.

Andrei tore through a line of brush and found his hawk on the other side in a crumpled mound of feathers.

His *sakk* was alive, only barely.

She would live. Andrei would make sure of that.

He knelt down and picked her up in his arms. He cradled the bird in the same way he'd done his sons when they were infants.

He already had the men who weren't injured gathering moss to make a healing paste for her. She would be fine.

She had to be.

Andrei could already feel the emotions changing in the bird's small head. Hope appeared again from the warmth of Andrei. She snuggled deeper into his arms.

Andrei stood up and carried her back towards his men.

Now that he'd found his *sakk*, Andrei's mind went back to the mission. They'd almost had the girl.

His men had reported soldiers arriving right as the wolverines had the girl cornered. Erlonian soldiers had appeared as if by magic from the forest. A Lakmian Jinete and a handful of Erlonian musketmen had saved her.

Andrei shook his head and rocked his hawk slowly. He walked steadily back towards his men so as not to disturb the bird. She needed rest.

Andrei's next move would be to get the hawk comfortable and recovering. Then they would move off after the girl.

If she was with a larger group now, she would only be easier to track. The hawk would recover and be back up in the sky in a week or so.

And then they would make the girl and the soldiers who protected her pay for what they'd done.

"Find her?" Jerkal stood from his resting place against a tree when Andrei arrived back at his unit.

"Yes. She'll be fine."

The men were relieved at the news. A few came over and scratched the sleeping hawk's head affectionately.

"We're all accounted for here," Jerkal said once the other men had cleared out. He handed Andrei the bowl of moss that had been muddled to a slimy paste.

"Thank you." Andrei knelt and laid the bird gently in the dirt and began administering the healing ointment. "How long before we can move?"

"Soon. Can she travel?" Jerkal nodded towards the crumpled bird.

Andrei stayed silent for a little while, thinking through the situation. "She can move. She's tough, just needs rest. I'll carry her."

A low growl came from behind Andrei and he turned to find his wolverine pawing at the dirt and looking north. The mounts were ready to move again. They had a scent to follow.

"We can move whenever," Jerkal said.

"Good. Get the men ready. The girl can't escape us, it's just going to take a little while longer than we thought."

"Yes, sir."

Andrei bent over his injured hawk again. He spread the moss paste over the broken section of wing and around the bird's neck.

"And besides," he said. "Now we've got some revenge to take. They've hurt us, it's time to hurt them back."

Chapter 10

Make peace and only postpone conflict. Make war and win glory.

Engraving
Above the Entrance to the Lesser Basilica at Oxtow University

Elisa

The group of Erlonians fell into a routine while fleeing north. Lauriston led from the front of the group and the horses formed a winding train through the trees along the paths the forest offered. Desaix and a few cavalrymen scouted in front, and the rest of the men fell in behind their leader with Elisa always in the middle for the most protection.

The horse directly in front of her would hold the crossed double muskets of an Imperial Guardsman or the spears of a Lakmian. The horse behind her would have a long-musket sharpshooter or a cavalryman with a plumed hat. One of the generals, usually Lodi or Quatre, would ride next to her as well, Lodi being the most talkative of the group by far.

The forest land became rolling hills of rock and dirt and trees. The hills jutted up on their eastern flank to even higher ground and thicker trees. Lauriston didn't break off to the east yet. He followed a path almost directly north. From what Elisa could tell, they traveled a parallel path to the great Broadwater river somewhere to their west.

The first few days of travel were uneventful. The scouts saw nothing and the rear guard didn't report any sightings of Scythes or other Kurakin on their trail. Part of Elisa wanted to feel safe and believe the Scythes were done. But she knew she couldn't be that naïve.

On the fourth morning of travel, Lodi sat on a log across from her next to the fire.

"Watch this," he said. It was early enough that most of the camp was still stirring awake.

Elisa chewed on a bite of her trail biscuit and turned to look at the Lakmian. Lodi had a mischievous grin on his face and he nodded his head towards the other side of camp, where other soldiers were in the process of waking up and packing for the day's journey.

Elisa followed the nod and saw Mon bending over his pack just before a shriek pierced the camp, high-pitched and foreign in a group of soldiers. The yell would've had more of a place at a lady's luncheon at the palace.

Mon jumped back away from his pack as heads snapped in his direction. Laughter grew in a wave around the camp. Even the sentries in the trees joined in the chuckling.

Mon turned immediately and fixed Lodi with a glare.

"Mon hates spiders." There was a glint in the Lakmian's eye as he winked at Elisa.

"That's an even worse wake-up than a real rooster," one of the sharpshooters said from the flap of his tent near Mon.

Mon reached into his pack and pulled out what looked to be a bundle of strings. He let it dangle from two fingers and Elisa saw the outline of what could easily be mistaken for a very large spider but was in fact a group of twigs with eight dark strings attached.

"Welcome back, Montholon," Quatre said from beside Mon. He slapped the older general on the shoulder and continued laughing.

Elisa was surprised to realize she wasn't worried at all about the noise from the camp. The Kurakin that had chased her and Mon from the farm were now forgotten for a short while thanks to the company she shared. She laughed along with the men and returned Lodi's wink, noticing Mon was unsuccessfully attempting to hide a grin of his own.

She finished her biscuit and washed it down with a gulp of water. Her mind now went to other thoughts and she couldn't avoid the topic of Mon's history. She'd thought on the farmer a lot in the first few days of travel but hadn't gone to talk with him.

Elisa made herself stand up and walk over to Mon. She reached him as the old man threw Lodi's fake spider as far into the woods as he could.

"Good morning, Mon," Elisa said.

"Morning, Princess. I didn't wake you, did I?"

"No, I was already awake by the fire with Lodi."

Mon's mouth was set in a grimace. "Don't ever turn your back on a Lakmian. Every chance they can get they'll play a joke on you. Tricksters, every one of them."

Elisa saw through the glare on Mon's face. He was still experiencing mixed success in holding back a grin and remaining stern.

"Mon," Elisa said.

"Yes?"

"I wanted to thank you." Elisa looked at the ground and thought through how to say what she wanted to say. "For saving me, taking care of me, getting me away from the Horde."

Mon waved his hand as he stuffed a sleeping pad into his pack. "It was my duty. And besides, the plan was Lauriston's. I only followed orders." Mon nodded over towards the marshal's tent.

"But you took care of me. And I know I wasn't the best guest on your farm."

Mon gave a quick laugh. "No, you were fine. Maybe a bit moody."

Elisa laughed. Looking back now, it was clear she'd been a little more than just moody. She'd been forever annoyed at having to spend time with the too-talkative farmhands and the drunk farmer. And she hadn't helped with the actual farming or work around the farmhouse at all.

Mon stood up and began taking down his tent. "I'd say you weren't a problem at all. I knew you were Lannes's daughter. I should've expected you to be off hunting and in the woods half the time anyway."

Elisa laughed again, but her mind went to the thoughts that had been swirling nonstop in her mind since they'd been rescued by the Erlonian soldiers. She watched Mon fold the cloth of his tent neatly into a square and wondered about his past and what he'd never told her and what he still held inside.

He'd been a good farmer despite the drinking. That much was clear from back on the farm. But he was apparently a good general too. One that the soldiers and the other generals had an affection for.

"How come you never told me you knew my father?" Elisa blurted the question out in a rush. The moments of silence directly after magnified the awkwardness of the words.

Mon stopped his packing and thought for a second, but didn't seem put off by her bluntness. He looked up at her before speaking. "I had an irrational fear that you would get the idea that we needed to march off and save the empire. If you knew who I was, you'd insist we fight."

Elisa paused. That made sense.

She would've felt even more trapped and useless if she'd known Mon had stood next to her father during his previous battles. But she'd spent enough time with Mon now and she could see something else hidden behind his eyes.

Mon appeared to notice Elisa's attempt to look through him and hurriedly went back to his packing.

"We needed you safe, not off fighting with the remains of the army," Mon said without looking back up. "Lar's goal was to keep you hidden."

"Thank you, Mon," Elisa said even as her thoughts stayed on the parts of Mon's story that had been left unsaid.

She walked away from the old general and moved back towards her own pack to make sure she had everything ready for the day's ride. She tried to guess at what Mon could still be holding back inside himself and the reason behind keeping it from her.

What could've caused the shadow that passed over Mon's eyes when his past was mentioned?

Nothing jumped out to her immediately, but she knew the reason couldn't be obvious when it came to Mon. The old farmer was becoming more complex by the day.

She found Lodi already folding up her tent and stuffing it into her pack. He had most everything else organized neatly as well.

Elisa knelt to help him and opened her mouth to ask the Lakmian about his own history with Mon from the past. Before she could get a word out, a voice spoke from behind them.

"Good morning, Princess. Morning, Lodi," Marshal Lauriston said. He bent down and helped gather the spikes of the tent to be packed.

"Good morning, sir," Elisa said.

She made the last fold of the tent cloth and Lauriston held the pack open for her to stuff it inside. Her next thought was to ask both men about Mon and his mysterious past. She looked across the camp again to where Mon finished his own packing and turned back to ask Lauriston one of the many questions she had.

"Time to mount up," Lauriston said before she could say anything.

Lodi stood up. "Another long day of travel, Princess."

Elisa sighed and stood with them. Her legs were already overly sore from the first few days. Lauriston smiled once more and left to go rally the rest of the men.

Lodi carried Elisa's pack over to her horse and helped her climb into the saddle. The quiet of the morning and her thoughts on Mon had distracted her from the fact that she was still hunted.

Now that they traveled again, the images of wolverines and Scythes in the woods returned in a rush. She took an involuntary glance back towards the south and fell in line with the other soldiers for the day's journey. The forest was empty for now, but Elisa knew the enemy would still be out there.

Questions on the empire's past and stories from the veteran generals seemed so small compared to her country's current predicament. At least she was safe for now with the empire's best soldiers, its last marshal, and its remaining generals. And General Montholon, returned to fight for the end of the empire.

Elisa would fight with him. She fell in behind a sharpshooter on a brown destrier and tried not to think about the Scythes and their wolverines that hunted her through the woods behind the group.

Rapp

The clank of teacups and fine breakfast plates around Rapp was maddening. The room was quiet and bright and too far away from any army camp or barracks mess hall.

Queen Caroline and his sister Julia both sat with their hands in their laps and waited while the servants cleared the remains of the family's breakfast. Rapp wanted to scream. He wanted to run out of the room and leave the palace and head for the war in the west.

He should be fighting. He should've left a long time ago.

He would have already been marching west too, if not for divine intervention.

"Rapp, we have a delegation strategy meeting in an hour," Queen Caroline said as the last platter was carried away from the table.

"Yes, ma'am." Rapp gave her his best smile. "Apologies for missing yesterday, I was praying in the temple."

This wasn't a lie. Rapp had spent as much of his time in the temple as he could since the voice spoke to him.

The Ascended One hadn't offered any more guidance, but the cavernous building brought a peace to Rapp's thoughts he couldn't attain in the palace around his family. Plus Rapp's piousness irked his mother greatly, as she thought he should be more focused on the summit than the heavens.

The queen would be even more irked if she knew Rapp's plan to bring Leberecht into his divine task. Rapp wasn't going to mention the full story of the Ascended One's voice coming to him, but he would request Leberecht's help in finding the traitor and knew the ambassador would prove a great ally in the task.

While Rapp enjoyed the Moradan ambassador's company, his mother hated the man. He was still a republican in her eyes, despite his change of heart and service to the Moradan crown, and she hated how much he ate and how he acted in front of the royals. She would never be able to fully trust Leberecht.

This only made Rapp like Ambassador Leberecht even more.

Rapp excused himself from tea as soon as it was appropriate. "I have some letters to catch up on before our meeting," he told his mother.

"To the front? To General Neipperg?" his sister said, a little too quickly.

"Yes, with both fronts actually." Rapp didn't give either his mother or sister time to say more and left the tea room walking at a brisk pace.

He traveled out of the main royals' quarters on the second floor of the palace and took the grand staircase down through the entrance hall. He felt the chill of the morning wrap itself around him as the guards opened the heavy doors and he stepped outside. Sunlight flowed across the distant Wahrian plain from the east and the morning was as bright as it was cold.

Rapp turned right and headed down the main street in the direction of the Ascended One's temple. He took a glance at the holy building in the distance, but his eyes settled on his destination and the Moradan flag hanging over the door of the second house along the street.

A servant let him into the foyer of the delegate housing and exited deeper into the building to announce the prince's arrival. Leberecht came back quickly and burst through the door at the far end of the room.

"I figured you'd come and see me eventually." The jolly man moved towards Rapp and stretched his arms out for a hug. Rapp was engulfed quickly and felt the rolling stomach of the large man press against him. It was what Rapp expected being sat on by a Kurakin mammoth would feel like.

"Good to see you too, Uncle," Rapp said.

"How is my favorite royal?" Leberecht released Rapp and held him at arm's length. "Would you like a drink? Something to eat?" He beckoned Rapp to follow him and the pair walked deeper into the house.

Rapp had never been in the servants' quarters before, but the study in the next room seemed nice enough. It featured plush chairs, strong wooden tables, a large fireplace, and bookshelves lining the walls.

Leberecht waved to the center of the study, where olives and various slices of meat were laid out on platters. He motioned for Rapp to take a chair by the fireplace as he took the one opposite.

"I'm fine, thank you." Rapp wanted to get straight to the point of his visit. As much as he wanted to catch up with his old mentor, a divine quest took precedent.

Leberecht had other ideas.

"You know, this is my first time all the way up here, on the plateau. It's more beautiful than even I imagined." He leaned forward to reach the food platters and took up a handful of olives.

"You were never invited up even when you lived in the city?" That surprised Rapp. He took his seat across from Leberecht.

The ambassador laughed. "No, I was quite poor when I lived here. Skinnier, too." Leberecht slapped his gut once as he discarded an olive pit and put two more olives into his mouth. "I was born on a farm just north of here. Lots of poverty up there."

Rapp leaned forward and rested his elbows on his thighs. He looked directly at Leberecht and launched into the topic he wanted to bring up before Leberecht could continue.

"I have something important to discuss with you."

"To business immediately? I see you haven't changed a bit." Leberecht smiled around his mouthful. He set the olives back on the platter and turned to give the prince his full attention. "What do you want to discuss?"

"Something has come to my attention that's more important than us catching up." Rapp looked Leberecht in the eye and took a breath. "I believe there's a traitor at this summit."

Leberecht's eyebrows rose, but he didn't say anything. His mouth hung open.

"I trust most of the diplomats here," Rapp continued. "But I have reason to believe that some faction or someone within a faction doesn't have the Coalition's best interests in mind."

Leberecht shook his head and seemed to come out of his daze. He blinked and cleared his throat. "What makes you say this?"

Rapp had thought all week on how to answer this question without telling Leberecht about the divine voice. He'd settled on the best response he could think of and now hoped it would be enough.

"Any time a group of diplomats comes together, there are always competing interests."

Leberecht shrugged. "Naturally."

"But with a summit this important, this historic, I fear there may be some who have more sinister plans afoot."

Leberecht nodded once. He looked down at the ground and scratched his clean-shaven chin. "I can agree with that. But why are you coming to me with your concerns? Go to your mother—she's the summit's host."

Rapp shook his head. He looked at the soot-covered stones of the dead fireplace to his left. "Mother and I can't agree on much right now, ever since she forced me to return here from the front." Rapp gripped the arms of his chair as if they were hilts of swords. He looked back up at Leberecht. "And besides, I don't want the whole palace to be searching for a traitor. That will only give up the game and let the enemy know we're looking."

Leberecht pursed his lips and nodded again in agreement.

"I want your help, though. Help me watch the members of the summit. Help me find someone passing information to the Erlonian loyalists or trying to undermine the Coalition to gain more power in the future. Help me burn out the traitor."

Leberecht smiled and didn't give the request as much thought as Rapp had assumed he would. The ambassador clapped his hands together almost immediately and took in a breath. "Of course, Your Highness, I'm honored you thought me a strong enough diplomat to assist you. Who are your main suspects?"

* * *

Rapp left Leberecht's house a few hours later. The sun was close to its apex now and Rapp's head spun with the thoughts from his discussion with the ambassador.

Leberecht had agreed with Rapp's main suspects of Thirona and Ambassador Trier and he'd proposed a few more names that seemed plausible and worth watching.

Rapp was confident that his choice to bring Leberecht in to help with his mission was the correct one. The ambassador was someone Rapp had always been able to count on and had always been a good mentor and friend.

Rapp climbed the steps up to the palace and nodded in return to the bows from the guards. His boots echoed loudly across the entrance hall and off the steps of the grand staircase.

He'd missed his mother's strategy meeting with her delegates, but that was no matter. Rapp would tell her he was praying again.

It felt good to talk through his thinking with someone he trusted. He was now moving forward with his divine task. He felt like he'd made progress today.

Always attack. Always push forward.

That is what the Ascended One preached. That is how the god conquered the Continent and ascended to the heavens.

Rapp would emulate him and complete his task.

Tomorrow, the summit would continue and Rapp would push onward with his search for the traitor. He would be another day closer to fulfilling the divine request and gaining glory from the Ascended One.

Chapter 11

Lannes owed much of his early military success to his alliance with the Lakmian tribes. The young emperor succeeded in gaining the trust of the fair and martial race where centuries of statesmen had failed before.

Tome of the Emperor
Nelson Wellesley

Elisa

Elisa's escort stopped for lunch near a small stream in the woods. The horses were watered and fed and the soldiers not on scouting duty stood in small groups, talking quietly or resting against trees.

Elisa drifted between the groups but didn't join any conversations. Mon and Lauriston and a guardsman were on the far side, sitting under a tree. Quatre and some of the sharpshooters dealt out a quick game of bisset, as they always did. Elisa finished the last of her trail biscuit and stepped into a small patch of grass in an opening in the trees away from the main group.

The opening was a few paces across and allowed a spot of sunlight to shoot through the canopy and warm the back of her neck. They'd been traveling for five days now and her thoughts still wouldn't stop running through the events of the past few days over and over.

The vision appearing in the woods for the first time.

Running from the farm.

The escape from the Scythes.

Marshal Lauriston and her father's greatest warriors now traveling with her.

The Farmer Montholon was not just a farmer.

He knew the marshal, Mon had fought with him.

Too many thoughts, too much to think about.

113

Elisa needed a distraction. She drew her sword and watched the steel gleam in the ray of sunlight.

Erlon was falling. Her father's empire would soon be nothing but dust. Plancenoit had been sacked and Elisa was on the run, chased by Kurakin Scythes.

But Elisa's guide had said she was important at the *start* of the war. That one phrase stuck in her mind and gave her an inkling of hope, or at least mystery.

Had the guide misspoken? Should she even trust a strange vision who appeared to her in the woods? That kind of thing only happened in legends or in the Ascended One's tome, and her guide was definitely not a messenger from the Continent's war god.

He was Lakmian, to start, and didn't seem to be inclined to warfare or fighting of any kind. But if he wasn't from the Ascended One's legion, then where was he from?

It was too many questions for Elisa's mind to think through them now. Everything made her head hurt.

She spun her sword and took up a practice stance with the sunlight gleaming off the blade. She glanced at the closest group of soldiers. None of them were paying attention to her. Her mind cleared and only focused on the weight of the blade.

She went through her first step. A slow circle with parries against an imaginary enemy. She pictured attacks in her mind and let her sword turn them away.

She completed the move and started back the other direction. Slow steps. Deliberate parries. And a thrust or two between. She ended up with her feet back in her original position.

Elisa took a deep breath and felt her mind settle down a bit. Her first practice series was complete and the imaginary opponent fell away. She looked up and was startled to find Lodi standing in front of her.

"Hello." The Lakmian had a big smile on his face.

"Sorry, General." Elisa felt her face grow red. "I was just practicing."

"No, I'm sorry. I didn't mean to interrupt." The Lakmian pulled his spear out from his back. "Care for a sparring partner?"

Elisa's mouth hung half open. She'd had training partners back at the palace, but they'd always used practice swords. And she'd never fought against an opponent with a spear. Let alone a Lakmian.

"It's okay." Lodi spun the spear once and Elisa saw the lean muscles in his arm tense in a strength she couldn't hope to match. "Your sword won't hurt me. And I can show you some of our Lakmian moves."

Elisa felt a ridiculous flutter of fear in her chest. Lodi was an ally to Erlon, he was one of her father's friends and a general in his army. But standing in front of an armed Lakmian would have that effect on any person.

Elisa didn't want to be afraid. She buried the flutter in her chest and nodded to Lodi. The Lakmian smiled.

He spun his spear faster than Elisa thought possible and ended in an attacking stance. She brought her sword up and shifted her feet into a defensive position, but would've been entirely too slow had Lodi actually attacked her.

Elisa's heartbeat had picked up. This still didn't seem like the smartest idea.

Lodi raised an eyebrow at her. Elisa's thoughts ran wild, half of them screaming for her to not even try against the Lakmian techniques. She beat the thoughts away and took in a breath.

She smiled at Lodi.

Her thoughts were clear again. She thought on what her father and her training masters in the palace had taught her. They'd started her young, especially for a girl, and Elisa had loved every minute of their drills.

Ever a Lannes, Elisa decided to make the first move.

She lunged forward with a quick step. Her sword darted into Lodi's stance. The Lakmian appeared to only shrug one shoulder in response and Elisa's jab was pushed sideways.

Lodi's spear returned to the same position. Elisa was sure it moved, but her eyes didn't track the parry at all. It was almost like the wind had pushed her sword away.

Lodi raised his eyebrow again. Elisa's heart rate hammered. By now a few of the other soldiers had noticed them and were watching. She couldn't back away now.

She took in a breath. Before she could fully exhale, the Lakmian attacked.

Elisa parried the thrust clumsily. She stepped back and felt her stance waver and her balance shift. Lodi spun with the momentum of his thrust and pressed into her. The butt of his spear came up and around and stopped right in front of Elisa's face.

She didn't duck and she never could've gotten her sword up to block the attack. Lodi would've put her on the ground if it had been a real fight.

One of the soldiers nearby applauded Lodi's win. Elisa's face reddened. She took another step back and reset her stance.

"I didn't go easy on you," Lodi said.

"I didn't expect you to." Elisa wiped a strand of her hair from her face and prepared for another go.

"I can teach you that move," Lodi said. He stood in a neutral stance with his spear under his arm.

"With a spear?" Elisa straightened her own stance.

"It works with a sword." Lodi shrugged. "All our movement techniques can be used with any weapon. They were created for hand-to-hand combat originally."

Elisa had read about the famous Lakmian fighting methods. She'd seen the Lakmians in her father's army practicing their breathing and steps and fighting movements during drills. She'd heard stories about how fierce they could be in battle and how hard they were to defeat.

The memory of Lodi's spear taking down the wolverine charging at Mon returned to her. He'd thrown it from a long distance and from horseback, too. Without Lodi, she and Mon would be dead.

She met the Lakmian's eye and nodded.

"The key is in your feet." Lodi took three slow steps and repeated his earlier twirl. This time it was slow enough for Elisa to follow. "Think of your body like river water, flowing where the banks of the land take you. Your feet are the guiding rocks on the bank."

The metaphor didn't completely resonate with Elisa, but she watched Lodi's feet and tried to copy the steps.

Three steps. One. Two. Three.

Elisa almost fell over on the third step. It didn't seem hard, but somehow her balance felt off. She glanced back towards the main group and was thankful the soldiers had gone back to talking among themselves.

Lodi gave her some pointers and she tried again and did better this time. The third time felt perfect, but Lodi had her go again and again until she felt dizzy.

"The actual attack adds another element. Use your arms to guide your weapon. Same as your feet guide the flow of your body."

Lodi showed her the movement and had her practice. Elisa felt she had the hang of it, but wasn't moving as fast as Lodi yet. She'd have to practice this along with her normal movements now.

Lodi did the steps with her over and over and continued to give pointers until Lauriston called for the group to mount up again for the afternoon ride.

"Thank you, Lodi," Elisa said as they walked back to their horses.

"Of course. I can show you more if you want."

"I'd love that." Elisa glanced towards the front of the group and saw Mon mounting his horse next to Lauriston. The brief distraction of training hadn't made her forget her questions surrounding the old farmer. Now seemed as good a time as ever to ask more about him. "Did my father have you teach the Lakmian fighting methods to his soldiers?"

"Some units," Lodi said. "Like the guard."

That was the answer Elisa had been hoping for. "So Montholon knows them?"

Lodi chuckled. "He knows a few. Although he's probably forgotten most of it by now. I bet his flexibility is a bit rusty too."

Elisa couldn't picture the old general moving the same way Lodi did at all.

"You knew Mon well, back when he was in the army?"

Lodi looked at her. His smile weakened and Elisa knew he understood where her question came from.

"I'd imagine he didn't tell you his full story," Lodi said. His expression and the tone of his next comment surprised Elisa. "Be careful digging those stories up, Princess. Mon has a long history in the army, with your father too. And not all of it's glorious like the stories."

Elisa could see the warning clearly behind Lodi's eyes even as the Lakmian returned to smiling. Lodi knew Mon's full story. He'd probably been there for most of it.

"Give Mon his peace if he wants it. He'll tell you when he's ready, but don't push him," Lodi said.

Elisa nodded. That sounded like sage advice. She could respect boundaries, but the thoughts and questions didn't stop stomping around her head at all.

The pair finished readying their horses and mounted up. The line of Lauriston's men reformed and the trek north resumed. Elisa thought on Mon and what could possibly have happened to merit Lodi's warning to her.

Lodi turned the conversation back to more tips on the Lakmian attack move he'd just showed her. Elisa listened and responded to his advice, but half her mind remained on Montholon. Lodi had only piqued her interest even more.

She would respect Mon and not ask him directly. That seemed like the right thing to do for now. But she wondered if she could figure out what happened on her own somehow.

The group continued north and Elisa rode next to Lodi and dwelt on her thoughts. Her mind ran wild with Mon's history and his younger days fighting with her father's army and the mysteries of how he ended up on the old farm.

Rapp

Rapp exited the palace and felt the thick evening air cling to him. The day had been unseasonably hot and humid as the last bits of fall fought to hang on before the chill of winter set in fully.

Rapp turned and moved towards Leberecht's quarters. He took a quick glance over his shoulder to the western horizon beyond the front of the palace. The dusk sky exploded with bright colors of fire around massive thunderheads.

The prince felt a familiar longing, the strong pull of the war that simmered beyond that horizon. The voice in the back of his mind screamed for him to leave the plateau and find a fight.

But a stronger voice kept him anchored at the summit. The voice of a god.

Rapp glanced at the Ascended One's temple at the end of the street and set his thoughts straight. He needed to focus.

They'd made minimal progress in the days since Rapp had first spoken to Leberecht about his quest to find the traitor at the summit. He needed to work faster, but Rapp didn't know how. They had to find the traitor within the summit soon. Rapp felt a fear of failure creeping up from the back of his mind.

"Good evening, Prince Rapp." Ambassador Mikhail was waiting outside Leberecht's door. The Kurakin gave a low bow and swept a hand out behind him in a gesture too formal for the setting.

"Good evening, Ambassador."

Leberecht opened his door right after Rapp spoke and beckoned them both inside. Mikhail swept his coat aside and entered first. Rapp followed closely behind and the glint of the smooth black hilt of the Kurakin's dagger caught his eyes once again.

"What news?" Rapp didn't have time for small talk. He dove straight into business.

Leberecht had an annoying habit of discussing his opinions on the summit progress with Mikhail before starting in on Rapp's quest to find the traitor. They needed to get right down to the more important matter this evening.

"Nothing new from me." Leberecht led them through the house and out onto the back patio, where he had a full platter of cheese and cold-cut meats on a table.

"Nothing from the men I've been watching," Mikhail said.

Leberecht had insisted on bringing the Kurakin into their plans to observe the summit members. Rapp was assigned to watch Ambassador Trier while Leberecht had taken to shadowing the Sorceress Thirona. Mikhail followed two other Wahrians and another Brunian, but they were lesser suspects that Rapp didn't fully believe were worth the time.

Leberecht offered them both a glass of wine from a bottle next to the cheese. Mikhail agreed, but Rapp refused. He didn't have time to cloud his mind with drink tonight.

Rapp paced by the door back into the house while the other two sat. Leberecht poured the wine and then focused his attention on his cheese platter.

Marching with an army was always exciting, even when the enemy didn't appear for weeks. There were logistics to handle, men to move, artillery to position, and so on. This summit was nothing but boring watching and waiting.

And the worst part was the Ascended One hadn't given any more guidance to Rapp at all.

He'd spent every morning and most evenings in the temple, praying in front of the sword and statue. No voice visited him. No more orders came down from the heavens. There was only silence for Rapp's thoughts to boil over as his thin layer of patience evaporated into nothing.

Logistics make an army, but patience makes a general. Patience and the decisiveness to act when the time comes.

Rapp had read that passage of the Ascended One's Tome over and over and it didn't make him feel better in the slightest. Patience gained him nothing for his divine task.

"We should've seen something by now. There must be something we're missing." Rapp continued to pace and glared at the other two men as they sipped their wine on the patio.

Mikhail shrugged after finishing a gulp from his glass. "Maybe there isn't a traitor."

Rapp wanted to kick something. "No, the summit is in danger. Peace can't last, it's never lasted. We must find where the next war will come from."

"I agree, Your Highness." Leberecht's voice was calm and level. It didn't help Rapp's anger. The ambassador held out a hand to an open seat for Rapp to sit. "Come join us and we'll talk through how we can better smoke out the traitor."

Rapp didn't take the seat. He continued to pace.

"We have to make a move," he said. "We must be aggressive, as the Ascended One would be if he were still on the Continent."

Rapp needed to attack. He knew the Ascended One was looking down on this entire summit and frowning. Maybe the god had already given up on Rapp, since the prince couldn't find the traitor. Maybe Rapp was already back to being a worthless prince who would never win glory.

"I would advise patience," Mikhail said. He leaned back in his seat and thumbed the top of his dagger's hilt at his waist. "If someone is betraying a summit such as this, it will show in time."

Patience makes a general.

Except Rapp didn't have time for patience. Rapp needed to find this traitor now. He couldn't let the thoughts of failing the Ascended One grow from the back of his mind any more.

If he were fighting on one of the fronts, even the Lakmian Range campaigns, he'd have something to do. He'd have a musket to fire and men to order around. But this sitting around and talking at this summit accomplished nothing.

"I could agree with us having patience." Leberecht spoke around his latest bite of aged Moradan cheese.

Rapp almost did kick something then. He turned to walk out the door. He would've left the two men and maybe left the plateau and the summit and his mother altogether if Leberecht's next words had been any different.

"But I think the prince is correct, we need to be more aggressive."

Rapp stopped with his hand outstretched towards the door back inside. He turned back and looked at Leberecht with his eyebrows raised.

"Most of the delegation here is planning to go down to the market on Ascension Day. I think our traitor may show his or her hand then, potentially."

Rapp saw the merits in the plan immediately and started nodding as Leberecht listed his reasons. His doubts and frustrations started to fall away.

"We'll be off the plateau and around crowds of citizens. It'll be hard to monitor everyone, but if I were a traitor, that's when I would pass information to someone down in the city."

Leberecht had been monitoring the letters going off the plateau where possible, but it was hard to track everything. Rapp liked this idea. If they could catch one of their suspects doing something suspicious, it would allow them to focus on cornering him or her.

"When is Ascension Day?" Mikhail looked between Rapp and Leberecht.

"Three days." Rapp's mind was racing. He looked at Leberecht and found the ambassador smiling. Rapp smiled too. "I like this plan."

"Good." Leberecht rolled up a piece of spiced meat and ate the entire thing in one bite.

The strategic part of Rapp's mind started working again. He could see the market on Ascension Day as if it were a battlefield. The diplomats were arrayed like units of soldiers. Rapp was a general looking over them. His two advisors sat in front of him.

"Leberecht will follow the Brunians, like we've done before." Rapp spoke fast and before he even finished, he knew the plan was a good one. "Maybe even talk with Thirona directly and see if she divulges anything in that setting. I'll follow Ambassador Trier. Mikhail will stay on his previous assignments."

Leberecht nodded and smiled. "It's decided, then. What a wonderful plan." The ambassador stood and held up his glass for a toast. "In two or three evenings we may have saved this summit, gentlemen. To our good work together."

"And glory to the Ascended One." Rapp didn't have a glass to join the toast, but stepped towards the two men.

Mikhail stood with one hand resting on the hilt of his dagger while the other touched his glass to Leberecht's. "Such a funny northern custom, but here's to our good work together."

Rapp couldn't help but smile as the other two drank.

He left Leberecht and Mikhail to finish their wine and walked out of the house to return to his palace rooms. He had letters to the generals of the front to catch up on before bed and he wanted to think through the best was to catch Trier in the market as well.

Rapp walked with his head down and moved quickly back towards the front of the palace. He didn't glance towards the now dark horizon in the west at all. He didn't think about the distant war he was missing, either.

The prince was focused fully back on catching the traitor and serving the will of his war god.

Andrei

"The trail goes north." Andrei crouched down and surveyed the remains of the campsite. His Scythes scouted the outskirts and searched the trees around him.

Andrei stood and walked around the scuff marks and the charred remains of a fire on the forest floor. He held out an arm and snapped his fingers once. Scuffling came behind him and he heard the sniffing coming from his wolverine's snout.

The beast nuzzled the side of his leg and sniffed at his shoes. Andrei looked down at the wolverine and met his mount's eyes. He pointed to the ground in front of them and around the edge of the camp remains and snapped again with the same hand at the end.

The wolverine's nose went back to the ground immediately. He sniffed the very center of the camp and the remains of the fire before moving in a slow circle around the outer edge. Other Scythes were doing similar things with their own wolverines farther out in the trees.

There was no doubt in Andrei's mind the wolverines would be able to follow the trail. But could they move fast enough to catch the girl and her soldiers?

The bundle that hung in front of Andrei's chest shifted. He pressed a gentle hand against the cloth strung from his shoulders and felt the slight shake of the hawk's body. She nuzzled up tighter against his chest and he felt the little heartbeat through the cloth and feathers. Andrei sighed and adjusted the pack to make sure it would stay tight.

"Commander, sir."

Andrei moved towards the voice and found Jerkal bending down to pick something up off the ground just outside the main camp circle. He turned and showed it to Andrei.

"What is it?" Andrei reached out and took the object.

"I don't know, sir."

Andrei turned the thing over in his hands. It was a bundle of small sticks tied together with eight black strings hanging off in all directions.

Andrei looked up at Jerkal and shrugged. "Erlonians are such strange people. Have the beasts smell it for the scent."

"Yes, sir."

Andrei shook his head as he walked back towards his own wolverine. General Duroc demanded the princess and Andrei would deliver her, no matter how strange the trail became.

Then he would return home. Finally, he would make it back to his family.

The faded memories that came with the thoughts of home almost brought tears to Andrei's eyes. He had to press the thoughts back down and keep his eyes dry. It would be unbecoming for a Scythe commander to be seen crying by his men.

Andrei had to be strong and finish the mission. They had to find the girl for Kura and General Duroc.

He and his Scythes would ride through the night tonight and slowly catch up to the Erlonians. Andrei's own wolverine completed its circle of the camp. A low growl started from the beast's chest and it turned to face north with its snout up. Andrei smiled and laid a hand gently on the now still hawk bundled against his chest.

They had the scent. They had the girl's trail.

Chapter 12

A marshal's stoic demeanor is his greatest weapon. He must appear brave when he is afraid, confident when he has doubts, and erudite when he is confused and outsmarted.

A Marshal's Memoir
Alexandre Lauriston

Lauriston

Marshal Lauriston pulled his reins to his left and guided his horse around a boulder protruding into the path. His soldiers and the princess stretched in a line behind him as the light of a new morning shimmered through the tops of the trees.

They'd been lucky so far. They'd found the princess just in time and had been able to save her before the Kurakin Scythes closed in on her. The group had made it safely away from the scene of the rescue and had been able to put some distance between them and the Kurakin.

But now the marshal had to get Lannes's daughter all the way to safety. He had to somehow find the Erlonian army while avoiding the Kurakin chasing them and the Brunian and Wahrian army coming down from the north.

Lauriston looked up at the brightness of the forest canopy as his horse continued on the path. It seemed an impossible task, staring at the road in front of them. At least they didn't have a Scythe hawk watching for them in the sky.

The bird would return soon enough, though.

The sounds of a rider approaching from the west reached the marshal's ears. Lauriston kept up his hiking pace to keep the group moving. Soon Lauriston's cavalry general, Desaix, appeared through the trees and swung around to fall in next to Lauriston at the front of the column. His horse snorted out a few breaths and sweat glistened on its neck.

"Still marching north along the river," Desaix said. He'd been riding hard, but he was barely out of breath. Lauriston was always amazed at the general's natural ability on horseback. "Still pushing hard, he's got a large van out in front."

Lauriston nodded. General Duroc and the main Kurakin army were still pushing aggressively north along the Broadwater.

The marshal unslung his canteen and offered it over to Desaix. "Just as we thought. Any sign of the Scythes in the ranks?"

Desaix took the canteen and gulped down a long drink. "Not that we could see. We didn't get too close, though." He wiped his mouth on his sleeve and gave the water back to Lauriston.

"The Scythes will still be after us. Their hawk will be back up in the air soon."

The map of the land formed in Lauriston's mind and visions of the troops from all sides poured over it. The Erlonian group behind the marshal was just a small dot on the vast map covered in the great armies of the Continent.

"Thank you, General." Lauriston nodded to Desaix again. "How are your scouts?"

"Fine. Well-enough rested."

Lauriston smiled. "I doubt that. We'll need to keep pushing hard. I know you take care of your horses, but make sure the men get rest and food too."

"Yes, sir." Desaix pulled his horse around to relay his scouting report to the rest of the group.

"General," Lauriston said before Desaix completed his full turn. Desaix looked over his shoulder back at the marshal. "You get some rest as well. Maybe some food. You need to eat every once in a while too."

Desaix nodded and tipped two fingers up to his hat in a quick salute before continuing back down the line.

Lauriston was left alone with his thoughts again as he started back on the trail. There was nothing in front of him but the open path and the trees closing in around him. His mind would think on nothing but the map of central Erlon and the armies converging all around him.

The Scythes would be recovered from their wounds and would be pursuing the group with a new vigor. General Duroc marched the full Kurakin army in parallel up the Broadwater from Plancenoit.

Lauriston's army was in the Dune Forest. They would be in the dense parts to the east by now and would be well hidden in the hills south of the Branch River. Lauriston would have to find them, if they made it that far.

He didn't know where the Wahrian king's army was at the moment. The last he'd heard was a message from the garrison at Vendome. The Wahrians, with a combined Coalition force of Brunians, had been marching to besiege the northern city.

They would've taken it by now, Lauriston had to assume. Maybe they were marching south, already about to cross the Branch, and would meet Duroc along the Broadwater in the west. Maybe that was their plan, to combine and then swing back east to burn out Lauriston's men.

Whatever the Coalition's grand plan was, Lauriston had a task in front of him that would make the rest of the war pointless if he failed. He turned slightly in his saddle and glanced back up the line of men.

Montholon rode directly behind the marshal and was followed by a group of his old guardsmen. Next came a mix of Lakmian Jinetes and Erlonian sharpshooters. Princess Elisa rode in the middle, with the Lakmian Lodi by her side. Elisa was smiling at some story Lodi told while talking with his hands waving in front of him over his horse.

That was his mission right now. Protect the princess, then worry about the army and the war over the fall of Erlon.

Lauriston had to focus on his task. He had to complete his promise to Lannes. Was that more important than leading the last Erlonian army and trying to win this war?

No. But Lauriston knew he could find a way to do both.

The men would rally around Elisa. She was Lannes blood. Emperor Lannes had led the soldiers to greatness. She would be a source of great inspiration with Lannes in exile.

If she fell into enemy hands, that war effort would take a mighty blow. Lauriston wouldn't let that happen.

A plan formed in Lauriston's mind. His group needed speed. They needed to get as far north as possible before breaking east and entering the rolling hills of the Dune Forest to find the army.

Duroc marched the Kurakin up the Broadwater just west of their current course. The proximity was a risk Lauriston was willing to take for now. The Kurakin wouldn't be looking for them alongside their main army. The Scythes would be on their tail no matter which path they took.

Lauriston wanted to get as much distance between his group and the Scythes before their hawk returned to the air. That meant staying on their current course and using the flat land to run as far north as they could in as little time as possible.

That was the plan. Lauriston would stick to it.

The path rose slightly in front of him and Lauriston guided his horse around another boulder sunk into the earth and pressed on up the small incline. They reached the crest quickly and the marshal got a brief glimpse through a gap in the trees of the land flowing north in front of them.

It was a long road. Would Lauriston lead the group of his loyal soldiers and his friend's daughter to safety? Or would he fail once again and be the cause of their defeat?

The doubts erupted in his mind. They always did when he made a decision. He hated himself for it.

The doubts appeared like a sudden convergence of waves before a beach. Smaller swells pressed against each other to suddenly double in height and power and crash downward, pummeling against his plan.

Lauriston, supposedly the empire's greatest marshal, had failed before. He would fail again.

He shook his head to try to rid his mind of the thoughts. His horse trotted onwards. His men followed him as always.

They trusted him. They would follow any order he gave.

But Lauriston didn't always have the answers.

He'd led thousands of men to their death throughout numerous wars. The wars and battles flashed across his thoughts.

The Moradan Campaign. Battles in the swamps against insurgents. Disorganized but savage. Months of death tolls too high to count and nothing gained.

The Three Bridges of Brun. Sorcery and destruction. The drowning of thousands of Erlonians under Lauriston's command. The great Erlonian army broken on the banks of the Brunian Riversea.

The end of the empire. Emperor Lannes's capture and exile. It was all Lauriston's fault.

Lannes was brilliant. Lannes was unbeatable.

His fall had been Lauriston's fault.

The Southern Campaign had been Lauriston's plan. He'd orchestrated it. He'd assumed the Kurakin would never join the Coalition. He'd been the one to never plan for fighting mammoths on cold ice fields.

Lauriston had been the one to split up from Lannes during the retreat back to the safety of the north. He was the reason Lannes was separate from the army and vulnerable to capture when the Lainians betrayed him.

How different would the wars with the Coalition have been if Lauriston hadn't been the second-in-command? Would the empire still be strong if Lannes had trusted someone else?

Lauriston couldn't shake the doubts, but he forced himself to hold strong to his plan for Elisa and his men. He kept the nose of his horse pointed north. He weaved through the trees and tried not to think about the Scythes behind them or the Horde army just to the west or the mistakes of his past that had cost so many lives.

Lauriston nodded to himself. He was making the right decision. He was going to lead the group to safety. He was going to make up for his mistakes and get Lannes's daughter to safety. Then he was going to somehow save Erlon and turn this war around.

Or else it was all hopeless and Lauriston's mistakes had already doomed them all to fall with the empire, and Erlon would be no more.

* * *

They stopped for a quick break at midday. Quatre handed out hardtack for lunch and Lauriston walked among the men and made sure they had enough water and that their horses were well.

The actions were a welcome distraction from his doubts and him second-guessing the group's course.

When they started down the path again, Mon fell in beside Lauriston at the front of the group.

"Not sure what I'll do when this runs out." Mon took a swig from his ever-present bottle of wine. He held his reins in one hand and the bottle in the other.

"Lodi brought a few more for you," Lauriston said. He smiled over at his old friend.

The thought of a general drinking while on campaign would've been ludicrous back at the height of the empire's military strength. But Mon wasn't a normal general and this was a strange and desperate war.

And besides, Mon had a good excuse for his vice. Lauriston knew that better than most.

"I'm going slow, trying to make each bottle last," Mon said. "I was trying to drink less anyway, so this is a good excuse to taper back." Mon chuckled and took another swig.

"It's fine. You kept Elisa safe and got her to us. As long as you're sober enough to fight for her if it comes to that." Lauriston smiled again at the old man. "I think your return to the army has been quite successful so far, don't you?"

Mon laughed and shook his head. "I wouldn't call it a return."

"What else would you call it?"

Mon waved his bottle around in front of him and shrugged his shoulders. "I don't know. But I was happily retired until the empire fell apart. I enjoyed farming."

Lauriston raised an eyebrow. "Did you now?"

"It was quiet."

Lauriston kept his eyebrow raised.

Mon looked at him. "And terribly boring." A smile broke through the old man's scowl. He nodded. "It's good to be back."

"Good to have you back, General."

The two rode in silence for a long while. The group behind them was mainly silent as well. Lauriston had scouts out in front and to the west to spot any approaching enemies or danger. It would've been fine for the group to be as loud as they wanted.

But the days on the trail were starting to wear on everyone. Most kept their heads down and focused on their horse and the path.

"We should go rescue him." Mon's gruff voice cut through the silence of the afternoon forest.

"What?"

Lauriston had been thinking through everything that could go wrong the farther north he pushed the group. His doubts were a rising tide still and he struggled to keep them back when the trail was silent and he was allowed to think.

"We could go east," Mon said. "Sneak over the mountains and get to the coast. We could go rescue Lannes."

Lauriston laughed. "We certainly could."

The marshal's imagination ran with the images of the troop trekking over the Antres Range and sneaking through Laine and Morada and stealing a ship to sail to Taul. He could picture the surprise on the emperor's face when they broke through the main gate to set him free.

"That would be a story." Mon took a long pull from his bottle. It was nearly half-empty now.

"I'm not sure what it would accomplish, though." Lauriston reached up and scratched at the stubble on his chin.

Mon shrugged. "We'd all be together again." He took another swig from his bottle and then offered some to Lauriston.

The marshal felt a twang of sadness at Mon's words. He longed for a return to those days as well. The height of the empire, the entire northeastern part of the Continent under Erlonian control. It was all prosperity and military might with no other faction challenging Emperor Lannes and Marshal Lauriston at the head of a column of invincible soldiers.

That was all long gone now.

Lauriston reached over and took the bottle from Mon. He took a small sip and swished the liquid around in his mouth before letting it wash down his throat. He relished the burn and felt the world brighten in his eyes at the rush as it hit his stomach.

Mon's eyebrows were almost to his hairline as Lauriston handed the bottle back. "I didn't even think you liked wine."

"That's the most you'll ever get me to drink while on campaign." Lauriston smiled over at his old friend.

This conversation had been a welcome distraction for the marshal. He wondered if Mon had somehow sensed Lauriston needed someone to talk to.

"We'll win this war," Lauriston said. It felt good to say it out loud.

He turned to face forward again and kicked his horse a little faster up the trail. "We'll save Erlon and keep Elisa safe. Then we'll go get Lannes and return him to Plancenoit. How's that sound?"

"Sounds like the perfect plan to me," Mon said. He spurred his own horse faster to keep up with Lauriston.

The group behind them sped up as well and the entire troop of Lauriston's Erlonians marched farther north on the path to safety and continuing this war to save the empire.

Pitt

Pitt squeezed his legs and pushed his horse up the final stretch of the hill. The view of the river and town opened up below him.

His men were already crossing the stone bridge and marching through the town. They passed under the spire to the Ascended One in the middle of the town's square and moved out the road heading west, parallel to the river.

The Erlonians called this river the Branch and the town was called Neuse. Like most of what Pitt had seen of Erlon, the place would've been scenic if there wasn't a war raging all around.

General Win rode up the hill and pulled his horse to stop next to Pitt.

"A glorious Ascension Day, sir." Win tipped his plumed cavalry cap towards Pitt.

"It that today?" Pitt hadn't thought about the day of the week or the specific date in a long time. It was late fall in terms of the campaign season and that was all that mattered. "I guess it is. Happy Ascension to you, Win."

Win smiled and placed his hat back on his head. "The van is crossing now. We'll assemble in those trees to the west before marching onward to the Broadwater."

"Good." Pitt nodded.

"My horses are already down the road. We'll scout everything and hopefully find the last Erlonians soon."

Pitt knew the Erlonians would be far away from here. The army could march west and find the Broadwater, but he didn't expect Marshal Lauriston to be waiting around for them.

King Charles was moving too slow. Pitt would have to wait for him every few days. The king was giving the enemy too much time to regroup and flee on their own soil. Pitt wouldn't be surprised if they never found the Erlonian army. Or the Kurakin would defeat them first. The Horde had already taken Plancenoit, so it was only a matter of time before they surrounded the last marshal.

Pitt was going to return home with no glory won for his family. It didn't matter what he did now, nothing would change.

Pitt hung his head and followed Win across the bridge with his men. They passed through the town and Pitt didn't see a single Erlonian citizen in the stone houses. The land was deserted; all the people fled in the face of enemy armies approaching.

Pitt caught up with Win after supervising some of the crossing. They talked about their marching plans while they reached the road heading west at the edge of town. "We'll leave part of the first brigade here to hold the crossing and wait for Charles to arrive."

"Any idea when that will be?" Win flicked his reins to keep his horse on a straight path next to Pitt.

"He'll arrive when he arrives, that's all I know." Pitt shook his head and rubbed his forehead with a calloused hand. "All we can do is be a good vanguard for him. Let's find the Erlonians to the west, if they're out there. If not, we'll surround the forest and hope to trap them."

Win nodded. "I'll find them, sir." He saluted and kicked his horse into a trot and moved around the marching soldiers in front of Pitt to head off to the west.

Pitt slowed and turned his horse to look back at the town and the rest of his part of the army crossing the river into central Erlon. They'd made it; they'd conquered all the way to the center of the great enemy empire.

Pitt didn't feel like he'd accomplished anything.

This was a moment the Coalition had been striving to achieve for a decade. King Charles should be at the front here. It should be a glorious joint achievement, on Ascension Day no less.

Instead, there was a sinking feeling in Pitt's chest. A despair pulling him down because he knew that no matter what he did, no matter how the rest of the war turned out, he'd return home as a land general to a maritime nation with no glorious victories to call his own.

Pitt's conquering army continued to march through the deserted town. He'd continue leading them west and follow the Wahrian King's orders. Maybe he'd get lucky and find Marshal Lauriston and be able to fight the Erlonians in open battle. Maybe he'd get lucky enough to die a hero's death.

Pitt was starting to consider that kind of death a better option than returning home with nothing.

He sighed and turned his horse back to the west and away from the town he'd never see again. He had work to do and men to oversee. He shook the despair from his mind and pressed on like a good soldier should.

Chapter 13

I stand before you overlooking the greatest nation on the Continent, the greatest empire since the Ascended One's own. Yet, there is still more to conquer. There are more glorious heights for Erlon to scale.

Emperor Lannes's Ascension Day Speech
Plancenoit, Year 1113 Post-Abandonment

Elisa

Elisa couldn't help but keep thinking about how Erlon was already defeated.

It was a horrible thought, she knew, especially for the heir to the once-great empire.

But how could she avoid it?

She rode with the soldiers every day and got to know both the officers and the soldiers under them. She sparred with Lodi and learned more about the Lakmian style of fighting and practiced some sword techniques that would be useful when it came to battle with the Kurakin.

The officers were happy, it seemed. They joked with Mon and told old stories and Lodi played pranks almost daily. Lauriston kept the men well organized but content. It was like her father's old army, just on a smaller scale.

There was camaraderie here. There was an unimaginable hope and confidence in the future from these soldiers. They were going to fight onward, just like her father would. No one else seemed to be dwelling on the fact that it was already over for their empire.

Elisa couldn't avoid the dire thoughts, though.

Her father was in exile. Her mother had abandoned them and disappeared. All that was left was Marshal Lauriston leading this small group of stoic soldiers and whatever army waited for them in the north and east.

Elisa was the heir and was still alive, but what could she possibly do? She was a fourteen-year-old girl who'd been left by her parents. She wasn't a soldier, no matter how much practice time she had with Lodi.

Elisa looked up the line of soldiers in front of her. They'd just finished a short break for lunch and now pressed on for the afternoon. Light stretched the canopy above them and lit the path Lauriston still had the group following.

All these soldiers had broken away from the main army to come and rescue her. Marshal Lauriston *himself* had stopped a campaign with his army against the Coalition and led the group personally.

It was because she was the heir. She was Lannes's daughter, true, but Elisa had never felt like a leader of the empire. She'd never felt like an empress when her father was running things. As a little girl, she might have felt like a princess at the height of her father's power.

But now, with the empire on its last leg? She felt like nothing but a scared teenage girl running through the woods.

So why did these men smile at her and work so hard to protect her? Why were they ready to give their lives for her when she had nothing to offer in return? Why did Marshal Lauriston look at her with a distant hope in his eyes and the determination of the entire empire?

"I just realized it's Ascension Day."

The voice brought Elisa out of her thoughts. She turned to see Lodi riding next to her once again.

"Is it really?" she said. The question did a nice job of pushing away Elisa's negative thoughts. It replaced those thoughts with happy memories of Ascension Days past. "My father always liked Ascension Day."

"Oh, I remember, Princess." Lodi smiled widely. "That was always a fun time to be a soldier. Especially if we were back in Plancenoit."

"Lakmians celebrate the Ascension?" Elisa knew the Lakmians had their own religion and worshiped their own gods separate from the Ascended One.

Lodi tilted his head back and forth as if to say it was complicated. "Those of us who fought for your father did. But you're correct, we have our own gods that we worship. Old beings who walked the Continent long before your Ascended general rose to glory."

That's what Elisa thought she remembered learning. She couldn't remember many details about the Lakmian religion, but Lodi didn't give her a chance to ask further questions on the topic.

"Your father would let the army feast on Ascension Day," the Lakmian said. "The barracks chefs would pull out all the stops for the soldiers."

"It was wonderful."

Both Elisa and Lodi turned in their saddles to find Quatre behind them. The man had his eyes closed, imagining the large feast back in the Erlonian capital. Elisa had to stifle a laugh at how joyous and satisfied Quatre's face looked.

"The feasts were grand, I remember them in the palace," Elisa said. "Father would work most other holidays, but this one he spent with us, mother and I. Unless he was writing his speech."

"Ah, the speeches." Lodi's smile grew to match Quatre's. "They were wonderful. Even if we didn't have an active war going, every soldier in the army would want to charge through the stones of the Antres Mountains themselves for your father afterwards."

Elisa remembered marveling at her father's way with words even as a child. His ability to inspire the people of the empire. His ability to lead. It was something she still hadn't mastered, or even come close to understanding.

Her doubts about her capability for leadership came back in a rush, like a gust of wind. She had to fight to dampen them as she worried about tearing up on the trail. She didn't want these brave soldiers around her to see her cry.

Why was she acting like this?

She had other things to worry about. More important and short-term things, like the enemy Scythes chasing them and the Kurakin army invading her homeland.

Elisa told herself to focus on that problem and nothing else. She repeated it in her mind over and over until the doubts went back to the edges of her mind.

"The Ascension Day the year before Three Bridges was the best," Quatre said. His eyes were still closed in memory.

"That was the last grand feast we had," Lodi said.

The Lakmian's words didn't dampen Quatre's mood. "There was boar and pheasant and great big steaks."

"There was a beet salad too, if I remember."

Quatre's eyes finally opened, but just long enough to scowl at Lodi. Elisa held in her laughter as the Lakmian gave her a quick wink before letting Quatre continue with his daydream about celebrations past.

This company and conversation helped Elisa keep her doubts at bay. They continued talking and reminiscing for the rest of the afternoon and the group made good time heading north. Lauriston seemed pleased by the time they stopped for the evening.

She sparred with Lodi as the rest of the men made camp. She was getting better with his instruction. She could feel how much faster she was with the blade and her feet felt lighter already.

The movements and mental concentration kept her focused on the right things. It kept her mind from the doubts that lurked in the back of her head. She still knew they were there, but she could continue to ignore them with the help of these men and the activities of the trail.

Her father would tell her to put on a good face for the men. That's exactly what he would do in her situation. He would lead the men to victory and never waver. He would show nothing but strength.

"How's the practicing going?" Mon asked her that night when she returned to the main camp circle for dinner.

"Good so far. Lodi's teaching me a lot." Elisa sat down next to the old farmer and dug into her meal of a rabbit stew made by some of Desaix's scouts.

"Good. Hope you won't need it, though." Mon winked at her and Elisa smiled in return. "We're making good time. There's a Kurakin army close, but Lar thinks they won't find us if we move quickly."

"And the Scythes?"

"Still behind us." Mon shrugged. "But we can outrun them and then hide in the east."

Elisa nodded and hoped that was true. She spooned some more of the stew into her mouth and felt it warm her body.

She briefly considered asking Mon more about his history with her father and the Erlonian army, but stopped herself. Lodi had warned her about the topic and she didn't want to ruin what had been a good day by bringing up a dark part of the farmer-general's past.

Elisa kept quiet and chose to focus on happy memories of Ascension Days past in Plancenoit back when her family was still together and her mother was still here and her father was the most powerful man on the Continent. She smiled to herself and ate more of the wonderful stew, her doubts from earlier almost completely forgotten.

Rapp

The crowded lift groaned as it fell towards the city. Rapp stood next to his mother and sister with Leberecht on the other side. Ambassador Trier and a diplomat from Brun stood in front of them with the rest of the delegation crammed in on either side.

"A fine day for a tour of our city," Trier said to the other diplomat.

Rapp wanted to punch the ambassador right in his smile. He wished he could arrest the traitor right here and get his task over with.

But he had to be patient.

A general waits to make his move at the appropriate time. Never before. Never after.

Rapp used the words from the Ascended One's Tome to calm himself. He had to see out Leberecht's plan for the day. The Ascended One would stick to strategy and be patient were he in Rapp's position.

And it was Ascension Day, after all. The war god would certainly guide Rapp to victory on his quest.

The summit delegation was taking a day-long break from their marathon debates on the future of the Continent to honor the holiday. Queen Caroline had organized a trip down to the main market of Citiva for anyone who wanted to join.

Rapp would catch Trier in an act of traitorous espionage and his quest for the Ascended One would be over. Rapp would win glorious praise from both the god and the Wahrian people without having fired a shot or ordered his army to march.

"Ambassador Leberecht, has there been any news from Duroc since yesterday?" Queen Caroline's words brought Rapp out of his scheming thoughts and pulled his eyes from the back of Trier's head.

"No letters or reports this morning, Your Highness," Leberecht said. He leaned around Rapp to look at the queen with a hand rested on his protruding belly.

"Duroc and Father will cut Marshal Lauriston's army off. They'll be trapped in the hills," Rapp said. "And Mikhail has assured me that Duroc's men will find the emperor's heir soon as well. The empire will be all but finished at that point."

Leberecht nodded. "Duroc has the Scythes tracking the girl. There's only so far she can go."

"She's gotten this far." The queen had her eyes forward and her lips pursed. It was the familiar expression she always wore when Rapp or anyone else discussed military matters.

Rapp didn't have an argument back for that statement. The summit had been waiting for weeks of news of Princess Elisa's capture.

Not that it mattered. Rapp told his mind to focus. Everything in the western part of the Continent would be secondary if he could complete his task for the god.

The war was over. The Erlonian princess would be captured. Rapp had to only catch the traitor who sought to break the Coalition apart.

The prince looked across the lift to where Mikhail stood at the front left corner. Thirona was near him, surrounded by the usual group of Brunian delegates and a few other random male representatives from other countries. The Kurakin claimed General Duroc was doing everything he could to find the princess. But could that be a ruse?

Could the Kurakin be the traitors the Ascended One's voice had warned him about?

The thought made the prince's head spin. He stopped the idea before it could go further. It was too complicated of a thought and nothing good would come from dwelling on it.

Rapp needed to focus on Trier today. If Trier proved innocent, then Rapp could move on to other suspects. Today he would only think on the small ambassador with wisps of white hair in front of him.

The lift shuddered as it approached the city. The group of diplomats and royals stayed silent for the last few feet before it hit the ground. A line of guards waited to escort them into the market.

The doors of the lift pulled open and the group pressed out. Rapp finally felt like he could breathe properly again, not pressed between a bunch of people.

The smell of the city engulfed him. The dirt in the streets, the sweat of the people moving about, the commotion of the market beyond. It all rushed into his head at once and was almost too much to handle after so long up on the plateau.

Thirona and Mikhail were in the front of the group. Rapp walked behind his mother in the middle in the long procession. The guards pushed into the crowd where they needed to, but most of the citizens parted for the group. Rapp could see people standing on their toes to get a glimpse at the royals and the foreign sorceress and the other ambassadors.

The market was an organized group of tents in the center of the main square of the city directly adjacent to the plateau lift. The square sat at the end of the city's major street through the northern part of the city.

The tents were arrayed in an outer ring on the edge of the square, with two more inner rings circling the grand Citiva Fountain in the middle.

The guards led them across the square to the tents and the diplomats dispersed. The foreigners who'd never been to Citiva, some never having been to Wahring at all, were eager to see the wares of the market.

Guards broke off with the various groups. Rapp stayed with his mother and sister while Leberecht walked over to join Mikhail with Thirona's group. The large ambassador gave a short wink back to Rapp as he left.

This was it. They would finally see the traitor the Ascended One had warned about make a move. Rapp would catch the spy within the Coalitions summit.

Or so the prince hoped.

"What section should we walk through first, my dears?" the queen said.

Rapp left her without a response. Trier was already moving around the eastern edge of the square, looking at the outer rows of tents.

"Let's go to the jewelers!" Rapp heard Julia say to the queen as he walked away.

Rapp kept his distance from Trier and acted like he was interested in the turnip stands in front of him. Two guards shadowed the prince and two more shadowed Trier and the other diplomat with him.

Nothing suspicious happened for the first hour spent in the market and Rapp almost gave up his shadowing. He became frustrated again as Trier made a slow pass around the market, pointing out certain things to his companion and stopping at certain places to make a remark on the architecture or history of the buildings that lined the square.

It was all pointless banter from a man who thought himself important.

They came to the northern section of the square and Rapp's eyes were drawn towards the wide opening for the main street running away from the square. He could march straight out of the city right now and head to the front with an escort from the city guard.

Decisiveness makes a general.

The proverbs of the war god's Tome echoed in his ears. Rapp could leave the summit behind and ride west to help with the eastern front. It would be simple and easy, but even as his feet were drawn towards that freedom, a voice pounded in his head. The memory of the power behind the actual words of the Ascended One kept Rapp in the square.

His eyes found Trier just in time.

Rapp saw the Wahrian ambassador break away briefly from the other diplomat with him. There was a group of royal staff holding baskets outside a butcher's tent. They were kitchen staff from the look of their uniforms, sent to stock up for the summit feast that evening.

A servant turned and smiled brightly at Trier. The ambassador said something and the woman's smile brightened even more.

Rapp saw a flash of white in Trier's hand. A paper. A note of some kind.

Rapp's breath caught. The commotion of the market around him fell away and he watched Trier and saw him press the note into the servant's hand.

A message. What would an Ambassador of Wahring be doing passing a note to a lowly servant girl from the kitchens?

Nothing good, Rapp decided. Nothing good at all.

He felt himself smiling. His shoulders shuddered as a weight came off them. He wanted to yell out in victory and howl up towards the sky.

The noise of the market came back and he felt the full importance of what he'd just witnessed. Trier was a spy. He was passing information to someone through the palace's serving staff.

Ambassador Trier, a Wahrian citizen, was the traitor the Ascended One warned about.

Rapp couldn't hold his smile inside. He shadowed Trier the rest of the way around the outer rim of the market, but nothing else suspicious happened. That didn't matter.

Rapp couldn't wait for his chance to tell Leberecht the good news. Tonight they would talk through a plan on how to expose Trier to the rest of the summit.

Rapp would be a hero. Not a war hero, but glory would descend from the heavens nonetheless.

The prince continued walking through the market for the rest of the morning with his smile wide on his face and enjoyed the sunlight and clear weather and the sights and the sounds and the smells of the citizens of his realm.

Chapter 14

If all seems to be going well while on campaign, then it is assured that forces somewhere, hidden from your view, are conspiring against you.

Maxims of War, Entry Five
Emperor Gerald Lannes

Pitt

Pitt's army reached the Broadwater quicker than expected. Charles allowed the Brunian vanguard to range farther out than before and Pitt could move about with a little more freedom along the wide river. Pitt kept his cavalry out in front with the hope of finding the last of the Erlonian army somewhere out there.

They found nothing.

The Brunian vanguard camped along the banks of the river and Pitt stared out over the vast waterway every night for three nights as they waited for the Wahrians to catch up to their position.

The king's main column had reached the Brunian camp and set up in an adjacent group of fields slightly upriver. Pitt stood on the banks of the river and listened to the sounds of the Wahrian camp. Their soldiers were loud and undisciplined next to Pitt's Brunians.

Pitt let out a long sigh and turned from the water to find his horse. He rode towards the Wahrian camp and straight to the king's tent. Charles had asked Pitt to dinner and Pitt tried to steel himself for another night of gluttony and unproductive talks on other subjects besides the war.

Within the royal tent, the king lounged with a glass of wine on his normal chair and hummed one of the royal tunes to himself.

"Your Majesty." Pitt ducked his head in a quick bow at the tent's entrance.

Charles brightened and sat up straight at Pitt's words. "General Pitt, come and sit. Such a fine evening and I've such a nice Weyrother vintage for us to share. This is my last bottle. Are you hungry? I'm famished. I shall have food brought in."

The king waved at a servant standing in a corner and the man ran from the tent. Pitt walked forward and took a seat across from the king. He kept his back upright in a rigid posture opposite the lounging royal in front of him.

"How's your Wahrian army?" Pitt tried to hold his voice steady and keep the frustration out of his words. By now, exasperation was almost his normal tone.

"Tired, but resting now. Cold nights and windy days on the trail. And too much time in a carriage for my taste. What news from you Brunians? Any word from the western flank across the river?"

"Nothing yet, sir." Pitt tried to wrap his head around a king complaining about riding in a plush carriage while his soldiers marched on dusty roads for miles and miles.

"We'll hear from them soon." Charles waved a hand in the air as if throwing the thought away from his body. "Oh, I almost forgot. Here, read this."

The king held out a letter. Pitt had to stand and reach out to take it from him, as the royal wouldn't lift his back from his chair. Pitt froze when he saw the seal on the envelope.

Black wax.

The symbol of Kura was clear even in the dark seal, an open winged hawk soaring above jagged cliffs of ice.

He looked at the king and ripped out the letter with shaking hands. "When did you receive this?"

"A few days ago, I think." The king had returned to focusing on his wine and humming to himself.

"A few days?"

Pitt read the letter twice over. He couldn't believe the words. His eyes pored over the sentences and pangs of frustration beat against his skull once again. The Kurakin army was nearby and General Duroc wanted to plan a joint campaign to find the last Erlonians before the end of fall.

"How did you respond?" Pitt had to work hard to keep from yelling. "What are we going to do? They could almost be to the rendezvous by now."

"We'll meet them at an inn, it's a few miles south of here, I think."

Pitt felt his grip trembling around the note. A Kurakin envoy had arrived and King Charles hadn't even told his other allies. General Duroc wanted to meet and plan the end of the campaign together and Charles was still content to drink wine and march slowly.

"I'll confirm tomorrow and we'll meet them on the next day. Then the war will be all but over." The king took another sip of wine and smacked his lips to savor the taste. Pitt thought it rather made him look like a clucking chicken.

He was finished with the Wahrian king. He needed to go back to his men and start planning for the meeting with the Kurakin Horde immediately. He needed to stop wasting time.

But as Pitt made to rise and take his leave, the king's servants entered the tent with food and Charles insisted that Pitt stay and enjoy the rich meal with him. It was rude and unwise to decline an invitation to eat with royalty. Charles was most certainly the type of king to take offense to a spurned invitation.

Pitt was trapped once again.

He had to listen to the king talk about military strategy while the thoughts on the meeting with General Duroc and the Kurakin army raged in his head. Charles talked about the past victories of his famous ancestors with an air of mastery and intellect, as if he were the Ascended One himself. Pitt disagreed with the majority of his opinions and interpretations of historical facts, even without the grandiose posturing.

Charles was the victorious conqueror. The slowest marcher in the world. The least intelligent general of his age. And Pitt had to bow to his every word as he sloshed his wine and sprayed crumbs all over the floor. All because he was royal.

The night stars were in full bloom when the meal finally ended and Pitt was allowed to leave to return to his men. He stepped out of the tent and stared up at the lights in the sky and wanted to scream.

The Wahrian soldiers were still loud outside in the camp. Undisciplined and unprofessional. No wonder the Erlonian Emperor had conquered their country so easily.

Pitt spit on the ground outside the tent door and shook his head. He went to find his horse and make his way back to his men to put a little space between him and these dreadful allies of his.

Elisa

The call for a break on the trail came back down the line. Elisa slid off her horse and handed the reins over when Lodi offered to take her mount for her.

No wind moved through the forest today and the sun was high over the trees. The still air almost felt like the warm early fall and made Elisa forget that winter was almost here.

She looked up the line of men watering horses and eating trail biscuits and talking quietly to each other. Mon was at the front again and had his head bowed in conversation with Lauriston.

Elisa stepped out of the immediate trail area and into the trees. The noises of the men fell away behind her and the chorus of the forest overtook her ears. It calmed her head down and dampened her feelings of fatigue.

Seeing Mon and Lauriston deep in discussion made her think on the questions around Mon's past once again. They were always popping into her mind, especially when she was alone.

Elisa drew her sword and held it up in the low forest light. She walked a little further from the soldiers and found enough open space between the trees and undergrowth.

Practicing Lodi's Lakmian fighting move was the perfect distraction. She could always fall back on her sword and the moves Lodi was teaching her if she found herself dwelling too long on thoughts about the Kurakin chasing her or the pressure of being the heir of a dying empire.

Elisa stepped slowly at first and put one foot after the other. She brought her sword around on a steady arc.

The next pass she sped up. She tried to control her breathing. It grew more difficult and she stumbled on the third pass. She righted herself and started again. The fourth time was better.

"If I tried that, I'd get dizzy."

Elisa winced and turned towards the voice with a reddening face. She assumed one of the soldiers had approached and seen her practicing.

But then she felt the cool breeze along the back of her neck.

Her Lakmian guide had returned.

"I'd almost forgotten about you," Elisa said. She sheathed her sword.

"You haven't needed me in a while." The vision waved a hand back towards the group of soldiers through the trees. "You're in good company."

"Aren't you worried they'll see you?"

The guide looked back towards the men as if contemplating the thought. "No," he said with a shrug.

Elisa smiled at how nonchalant the vision was. She was glad he appeared. He would be something else to take her mind off the questions and fears overtaking her mind.

"I've taken your advice, I guess," Elisa said. "Flee north. Have we gone far enough?"

"Taking my advice is always a good idea." The guide smiled. "But no, you haven't gone far enough. As long as those Scythes still give chase, you're still in danger."

"So are you here to tell me to keep going?"

"Yes." The vision leaned a shoulder against a tree and crossed one foot over the other. "But I also want to give you a little bit of a warning."

A warning?

That didn't sound good. Elisa fingered the silver seal on her pistol as the guide talked.

"Things are about to change. They're about to pick up pace. I want you to stay focused and vigilant."

"What do you mean? How will things change?" Elisa didn't have the slightest idea what the guide meant by any of this.

"You'll see."

Elisa didn't consider this a very good warning. She opened her mouth to tell the vision this but saw he was already fading away. He wasn't giving her any time to ask another question.

"Thanks, I guess," she said instead of voicing her complaint.

"You're welcome. Stay alert, Princess. You must survive this coming war." The guide faded away and left Elisa standing alone in the circle of trees with more questions than answers.

"This coming war?" Elisa said to the empty air. "What in the Ascended does that mean?"

No answer came back to her. There was only the still air of the forest and a bird chirping happily in a tree above her. Elisa stood still in thought, but nothing made sense about what the guide had said.

Maybe this was why her mother always said not to trust visions.

"Practicing more, I see." Lodi's voice cut through Elisa's thoughts. She didn't know how long she'd been standing alone staring at the tree the guide had been leaning against.

"Everything okay?" Lodi said when he reached Elisa and saw the confused look on her face.

"Yes." Elisa shook herself back out of her thoughts and nodded to Lodi. "Everything's fine."

"We probably shouldn't let you wander this far into the woods alone, you know. The Scythes are out there hunting you still." Lodi smiled as he said the words.

"I'm sorry," Elisa said.

"Don't be." Lodi pulled his spear from behind his back. "Lauriston wants to get back on the trail. But we have a second to spar if you want to practice."

Elisa's mind was still half on what the guide had said.

Things are about to change.

You must survive the coming war.

There it was again, a mention of a future war when this war in Erlon was already almost finished. What was Elisa supposed to make of that?

She had to shake her head again to keep her thoughts from dwelling on the ominous words.

She looked at Lodi. The Lakmian was already in his fighting stance with his spear out in front of him. The guide's words flashed once more across her mind.

But the thoughts disappeared quickly and she drew her sword with a smile.

"Yeah, we've got time for a few rounds," she said.

Elisa attacked and Lodi parried and their sparring session began.

Rapp

A social hour was scheduled following the day's discussions and all the summit members converged on the dining hall in the evening and found a buffet of fine foods from across the Continent and drinks of every kind. Rapp was beginning to realize that diplomats drank even more than soldiers on leave.

The prince moved around the buffet table filled with various small bites and found a spot in the corner where he could observe Ambassador Trier. He kept his focus on the traitor but took in the rest of the room in his periphery.

Thirona's tall form with her typical bright dress stood surrounded by other delegation members. Rapp's mother the queen was in an opposite corner, talking to the ambassador from Laine and a few smaller Moradan representatives.

Leberecht and Mikhail weren't in the room yet, but Rapp expected to see them walk through the door soon. When the last summit meeting of the day had adjourned, Leberecht had stood and shaken hands with those around them. He'd winked at Rapp across the table and given a secretive glance towards Trier.

Rapp's job tonight was to track the man. Leberecht and Mikhail had both shared Rapp's joy after he'd told them of what Trier had done in the market. They'd talked for hours that night and planned how to make a move and catch Trier in the act, so as to be able to have him arrested.

Leberecht had told Rapp to shadow Trier even tighter now. The second they saw Trier passing more information, they would move to arrest him.

Rapp refused a glass of wine offered by a waiter. His eyes fell back to Trier across the room. The ambassador shifted in his stance and nodded quickly to the group he was talking to.

Trier turned towards the door and Rapp's breath caught. The ambassador was leaving far too early, far earlier than normal for his drinking habits.

The prince stepped out of his corner and followed across the room. Trier ducked around two ambassadors from the Southern Confederacy on his way out the door.

The queen glared at Rapp as he made his own exit. She would assume he was leaving early to go catch up on military reports or visit the temple. Rapp didn't care if she was angry or not. That wasn't important.

All that mattered was the back of Trier's head and for Rapp to find out where he was going and who he was going to talk to and catch him before he could pass on any more information to enemies.

This was it. This was the climax of Rapp's task for the Ascended One.

Rapp expected the ambassador to make for the main entrance and meet another informant. Instead, Trier turned out a side door used by the servants. Rapp had to stop and think where the door led, as it wasn't a route he usually took within the palace.

He looked out the window next to the door and out into the courtyard beyond. It was a small brick patio with a few shrubs along the far wall. A break in the brick formed an opening to allow various supplies to be wheeled in for the kitchen.

Ambassador Trier stood alone in the center of this servants' courtyard. He wrung his hands together in a nervous gesture and watched the opening opposite him.

What was he doing? Waiting on a meeting to pass along the latest news from the summit?

Back inside, Rapp ignored the guards and servants passing him in the hallway. He kept his eyes on the traitor below him.

Trier turned towards something out of sight from Rapp's window and smiled widely. It was the same smile Rapp had seen down in the market. The same servant woman appeared and ran into Trier's arms.

The low light of the evening made it hard to see her, but Rapp saw the truth of what was happening immediately. She had a full bosom and a bright smile and her hands immediately latched tightly around the ambassador's neck above her. They hadn't done this in the market; this action was reserved for private quarters.

Ambassador Trier was supposedly happily married to a distant relative of the royal family.

It was an affair.

Rapp ran through everything he'd seen Trier do. All the strange behaviors. The passed note in the market. The early exits from other meetings and social gatherings. His distracted demeanor.

It wasn't a grand scheme to undermine the Coalition.

It was only lust for a serving girl. A simple serving girl.

The pair released each other at last and Trier pulled the girl towards the gap in the wall. She followed willingly and Rapp lost sight of them. The back of the serving smock tied tight around the girl's waist was the last thing Rapp saw.

The prince tore his eyes away from the now empty courtyard and the world spun around him. He would've spat on the ground in disgust if he hadn't been in an ornate hallway with a lush carpet at his feet.

Instead, he held his rage inside but felt himself strain at keeping it under control. He'd wasted his time following that stupid ambassador. He'd wasted his time with the pointless summit. And he'd failed the Ascended One.

The prince looked back towards the sound of the drunken social gathering down the hall. His mother would be in there, happily entertaining the foreign guests, oblivious to the fact of a traitor in her midst.

Rapp was no closer to finding the man or woman the voice of the god had warned about.

He turned down the opposite direction and started walking. There wasn't a destination in his mind. He just needed to walk and burn off some of the steam rising up inside of him.

He charged through the hallway and ignored the smiles and bows from the servants and guards and others he passed. He moved out into the great entrance hall and out the front entrance into the beginnings of the night and the first stars poking out above him.

He wished he knew where Leberecht was. He wanted to yell at the man for allowing him to waste time following Trier.

Rapp turned right off the palace entrance stairs and moved down the street between the diplomatic housing. He kept his eyes away from Leberecht's house as he passed. The temple to the Ascended One rose in front of him from down the street.

The entire walk was filled with confusing thoughts. Rapp played back his observations of Trier over the last few weeks with disgust. He threw the memories away and tried to forget them.

He thought on the other summit members he should've payed closer attention to. Thirona and the Brunians. The Southern Confederacy. Even Leberecht and the Kurakin Mikhail.

Maybe he should've started with Mikhail. Could the Coalition really trust the Kurakin Horde? Mikhail certainly behaved in a civilized manner, but he was still a barbarian from the south.

The Kurakin culture was different. Their goals for the Continent would be different.

Rapp shook his head as he approached the temple steps. Mikhail didn't seem like the type for betrayal. He'd been genuine in all Rapp's interactions with him.

Besides, the Kurakin were the main reason behind the Erlonian Emperor's fall in the first place.

He picked up his pace and climbed the temple's steps two at a time and pushed through the doorway.

The worship chamber was silent and still and dark. The god of the Continent rose above Rapp and blocked his view of the altar behind. Rapp walked forward and met the eyes of the god.

The prince needed help. He pleaded for guidance from the stone visage of the warrior god, but nothing came. The temple remained silent.

Rapp wanted to throw something up at the stone face. He should've left the plateau and headed to the war front long ago. He should've left his mother to fend for herself at the *peace* gathering.

The prince reached the statue's base and took a last look up at the god's eyes before stepping around it towards the Tribune's dais. He would pray and ask for guidance one more time. But if nothing came, he was leaving.

Rapp froze when he saw the dais.

Everything was in place and still except for one thing.

The sword of the Ascended One was gone from the wall.

Rapp spun and looked around the cavernous temple. He was alone. There was no thief running out any of the doors. The sword was probably taken earlier in the evening. Or had it been gone even longer and no one had noticed?

Rapp didn't know what to do. His legs moved on their own accord and he ran from the temple. He threw open the doors and started hollering into the night. He ran back down the street, the worries of the summit and the war all but gone from his mind for the moment.

The god's sword had been taken. Wahring's most sacred possession was gone.

Rapp yelled and yelled and saw the flicker of torches from the night guard twinkling up ahead as they ran from their posts. Two guards stood at the end of the street.

"The sword! The sword is stolen!"

Neither guard moved. Their expressions were only shadows in the torchlight.

"Someone's stolen the sword!" The prince pointed back at the temple behind him. This finally got a reaction.

The guards' eyes went wide and one turned and ran for the palace.

Rapp made to follow, but something behind the remaining guard stopped him in his tracks. A black mound lay in the shadows by the plateau gate.

Rapp knew what it was even before he even approached it. It still took him a few seconds to comprehend it, but it could only be one thing.

He grabbed the torch from the guard and walked slowly towards the mound. The flames close to his face blacked out the view as he approached, but eventually the light fell on the dead bodies.

Two guards on either side of the lift lay dead. The left was on his stomach with blood pooled underneath. The right was on his back, staring up at the stars with eyes wide open.

Rapp raised the torch and saw the plateau lift was gone. Rapp now knew the sword was off the plateau. The men who'd taken it had killed these guards as well and fled down.

And Rapp knew who had done it.

He took a step closer as he heard more guards rush out of the palace behind him. The crowd moved towards him as he knelt and reached out and touched the dagger protruding from the dead man's chest.

Rapp recognized the dagger. He'd seen it numerous times over the past weeks. It'd hung on the belt of a man he thought was an ally but always should've suspected capable of a betrayal such as this.

The crowd of guards came up behind him as others ran towards the temple. They would want direction from him, but Rapp's mind was shattered by fear and disbelief.

He removed his hand from the black hilt of the Kurakin's dagger and tried to understand the full scope of this betrayal, but nothing would work. Leberecht and Mikhail's absence together now spoke volumes. They'd been plotting against Rapp this whole time.

It didn't seem possible.

The prince fell to one knee and hung his head in shock as the chaos continued to grow in the darkness of the plateau behind him.

Chapter 15

Lannes believed in aggression. He believed in taking the initiative. There was a reason his first military maxim was 'On the battlefield, favor goes to the general who strikes first.'

Tome of the Emperor
Nelson Wellesley

Pitt

Pitt rode south along the Broadwater with a small group staff from King Charles's retinue and the king himself. They trotted at a leisurely pace.

"It will be a grand strategy summit. The great leaders of the defeat of Erlon in one room, planning the end of the empire." Charles led the group on a white horse. The mount pranced about, holding its head above everyone else in a much similar manner to its royal rider. The horse was too pretty by half to be leading an army.

The meeting location was an inn on the Broadwater, north of the crossing near the town of Ligny. Surprisingly, they arrived early despite the king's slow pace.

They entered the building and Charles ordered his staff to start preparing food. He'd chosen to bring along his cooks instead of the Royal Guard.

"A summit calls for a feast," he kept saying as he walked around the main room. "I want this to be the best meal Duroc has ever tasted."

The Wahrian aides pulled many of the tables together in the center of the open dining area and unfolded the campaign map. Charles oversaw them scrambling around the table, placing the wooden troop markers on known locations of enemies and allies.

"It's great to be on the winning side, eh, Pitt?" Charles slapped a hand against Pitt's back and drank from his freshly poured cup of morning wine.

"Certainly, sir." Pitt waved the Wahrian aide with the wine jug away from him and looked over the large map.

"What glory, to lead from the front of a victorious campaign." The king belched and reached to pick up one of the blue Erlonian markers from the map. He turned it over in his hands and then placed it back on the map in an incorrect position.

Pitt resisted the urge to correct the piece and looked over the rest of the map instead. He saw the clump of Wahrian and Brunian markers south of the Branch. They were spread along the Broadwater running down the middle of Erlon, with a small Brunian marker holding the town of Neuse back in the east.

The Moradan and Brunian navies sat off the western coast and another joint Brunian and Wahrian army marched south along the western edge of the empire. It was a couple divisions' worth of men and they had just crossed the Broadwater in the north where it curved west towards its meeting with the sea.

The last markers to be placed on the campaign map were the Kurakin. A black flag was dropped on Plancenoit and every other major Erlonian city and port in the south. Over half the country was covered in the markers of the black Horde.

Pitt frowned. The main force under Duroc was placed just north of Plancenoit, miles away from the Wahrian-Brunian position near the northern Broadwater. Duroc was going to walk through the door of this inn soon, why were they placing his army near Plancenoit?

Pitt shook his head and rubbed his temples. It wouldn't be productive to speak up about this small matter. The king would get annoyed and insist he was right no matter how wrong he was.

A guard came in and announced the approach of the Horde. King Charles straightened and set down his wine. He rubbed his hands together. "Are we ready?"

"Yes, Your Highness."

"Yes, Your Excellency."

"Yes, Your Royal Highness!"

The staff around the map table made final adjustments to the army placements. Shouts and clanging pots from the kitchen wafted through the door. Pitt followed Charles out the front door to greet their allies.

The Kurakin delegation came in on horseback. A flag bearer rode in front with the black of Kura flowing behind him. General Duroc came next in full battle uniform with a Kurakin bearskin hat and flowing black cape. Pitt wondered if the Horde's leader ever wore anything but his military clothing.

The horses shook the ground under Pitt's feet. Duroc had brought plenty of men. Charles stood straight and smiled while the column approached.

The Kurakin general dismounted and took off his riding hat and walked towards the pair. "Generals. Good morning." His voice was low and rough and his smile barely showed his filed teeth through his beard. He towered over King Charles.

Pitt raised his eyebrows at the lack of royal decorum in the address. He braced for Charles's angry outburst in response.

"General Duroc, how nice to see you," Charles said instead. He stepped forward with an excited smile on his face and shook Duroc's hand.

"General Pitt, sir. Pleased to meet you." Pitt shook the Kurakin's hand as well. The man's grip was iron.

"A Brunian. Good to see your forces are combined." Duroc turned and held out an arm for King Charles to enter the inn first.

"Yes, under myself, of course." Charles handed his hat to an aide and swept back into the inn and up to the map table. "What is the latest from your army, Duroc? Any remaining Erlonians to give us trouble?"

Duroc took off his riding gloves and folded them neatly into his jacket pocket. His men filed in behind them and circled around the edges of the room while Duroc leaned over the map.

"Well—"

"We took Vendome with a morning attack. Cannon smoke joining with the mists rising off the fields."

Charles pointed down at the map and Pitt winced after realizing he was pointing to the wrong city. The king wasn't even looking at the right region.

Duroc let the king continue and didn't show annoyance at being interrupted. Charles barely looked at the other two as he talked. He went through their march and the positions of the army and got very few of the details correct.

Pitt looked up from the map and up to Duroc while the report was given. The Kurakin didn't correct Charles's mistakes, but Pitt could see that Duroc knew everything. There was no surprise on the Kurakin's face and his eyes scanned the map layout calmly. He knew the positions of Charles's men better than Charles did.

Movement brought Pitt's eyes to the door. More of the Kurakin soldiers entered the inn. They spread out and closed the gaps in the Kurakin encirclement of the room.

The armed soldiers took their hats off but left their heavy coats on their shoulders. All had sabers and pistols hanging from their hips under the mammoth fur uniform.

A chill washed up Pitt's spine.

Duroc's patience for the Wahrian king finally broke. He cut the king off mid-sentence while Charles explained the finer points of the coastal campaign strategy.

"This map is incorrect."

Pitt looked at Duroc and saw his eyes had changed. They were darker. More focused. Dangerous looking.

The chill on Pitt's spine came again. A dread joined it.

The Kurakin leader approached the table. Charles stayed quiet. Pitt looked around the room at all the Kurakin surrounding the small group of Wahrian royal staff. He stood rooted to the spot with his mind racing. Duroc reached out over the map with a large hand.

"My armies are here. May I?" Duroc didn't wait for Charles to answer. He moved the main army marker north on the map. Farther north than even their current position in the inn. "There are also more troops here and here, but I assume we're out of markers?"

"Yes, sir," a Wahrian staffer said. The voice sounded like a squeak next to Duroc's.

Pitt looked where the Kurakin general had indicated on the map. It was the western plain of Erlon. A big open space on the other side of the river full of cities that sat empty on the Wahrian map.

"Your soldiers march fast." Charles chuckled. He stepped up to the table and looked over everything. "You are formidable allies."

Pitt looked back to the center where their own army now sat surrounded by the Kurakin black markers Duroc had shifted north. He looked at Duroc. The Horde general met his eyes and Pitt felt the dread again. The Kurakin smiled and Pitt went cold at the sight of the filed teeth.

The scene shifted and Pitt saw what was about to happen for the first time. He realized what the chill along his spine was warning him of.

The Kurakin around the room opened their jackets and the metal of their pistols gleamed bright in their holsters. Charles's staff were oblivious and unarmed. Charles was busy staring at the map with a stupid smile on his face.

It couldn't be. This wouldn't happen. They were all part of the same Coalition.

They were allies.

But the Horde was different. General Duroc was different. Pitt looked at the man who'd defeated Emperor Lannes and knew exactly what was about to happen.

Pitt stood frozen. The weight of his own pistol felt heavy on his hip.

"You have a choice, Your Highness." Duroc spoke slowly. He was now looking at King Charles. "My army outflanks yours along the river, we have the stronger position and the numbers."

"I beg pardon?" Charles's dumb smile didn't waver.

"You will stand your men down and have them surrender to my forces. Or they will be slaughtered." Duroc stood perfectly still.

Charles's face fell. "What?"

Pitt saw the movement as if in slow motion. The Kurakin around the room drew their pistols in unison and leveled them at Pitt and Charles and the Wahrian staffers around the table. Pitt heard one Kurakin cock his weapon from directly behind his own head.

"Duroc, what is this?" Charles's face grew red. His confusion turned from anger to fear.

"Erlon will be conquered by the Kurakin. This Continent is ours." Duroc still hadn't moved. "Your army can be a part of that, or it can be slaughtered here and now. That is your choice."

Charles didn't have a response. Pitt watched his face turn almost purple.

Duroc finally moved. The general drew a pistol from his side and cocked it. He held the barrel down and rested it on the table. It faced the king's direction. "You have a choice, Your Highness. A choice for Wahring. Will her army die with her king? Or live to fight on?"

Charles still didn't respond. He stood rigid, but his eyes were going back and forth between the gun barrel on the table and the general holding it.

The Kurakin leader waited only a second for the king before bringing the pistol up to point at the king's chest. He seemed to shrug, as if he didn't care if Charles answered one way or the other.

"It's up to you, Your Highness," Duroc said.

The full weight of the betrayal hit Pitt. His legs wanted to collapse. Fear pulsed through his entire body.

It took all his will for Pitt to move his hand. He went for his pistol. He could shoot Duroc, he could cut off the Horde's head. He could stop this betrayal.

It was the only option he had.

He gripped the handle of his gun and pulled it out. A rush of movement came behind him before he could complete the move.

There was a thud and a pain in the back of Pitt's head. Metal against his skull.

Pitt's world went black as he collapsed to the floor, his pistol clattering across the wood away from him.

* * *

Pitt felt his arms going numb already from the tightness of the rope that held them behind his back. He felt the terror of being strapped to a horse without being able to use his arms. He felt the cold wind whip by his face as the Kurakin made a frantic gallop back towards his camp.

Pitt felt it all and understood none of it.

Fear and disbelief outweighed everything.

The Wahrian king was tied to another horse whose reins were held by a Kurakin soldier galloping next to him. Pitt had never seen a king look less regal.

From what Pitt could tell, he'd awakened not long after being knocked out. He'd been carried to a horse behind the blubbering king and they'd both been thrown up into a saddle with their hands tied.

The rest of the party the king had brought to the inn were left behind under armed guard and Duroc carried the king and Pitt off. The Horde army waited for their arrival only a few miles down the road.

They cheered the return of their general and the great prize he carried tied to a horse.

Pitt had never fought in a battle with Kurakin present. He'd barely ever seen anyone from the bearded race. But he now understood why they were called "The Horde" by northerners.

Their soldiers lined the path into the tents of the camp with black mammoth fur coats and full beards hanging over their necks. Filed teeth gleamed in the sunlight as they threw jeers at the fallen Wahrian king and Brunian general.

The taunts sounded like grunts and roars and laughter. These men were happy and expecting a show.

But what kind of show was Duroc going to give them?

The Kurakin leader continued his gallop even after entering the camp. The line of horses went straight to a large tent at the center and Pitt and Charles were pulled off their mounts and thrown inside after the general.

It was Duroc's command tent. The general went to a desk in the center of an open and clean-looking working space. A single lamp provided light.

"The king can sit."

King Charles was pulled forward and pushed into a chair opposite Duroc at the desk. Pitt was held by the door. A Kurakin soldier had a tight grip on his shoulder.

"This is an outrage." The king finally found his voice, but the strength of his words was dampened by a crack that took his tone an octave higher.

The soldiers in the tent chuckled and even Duroc smiled.

"I have drafted orders for your army to stand down and surrender." Duroc turned three different pages around to face the king's seat while he spoke.

"I said this is an outrage, untie me right now!" Charles's volume increased and he struggled against the ropes that held his arms.

Duroc nodded to a guard. "Untie him."

The soldier stepped forward and cut Charles's bonds. Pitt's eyebrows shot up in surprise. Charles looked surprised his demand had worked as well. He flexed his hands and tried to stand but was roughly shoved back down by the soldier.

"You will return me to my army at once." The king's voice cracked again.

"Sign these orders and we will." Duroc's voice was level. He pointed to the papers in front of Charles. "Like I said back at the inn, you have a choice, Your Majesty. Save your men by signing the papers."

Pitt couldn't see what the papers said. A pen was brought over and placed before the king. Charles looked at the soldiers around him and back to Duroc.

"I'll sign, but you must return us to my army."

Duroc shrugged and nodded his agreement.

"And we'll forget this whole indecent matter. From one leader to another." Charles leaned forward and picked up the pen and looked at Duroc. The Kurakin general nodded again.

Pitt couldn't believe it. He wanted to yell out for the king to stop. But before the words could be formed, it was done.

The king signed the first and went right on to the next two without a second thought. Charles didn't even read what he was signing.

It was done.

The tent spun around Pitt's head.

"And now." Duroc stood up from his chair and towered over Charles. "For the show I promised my men."

Duroc flicked his hand and his soldiers responded. They grabbed Charles roughly and tied his hands again. The king scream in protest but could do nothing to stop them.

Pitt was yanked out of the tent and cheers rang out from the Kurakin camp at his appearance. The yells grew even louder when the king appeared.

Pitt got a good look at Charles's face now. It was still red with anger but was quickly becoming pale as fear set in for a man who was used to complete control in his life.

Pitt was sure his own face showed the same fear.

The soldiers hauled them through the camp. Kurakin soldiers on all sides jeered at them. One soldier threw a ball of mud and it splattered all over the king's chest.

The group turned a corner and Pitt got a first glance at their destination. A wooden gallows platform.

Pitt had felt fear before. He'd been in enough battles to know the feeling with familiarity. But this was different.

His current situation was hopeless. He was going to die next to a coward king.

Pitt was stopped at the base and held in place. The Horde army pressed in around the gallows. Charles was hauled up the stairs. The king was kicking against his holders now. He protested with everything he had left and his red face turned pink from strain.

Pitt looked around at the soldiers pressing around the platform. All bearded with dark eyes. Large soldiers with gleaming swords and axes at their belts and teeth filed to points.

Except for one.

One was unarmed and clean-shaven. He stood close by Pitt in the crowd and laughed with a glint in his eye. His long, smooth hair flowed back from his head and stuck out against the matted and tangled locks of the other Kurakin. A crazy smile showed off his pointed teeth.

Duroc passed Pitt and stole his attention back to the gallows. The general followed the king's path up the stairs at a normal pace. He reached the top and nodded to the soldiers to put the noose around the king's neck.

Duroc held up his hands and his army grew quiet immediately. Charles struggled against the rope at his throat.

"We have a new war on our hands." Duroc's voice carried easily over the crowd. It was powerful and deep. "This man is not fit to be our ally."

The soldiers erupted in cheers of agreement and Pitt felt the ground underneath him shaking. Duroc let the noise die down before continuing.

"Wahring. Brun. Erlon." Duroc swept an arm to show the countryside surrounding the camp. "They only stand in our way. We will crush them."

The soldiers cheered again. Charles shook underneath the noose around his neck.

"A new war begins today. One we will win." Duroc pointed back to Charles and smiled. His teeth were white knives sticking out of his beard. "If you don't believe me, watch what we do to the Wahrian king."

The lever was pulled. The platform trap door snapped open with a crack. Charles dropped and the rope tightened. The king's red face turned purple. Cheers shook the ground once more.

Pitt struggled against the ropes behind him and the soldier that held him. He didn't know what he was struggling for.

It was hopeless.

It was all hopeless.

He wanted to scream, but his throat was dry. The Wahrian dangled and jerked under the platform. Pitt felt like he himself was already still and hanging from the rope.

Charles had slowed the Brunian and Wahrian armies down. He'd let Duroc take Plancenoit first. And now their allies had turned against them and had executed the king in front of laughing Horde soldiers.

Pitt wanted to fall to his knees but was held upright by his captors. He wanted to run away and find his countrymen and scream for them to flee and to hide.

Charles kicked one last time and hung still. It was over. The Wahrian king was dead.

The soldiers continued to cheer. Duroc walked off the stage and down the stairs and passed Pitt and the guards again.

"General, what do we do with this one?" one of the soldiers asked.

Duroc turned and looked at Pitt as if seeing him for the first time. He shrugged. "Do with him what you want."

A smile formed on the soldier's face and Pitt was dragged away through the mud of the camp. His last glimpse of King Charles was his purple face growing darker as he hung over the Horde army's celebration.

Chapter 16

An army's strength is in the discipline of the brave.

General Gerald Lannes, spoken to his officers before the Battle of Riom
Year 1098 Post-Abandonment

Pitt

A cool mist hung over the Kurakin camp the next morning. The celebration had turned to focus and preparation for a march and now all was still after a night's rest.

Pitt was tied to a tree.

He pulled against the ropes that held him but found no luck. He could barely move, let alone feel his arms.

A Kurakin coughed from behind the tents in front of him. His gaolers barely stood watch over him. The rest of the camp stretched beyond. The top of the gallows on the far side poked up above the black tents and still held a single black figure.

Flashes of King Charles's death came to Pitt's mind. He shuddered and wanted to vomit, but there was nothing in his stomach.

The Horde army had celebrated after the hanging, but not for too long. Most of the camp had broken things down and marched off north. Pitt had no doubt where their destination was.

They were going to attack Pitt's men. His soldiers. His army.

They were going to surprise their former allies, the same as they'd surprised King Charles. The central army of the Coalition would be shattered. The Brunians and the Wahrians and the rest of the Coalition would have the same fate.

It was hopeless.

All Pitt could do was knock his head against the tree trunk behind him and pray to the Ascended One that the armies could retreat north and somehow get across the Broadwater or Branch without losing too many men. He sighed and his breath formed a cloud in front of his face.

He'd left for this war hoping to find glory. Every breath Pitt had taken was towards gaining victory for Brun and avenging the wrongs of the Erlonian Empire and earning medals on his breast for women to admire and to further his family's future.

He'd accomplished none of it.

In the end, he would die with nothing. He'd be remembered as a general who led his men into a Kurakin trap and lost without firing a single shot. His sisters and mother would have to live with the shame. At least Pitt would already be dead and not have to see it all back home.

Pitt didn't weep, even though he wanted to. He shivered against the cold of the morning and watched and waited for the Horde hangman to come his way.

They didn't come for him until well after breakfast. A group of soldiers came out of the camp tents and untied him. They stood Pitt up and held him on his feet.

One of them pulled out a knife and cut the ropes from Pitt's hands. "You're free to go."

The words didn't register in Pitt's head.

The ropes dropped to the dirt. Pitt shook his arms and tried to get feeling back to them. He felt wobbly on his feet and knew he must've misheard the Kurakin.

Another Kurakin stepped forward. This one had the bars of a captain on his shoulder. "You may go. But we'll need your coat."

The cloak was pulled from his back and Pitt hugged himself against the cold.

The captain looked around at his men and smiled again. "Actually, we'll need your boots too."

They took his boots and more. Everything but his undergarments. Pitt shivered in the cold and felt the mud sticking between his toes.

A dog on a chain was brought forward. The animal smelled at Pitt's legs.

Pitt felt the hairs on his neck stand up. A cold wave hit his spine. He now knew what was going to happen.

The Kurakin started laughing when they saw the recognition in Pitt's eyes. "We'll give you a few hours' head start," the captain said.

The laughter increased.

Pitt didn't need to be told a second time. He took off away from the men and ran as fast as he could into the forest. The dog's barking followed him. The Kurakin continued their laughter as they prepared their horses and weapons for the hunt to come.

Elisa

The morning was bright and chilly. Elisa rode directly behind Marshal Lauriston as he talked quietly with Desaix in the front of the group. Mon was to her left with a bottle clanking around in his lap.

Desaix galloped away from Lauriston to return to scouting. The marshal rode alone at the front now with his head down in thought. Elisa nudged her horse faster to catch up with Lauriston at the front.

"When should we cut east?" she asked when she pulled level with the marshal. She'd assumed they would've already moved away from the Broadwater and hidden in the deeper forest, but she trusted Lauriston to make the right decision.

But since the guide's latest warning to her, she knew something was about to happen. Maybe the group should already be heading east and away from potential danger. She wanted to hear Lauriston's thoughts on his own plan.

"When we approach Bres, I think." Lauriston didn't sound fully confident in the answer.

"And we'll be able to find the army in the forest?" Elisa knew the Dune Forest to be vast and difficult to traverse.

"The agreed-upon location is Lake Brodeur. That's on the other side of this part of the forest. The army should be split up throughout the forest, so we may find them sooner."

"And if their plan has changed?" Elisa's voice was low. She didn't want the scenario to be true.

"Then we'll have to find them some other way."

They rode some more in silence. Traveling up and down small hills. Passing over small creeks and between thickets and clumps of underbrush.

"Your father would ask me for advice while we were on campaign." Lauriston spoke at last through a long exhalation. His voice was tired and worried. "We would discuss the next move, the mindset of the enemy general and how to defeat him. He seemed to always know the right answers. For any situation, even against Duroc."

Elisa didn't know how to respond. Memories flooded her mind and she felt heat come to her cheeks at the mention of her father. A vision of him riding next to her through the imperial forests outside Plancenoit flashed across her mind. She was younger. She laughed and her hair waved behind her as they galloped through the trees.

"I keep asking myself what he would do right now. What would he have us do?" Lauriston shook his head and stared down the path in front of them. "He wouldn't give up."

"No." Elisa knew that much was true.

Lauriston turned his head and looked at her. She could feel his eyes searching through her own. There was pressure there, like he expected her to have answers. He wanted her to be her father, to save them all in some miraculous and brilliant move.

But there was nothing to offer. Elisa was as lost as the rest of them. She wasn't her father. She was useless, especially in a war like this one.

"It's okay," Lauriston pulled his eyes from hers. "We'll find a way."

Elisa fell back behind Lauriston and let the marshal ride alone at the head of the group. Mon continued to sip from his bottle and Elisa lost herself in memories of her father from when she was younger and the world was a simpler place.

Around midday, Desaix came galloping back through the trees with two other scouts. "Kurakin ahead." Desaix reined up his horse.

Everyone stopped and grew quiet. All of Elisa's worries disappeared and were replaced with a cold fear.

"How many?" Lauriston said.

"Not sure, not a whole regiment. There's a dog with them. Almost like a hunting party."

Both men looked unsure what to make of the information.

"Should we keep moving?" Desaix said.

Lauriston looked back at his line of soldiers. "For now." He spurred his horse back into motion.

Desaix fell in with the group and they continued moving. After another hour, a second scout came back to report on the movement of the enemy.

"They're close," the scout said.

As he said it, the distant howl of a dog came through the trees.

"Coming this way?" Lauriston's eyes didn't leave the scout's face.

"Yes, about the same size as us." The scout nodded back to the line of their own troop. "They keep changing directions, definitely Kurakin though."

Lauriston didn't wait long to think through things. He called out orders to the men immediately and the whole group moved up to the crest of the next hill. Elisa was ordered to stay with a group of the sharpshooters while the rest of the soldiers rode down into the small valley below.

The barking of the Kurakin dog grew louder.

Elisa watched Lauriston lead the men down through the trees. She could see all the way to the bottom where a creek broke apart the forest floor.

The sound of horses came through the trees. Lauriston stopped his group. The dog was no longer barking. Silence filled the forest. Elisa watched the group below them spread along the creek and face north. Lauriston held up his hand at the front of the line.

The dog bark returned, closer now. Lauriston drew his pistol and the rest of the soldiers followed suit. Elisa scanned between the trees but saw nothing.

Something white appeared and bounced between the dark outlines of the trees. The shape turned into a man. Lauriston drew his pistol.

The man wore only undergarments and was covered in mud. He screamed and flung himself onto the ground next to the creek a few feet from Lauriston's horse.

"Help me!" the man yelled. "Help me! Help me! Help me!"

Lauriston

The man fell to the ground in front of Lauriston. His horse tried to shy away but Lauriston gripped the reins tight and held her in place.

He focused on the tree line, where the sound of the hunting dog was coming closer. "Make ready." He kept his eyes forward while issuing the order to his men.

The soldiers already had their weapons leveled at the far part of the clearing. Lauriston pulled back the hammer on his pistol.

The hunters appeared at a full gallop. They came around the bend of the creek and pulled up quickly. A dog came barreling onward and Lauriston was about to shoot the animal when the lead hunter called it to a halt with a whistle.

Lauriston looked at the hunters. They were wearing thick black furs.

Military uniforms.

Tall bearskin hats.

Lauriston knew the uniform well. He'd hoped to never have to fight them again.

The Kurakin numbered fifteen or so, about the same size as Lauriston's men. But the Erlonians had their weapons already drawn.

The naked man in the middle still cowered. He pulled himself across the ground closer to the Erlonian side.

One of the Kurakin stepped forward. Lauriston saw the bars on his shoulder. A captain.

"We've no quarrel with you," the captain said. "Leave that man to us and go. There won't be trouble if you leave now."

The soldiers behind Lauriston shifted a little. His own horse moved her head in response to the tension between the groups. He didn't believe the captain's words for a second.

"Well, shit," Lauriston said to himself under his breath.

Silence and stillness filled the creek bed.

Lauriston raised his voice so the enemy captain would hear. "No."

He said the response with force.

The Kurakin didn't seem surprised. "So be it."

The men in his group moved their horses two steps forward to draw even with their leader.

Everything sat frozen for a moment. The two groups looked at each other and waited for the other to move first. The dog stood with rigid legs in the middle. The cowering man continued to cower and crawl slowly towards the Erlonian side. The forest was dead silent around them.

The Kurakin charged.

It came quickly and without an order. They moved all at once. Their horses roaring forward. Lauriston yelled and the Erlonians let loose a volley.

Smoke from his pistol shot flew into his face. He didn't see if his ball had struck the captain. The Erlonian horses galloped forward. Lauriston's mount churned up mud from the creek.

More shots exploded around him and the thunk of bullets hitting flesh accompanied screams from both sides. Clashes of metal and flesh joined the chaos as the two sides collided.

Lauriston emerged from a cloud of smoke and found the Kurakin captain directly to his right now. The enemy's right shoulder was bleeding. His pistol was already leveled at Lauriston.

The marshal ducked to the side and slid behind the flank of his horse. He pulled the reins and the animal swerved. He heard a crack and the ball whizzed overhead.

Lauriston continued through the Kurakin line and out the other side. He pulled himself back upright and drew his second pistol as he turned. The Kurakin captain was lost in the smoke.

Lauriston brought his pistol up and fired into the back of another Kurakin nearby. The enemy fell forward on his mount and the body was carried off into the forest by the panicked horse.

There was death everywhere. Horses down and screaming. Men on foot fighting men on horses. Men fighting with fists and no weapons in the mud. Lauriston drew his sword and charged back into the fray.

He swung down on a Kurakin who'd just fallen from his horse. A bullet snapped by his head. He parried an ax swing from a mounted enemy. Mud was flung up into the smoke-filled air.

Lauriston spurred his horse further into the fray and swung down on another Kurakin. The enemy fell with a slash across his face. Lauriston closed the gap on two Kurakin fighting one of his sharpshooters, but before he could reach the soldier, his mount stumbled on fallen bodies and threw Lauriston forward.

He rolled over his shoulder and dropped his sword and landed facing the same direction in a crouch. He turned and saw his horse tumble and come back to her feet and gallop away from the fight. Lauriston scrambled to find his sword on the ground.

He heard hooves and a yell behind him as he grasped the hilt in the mud. He turned and brought the blade up in front of him and parried an enemy horseman's swing. The force of the attack knocked him down.

He rolled and stood. The horseman made a wide swing around and came back towards him. Lauriston counted the seconds while he drew his pistol. He drew a powder cartridge from his pocket. He upturned it into his gun while keeping his eyes on the approaching Kurakin horse.

The enemy's sword went up. His horse came closer. Lauriston dropped the ball down the barrel and stuffed the rod in after. The horse was on him. The sword was high above Lauriston's head and swinging down. Lauriston stepped aside and felt the air from the swing and the horse passing by him and moving on its way.

He went to one knee and pulled the hammer back and fired at the rider's back. The enemy fell from his horse, dead.

Lauriston dropped his pistol and switched his sword back to his main hand. He spun around and looked for the next enemy. He found them behind him.

Two Kurakin soldiers both with pistols pointed at his chest.

Shit.

One of the Kurakin grinned. Lauriston waited for the shots to come. He kept his eyes open and on the enemy in front of him, his sword held at his side. The rest of the battle fell away and was lost to him.

Crack.

Smoke came from the trees to his right. The two Kurakin went down sideways. Blood spurted from wounds in their heads.

Sound came back to Lauriston. He ran forward and picked up the two enemy pistols. He turned to his right and saw Elisa and the sharpshooters come through the trees down the hill. Lauriston watched Elisa level her second pistol and fire into the back of another Kurakin.

The enemy were on the ground all around them. Moans and screams and the last clashes of swords carried through the haze of smoke. Erlonians stood over fallen Kurakin and finished them off.

The fight was over. Silence returned to the forest and the haze of smoke drifted off on the wind. The Erlonians breathed heavily and many had fallen to their knees. Lauriston felt a tension leave him and he wanted to collapse.

But there was work to be done. Soldiers moved to the injured Erlonians and started dressing wounds. Even through the chaos, Lauriston's head was telling him to get the wounded and fly from this place. The fight had been too loud and they were too close to the Kurakin's main army.

He started giving orders. They would gather what they could and bandage up what needed to be bandaged. They needed to move fast.

Lauriston turned and saw the nearly naked man standing at the edge of the group as the Erlonians tended to the wounded. He'd forgotten about the man who the Kurakin had been chasing. Lauriston went over to the man and took off his own coat and put it around his bare shoulders.

"Thank you," the man said.

The accent rang out in Lauriston's ears. There was less bite in the words than an Erlonian would use. It made things sound noble and poetic.

Lauriston looked at him in confusion. "You're Brunian?"

The man gave a nod. "Thank you," he said again.

Lauriston didn't know what to think. But answers would have to wait. For now, they only needed to grab the wounded and get far away from here before more Kurakin attacked.

Chapter 17

Don't poke the sleeping bear.

Lakmian Proverb

Nelson

White sails unfurled and filled with the steady wind. Salt air flicked up over the bow and the ship tacked away from the island. Nelson felt free now that he was back on the open sea and away from the stone walls and cold rooms of the fortress.

The same could not be said for Emperor Lannes.

Nelson turned in his seat and observed the emperor staring out the stern windows in the royal quarters as the Brunian ship sailed northward. Lannes turned away and resumed his seat at the desk across from Nelson. The former emperor leaned forward and rubbed both hands over his face.

"I thought you would've enjoyed that view for longer." Nelson nodded back towards the stern window and the receding island fortress on the horizon.

Lannes smiled. "Standing up makes my stomach worse."

"I see."

Lannes stole a quick glance back at the sea outside the windows right as the ship lurched over a large swell. He shook his head and went back to staring at the back of his palms.

Nelson chose to let Lannes deal with the beginnings of his seasickness in silence. The king turned inward and gathered his own thoughts. Now was the crucial part of his plan. Now everything would come together and his large gamble would either pay off or doom his side of the war from the start.

King Nelson had chosen to skip the peace summit after his spies in Morada had alerted him to a possible betrayal from within the Coalition. He hadn't known the details, but enough pieces were there for Nelson's diplomatic intuition to kick in.

He'd chosen to not attend the summit nor to attempt to stop Leberecht and the Kurakin's betrayal himself. He'd sailed to Brun instead to meet one of the most fascinating characters the Continent had ever produced. A man who would be useful in the wars to come. A man who was one of the only military leaders alive who could outsmart Duroc and the Kurakin and save the Continent.

A man who didn't have very strong sea legs at the moment.

The ship rolled over another swell and Lannes took in a deep breath and held it inside. He kept his eyes down. The breath escaped and he dry-heaved once, holding a fist over his mouth.

"There's a bucket." Nelson pointed to the port wall of the room, but Lannes kept staring down at the floor.

"I'm okay." The green hue of the emperor's face didn't agree with his statement. "Just need to keep my mind off it."

"Smart."

Nelson shifted the paperweights around on the desk. They held down various letters and maps and drafts of royal orders from the frequent rolls of the ship. He had too much work to do.

"I assume you knew about the betrayal through your network of spies. Or someone from Morada passed along information."

Nelson looked up from his papers and found some of the color was returning to the emperor's face.

"Yes." Nelson nodded. "Being allies for so long gives you plenty of access to inside information on your friends."

"And of all the things you could've done to stop the betrayal and prepare to fight the Kurakin, you chose to come and talk to me." Lannes raised his eyebrows and kept his eyes locked on Nelson.

The king's advisors had said the same thing. Sorceress Thirona had been the strongest opponent to this part of the plan.

"I wanted to consolidate allies," Nelson said. He moved the stone paperweight next to his right hand slightly to the left. "I couldn't stop the schemes already in motion and I feared telling other Coalition members would only muddy the waters even more."

Nelson was surprised to see Lannes nod in agreement. It was the king's turn to raise his eyebrows back at the emperor. He'd expected Lannes to disagree with Nelson just like everyone else did.

"You chose to prepare for the battle rather than try to prevent it," Lannes said.

"Precisely." King Nelson nodded. "I thought keeping you alive instead of letting Moradan poison be slipped into your food was the better move."

Lannes's eyes drifted back to the stern window, but he quickly snapped them back. He looked like he regretted the brief glance outside and chose to keep speaking instead of dwelling on the rolling sea outside.

"You'll need Erlon in this war," Lannes said.

Nelson nodded once. "Your armies will be key."

Silence fell on the quarters. Nelson watched the emperor's mind work. The man had somehow guessed at parts of Nelson's plan early on and kept quiet. But now that the Kurakin betrayal was out in the open, the emperor was seeing the full field for the first time.

Lannes tilted his head and the side of his mouth turned upward in a wry smile. "I can help you with Erlon, of course. My people, my soldiers, will follow me and my officers."

Nelson agreed. Lannes as a figurehead would be invaluable.

"But my real value is elsewhere." Lannes didn't continue the thought. The other half of his mouth joined in his smile now and the emperor showed his teeth to the king.

Nelson knew what Lannes was thinking. It was the part of his plan that he doubted the most. It went against everything Brun had fought for the previous decade. It was something none of his citizens would agree with and all of his advisors, especially Thirona, would oppose.

But it was the only way.

"My real value is elsewhere," Lannes said again. He met Nelson's gaze across the table and the king waited for him to form the same question Nelson had been asking himself every night for months.

Lannes, the greatest military commander on the Continent, took a breath in and spoke quietly. His voice was barely audible over the sea wind outside the stern window.

"Are you going to let me fight again?"

Leberecht

Leberecht's carriage rattled down the road as he basked in the glory of his victory. His plan was finally in motion, the Kurakin turn had finally happened.

The carriage slowed and a knock came on the window. Leberecht moved the curtain aside and opened the glass to find Mikhail outside, sitting on a horse. The Kurakin's hair hung down in tangled locks from his head. He wore a black coat against the drizzle of the rain falling.

"Good evening, Mikhail." Leberecht offered his gloved hand out the window and shook Mikhail's.

"Evening, sir."

It was strange seeing the ambassador now dressed in the normal Kurakin attire. He wore a black military uniform with heavy riding boots. The now-empty dagger scabbard was replaced by a long, curved sword not dissimilar from the cavalry swords used by the northern armies.

The sight of Mikhail's blade made Leberecht's eyes shift to the bundle of cloth seated opposite him in the carriage. Leberecht always felt drawn to unwrap the religious sword and strap it to his own belt. He felt it was a good trophy for the man who had accomplished the betrayal of the Wahrian Realm.

Leberecht didn't truly believe it was the Ascended One's actual sword. The chances of the blade surviving and being kept in such great condition over the centuries were quite low. Leberecht believed it was merely a propaganda tool used by the Tribune to inspire piety.

But Duroc had requested the blade be stolen and it was easy enough to steal. Leberecht had been happy to agree to such simple terms, as it meant full cooperation from the mighty Kurakin.

He looked away from the wrapped bundle and back at Mikhail.

"Scouts made contact southwest, just off the road in the Lainian hills." Mikhail wiped moisture off his forehead and made a clicking sound down at his horse to keep its path steady next to the carriage.

"Your army?"

Mikhail nodded. He looked up the road to the west. "We should reach their picket lines tomorrow morning, I hope."

"Good. Thank you, Mikhail."

This had been a part of the plan that had kept Leberecht up at night. He'd never worried about fooling the Wahrian royals or the Brunians or even the parts of the Moradan leadership that would oppose this betrayal. Instead, he'd worried about the chaos at the start of this new war.

Reports from the front were few and far between. The few letters Leberecht had received in the two days since leaving Citiva had been vague at best and useless at worst. He felt blind in his march west. He just had to hope they wouldn't be found by the Wahrian army.

But the Wahrians were in even more turmoil than Leberecht's side. Leberecht had known this great betrayal was coming. He'd orchestrated it from the beginning, since before the Erlonian Emperor had started his exile on Taul.

Prince Rapp, or *King* Rapp now if Duroc had completed his side of the plan, hadn't suspected a thing. The Wahrian queen had never trusted Leberecht, but she never would've dreamed a lowborn Wahrian would be capable of such a betrayal.

There were risks along the entire journey. Plenty of places where things could've fallen apart. Rapp had even suspected a traitor attended the summit. That could've undone Leberecht's carefully laid schemes easily.

But Rapp had made a fatal mistake. He'd confided his beliefs in the actual traitor and never stopped to investigate the man right in front of him.

It'd taken all of Leberecht's willpower to not laugh in the boy's face during their discussions about the traitor. Leberecht had often wanted to scream at the boy and tell him how stupid he was. Rapp was full of royal arrogance.

Leberecht's carriage slowed again and he looked around the curtain to find that night had fully fallen.

"We'll camp here; it's a good spot off the road," Leberecht heard his driver say.

A group of horses galloped by. Mikhail gave orders to the guard around them. Leberecht stepped out of the carriage to stretch his legs.

He smiled at the world around him. To the north, through the dense forests of western Wahring, sat a portion of the Wahrian army. Back to the east, down the road Leberecht and Mikhail and the Kurakin guard with them had just traveled, sat Citiva and the Wahrian royals in turmoil.

How Leberecht wished he could see the faces of the Wahrian royals now.

He was surprised to find himself actually feeling sorry for them, especially the boy Rapp. He was a good kid, or at least wanted to be.

Maybe he would've even made a good king, if one believed in hereditary monarchies.

Leberecht shook his head and smiled even wider at the thought. If Rapp wanted to be king, he'd have to fight for it. That was what the boy had wanted throughout the whole summit. In a way, both Rapp and Leberecht were getting what they wanted through Leberecht's schemes.

But only one would win.

Leberecht would ensure he proved victorious. He'd planned for too long to lose the war now. He had the Kurakin on his side, he had every advantage. Now he just needed to direct his allies to victory.

A question passed through Leberecht's mind that he knew the answer to, but he imagined all the royals across the Continent were now puzzling over it themselves.

Why?

Why would Leberecht do this? Why would the Kurakin betray the Coalition after all those years of neutrality in the far south? Why would a Wahrian-born diplomat rebel and betray his country and start another war just as peace seemed to be descending on the land for the first time in centuries?

Because the royals of the Continent needed to go.

That was Leberecht's answer. The royals themselves wouldn't understand it, but it was the truth behind this coming war.

The people didn't need the kings and queens anymore. They could choose their own leaders, like the Kurakin chose their generals to lead them.

The big irony here was that Leberecht actually supported how the Erlonian Emperor had risen to power. He disagreed with Lannes proclaiming himself an emperor—that was such a dirty word used by ancient tyrants from before the Ascension—but the Erlonians had actually voted to put him in power.

Lannes had earned the power. That was worlds better than the late King Charles Franz being a monarch simply because of who his father was.

Leberecht's stomach grumbled and it sounded like far-off cannon fire. He shook his head and turned to reach back into the carriage to grab his pre-dinner snacks. A small wedge of cheese and a link of salami was exactly what his stomach was grumbling for at the moment.

"We'll camp here," Mikhail said as he trotted back from relaying orders to his men. He dismounted and walked with Leberecht down into a grove of trees just off the road.

"Let's get an early start tomorrow," Leberecht said. "We won't need to unpack much, let's get to the army as early as possible. No need to risk being captured this close to safety."

Mikhail nodded and waved away Leberecht's offered slice of salami. The Kurakin walked off to relay Leberecht's wish to the carriage driver and the other officers.

It was strange, trusting a Kurakin. There were centuries of northern beliefs that screamed at Leberecht to stop and run away any time Mikhail smiled and showed his pointed teeth.

But General Duroc and the Kurakin army were Leberecht's key to overthrowing the power structure on the Continent. He needed their mammoths, Scythes, ferocious soldiers, and military excellence to fight the remains of the Coalition.

The Kurakin never should've been offered a spot in the Coalition in the first place. Emperor Lannes had backed Brun and Wahring and every other northern faction on the Continent up against a wall and forced them to call upon the great southern beast for help.

Leberecht's great scheme had appeared to him as if it were divine intervention when he'd heard the news that Duroc would treat with the Coalition leaders. Leberecht wouldn't completely rule out the idea that the Ascended One was guiding the recent events on the Continent. Things were almost too perfect for the god to not be involved.

But Leberecht also knew that he was one of the only men to be able to pull off this brilliant plan. No one else was as politically savvy or as smart as he was. The escape from the Wahrian plateau with the Ascended One's sword proved that by itself.

Leberecht smiled again and felt a now familiar cramp in the small muscles of his cheeks. He'd been too happy lately. His face wasn't used to smiling continuously for days on end. The pain felt good and only made his mouth turn up even more.

He ripped off another chunk of cheese and tossed it into his mouth. He chased it with a bite of the salami. The mixture was flawless and would serve to please his stomach before the servants could get dinner ready.

One more night, Leberecht told himself. Only one more night and then they would reach the Kurakin army on this side of the Antres Mountains and it would be finally time to fight.

Then Leberecht and Mikhail and the generals from Kura and Morada could unleash the next phase of their plan and march towards their ultimate goal.

They would campaign against the Wahrian army and defeat them before winter struck. It would be quick and painless, at least for Leberecht's side.

Then the former farmer's boy born north of the capital would march on Citiva itself and overthrow the royals of the Wahrian Realm.

Rapp

There were too many emotions for Rapp to deal with without shutting everything out. Confusion. Sadness. Anger.

Fear.

The gathering of Wahrian leaders from Citiva and beyond sat in the pews of the temple of the Ascended One. Rapp watched the backs of their heads from the back of the sanctuary.

The Ascended One's statue towered over the scene. He looked down on the temple and the Wahrians gathered to coronate a new king. The god didn't have eyes for the commoners, whether they were important dignitaries or not. Rapp knew the god only watched one person.

The person who had failed him.

Rapp hung his head and buried the thoughts deep inside his gut. They were replaced with others that were almost as distressing.

The news of the Kurakin ambassador attacking the palace guards had been disturbing and confusing by itself. But when it was confirmed that Ambassador Leberecht had left with the Kurakin, things had devolved into chaos.

Morada was splitting along with the Coalition. All the work of the peace summit had been for nothing. The Kurakin official declared war on the Coalition factions the next day. The delegations fled the plateau and the talks ceased. Only the war councils remained in contact with each other.

Then the worst news of all arrived.

King Charles was dead. His army was betrayed and scattered. Numerous were dead and captured at the hands of General Duroc himself.

The Kurakin had hung Rapp's father in front of their army, making Rapp the king.

He'd dreamed of the day of his coronation since the time he'd been old enough to understand what being king had meant. He'd always known he'd do a better job leading Wahring than his father and mother.

But now that the time was here, long before Rapp expected it, he felt the weight of the entire world pressing down on him. It was suffocating.

The Wahrians shifted in their seats. A few looked backwards at the royal gathering at the doors. They looked impatient.

Rapp wasn't ready for this. He would never be ready for this.

The soon-to-be king felt a soft hand on his shoulder. He turned his head and found his mother behind him. The now ever-present sadness still hung in her eyes, but she smiled at her son. Her hand gave a soft squeeze on his shoulder as the music started from the string quartet in the alcove by the door.

The commoners stood up and turned towards the back to watch the procession. The widowed queen started down the aisle, flanked by two soldiers. Rapp's sister Julia gave him a kiss on the cheek and followed her mother.

The Royal Guard went next. Everyone was dressed in black, the normal yellow of the Wahrian colors stricken from the palette for mourning.

Rapp was left at the back of the temple alone. The towering statue's eyes bore into him. He felt very tiny all of a sudden. He wanted to run away.

He'd failed the task given to him by the god. He'd failed to prevent the war the god said they couldn't win. Now Rapp would be king and he'd march off to fight that war.

It was exactly what he'd wanted for so long, a war and a throne. And he found his knees shaking as he stood just inside the doors of the temple and the eyes of the Wahrians in front of him stared at their new king.

The music changed. Horns blew and joined the sad strings. The commoners bowed their heads. Rapp's legs stiffened.

He finally started forward and almost broke into a run. He felt like he was moving downhill. The walk passed quickly and he didn't remember a single face he saw in the crowd. It was all a blur.

Rapp was on the Tribune's dais behind the statue before he could process his own actions. The Ascended One's priest held the crown up and said a few words. Rapp knelt and looked up at the priest. The blank wall where the Ascended One's sword used to hang screamed out from behind the Tribune and dominated the scene.

Then the crown was on his head. The horns started again. The commoners cheered. The noises echoed in Rapp's ears.

The royals proceeded back out of the temple. Rapp was thankful for the traditions of the realm being short. If they had been drawn out any longer, Rapp would've ordered them cut. He had work to do.

Only the momentum of action would keep his mind off the terrible thoughts dwelling inside the new king. Only decisive action would get revenge on Mikhail and Leberecht and win this war for Wahring.

"Rapp," the queen said after they'd exited back out into the bright sunlight of the fall day.

Rapp ignored his mother and marched down the street of houses that had been abandoned by the summit members. The housing had reverted back to holding the servants of the palace or were now empty and waiting on the next royal guests.

The plateau felt hollow now. Rapp never would've believed he'd want all the stuffy diplomats to be back around him, but their company would mean the Coalition was still in control. It would mean there was order in the world.

Rapp forced his mind away from those thoughts as well. Too many other terrible things flashed before his mind, though, and he couldn't hold them back. His father hanging from a tree. His weeping mother. Leberecht lying to Rapp's face.

Rapp couldn't believe he'd trusted the scheming republican for his entire life. Rapp couldn't believe that the large and jolly diplomat was now an enemy of the realm, that he'd sided with the Kurakin.

Rapp entered the palace's great hall without a glance behind him. He started right in on his work.

"Prepare the guard to march, we leave in the morning." Rapp turned and glared at the city guard's commander.

"Yes, sir."

"Split the palace guard as well, I want the honor guard with me."

The commander of the palace guard nodded. "Yes, sir."

"Rapp."

King Rapp turned slowly. He'd heard his mother's heels approaching across the entrance hall floor but had hoped she wouldn't interrupt them.

"Do you really need to march off to war immediately?" The sadness still hung behind his mother's eyes, but now it was directed towards him.

Rapp was now king. He didn't need his mother's approval anymore.

"Yes." Rapp made to turn back and continue ordering his military leaders into action, but his mother spoke again.

"Your father marched off and didn't come home." The queen's voice broke. Julia stood behind her with wet and red eyes as well.

"I won't lose this war like father would," Rapp said. The bite in his voice didn't make him feel any better, but he needed to show strength and confidence in front of the soldiers around the royals. "I will crush Leberecht. I will crush the Kurakin traitors. And then I will march west and defeat General Duroc and send the Kurakin back to their frigid place in the world."

The queen's mouth opened but she didn't speak. She knew there was nothing else she could say.

Rapp turned back to face his commanders. Speaking these words was helping to calm his nerves. War would solve everything. "You'll get your peace, Mother. We'll just need another war to get there."

Chapter 18

An army's true test doesn't begin until facing an unbeatable foe.

The Ascended One's Maxims
Verse Seventy

Lauriston

The drum of the horses pounded relentlessly.

Lauriston's back screamed out for a reprieve, but none would come. They had to keep galloping and get farther into the forest and away from any Kurakin who came to investigate the sounds of the fight.

Lauriston had to get his men away.

Lauriston stole a glance back and saw the group was still with him. Those who were uninjured rode upright and strong. Some held the reins of empty horses, whereas others were hurt and struggling and hunched over the necks of their horses, barely holding on.

Lauriston couldn't make the injured go much farther. That realization was creeping up from the back of his mind. But he also knew he needed to put more ground between them and the Kurakin and the Scythes who were surely still on their trail.

For a short period, Lauriston had almost forgotten about what tracked them. The wolverines would surely have their scent now; there was plenty of blood to go around back there. The hawk would be flying again soon, too.

Lauriston would cut east now. No sense in trying to gain ground moving north in the open area so close to the Broadwater. It was too dangerous.

Doubt.

It was Lauriston's least favorite feeling, but one he was becoming all too familiar with.

He'd led his men too close to the Kurakin army. Now he would need to push his men to get them to safety and right the mistakes he'd made leading them.

Lauriston snapped his reins and his horse picked up even more speed. They needed to get deeper into the forest.

The light of the day died quickly. The forest canopy grew thicker and evening became night almost instantly.

Lauriston finally reined up and the pounding of hooves stopped. He dismounted and felt his legs shake against the ground. They felt weak and hollow, but there was no time to sit down and rest. His work was far from over.

One soldier fell from his horse. A shout came through the gloom of evening. Lauriston couldn't see who'd fallen. Bodies scrambled to help the man and Lauriston was relieved to hear the man cough on the ground. He was breathing, at least.

"Clear out." Lodi's voice was calm and steady. He was at the soldier's side in a flash and knelt down to help him.

The group stood around the scene. No one moved. It was like a dark painting with the features smeared in shadow.

Lauriston had to get the men to action.

"Quatre." Lauriston forced his voice to be steady like Lodi's.

"Sir." Quatre stood up from next to Lodi and approached the marshal. He favored one of his legs.

"Are you hurt?" Lauriston said.

"No."

It was clear the general was in pain, but his eyes told Lauriston not to press the subject. Quatre was more worried about the others than himself.

"Get a group to water the horses. Give me a count on the mounts and their status."

"Yes, sir." Quatre nodded and took Lauriston's reins from him and limped away.

Lodi had the fallen soldier rolled over on his back now. Most of the others were standing still and watching.

"Mon." Lauriston looked directly to his left to where the old general stood.

"Sir." Mon's words were muffled. The old general stepped closer to the marshal and Lauriston saw his face was bloody from a broken nose.

"I'm fine," Mon said quickly after seeing the way Lauriston looked at him.

"Are you sure?" Lauriston could see blood running freely from the old man's nose.

Mon looked Lauriston directly in the eye with a hard glare as a response.

"Okay then," Lauriston said. "Gather the soldiers who don't need care and set a watch. Focus on the western path we just traveled."

"Yes, sir."

"I want plenty of warning if we were followed."

Mon moved off and started pulling men into motion with him. Finally, Lauriston's troop started to come out of their stupor.

Soldiers moved to help each other. Lodi had the fallen soldier up in a sitting position to drink water. Elisa knelt next to them and held the canteen. A soldier close to Lauriston dropped to the ground and leaned against a tree.

It was one of his sharpshooters. Lauriston took a step towards him and knelt.

"Are you hurt?"

The sharpshooter shook his head. "Never better."

Lauriston handed his canteen over for the soldier to drink. When the man leaned his head back to drink, Lauriston noticed the cut on the side of his head.

Lauriston looked behind him. Lodi had moved on from the fallen soldier but was attending to someone else. Lauriston reached into his back pocket and pulled out his field kit.

"You're cut." Lauriston shifted over to the man's side.

"You sure you're trained for that, Marshal?" The sharpshooter chuckled.

Lauriston smiled as he tore apart a strip of gauze for the bandage. "No, but you're stuck with me until Lodi gets over here."

"I guess I'll trust you." The sharpshooter smiled and shifted his head so Lauriston could see better in the dying light.

The bandage was easy enough to apply. Lauriston would have Lodi look at it later to see if it needed to be replaced.

Lauriston moved on after ensuring the sharpshooter was comfortable. Two more soldiers leaned against a tree nearby. One had what looked to be a couple broken fingers on his gun hand and the other had a black eye that was already swollen shut and turning purple.

Lodi would be needed to set the first soldier's fingers, but Lauriston knelt to look at the other's eye. He relieved the swelling by making a short cut just above the eye. It would make seeing clearly for the next day's ride easier on him.

"Sir." Quatre approached Lauriston as he finished stitching up the soldier. "Horses are in good condition. We've actually picked up a few extra. Big Kurakin mounts."

"Good. Thank you, Quatre."

"We're feeding them now. We'll be good to keep traveling when we need to."

That was good news. Lauriston thanked Quatre again and let him go off to finish the work. The uninjured soldiers were starting to unpack their tents now. It was fully dark and the troops were just shadows moving about on the outskirts of Lauriston's vision.

Fatigued threatened to take him as the day's adrenaline finally wore off. He'd have to fight it off. It would be a long time before the marshal could sleep.

* * *

"The injured can still travel." Lodi sat in the dark and sorted bandages. "They can all fight too, if needed."

"Hopefully it won't come to that." Lauriston could barely see Lodi's face in the dark. The soldiers were finally still and trying to find rest around them.

The forest floor was covered in blackness. The creatures of the forest were silent, as if holding a vigil for the men Lauriston lost.

The marshal took a deep breath.

"What are our casualties?"

He'd been holding the question inside but couldn't wait any longer. He thought he knew the answer. He'd seen the bodies at the scene of the fight. He'd felt the holes in the men and seen the riderless horses that remained with the group.

"Ange and Jerome from your sharpshooters."

Good men. Veteran soldiers.

Lauriston closed his eyes but held his other emotions in check.

Lodi continued. "Three guardsmen and one of Desaix's scouts."

Lauriston nodded. He hated to have left their bodies bare and open on the ground, but he'd had no choice. Sometimes a general had to make tough choices.

"Are you okay, Lar?"

Lauriston opened his eyes. Lodi's question surprised him. He could only see an outline of the Lakmian's face, but the concern was clear from his tone.

"Yes. Only tired."

"I've never seen you dwell on a loss like this." Lodi continued to sort his medical supplies while he talked. "We've been in worse scraps before. Bigger battles."

Lodi was right. Three Bridges. Klostern. Ice Fields. Those had all been worse fights, far bloodier than a thirty-soldier scrap in the woods.

Then why did Lauriston feel defeated?

Because Erlon was already lost.

"I'm okay," Lauriston told Lodi. "Only tired."

Lodi wrapped a pile of bandages up and stuffed them into his bag. He nodded but Lauriston knew the Lakmian well enough to know that there were more questions he was holding inside.

Lauriston wasn't okay and Lodi knew it. His friend chose to respect Lauriston's silence, though.

The marshal needed to answer questions for himself. This group deserved a strong leader. One who didn't second-guess his own decisions. Or lead them too close to the enemy and get men killed.

Lauriston shook his head.

"We're here for you, Lar." Lodi stood up with his bag. "If you need us." The Lakmian walked off to go check on the injured soldiers who were still awake and left Lauriston alone with his thoughts.

It had been his decision to travel north before cutting east into the forest. He'd kept them close to the Kurakin. He'd allowed them to run into that hunting party.

But a general couldn't dwell on the past. Lauriston had been through this part of war before. He'd lost friends in battle.

His focus needed to be getting the soldiers away from the Kurakin instead of mourning. They needed to get away from the Scythes that surely had their trail now.

Lauriston could do that task, but as full night fell on the camp and the silhouettes of his soldiers faded and became only blackness, he couldn't help but dwell on his decisions that had led to this situation. This was his fault.

The empire was dead. The army was dying.

And Lauriston was their leader. A leader of the dead. A leader of nothing.

* * *

The next day was overcast and gray. A chill ran through the forest and every man wrapped a cloak tightly around their shoulders as they rode.

Lauriston didn't make the men gallop, but kept up a brisk pace. He was content with their progress east and allowed a stop for a brief lunch at midday.

His thoughts still lingered on the fight and the larger war and his decisions. He coped by focusing on the tasks at hand, on the flight from the Kurakin and ensuring they weren't followed.

Flashes from the fight in the creek bed still came back to him frequently. He had to ward them off.

"Lar."

Lauriston turned from feeding his horse to find Mon behind him.

"Have you talked to the Brunian?"

Lauriston had completely forgotten about the man they'd saved. He looked around at the group and found the Brunian still with them. The man stood away from the Erlonians towards the back with his horse and huddled under the Kurakin coat they'd taken off a dead soldier and given him.

"No," Lauriston said. "I haven't."

"Perhaps you should. Find out exactly what happened to him."

Lauriston had been so concerned about getting away from the creek that he'd forgotten the questions surrounding the event.

Why had a Brunian been running through the woods hunted by the Kurakin? They were supposed to be allies.

"I'll go talk to him. Thanks, Mon."

"He helped with the watch last night," Mon said as Lauriston walked off. "Seems like a decent fellow, for a Brunian of course."

Lauriston walked through his men and approached the Brunian. The man stood when he realized the marshal was coming to talk to him.

"Marshal," he said with a nod.

"You know me?" Lauriston stopped a few feet short of the Brunian.

"Of course." The man smiled. A Brunian accent always made words more elegant-sounding somehow. "You're famous even among your enemies."

"I guess that makes sense." Lauriston shrugged. "Sorry for not checking on you earlier. Are you hurt? Need anything from us?"

"No, I'm fine. Thank you for saving me."

Lauriston nodded and waved the thanks away. Brunians were always said to be too polite and formal. Lauriston needed to get straight to the point. "Why were your allies chasing you?"

The Brunian's smile fell away. He wrapped his coat tighter around his shoulders and Lauriston saw the familiar look of a man turning in on himself to protect from memories. Lauriston was very familiar with that feeling at the moment.

Maybe he needed to be more tactful in his questioning.

"What is your rank?" Lauriston said. He'd start with an easier question instead.

"General. I was with the Fourth Army, marching with King Charles and the Wahrians."

The Brunian continued with the story then. His tone was steady and he talked slowly, as if reading the events from a history book. Lauriston didn't stop him and let him talk it all the way through, even when he got to the truly unbelievable parts involving Duroc and the Kurakin.

The Wahrian king had been betrayed by Duroc. That didn't surprise Lauriston as much as the next part.

Duroc had hanged King Charles. He'd murdered a foreign leader.

And now the Horde turned to attack their former allies.

None of this made sense.

The Brunian finished and Lauriston stayed silent in thought. He turned to look at his remaining men. They rested and ate and fed their horses and talked with each other.

Lauriston didn't sense any ruse behind the Brunian's story. He'd been betrayed and the Coalition that had opposed Erlon for a decade now fell apart.

This betrayal was good for Erlon. Lauriston's enemies now fought each other and the Brunians would need Erlon to help fight the Kurakin if they hoped to survive.

Lauriston could work with that. The world turned brighter under the overcast skies of the day. Hope returned to Lauriston's mind. He was surprised at how quickly it reappeared. But he now saw a path forward.

Lauriston looked across the camp and saw Mon talking with Elisa and sharing a piece of his trail biscuit with her. Mon had reminded Lauriston to talk with the Brunian while Lauriston had been drowning in his own thoughts. The old man hadn't lost sight of the larger war. He had helped guide Lauriston back towards a path they could fight on.

A marshal couldn't be selfish. A marshal had to lead no matter what the situation.

And he had to be positive. He had to find the road forward on the campaign.

Even after a mistake, Lauriston had to be positive and encourage the men and lead them on. He would have to do that. He would have to push on.

He looked back at the Brunian. "Thank you."

"For what?" The general's eyebrows raised.

"Telling me everything." Lauriston nodded and scratched at his chin. "The war has changed now."

"It certainly has. I'm not sure exactly what it means, though."

Lauriston smiled. "Me neither."

He turned back to look at his group of Erlonians. They would push through this and find a way to keep fighting. There was nothing else to do.

"Thank you, General. I don't know what your story means for us exactly, but we'll figure it out. We've got to," Lauriston said. "The war has changed; we may actually be allies now, if our countries can stand the thought of it."

The Brunian nodded and pulled his coat tighter around his body as a wind blew through the camp.

Lauriston left him and returned to thinking on their next steps. They needed to find the Erlonian army. They would have to outrun the Scythes. From there, they'd have to find a way to fight. Maybe even form a new alliance with the betrayed Brunians.

That was still a long distance away, though. First things first.

"Mount up," Lauriston said to the entire group. "We've got more ground to cover."

The orders felt stronger to Lauriston now. He was more sure of himself. He caught Mon's eye and got a nod of approval.

Lauriston mounted his horse and turned back to the eastern path. He started down the trail and his men fell in behind him, the Brunian general included. They had a long road still in front of them. But the soldiers would push through it and Lauriston would continue to lead them onward.

* * *

Lauriston's mind settled down quickly after his talk with the Brunian. It helped to have a focus. A goal. A deadly enemy chasing you.

A plan for the larger campaign had begun to form in Lauriston's head.

The marshal had Mon to thank for his renewed focus. The old general had helped him to remember the goal of the group. He'd told Lauriston to go talk with General Pitt. A marshal always had his generals to thank for making campaigns and marches and battles easier.

Lauriston believed he'd settled on the course of action for his current group and the larger army. Now he just needed to convince his officers that it was the best course of action.

"Generals to me, Pitt and Elisa included," Lauriston said when he called a halt to the riding on the second evening after the fight. The sun was still dropping from its afternoon height, but he felt the men had earned the extra rest and he didn't feel the danger on their tail quite as much anymore.

They had room to breathe and discuss their next steps.

The other soldiers began setting up the camp and watering the horses while the generals walked over to Lauriston. Pitt stood slightly on the edge of the group and gripped his arms across his chest, shifting his weight from foot to foot. Elisa stood directly next to Lauriston.

Lauriston looked everyone in the eye while he spoke. "We push east through this part of the forest. We continue on this trail at a good speed."

Desaix nodded. Quatre scratched at the stubble on his cheeks. Pitt continued to shift back and forth.

Lauriston pointed at the Brunian as he continued. "General Pitt here was betrayed by his allies, in case you didn't notice during our fight back there."

Quatre, Mon, and Lodi all looked at Pitt. Desaix and Elisa kept their eyes on Lauriston.

"I've been doing some thinking on what that means for us. Duroc executed the Wahrian king. He's supposedly attacking his own allies now. And General Pitt doesn't think the central army from Brun or Wahring will be able to defend against it."

"So now we fight two separate enemies instead of one big Coalition," Quatre said. He glanced sideways at Pitt with narrowed eyes.

Lauriston couldn't blame Quatre or anyone else for skepticism. Brun was one of the empire's greatest enemies. A big part of the next stage of his plan was to get the men to see the new war that was now laid out across the Continent. A new war that gave Erlon a fighting chance to avoid collapse.

"That's one way to look at it," Lauriston said. He meant to continue with a rebuttal but Mon spoke up for him.

"No," the old general said. "It means we have fewer enemies."

Lauriston nodded. He'd known Mon would be smart about this. "That's what I think too. We may even have new allies." He looked back at the Brunian. "General Pitt, how will Brun take this betrayal?"

Lauriston pointed at the Brunian and expected a quick confirmation of his theory about an alliance against the Horde. Instead, Pitt looked very confused.

"I'm not sure." The Brunian rubbed the side of an arm and continued to shift his weight.

"I would assume it would be in our best interests to ally against the Horde." Lauriston raised his eyebrows at Pitt to emphasize the statement and his need for confirmation.

Pitt stayed silent. Quatre's eyes were still narrowed at him. Lodi looked at the ground in thought.

Mon broke the silence.

"I think that makes sense, Lar."

At least one officer agreed with Lauriston.

"Thank you, Mon." Lauriston smiled at his old friend. "Our focus now is obviously to get Elisa to safety and find the army. They shouldn't be far through the trees, but it'll be rough going."

"We'll find the path through, Lar," Desaix said.

Lodi and a few others nodded in confident agreement.

"Thank you, Desaix. The army should be near Lake Brodeur. We'll find them and plan a campaign against the Horde."

Lauriston took a breath. That was the easy part. The next part was more murky and confusing.

"From there, I think we push north and find the remaining Brunian army. Pitt here says they've taken Vendome and should be down along the Branch. If we can get there before the Kurakin can continue their attacks..."

Lauriston trailed off. The thoughts had sounded crazy in his head and now sounded even worse when spoken aloud. He shook his head and regained his voice quickly.

"My point is that two armies are better than one, especially against the Horde. If we can convince the Brunians to fight with us, we may be able to scuttle whatever campaign Duroc is planning with the Horde the rest of this season."

Mon nodded. Elisa and Lodi didn't move at all. Desaix thought for a second before nodding and Quatre continued to scratch at his stubble.

The group's eyes turned to Pitt. The Brunian seemed shocked to have the attention pivot onto him once more.

"I think that could work," he said. The lack of confidence was clear in his tone. Lauriston would have to work on that.

"That part of the plan is still days away, at least. Priority one is to find the Erlonian army," Lauriston said. "Distribute the plan to your men. We keep up the same marching strategy and watch our rear."

He nodded at his men and met their eyes to ensure there were no other questions.

He added one final point before they walked away.

"Watch the sky. The Scythes will have their hawk back in the air soon. That's the biggest danger to us right now, and I would bet they'll be back on our trail soon."

Lauriston thought he saw Elisa give a slight shiver at the mention of the Scythes, but wasn't sure. He continued as if he hadn't seen it.

"We lost good soldiers yesterday. Don't let their sacrifice go to waste. We get the princess to safety first." Lauriston pointed to Elisa. "And then we find a way to keep fighting. Onward, Erlon."

The men echoed the last words immediately. The officers and the princess were dismissed and Lauriston was left alone with his thoughts. He knew the idea of allying with the Brunians sounded insane, but it would increase their chances of winning the war and saving the country by tenfold.

Lauriston looked to the east and the dark tangles of the forest before them. They still had a hard journey before they found the army. Lauriston would do his best to see the men through and keep them in front of the Scythes.

The fight with the Kurakin over the Brunian had been a setback, but it wouldn't ruin his troop. Lauriston would push them on and overcome this. He would lead them and find a way to somehow win this war.

One step at a time, that was all they needed to focus on for now. Get the princess to safety and find the army. And avoid the Kurakin Scythes at all costs.

Chapter 19

A strong leader, by his presence alone, can swing the momentum of a battle.

Maxims of War, Entry Two
Emperor Gerald Lannes

Andrei

The bodies sat bloated in the creek bed. Andrei knelt at the edge and looked over the fallen soldiers.

"They took their weapons," Andrei said.

"Quite a fight." Jerkal nodded a few feet away.

"Yes."

A horse lay broken to Andrei's left. Wolves and vultures had already picked through the insides.

"They left quickly," he said. "Many wounded. They won't be far."

"You think it's the girl's group?"

"Yes."

The scene was a brutal one. Andrei had seen great battles and the destruction they caused. This was on a much smaller scale, perhaps thirty men fighting total, but there were bodies of men and horses everywhere.

And most of them Kurakin.

Whoever protected the girl was strong. They'd run into the hunting party tracking down the Brunian captive and had been able to fight them off. Erlon might be falling, but Andrei could still marvel at their soldiers' strength.

"What a mess." Andrei shook his head and stood up.

The bundle strapped to his chest stirred slightly but only shifted to a new position before returning to sleep. Andrei put a hand on the bird in the pouch and felt the strength returning to his animal.

"No sign of him, Commander," came a call from the other side of the carnage.

The Brunian captive was gone. Andrei's prey still eluded him. Duroc wasn't going to be happy.

The Kurakin captain who'd been responsible for the Brunian prisoner now lay dead in front of him with bullet wounds in his back. The whole scene was a mess.

"Jerkal, start on their trail. We must keep up pursuit. I'll go give the report." Andrei left the group. He walked up the hill to his wolverine and started the ride back to camp.

The Kurakin army had camped a few miles west by the river. This was only the rearguard now, as the main attacking forces were already pressing to clean up the Brunians and Wahrians just to the north.

Andrei rode through the camp. There was a buzz about the soldiers. Like the water piled up behind a damn about to be released to rush towards the sea. It'd be hard to stop this army.

General Duroc was alone inside his tent when Andrei stepped inside.

"Andrei." Duroc sat at a desk, writing out formal orders. A lone candle gave him light.

"No sign of the captive, sir," Andrei said. "It was quite a fight."

"The Erlonians with the girl helped him?" Duroc stopped writing and looked up.

Andrei nodded. "It's got to be."

"You'll find them soon." Duroc resumed his writing.

"Yes, sir." Andrei made to leave the tent. Quick meetings with Duroc were common. Efficiency was the key to a Kurakin army.

"Another thing."

Andrei stopped at the tent flap. This voice didn't come from Duroc. It came from Andrei's left. A figure walked out of the shadows of the tent's corner. A chill blew through the air and ran up Andrei's back.

The Scythe recovered from his shock and bowed to the clean-shaven god.

"You think too much on the rest of the war," the god said. "Your sole focus is the girl. Is that understood?"

Andrei looked at Duroc. The general was focused back on his writing.

"Is she still with the group we track?" Andrei turned back to the god.

"She should be. You track them and find her."

"Yes, sir." Andrei bowed his head and left the tent quickly. The chill lingered in his body even as he moved out and away from the camp.

Andrei walked back to his wolverine and moved off to find his men. They'd set off on the trail at once. There would be no rest for Scythes tonight.

Whatever scheme Duroc had planned, whatever games his god was playing, it depended on the Erlonian girl. Andrei didn't need to be told why. He only needed to do his job and find her.

The injured hawk shifted again on his chest. She burrowed deeper into the pouch and rested against his heartbeat.

Andrei was happy to track down the men who'd shot her. He would find the girl and the soldiers with her and he'd get his revenge and complete Duroc's mission in one great swoop.

Elisa

Elisa was back on the trail. Back to riding all day and the feeling that the enemy was about to appear out of the trees behind her at any moment.

The conversations with the soldiers helped, of course. But now the group was quieter as they nursed their injuries and fought through the exhaustion of the pace Lauriston pushed for. The quiet gave Elisa's mind freedom to roam to unhealthy subjects.

She thought back to the fight. There were horrible memories. She could see the colors in the strongest detail. Black coats clashing with blue. Blood and smoke flowing freely.

"You've never been this quiet, even on the farm," said a voice beside Elisa.

She looked towards the source and found Mon riding next to her on the forest path.

Mon had checked on her immediately after the fight, but as the group fled the scene and rode east, she hadn't had time to talk to him yet. Mon was usually busy at the front of the group, discussing things with Lauriston.

They were five days out from the fight with the Kurakin horsemen and today Mon rode next to her in the middle of the pack.

"Even when you were mad or annoyed with us, one of the farmhands would get a rise out of you." Mon clicked at his mount to keep it on the path. "But now you've been silent."

"I'm sorry, Mon." Elisa wasn't sure how long they'd been riding for the day. She'd been too lost in her thoughts. It felt like morning still, but she couldn't see the sun through the forest canopy.

"What troubles you?"

"Nothing."

Elisa knew she answered too quickly and Mon would see right through the short response. She turned her head towards him and gave a tired smile.

"Too many things."

"I'm sure."

Elisa raised her eyebrows at Mon's quick answer.

Mon shrugged. "Your parents are gone, your country is falling apart, you've just witnessed a brutal fight and there are a bunch of Kurakin on wolverines in the forest chasing us."

Elisa raised her eyebrows. It was impressive Mon understood that much.

She let out a sigh. "It's not just that, though."

"Try me," Mon said.

Elisa struggled to force her thoughts into words. It was hard to explain her current feelings. They kept slipping away and changing.

"The men," Elisa said finally. Mon's voice calmed some of her thoughts and she took a stab at voicing the biggest trouble that now screamed at her. It was a new feeling and she still didn't understand it. "We lost six soldiers. Three of your guardsmen. Jerome was nice to me. They all were."

"Loss and war go hand in hand." Mon stared down at his horse's mane. "But you know that. Your father is in exile because of war. You lost your palace, your home."

Elisa nodded.

"But this is different. Something more." Mon pulled his eyes back to Elisa and she noticed a new light behind them. Something darker, as if Mon was half in a deep memory and half in the present.

"I'm supposed to be their princess. The heir," Elisa said.

"You are our princess," Mon said slowly. He spoke like he couldn't understand Elisa's statement properly. The shadow was still within his eyes.

Elisa looked away into the trees. Maybe this was too hard to explain. Maybe no one could help her. Only a royal could and there were none of those left on this side of the Continent. Her family had abandoned her and left her to figure things out on her own.

She shook her head and looked back to Mon and decided to try anyway.

"They died saving the Brunian general. But also protecting me. All these men." Elisa nodded at the line of soldiers stretching in front of them. "They're making sacrifices, all for me."

She paused and was thankful when Mon didn't interject. Her thoughts needed time to gather.

"What if I can't live up to their sacrifices? What if Lauriston came south for a worthless princess, someone who isn't fit to lead? What if you sacrificed your farm for nothing?"

"So you'll give up? Because you don't think you can lead?" Mon said.

Elisa was shocked by the bite in his voice. She saw something dark again behind the old general's eyes. It had grown. She'd never seen this shadow before and couldn't understand it. The old general's knuckles where white where he gripped his reins. Some faraway memory had turned to anger.

"No," was all she could say.

The word blew away with the wind. Elisa knew it was a weak answer. Giving up was exactly what she'd been thinking about.

"I'm sorry," Mon said.

His eyes returned to normal. They were bloodshot and cloudy, with nothing hiding deep behind them anymore.

"No, I'm sorry," Elisa said. "I'm not thinking about giving up. Not while this group still fights on."

She hoped her words were true. She wanted them to be.

"The six we lost were not the first to die for Erlon. Thousands came before them, and that's just for your father's empire. History has millions dying for the west, sacrificing their lives for the country and the people." Mon returned to staring down at his horse. "My three guardsmen join others with the Ascended now, including all the guardsmen before them."

Mon's voice had the slightest break in it at the end. Elisa looked at him again and saw another flash behind his eyes. This time of sadness and loss and pain.

She wanted to ask him about his past then but couldn't find the words. It was too hard of a question and she didn't want to say the wrong things.

"Not fighting on, giving up after surviving..." Mon's grip had loosened on his reins. "That would be the worst thing to do. That would ruin their sacrifice. It's a burden, I know. For you even more so than a normal person. But we fight on for the same reasons they died. Walking away would be the worst thing to do."

Elisa knew the old general was right. She'd never heard Mon talk this way before. His voice was deeper and full of emotion she didn't know had been there. He stared at the path in front of them.

"Thank you, Mon," she said.

Elisa went back to her thoughts. Things were a little clearer now but still difficult. Mon was right, of course. She had to continue on. She had a duty to Erlon. She just had to figure out a way to not fail them.

They expected her to lead, to be her father. She didn't know how she would do it, but she had to find a way to keep from letting these soldiers down.

* * *

The group broke for lunch around midday. Lauriston ordered it to be a quick one and Elisa overheard Desaix pass along a report to Lauriston from one of the scouts.

"No sign behind us yet." The cavalry general spoke in a low voice, but Elisa was close enough to hear.

Lauriston nodded and said something, but Elisa lost the conversation.

At least that report was good news. Something positive for her mind to think on instead of the unknown of the future and the beasts that chased her and the men.

It was a distraction, but not a complete escape. Elisa stood away from the others and chewed on the dry biscuits. It was no use. Even after Mon's encouraging words, she couldn't hide from the feelings of overwhelming pressure.

Those feelings mixed with increased questions surrounding Mon's past now. The darkness behind his eyes during their conversation that morning only made her questions more pressing. What in his past could've caused him to react that way to her doubts?

What happened to Mon during her father's wars?

Elisa stepped away from her horse and put a big oak tree between herself and the group. The noise of the soldiers fell away. A cool breeze picked up and rustled the leaves on the forest floor.

Maybe practicing Lodi's sword techniques would help ease her mind. It would be an action to keep her mind off everything that wouldn't stop troubling her. She put her hand on her sword hilt.

"Mon's right, you know."

The voice startled her. Her blade came out in a flash and she pivoted instantly and pointed the sword at the source.

A figure stood and leaned against the large oak tree. It was the guide.

She'd forgotten about him in the rush of the recent events.

The vision held up his hands and smiled innocently.

"Is that any way to greet an old friend?"

"You startled me, that's all." Elisa sheathed her sword and stood there sheepishly.

"It's okay." The guide stood up straight off the tree and shrugged.

"Won't they see you?" Elisa nodded back towards the group of soldiers only a few feet away from the other side of the oak.

"This tree's pretty big. But I'll make sure they can't hear us talking. It's just for a little bit."

Elisa didn't know how to respond. She tried to think back to the last time the Lakmian vision had appeared. Was he even real? Was she hallucinating from all the recent stress?

Last time, right before the fight for the Brunian, he'd told her things were about to change. He'd certainly been correct about that.

"Mon's right." The guide crossed his arms over his chest and talked calmly in a low voice. "You can't dwell on the men lost. And shouldn't overthink the pressure of your royal birth."

The vision's voice settled Elisa's thoughts a bit. She felt the breeze blowing over the back of her neck and the air pent up in her lungs released slightly.

But she still had questions and doubts.

"That's easy enough to say," she said.

"That's true." The guide shrugged again. "You have more to give this world than you give yourself credit. Watch how the men treat you, how they look at you during hard times."

Elisa could see some of the men eating and talking and feeding horses around the side of the oak. Many still nursed injuries, but all helped with the horses and seemed to be in good spirits.

"You give everyone something to fight for. You're one of the only pillars of the empire left." The guide uncrossed his arms and leaned back against the tree again. He pulled an apple from his pocket and took a carefree bite. "I know it's hard and may seem unfair. But you can handle it."

Elisa felt a little better. Her thoughts calmed, at least for the time being. She still had far too many questions, though.

"And listen to Mon," the guide said through another bite of apple. "He's a good man, good soldier. He's a good friend."

One question pushed itself up to the front of Elisa's mind. The guide had already started to fade away. She didn't have much more time with him.

"Do you know Mon's story? Do you know why he left the army and became a farmer?" She blurted the questions out all at once.

The guide wasn't fully gone yet. He smiled at her and nodded but didn't say anything.

"Why did he leave?" Elisa said again.

But the guide wasn't going to give an answer. He blew away in the breeze and Elisa was left standing alone staring at the giant oak. The men milled about on the other side, oblivious to Elisa's conversation only a short distance away.

Someone called out the order to remount. Elisa trudged back to her horse and felt a little better, but still had her questions and concerns swirling around inside her head.

She found the mount grazing happily on a patch of grass. The soldiers led their horses to bunch back into a group and began preparing to mount back up.

Elisa's mind was still swirling with doubts and questions, but she had it more under control now. Talking with both the vision and Mon helped, even if her questions weren't answered.

She looked up to the front of the group. Mon stood next to Lauriston and chewed on a trail biscuit. The dark light behind Mon's eyes during their conversation told of a story from the past that he held inside. Something she'd said had triggered a memory and caused the dark tone he'd used when she'd expressed her doubts.

But his other comments to her that morning were correct. Elisa needed to fight on, no matter how much she doubted herself. The guide and Mon were showing her how important that was.

"Here, Princess. Tighten this to ensure it stays on."

A soldier pulled on a strap on her pack to tighten it on the back of her horse. The soldier had his arm in his sling but managed with the strap anyway.

"Thank you, sir," Elisa said. "How is your arm?"

"Fine, Your Majesty. It'll heal soon enough." The soldier smiled and moved back towards his own horse.

Elisa felt Mon's lesson and saw its truth firsthand. The soldier was hurt and in pain, but still carried his head high and walked with a smile on his face. He was confident in their mission and didn't care about his injury.

He believed in the importance of protecting her.

Elisa looked over the rest of the group as she climbed back on her horse. Others were injured and those unhurt helped the others back onto their mounts.

The group should look ragged and tired and defeated, but instead they remained strong.

Elisa climbed up on her horse. A soldier or two met her eye and nodded and smiled and faced east, prepared to follow Lauriston onward and protect her at any cost.

Elisa saw Quatre still walking with a strong limp. The general helped the soldier with his arm in a sling to mount up before climbing up on his own.

Quatre looked over at Elisa and gave a confident nod as he pulled his horse around to face east.

All the soldiers were focused. Elisa was their mission and their inspiration. They were going to get her to safety.

Elisa knew right then that she had to be stronger.

It wasn't exactly leading. At least not like her father led. But she now saw what her presence could do for the men. She now saw that her burden wasn't as heavy as she originally thought. All she had to do was keep living. Keep fighting.

Elisa resolved to do that no matter what happened in the coming weeks. She would keep suffering with these men until their goals were met.

If the empire was dying, they would all die together.

There was a chance to win this war still. And if Elisa could help with that, she would do it. She would fight with Lauriston and Mon and Quatre and the injured soldiers who protected her. She would keep fighting until the end.

Chapter 20

Hubris is the most detrimental trait possible in a military officer.

Maxims of War, Entry Twelve
Emperor Gerald Lannes

Rapp

It was a strange feeling to lead the army as king. Rapp had marched with his father a few times and even led a small force as a general before, but having command of the entire army, and the entire realm, was vastly different.

Rapp kicked his horse up the road and heard the cheers from the marching soldiers he passed. Their king touched his hat back to them in return and continued up the road to the front of the line of black- and yellow-coated Wahrians.

He felt powerful, like a god. This was as close to being the Ascended One as a mortal could get. Rapp loved the feeling.

He was also terrified.

Rapp was alone. He had advisors and other generals and everything, but he sat alone at the head of the entire faction. The war was his responsibility. The safety of his people fell solely on his shoulders.

He might have risen as close as possible to the war god's lofty throne, but Rapp wasn't getting any guidance or help from the heavens.

He'd tried to hear the god's voice again. He'd even expected the voice to return to him now that the war the god had warned about was starting.

On the morning he'd marched from Citiva, he'd prayed in the temple for over an hour and heard nothing. The great statue only stared down at him and continued to shame him for his failure at the summit.

The message was clear. The only thing left to do was win this eastern campaign.

Rapp had to show the god that he would be a great king, that he would bring glory to the Ascended One and return the Wahrian Realm to greatness despite his failure at the summit.

"My King." Neipperg bowed his head as Rapp slowed his horse to stop next to the general on the side of the road. Rapp still had to catch himself when he heard those words addressed to himself and not his father.

"General Neipperg. How's the march?" Rapp turned and looked back down the road at the line of soldiers marching west. A dust cloud kicked up and was carried back east on the wind above them.

"Good. The van should reach Vith tomorrow. We'll swing this group south and reinforce the lines to the east of the city."

Rapp nodded. "And the Lakmians?"

"So far they've stayed in the mountains. The Kurakin have swung back east and south. There's not much of a flank there, but the Lakmians could take it if they wanted."

Rapp tried to picture the campaign map in his mind but couldn't see all the details. His memory of the exact terrain was blurry at best. He shook his head. He'd have to get the aides to lay things out in his tent tonight.

"Who would they attack, us or the Kurakin?" Rapp turned from the view of his troops and looked at Neipperg.

The general shrugged. "I would hope the Horde."

"Same. But maybe they'll just stay up in the mountains and let us fight the Kurakin first."

"Hopefully."

Rapp liked Neipperg. He was one of the best generals in Wahring's next generation of military leaders. He wasn't much older than Rapp and was already renowned across the realm for valor in the wars against the empire.

He was so renowned that Rapp's sister had taken an interest in him, although Julia was interested in most of the realm's war heroes nowadays. Julia thought she was covert enough in her correspondences with the general that Rapp or their mother didn't know, but it was obvious enough from the first time Neipperg had dined with the royal family.

Julia was attracted to any male who showed an ounce of bravery and had a strong jawline. But even Rapp had to admit that when her gaze found Neipperg's face, it held a different kind of adoration.

Neipperg's battle wounds lent themselves to his mystic of valor and manliness, the most prominent of which was the eyepatch and scarring over his right eye. It was an old wound from his time before Rapp knew him, before he was a general.

The contemplative looks from Neipperg's one eye held more military knowledge than most generals Rapp knew. He would trust Neipperg's judgement over that of any others on the eastern side of this new war. Rapp was glad the man was with him and not in the west. Wahring would need his leadership. He was glad they were friends.

They could even be related someday, if Julia could convince their mother to allow a marriage. Rapp chuckled softly at the thought.

"What's funny, Your Majesty?" Neipperg raised his eyebrows at his king.

"Nothing." Rapp looked back to the column of soldiers marching past them.

These men adored Neipperg and would follow him into a tornado of fire sent by the gods if the general ordered it. It was because they trusted him; they believed he would lead them to victory, whereas they only followed Rapp because he was king. Rapp had earned nothing yet. Neipperg was something more than a general.

He was everything Rapp wanted to be.

Except for king.

"We'll continue as planned. Strengthen Vith and keep the Kurakin in the south. Then we press them." Rapp wanted to end this campaign quickly. He wanted an early victory to show his people the Horde could be defeated.

"Yes, sir. I'm going to keep the van out with frequent scouting. I don't want any surprises from the Horde or the Moradan rebels."

Rapp nodded his agreement. "Don't use too many men. I want to make sure the defenses are well stationed when the Kurakin attack comes." The king took off his hat and ran a hand through his head.

Rapp was tired. They'd been marching hard for almost a week. He was also getting impatient again and was ready for a real fight. He wanted to win a grand battle as king and hear the praises from his soldiers.

Soon, he told himself. Very soon.

They would get to Vith and press out from there. The Kurakin and the traitor Leberecht waited in the south. Rapp would have his revenge soon enough. The great climax of the beginning of his reign would come.

Neipperg bowed his goodbye and rode off to continue overseeing the march. Rapp watched him go and his mind went to the future and the glory that awaited the new king in the next few weeks.

This would be a glorious war. It would be important enough that the Ascended One couldn't keep ignoring the young king and would have to speak to him once again and guide the rest of the war effort.

Rapp couldn't wait for the first cannons to sound. For the charge of cavalry and the yells of men.

The king watched the dust rising up from the pounding of his soldiers' boots and reveled in the feeling of being in complete control. Victory was coming for him. He just had to be patient and wait for the battles to start.

Pitt

Pitt still woke up every morning and had to think about where he was and who the voices outside his tent belonged to. He had to remind himself about the Kurakin turn in the world and the brave Erlonian soldiers that were now his allies.

His next feeling was always a warm happiness.

Pitt was ashamed of it. He should be filled with worry and fear for his country given what he'd witnessed Duroc and the Horde do to the Wahrian king. But his mind only wanted to focus on what was right in front of him.

Marshal Lauriston and the Erlonians.

He was traveling with Marshal Lauriston, Emperor Lannes's right-hand advisor and commander.

General Desaix the cavalry commander was with him. There were legendary Imperial Guardsmen, sharpshooters, and Jinetes and their leader Lodi, master of the Lakmians.

These were all legendary enemies of Pitt's country. Men who'd struck fear in the people of Brun for more than a decade and fought some of the Continent's greatest battles.

Desaix had led the cavalry flank at Stetton. Lodi led the Lakmians through the swamps of Morada.

Marshal Lauriston had been with the emperor from the very beginning. He'd seen Three Bridges. He'd marched on the Ice Fields against Duroc. He'd been part of the force that occupied Citiva for the first time in centuries.

Pitt couldn't contain himself, even in the face of danger. He'd never been with more famous company. He went through these giddy thoughts every morning.

Over a week after his rescue, Pitt rolled out of his tent and wrapped his coat around himself against the cold fog that hung outside. The majority of the soldiers were still pulling themselves awake. Pitt walked towards the fire and found Marshal Lauriston sitting by himself.

"Mind if I sit?" Pitt said.

"Of course not." The marshal nodded towards Pitt and continued building the fire back up from the previous night's coals. "It's still a strange sight, seeing you in this camp. Especially in that black coat."

Pitt looked down and remembered where his coat had come from. The Erlonians had pulled it off a dead Kurakin after the fight when they'd saved him.

The thick mammoth fur was heavy on his shoulders and still smelled of death, but it was warm and comfortable and worlds better than being without one. Or being dead in a ditch after being hunted down by Kurakin dogs.

Pitt looked at Lauriston and shook his head. "A Brunian general wearing a Kurakin coat traveling with a group of Erlonians. I'm not sure what the world's come to."

"Chaos." Lauriston chuckled.

"Chaos. Most certainly." Pitt nodded and a silence followed after Lauriston's laugh died.

The fire crackled to life and Lauriston fed it more kindling.

Memories of Pitt's cold flight through the woods before he was saved flashed before Pitt's eyes. They appeared like bursts of nightmares every so often.

"When were you promoted to general?" the marshal said eventually to pull Pitt from his thoughts.

"Recently, before the western offensive," Pitt answered quickly. He tried to keep his failures as a general from rushing up in his thoughts. Dwelling on his captivity with the Horde was almost preferable to the memories of his failures while marching with the Wahrian king.

"Ah, so this was your first campaign."

"As a general, yes. I marched against you during earlier campaigns, though."

Plenty of Brunian defeats, plenty of embarrassments against Erlon in Wahring and Morada for the Coalition. Pitt didn't need to say those thoughts out loud, though.

"I see." Lauriston's voice was calm. His hands were steady as he fed the growing fire.

"I was at Three Bridges," Pitt said.

"Naturally." There was no change in the marshal's demeanor, no hint of emotion in his voice, no betrayal of turmoil from the memories.

Pitt chose to continue listing other battles. "But also Riom. And Stetton. There I had a view of Desaix's charge from the right."

"From the Brunian right?" Lauriston looked up from the fire with eyebrows raised. "Must've been terrifying."

"Yes."

Lauriston had been the general in command at Stetton. That was only a year after Lannes took the throne as Erlonian Emperor. It was before the rank of marshal had been created by imperial decree.

"Where were you at Riom?" Lauriston bent down to blow low through the coals. The fire grew stronger and he warmed his hands over the flames.

"The center, on the bluff. But we were ordered to reinforce our attack on your right early on." Pitt leaned forward to share in the warmth.

Riom was earlier than Stetton. Pitt was only a captain then. This battle was another memory that showed King Charles's failures. Pitt couldn't escape the Wahrian king, even after his death.

"I led the attack on the center that morning."

"I know. You won the fight for Lannes. You crushed us."

"That was quite a fight." Lauriston stood and threw a larger log onto the fire.

Quite the blunder on Charles's part, Pitt thought to himself. It lost the man his throne, started the descent that would eventually send his family into exile for a decade.

Pitt shook his head. "You mean a slaughter," he said as he watched a group of sparks rise up towards the sky.

"Well, yes. Lannes had the battle all planned out, exactly how it ended up happening. We merely just went where he told us and fought."

"That's being modest. Your attack was executed flawlessly." When Lauriston didn't respond immediately, Pitt asked another question. "What was it like, being with the emperor in the beginning?"

Lauriston resumed his seat and thought for a second. "He wasn't emperor yet at Riom, but he was meant to lead from the beginning. That whole campaign was nothing but masterful strategic work. He and I hadn't known each other long, but we were already a good team. He taught me a lot about leading soldiers."

"And he laid out the entire strategy of Riom beforehand?" Pitt thought on the military diagrams of the battle. It had been a flawless victory. And a horrible defeat for Brun and Wahring.

"Yes. I helped a little, but the full idea was his. The entire plan was his." Lauriston wasn't looking at Pitt; the marshal stared into the new morning fire.

Pitt could see the reverence in his eyes. This man in front of him was a great leader in his own right, yet he still deferred to Lannes.

Pitt paused as he saw something else flash across the marshal's face. He could have been mistaken, but there was something else under the reverent expression Lauriston held for Lannes. Something darker, like a flicker of doubt?

No, that wasn't possible.

This was the second most successful military mind on the Continent at the moment. Marshal Lauriston was only behind Emperor Lannes himself.

Pitt cleared his throat and wanted to say something more. He wanted to apologize for his country's role in taking Lannes away from Lauriston and the rest of Erlon. Apologize for what happened at Three Bridges and for pulling the Kurakin into the conflict. But the words wouldn't form in his throat.

The moment was lost. The fire licked at a full stack of logs now and other soldiers began to join them as the camp woke and started the day.

"I think it's time we packed up." Lauriston stood and greeted his men. "We must make good time today."

The marshal moved away and Pitt felt awe for the man, but another emotion pushed its way through once Lauriston was gone.

Pitt envied Lauriston.

The marshal had his glory. He had stories and legends surrounding him. Pitt had nothing.

And there would always be nothing for Pitt if he didn't somehow take this opportunity with this new war and win glory with these Erlonians.

What would his sisters have done if he'd died in the woods at the hands of the Kurakin? What would his mother have left to support her? Pitt didn't want to think about it.

He needed to somehow pull himself out of this hole and stay focused on the positives. This new war was his second chance. Marshal Lauriston was fighting to save Erlon and Pitt would join him. All of Brun needed to accept the help of the Erlonians against the Horde now.

The marshal handed out breakfast to the soldiers as they took seats around the fire or worked to take down their tents for the day. Pitt accepted his ration of hardtack and stared into the fire and ate his breakfast in silence as the rest of the camp moved around him.

* * *

When the group of soldiers started on the path for the day's march, Pitt's thoughts drifted away from his own failures. Instead he chose to focus on the chaos of this new war erupting from the Kurakin betrayal. He was thankful for these new thoughts, but there were still plenty of unanswered questions to dwell on from this topic as well.

The Kurakin had betrayed the Coalition and shattered everything that had been accomplished since the capture of Emperor Lannes and the invasions of Erlon. The war had somehow flipped on its head. These Erlonians around Pitt now needed to be his allies. Brun needed to fight with them to defeat the Kurakin.

Even if the two historic enemies chose to work together, it still may not be enough.

Pitt had seen the might of the Kurakin. He'd had seen General Duroc at their head. He'd seen the bloodthirsty Horde erupt in cheers as King Charles dangled at the end of a rope.

He didn't see how anyone could fight that army. He didn't see how Brun could win.

Pitt shook his head as his horse followed the trail after the line of soldiers stretching in front of them. The Erlonian general named Montholon rode next to Pitt and offered him the bottle of wine that the general always carried. Pitt shook his head but smiled at Montholon to show he was thankful for the offer.

It was strange for Marshal Lauriston to allow this old general to drink so much. But Pitt had seen Lauriston and Mon deep in conversation late into the evenings or during the long hikes during the day. Lauriston trusted this man's opinion, even when he was in the bottle. There was something more behind this General Montholon that Pitt wasn't aware of yet.

The other officers and soldiers had all been just as nice to Pitt so far. The Erlonian princess had made sure he was uninjured after the fight and offered him food. The Lakmian Lodi had checked for hypothermia from the cold flight without clothes. The general named Quatre always asked if Pitt wanted to join in his card games at night.

These were good people. Pitt would fight for these men. He owed them at least that much for saving him.

But would Brun feel the same way?

Would Pitt's soldiers, wherever they were now, follow him into a new alliance? Would King Nelson agree with that course of action? Would the other Brunian generals?

Was King Nelson even aware of the Kurakin betrayal yet? What would the people back in Trafal and across the Brunian island think?

Pitt's head spun when trying to think of all the political ramifications of this new war. That wasn't his job; he didn't understand the larger Continental concerns with treaties among the large factions. The only thing he could focus on right now was the trail in front of them.

Marshal Lauriston seemed to be focusing on the short term as well. He was pushing to get the group to safety and find his army in this forest first. Then he was going to worry about the rest of the war.

Pitt would do that too. He would seek to emulate the marshal and see where this new course took him.

The trail narrowed between two trees and Pitt slowed. He nodded to Montholon beside him and the general tipped his hat in thanks as he passed between the trees first. Pitt kicked his horse back into motion and followed the old Erlonian.

They continued down the path for the rest of the day and Pitt's thoughts tried to keep raging, but he was able to remain focused. Kurakin Scythes chased this group. They needed to find the Erlonian army. That was the goal. That was all Pitt needed to concentrate on at the moment.

Chapter 21

Leadership is appearing strong when you have doubts. It's never leaving your men. It's fighting on no matter what.

From Emperor Gerald Lannes's Personal Journal
Year 1114 Post-Abandonment, days after his defeat at Klostern

Leberecht

Leberecht stepped out of his tent and took in the sights of the Kurakin camp around him and felt the air pulsing with the power of an army before battle. He wasn't an experienced warrior—this was his first time on a full campaign— but even he could recognize the energy of a group of soldiers who would win the coming fight.

It terrified him.

The Kurakin Horde was an unnatural force. It was unnerving enough talking with Mikhail alone in a tent or traveling on the road, but now that Leberecht was here, he began to question his decision to take the Kurakin on as allies.

He didn't truly regret his grand scheme and the war he'd launched against the remaining members of the Coalition. But the idea of fang-toothed and hairy Horde soldiers streaming across the Continent to sack its great cities still unnerved him.

There were no mammoth units here, no Scythes on wolverines. The normal soldiers were enough to keep those thoughts alive, though.

Leberecht walked through the camp on most mornings. He saw the common Kurakin soldiers interacting with each other. They ate a breakfast of nearly raw meat that was only seared for seconds on a skillet. They marched in disorganized lines but were always on time. The units roamed around in packs like wolves. They trained daily, either running or lifting heavy bags over and over and drilling in open fields.

The aide assigned to Leberecht had the unfortunate habit of sharpening his bayonet and his ax outside of Leberecht's tent flap to start every day. Leberecht woke on the fourth morning after his arrival to the main army and found the Kurakin grinning up at him over a gleaming ax blade once again.

"Good morning, sir," the Kurakin said.

At least they had given Leberecht someone who spoke the northern language well enough.

Leberecht's stomach grumbled. He'd finished the last of the cured meats he'd carried with him from Citiva the night before and he now dreaded having to survive on the diet of the Kurakin army until more of the Moradan army arrived.

"Breakfast, sir?" The Kurakin stood and swung his ax with a *thunk* down into a stump that was extremely close to Leberecht's left leg.

The aide walked over to the fire and boiling pot around the side of the tent. "We have stew."

"What kind of stew?" Leberecht had to talk louder over the sound of his stomach. He smacked it to see if it would quiet down any. It didn't.

"Rabbit. With *prak.*"

"With what?" Leberecht leaned over the pot as the aide picked up the ladle.

"Oh. Um. *Prak,* that is... Um..."

Leberecht watched the contents of the pot as they were lifted up and stirred by the aide's ladle.

"Vegetables?"

"Yes, that's it! Vegetels!"

The Kurakin was close enough. Leberecht didn't feel like correcting his pronunciation.

"Thank you," Leberecht said as he took a bowl of the stew from the aide. He dug into the breakfast immediately before his stomach could start screaming again.

"I'd thought you might prefer something a little more cooked than our normal breakfast," a new voice said.

Leberecht turned to find Mikhail walking around an adjacent tent. The Kurakin held a bundle of papers in one hand and his eyes were too bright and full of energy for the early hour, in Leberecht's opinion.

"Thank you, Mikhail. That was very thoughtful of you."

Leberecht went back to the pot to top off his serving of stew and then walked with Mikhail as the Kurakin motioned for Leberecht to follow him down the rows of tents. They passed a pack of soldiers heading the other direction. Every one of these Kurakin carried a heavy-looking trident on their shoulders and laughed among themselves as they moved off towards the edge of the camp.

Leberecht almost asked what the unit was off to do but then thought better of it. He'd learned that it was better to not ask questions around the Kurakin army, as the answers were often terrifying.

"The generals should already be gathered. They'll want news of your Moradan troops." Mikhail turned and took them towards the command area at the very center of the Kurakin camp.

"Certainly," Leberecht said through one of his last bits of stew.

He'd been unaware there was a strategy meeting. Luckily he'd caught up on his letters the night before and could now be more focused on the army's campaign against Rapp.

"And no news of the Erlonian princess from Duroc?" Leberecht said as they approached the command tent.

"Nothing new."

Leberecht nodded. He'd been hoping for some good news from the west regarding the princess, but so far nothing had arrived.

The pair reached the command area and found the officers standing around a fire in the center of a circle of tents. There was a large tent for the lead general, a Kurakin shorter than Leberecht would've imagined a Kurakin general to be but with very mean-looking eyes.

"Mikhail, Leberecht. Good, we can get started now," the general said as the pair arrived. He turned back to the others around him. "We'll all speak the northern language since we have allies present. Speak up if you don't understand something."

Leberecht finished slurping up the last of his stew and nodded his thanks to the general.

There were no campaign maps and the general didn't give a grand speech. Leberecht had a hard time following the discussion, as the general and his officers appeared to already have numerous plans in motion. After a few minutes of being lost, Leberecht found it hard to focus.

His stomach grumbled up at him. He restrained from smacking it again. This was why he preferred politics to war—it was much easier to understand the strategies at play during a summit meeting compared to this.

"What is the latest from the Moradans?"

Leberecht jumped and cleared his throat as the group's attention turned back to him. "Marching at a good pace. They're on the Vitha road and should be here in three days or less."

"Good."

"They're moving fast and we'll need them. King Rapp won't sit in Vith very long. He'll want to attack and push us south."

The general nodded. He tugged at his long beard and looked down in thought. "I understand. That timing works perfectly, actually."

Another officer said something in the Kurakin language. It sounded like nothing but grunts to Leberecht's ears. The general nodded in response and grunted something back.

"You've given them an idea," Mikhail whispered to Leberecht.

"I have?" Leberecht looked to the men but still could make nothing from their conversation or facial expressions.

The Kurakin general spoke to a few of his officers in turn. He finally switched back to the northern language to address the entire group. "Keep with your movements. We break camp tomorrow with the main force."

They were going to break camp? Leberecht had assumed they would sit in this current position and let King Rapp attack and be pulled south. Where were the Kurakin going?

The general turned back to Leberecht. "We must write to the Moradans and tell them to cross the Vitha at Bratiz. You can help me draft the language."

"Cross to the north?" Leberecht's mouth hung open. That didn't make any sense to him. Why would they want their army north of the river and in open Wahrian territory?

"Yes. We must move quickly." The Kurakin general was shifting side to side in his stance. He looked like he was ready to spring into a fight right that instant. "My forces will be in place tomorrow. And you're right, the boy king will attack soon."

"Where are you going?" Leberecht needed a map. He needed markers for the armies on this campaign, especially if the Horde was changing plans on the fly. Even when the Kurakin general was speaking the northern language, it was hard to follow him.

The Kurakin general spoke with his other officers again and some of them dispersed. He turned back to Leberecht.

"We're spreading out. The army will relocate and be ready." The general smiled at Leberecht. His remaining officers mirrored the expression behind him and Leberecht had to stifle a shudder at the rows of fanged teeth pointed in his direction.

"You're right, the Wahrians will be aggressive," the general said. "And they'll walk right into our trap."

Elisa

Elisa hadn't thought it possible for her legs to become more sore, but as the days stretched on and the group continued to trek through the hills, she began to contemplate a further meaning of pain.

She kept her discomfort inside, though. It was what Lauriston was doing. It was what all the still-injured soldiers were doing. It was what Mon, the oldest among them, would want her to do.

She had to be strong. These men were here to protect her, to get her to safety. The least she could do was to not complain about something as silly as a rash on her leg from her saddle.

"We'll work on another turn next," Lodi said from the horse next to her. "You've about got the first one down."

The group was in their normal positions. Lauriston and Mon at the front of a long trail of horses. Elisa in the center surrounded by the Jinetes.

She'd been sparring with Lodi most of their recent evenings. It took all of her strength to not collapse after the day's journey, let alone lift her sword arm and step lightly through the Lakmian fighting moves he taught her. But Elisa wanted to keep training. She needed to keep improving.

The other soldiers had taken to watching their sparring sessions often. It was entertainment and a release from the long journey of each day for them.

Elisa now fully understood she was also a source of inspiration for the men. To see the daughter of their exiled Emperor working so hard to keep fighting would help push the men onward. It would make their packs a little lighter. It would push their feet just a little faster and farther each day.

She still had her doubts about herself, about Erlon's chances of survival. She was able to bury most of them in her mind, but Elisa always knew they were there. She was only a little better at appearing confident and strong on the outside now than before.

The activity with Lodi at night helped as a distraction, as did the conversation during their travels like their discussion today.

"The pirouette works well against the Kurakin, especially the soldiers with axes," Lodi continued.

Elisa often just let the Lakmian ramble. It passed the time quite well usually and proved no different on this day.

That evening, she helped the wounded set up their tents. There were only a few soldiers with lingering injuries left—a broken arm that still needed time to mend or an injured knee that flared up with the long days of riding. Elisa helped where she could and tried to make the soldiers' lives a little easier.

After her normal session with Lodi, she ate a quick dinner with the soldiers. A sharpshooter who'd broken his arm in the fight with the Kurakin soldiers stood and told a story of a battle from long ago against the Wahrians. It sounded like the Battle of Stetton or some other fight from before Elisa was born.

Elisa watched Mon while the story was told. The old general nodded at certain parts and smiled at others. He grimaced often too.

Another form of distraction for Elisa had been her returning to the questions surrounding the farmer turned general. She'd tried to ask the remaining guardsmen about Mon's military record and when he'd left the army, but had received the same responses that Lodi and the others had given her. They would talk about the early battles of the war and their time with Mon, but as they approached the latter parts of the empire's glory years, their faces would fall and they would refuse to continue discussing Mon.

She knew now that she should've just asked Mon directly long ago. But she thought her friend and mentor should want to tell her about his life. She wanted him to come to her himself and tell her about his relationship with her father and why he'd kept it hidden from her.

And why everyone's eyes fell when she asked why he'd left the army.

It seemed like a pointless topic, given that they were on the run from foreign invaders riding wolverines while the empire collapsed around them. But Elisa was thankful for the distraction. She needed to think on other things besides what came next when they found the army, what came next if she escaped the Scythes that chased her.

Or what would happen to her if they couldn't escape from the Scythes at all.

"Lodi's unit held strong," Mon said, interrupting the sharpshooter's story. "That was the center of the battle, the entire thing swung on their spears."

Lodi nodded over at Mon.

"That's true." Marshal Lauriston leaned forward into the firelight. "We'll need that kind of stance again in this war, I fear."

"And the Lakmians will provide it." Lodi raised his cup and the Lakmians around the fire mirrored him.

"As will the guardsmen."

Heads around the circle turned towards Mon. The old general raised his bottle of wine up in another toast. The few guardsmen left in the group did the same with their cups.

"As will everyone." Even Elisa was surprised when her voice cut through the group. She usually stayed silent during dinner and preferred to listen to the jokes and the old stories from the men.

Something felt different about tonight. Hearing Mon's proclamation had made her want to speak up. It made her want to lead.

"We're all guardsmen now." She looked around the group and into the eyes of every soldier. Lodi and Lauriston and Desaix and everyone met her gaze. A grin grew across Mon's face. "We're all that's left to guard the people of Erlon. We fight on. Always onward."

"Onward." The voices were low and in unison and the word carried out into the night beyond the fire.

The entire group raised their glasses. Mon held his bottle high before taking a long swig. He wiped his mouth on his sleeve after and smiled even wider over at Elisa.

It was dark outside of their fire and the nights were getting colder, but Elisa felt a hope wrapping around the group. These soldiers were ready to fight. Elisa would fight with them.

They were almost to the army. It was almost time for the Erlonians to march to war again. It was time for Elisa to put what Lodi and Mon and Lauriston and everyone had taught her to use.

* * *

Elisa's head hurt as she mounted her horse the next morning. She'd taken a few too many pulls from Mon's bottle the night before around the fire. From the looks of the soldiers in front and behind her, a lot of the group was the same way. They would recover quickly enough—they always did.

She rode next to the sharpshooter with his arm in a sling. Lodi, who rode up at the front with Lauriston this morning, said the soldier would be able to remove the sling soon. The arm was almost healed.

This was good news. The group was going to need all the healthy soldiers they could get.

The scouts returned near midmorning. Elisa's legs were already aching and she listened to more stories of past campaigns from the sharpshooter as a distraction from the throbbing of her thighs. She wasn't aware a scout had returned until Lauriston called a halt for the group.

Elisa slowed her horse and looked up the line of men. The trail inclined slightly and gave her a good view of Lauriston's face as he talked with the scout.

It was clear instantly that something was wrong.

Lauriston grimaced in response to something the scout said. The marshal was always stoic. He never reacted like that.

Mon sat on his horse next to Lauriston and looked at the ground and shook his head. After the scout had finished, Lauriston turned and said something to Lodi. The Lakmian pulled his reins around and rode down the line.

He swung around wide and stopped next to Elisa. "The Scythes are close."

Elisa hadn't expected good news, but the words still stung the air around her.

"Desaix's men just saw the hawk south of us." Lodi looked to the sharpshooter next to Elisa to make sure the message would be passed farther down the line. Everyone around them was suddenly quiet and stern. "It's flying again. They're close. They'll find our trail soon."

Andrei

Andrei closed his eyes and felt the joy of soaring above the world once again. His hawk screeched and rose higher on the wind and watched the forest stretch over the rolling hills below.

The screech wasn't a warning or a message about the enemy they tracked. It was an expression of jubilation at being able to glide up to the clouds again.

Andrei wanted to laugh and yell and screech along with his bird, but he held it inside. The other Scythes were around him on the ground and waited for their instructions.

The hawk soared higher and moved east with her eyes on the forest below. No sign of the girl or her protectors yet.

They would find them soon. Andrei was confident.

Back on the ground, a Scythe coughed. A wolverine gave a low growl and pawed impatiently at the ground. Andrei ignored them.

He only focused on the wind ruffling through his *sakk's* feathers and the green landscape rolling along underneath him.

The bird's eyes couldn't see through the thick canopy, but there were gaps in the trees every so often. She kept her focus on these spots and waited for movement.

There. A flash below the trees.

Andrei's heart picked up in unison with his bird's. The hawk tilted its wings and made a wide loop. She focused on the spot where movement had been seen and waited.

Another shift. The hawk was in better position now. She saw a horse and a rider wearing blue clearly pass below the canopy.

Andrei smiled. He felt the Scythes around him react to the smile. They knew what that smile would mean. Someone's wolverine pawed at the ground even harder.

The hawk made one more loop. Andrei calculated the distance between that position and the Scythes. Not far. Not far at all.

Andrei opened his eyes and smiled fully, showing the fangs of his teeth to his soldiers.

"We've got them."

A wolverine growled. A few Scythes drew swords.

Andrei smiled even wider. "Ride. Today is a fighting day."

More growls came from their mounts and the Scythes turned east and followed Andrei into the trees after their prey.

Chapter 22

Only a certain kind of creature can survive a Kurakin winter. This gives the Horde a natural advantage over the northerners.

History of the Southern Expanse
Anton von Zach

Lauriston

Lauriston ran over the plan in his mind as they galloped along the ridge. He wasn't fully comfortable with the idea yet, but it was all they had.

The morning had been quiet. They'd traveled through lunch and Lauriston had almost believed they were safe and could escape being seen by the enemy bird through the thick canopy of the forest. Then the screech from the Kurakin hawk came down from the sky.

Lauriston would split his men up and use their knowledge of this part of the country to their advantage. The Scythes were good trackers, but they were on foreign territory.

Take advantage of your advantages.

Emperor Lannes used to repeat that while on campaign. Lauriston knew his group's only chance was to lose the enemy in the deep and densely forested hills. They needed to somehow hide or escape from the trackers on their tail.

The idea had come from Desaix. There was a watering hole nearby used by cavalry messengers moving through this part of the country. If the Erlonians could throw the Scythes off their direct trail, they'd be safe to hide there.

They'd need luck on their side. Throwing wolverines off the trail with a hawk tracking above them would be tricky.

The group flew along the ridge. Lauriston felt the ground rolling forward in front of him as the land crested and dropped. To his right was a rock wall protecting the climb up the far hill. Branches whistled by his head.

He heard his first roar of an enemy wolverine.

Fear gripped him, but not from the sound the beast made or approaching death. By the time a man became a general, he was much beyond that kind of fear.

Lauriston was instead afraid his plan was a mistake, and he knew that was the worst kind of fear for a general.

He'd thought he was done doubting himself.

They could be heading directly where the Scythes wanted them to go. It could all be a trap. A funnel to corner the Erlonians. Lauriston could be leading his men to death.

He snapped his reins and pushed his horse faster. It was too late to second-guess himself.

Lauriston had a sudden flashback as they galloped further down the hill. He saw Lannes's army retreating across southern fields, heading north towards warmer climes and the safety of the empire. He saw generals and marshals riding beside Lannes and making plans to get back to safety.

He saw them making the wrong plans, the wrong decisions. They split up to outsmart the enemy and Lauriston led the main army onward, never to see his friend the emperor again.

Lauriston snapped back to the present and saw the fork up ahead. The ridge broke off into two, with one shelf shooting down into the valley on the left and the other continuing at the same level.

Lauriston glanced back from his saddle. He caught Lodi's eye and received a nod. The Lakmian would take the princess and one part of the group. Desaix and Lauriston would take the other. The marshal got a nod from Desaix as well.

No time to second-guess anything anymore. All a leader could do was act in the moment.

Lauriston let out a yell and pointed his horse towards the left path. He felt his stomach lift as they dropped into the valley at speed. The others, Lodi at their front, chose the right-hand path. Lauriston's eyes caught the tail of the group as they passed out of sight around a bend above him.

The group was separated now. Just like when Lauriston had separated from Lannes. No going back now.

Lauriston saw a rush of shadow to his left lower down the hill. Three Scythes on wolverines were moving fast parallel to them. Lauriston leveled his pistol and fired a wild shot. There was no accuracy at this range, but the hope was to get the enemy heads down and slow their rush.

Lauriston's horse pounded down the path and tried to put distance between them and the beasts on their tail. There would be more Scythes out there. Lauriston's hope was that the rest of the enemy would converge on his group instead of Lodi and the princess.

More shadows appeared in the trees below them. Lauriston pressed on. More pops of pistols came from his men behind him and Lauriston focused on reloading his own weapon.

The map of the land stretched out in his mind. The farther they galloped down this path and to the east, the more space they would put between these Scythes and the princess.

Another roar ripped through the trees towards them. Lauriston's horse broke through a clump of trees and found the ground leveling off. There was an open space here. A crack in the forest where tall grass had grown across the land.

Lauriston was halfway across the field when he saw the movement on his periphery. Behind him over his right shoulder, a wolverine burst from the trees. It made a line for the last soldier in Lauriston's group.

The marshal broke off and waved a hand signal for the others to keep going. At this speed, his horse made a wide turn. The last soldier wasn't going to make it. Lauriston was forced to watch as the horse bucked with fright as the wolverine lunged.

The soldier was flung into the air. By the time Lauriston had completed his turn and brought his pistol up, it was too late.

The wolverine was on the Erlonian before he hit the ground. Lauriston yelled and leveled his pistol. He aimed at the mount but saw the Scythe shift at the last second. The enemy soldier had seen Lauriston and lifted his musket.

Lauriston snapped his arm up and his shot took the Scythe rider in the throat and flung him backwards. His body crunched to the ground, but his wolverine had already torn into the Erlonian soldier Lauriston sought to save.

The marshal brought out his other pistol and fired at the beast. The ball struck its eye and caused a roar of pain and drew its attention. It was too late for the man, but Lauriston could still kill the animal that took the soldier's life.

Lauriston replaced his pistol in his holster as the black beast charged him. He brought out his musket from the right side of his saddle. He spun the weapon up to place the butt against his shoulder socket.

This was his last shot. There'd be no time to reload.

If he missed now, things would be over for him.

The wolverine's claws tore through the dirt. Its mouth open and full of blood. Its teeth sharp and ready.

Lauriston fired. The ball went into the other eye of the beast and dropped him.

Momentum carried the wolverine forward, sliding through the grass. The animal growled and clawed at the ground and kicked and convulsed. It was done. Only the dying was left.

Lauriston let out his first breath in what felt like minutes. He strapped his musket down again and jerked his horse back into a gallop. There were still plenty more Scythes out there.

He caught up to the group. The enemy was sweeping up the side of the hill behind them now. The climbing skills of the wolverines was impressive.

Lauriston would give them the higher ground. He just needed space to gallop deeper into the hills. Their horses would outrun the enemy on flat terrain.

They rounded the base of the slope. The trees were thin here and it became easier for their horses to run at speed. They'd almost made it.

"Fly!" Lauriston called out and the men and horses pushed faster.

They galloped and got the space they needed. The Scythes came down off their hill but fell far behind in flat forest.

The horses split up again and confused any trail they would leave before circling around the valley and reaching the hidden watering hole among the rocks of the hills.

The trees became thick again and Lauriston hoped it would be enough to hide their movements from the hawk still circling above them. He said a silent prayer to the Ascended One and hoped that the other group hadn't run into trouble while away from his decoy.

He approached the spot and held his breath. There were streams running from the top of the hills to the east. They gathered into a strong run of water down the sloping land and rocks jutted out of the earth to form cliffs. A waterfall fell and a pool sat at the base of the formation.

Behind the waterfall was a cave system. It was a picturesque enough scene, but secret and hidden from all but the Erlonians.

Lauriston's group led their horses on foot around the edge of the pond and passed through the falling water. He didn't hear anything of the others over the noise.

The marshal held his breath once again. He took the last step into the cave and stopped.

Where were they?

His eyes adjusted to the light and he stepped farther forward and saw the outlines of his friends and soldiers in the far shadows.

They were all safe. Even the princess, who sat happily at the far end against a wet wall and smiled at Lauriston as he walked deeper into the cavern.

Andrei

The wolverines calmed down. They still had a scent, but the bloodlust that made them so fearsome would abandon the beasts after a while. Now they were tired and annoyed and difficult to control.

Andrei still held out hope they could somehow find the Erlonians.

His hawk guided him to the section of forest where the group had last been seen, a flat part of the forest where the trees thinned for a stretch.

Their prey had split up. Andrei had only ever seen a small group of soldiers. The half they'd chased had scattered and been impossible to follow for even the hawk. They would now be rendezvousing with the others to try and hide.

Andrei ordered his group to split up and scan the forest. His *sakk* would stay in the air. They would work all night if they had to, hoping the Erlonians made a mistake.

No scent was picked up. No sign of the horses was found. Any trail that existed led in circles. Andrei's hawk saw no movement anywhere. Frustration grew in the pit of Andrei's stomach.

Night had fully fallen when he found the waterfall and pond.

It was a peaceful scene. Babbling water in the moonlight. Andrei listened for any signs of life. Any signs that the Erlonian soldiers and the princess had been here.

None came.

The wolverines smelled nothing. Andrei led the group around the water and kept an eye on everything. Something about this place was sticking with him. Something he could feel but not explain.

No tracks appeared. But then they wouldn't if their prey had used the streams here as a trail. No smells reached his wolverines. This area was just like the rest of the woods, silent and devoid of their quarry.

There were plenty more areas to search. He took one last glance at the waterfall on the far side of the pond and turned back to search the next area of forest.

Elisa

Elisa sat and listened for the sounds of Scythes outside their hiding place, but nothing could be heard over the falling water.

She helped Lodi redress some of the bandages of the soldiers. The sharpshooter with the sling had ripped his arm free during the chase and needed to be bandaged up again.

"Thank you, Lodi. Thank you, Princess," the soldier said when they'd finished. He sounded tired but happy.

Elisa walked across the cave back to where she'd put her pack down. The space was quickly losing light. No fire or torches were allowed in case the Scythes passed close to the waterfall. Evening fell outside.

Elisa found Mon sitting against the wall near her pack. She decided to join him.

"It means a lot to the men to see you helping the injured." Mon had his eyes closed and his head leaned back. He only cracked one eye when Elisa sat down next to him.

"I'm happy to help," she said.

"It does more than you know." Mon opened his eyes and leaned his head forward to look at the dirt between his legs. "Your father was good at that too. He made you think he was just another man in the army. He would speak with every soldier, all the way down to the cooks."

Elisa didn't know how to respond. The day had been a rush of danger and adrenaline with the flight away from the Scythes and now the emotions at the mention of her father threatened to overtake her tired thoughts.

"I'm not thinking about giving up anymore, Mon," Elisa said. She spoke quickly and mainly in order to keep the tears for her father from breaking loose.

"Good." Mon nodded.

"Erlon may be dying, the empire over. But as long as there are soldiers fighting, I will fight with them." Elisa watched Mon's silhouette in the dying light of the cave. "I'm not a general like my father. Or a sorceress like my mother. But I can still fight and lead and work for the people."

Mon nodded and Elisa thought she saw his mouth twitch into a tiny smile in the dark. The old general didn't respond and the pair grew quiet for a long time.

Elisa had many thoughts all at once. Memories from the last few weeks all blurred together. But even as they sat huddled in a damp cave and her enemies prowled with wolverines out in the forest beyond, Elisa felt a happiness.

She somehow felt a strong sense of hope.

"We'll get out of here tomorrow," Mon said. His voice broke the silence. The cave was almost fully dark now. "If we escape the Scythes and find the army, I'll tell you my story."

Mon's head turned to look at Elisa. She could barely see his eyes in the darkness and couldn't read his emotion. Elisa nodded to him.

"The full story, why I left your father and the army," Mon said. "I think you've earned that much. You deserve to know why I didn't tell you. Why I kept it inside."

"Okay."

The response sounded stupid after Elisa said it, but she didn't know what else to say.

She was feeling too much.

Fear. Uncertainty. Fatigue. Soreness from the long days of riding.

But also hope.

Elisa had confidence in the soldiers around her. She had confidence in Mon and Lauriston to lead them to safety. And she knew they had confidence in her to stay with them and help Erlon continue fighting.

That was good enough for now.

She didn't need to know the reason why Mon left the army. She could trust that he was a great warrior.

If Mon told her the story, that was his choice. For now, Elisa would focus on helping to lead the men to safety and finding the rest of the army. That was all that was needed from her at the moment.

* * *

In the morning, they packed up in silence. They brought the horses out of the back of the cave and walked out into the sunlight.

Elisa half expected to see the entire Scythe unit waiting for them with weapons drawn, but the forest was clear and quiet.

Lauriston didn't need to order the men to make ready. They mounted up and the marshal led them off into the trees.

Elisa still felt afraid and knew they were still being chased. But her strong sense of hope had stayed with her through the night.

Whatever this day brought, Elisa would face it with her friends and protectors. They would keep fighting on for Erlon.

Onward.

That was the cheer of her father's army. They would keep pushing onward.

If the hawk spotted them again or if the wolverines picked up their scent, they would have to run again or stand and fight. Whatever happened, Elisa was ready.

The group left the watering hole with the hidden cave and moved back into the forest. Elisa took one final glance back behind her and saw the water falling from the rocks and the ripples through the pond under the tall trees.

Andrei

Andrei watched from a tree above the pond as the group of horses passed below him.

He'd been right. He'd known there was something about the pond and the waterfall. The stiffness from sitting on a limb all night was going to pay off.

He counted the soldiers and watched the last horse slip out of his view and waited while counting his breaths. When he was sure the group was gone, he descended the tree and took off west through the forest at a jog. He had some good news to tell the rest of the Scythes.

Chapter 23

Attack where the enemy least expects it and victory will appear.

The Ascended One's Maxims
Verse Fifteen

Rapp

The day was finally here. King Rapp walked along his lines and inspected his men. The soldiers were ready to fight and die for their king and avenge the death of his father.

They were ready for war.

"Bring the latest report up from the pickets." Rapp stared out over the field before him. The aides scrambled away to follow his order.

He watched the mist rise up from the trees beyond the field and disappear into the morning air like smoke from a funeral pyre. His army sprawled all around him in black lines and their shadowy forms in the fog made them look like statues carved from stone.

His warriors were very much alive. They would fight for him today. They would be brave and strong, as if they were mightier than the Ascended One's host. They would charge against the Kurakin Horde lines and break the enemy.

This would be a glorious first day of Rapp's first campaign as king. This was only the initial battle in many more victories to come for Wahring's new king. But the first was always the most important.

"No sign of the Kurakin yet, Your Majesty."

Rapp turned away from his battlefield and to the aide behind him. "Nothing from the pickets?"

"Nothing, sir."

Strange.

He'd assumed the Kurakin would attack. They were historically the aggressors while at war. They had marched north to attack the Vitha Valley back when they were allied to the Coalition and they'd always been the aggressors in the Lakmian mountains.

"They're the invaders here." Rapp turned back to the south and the open fields before his army. "They'll attack soon."

King Rapp could be patient for an hour or two more. He'd waited a long time to fight a war for Wahring. He could force himself to wait a little while longer.

General Neipperg returned from the western flank at midmorning and reported to his king. The mist had fully dissipated and the land continued to stand open and clear before the Wahrian lines.

"Cavalry scouts have the Kurakin just through the trees." Neipperg started talking before his horse came to a full stop next to Rapp. "They're concentrated in the center."

Rapp's mind worked through the information as he yanked on the reins to keep his own horse steady next to Neipperg's. The general scratched at his eye-patch and waited for his king to reply.

"We should attack. We should press them."

Neipperg's face betrayed no reaction. His one eye stayed locked on his king. "If Your Highness commands it."

The plan fully formed in Rapp's mind all at once. It was as if the Ascended One had sent him an image of how the battle would play out, of how the battle would be won.

The Wahrians could use the forest to mask their approach. Neipperg's division in the west could sweep around and hit the enemy from the flank. They would push the Kurakin back against the river and crush them.

This history books would call this King Rapp's day.

Neipperg looked down quickly and his eye moved side to side in thought. He looked back up at Rapp.

"Your Majesty," Neipperg said, but Rapp help up a hand to show he was thinking.

"You swing around and press them from the west. Our main column will use the trees as cover and rush them in the center. We'll shift the artillery up between us."

Yes, this was a good plan. Rapp could see all of it like it was laid out on a map table with detailed markers showing each of the sides. It would be perfect.

Neipperg cleared his throat. "They may want us to be aggressive, Your Majesty."

Rapp looked over at Neipperg. The general's one eye stared back at him with concern shining behind it. Rapp was surprised to see Neipperg was serious about his critique of the plan.

Was he afraid to attack? Did he think the Wahrian regiments not up to the task of fighting the Horde?

There weren't any mammoth units here. No Scythes either, if the scouts were to be believed. Only normal Kurakin units.

What was Neipperg afraid of?

Maybe he wasn't as strong of a general as Rapp believed.

The king waved a hand to push away Neipperg's concerns. "We'll crush them. Draft the orders. I want us moving by midday."

Neipperg hesitated. Rapp almost yelled at him for even thinking about arguing with a king, but the general recovered quickly enough.

"Yes, sir. You'll have the orders to review within the hour."

"Thank you."

Neipperg rode off and Rapp's horse shifted underneath him. He yanked on the reins again and held the mount facing south. The bright sun beat down on his men and gleamed off the rows of musket barrels pointed at the sky.

It was a fighting day.

Before the sun would reach its apex, his army would be on the move. Rapp wished he could lead the charge himself and feel the pulse of the battle from the very front of the lines.

But he was king. His life was too important to risk being on the front lines.

Rapp would watch the fight unfold from behind and adjust as needed. If the Kurakin general opposite him tried something to stem his attack, King Rapp would adjust.

Only a few more hours, King Rapp told himself, and then he would be basking in victory as his army chased the fleeing Kurakin south.

Leberecht

Leberecht hadn't trained as an officer in an army. He'd barely studied military history at all. He knew next to nothing about battle tactics or campaign strategy.

And yet he was about to win a battle over one of the great powers of the Continent. He was about to defeat a king.

Leberecht's carriage bounced down the road as he flipped through the pages of letters and orders and formal documents laid out on the seat opposite him. It was difficult communicating with the Kurakin through letters. Most of the generals could at least speak the northern tongue, but only Mikhail and a handful of others could write it.

Despite this significant issue, Leberecht was confident his side of the war would win the day.

The Kurakin were cunning strategists. They knew warfare backwards and forwards, far better than any northern commander Leberecht had seen. He chuckled to himself at the irony.

The northern factions worshiped a war god that preached about winning glory through battle. Yet these barbarians from the far south were better organized, better trained, and led by better men than any of them, especially Leberecht's birth country.

The only northern leader who could stand up to the Kurakin would've been Emperor Lannes of Erlon. But even he had been defeated on the ice fields. There would be no stopping the Kurakin now.

Leberecht picked up a page and read through the army's orders once again. Mikhail had transcribed the message from the original Kurakin scrawl into lines of neat cursive.

A portion of the Kurakin were amassing directly in front of the Wahrian lines. More were sweeping east along the river and the Moradans were marching into position as well on the northern side of the Vitha.

Leberecht didn't need a campaign map to see what was about to happen. King Rapp would be confident. If there was one thing Leberecht understood about the boy, it was his hubris.

He understood a great deal more about the new king, of course. Leberecht's intelligence had run circles around the Wahrian royals for years now and it was finally time for action. Though the thing that would lead to the family's downfall most directly was their king's hubris.

Maybe everyone would be overconfident and rash if they were born into royalty on top of a plateau above a capital and told they ruled by divine right. But the Franz Dynasty of Wahring seemed especially susceptible to overconfidence and arrogance. Charles had been incompetent and somehow still arrogant. Rapp was at least a little stronger, but was still blind to the changing world around him.

That was all about to end, though. Leberecht was here to alter the course of the Continent, change the way the common man viewed the royals across factions. The Wahrians and the Brunians and the royalists still in Morada were all about to be overthrown.

A knock on the window of the carriage brought Leberecht out of his scheming.

"Yes?" Leberecht pulled the curtain aside and found one of his aides trotting alongside him on horseback.

"We're close to the Moradan column, sir."

"Good, let me know when we hear from their general."

"Yes, sir."

Leberecht shifted his hand and was about to let the curtain fall back over the window before the aide spoke again.

"And sir?"

Leberecht raised his eyebrows to tell the aide he was listening.

"We've heard cannon fire in the west. Sounds like the battle has started."

Leberecht smiled. He felt the minuscule twang of pain in his right cheek and reveled in it. The battle had started, it was finally time for King Rapp to meet his fate.

"Then we better hurry and reach the lines. Tell our men to double time. And find me the Moradan commander."

"Yes, sir."

Leberecht let the curtain fall back and his carriage interior returned to shadow.

The Wahrians would lose the war today. Leberecht would take control and be one step closer from overthrowing the power structure of the Continent altogether. There was no stopping him. It was time for victory.

Rapp

Cannons rumbled on the right flank. Rapp's horse pounded up the road with his aides close behind. The shadows of soldiers moved through the trees all around them. Rapp's first great victory had begun.

Rapp reined up at a ridge that peaked over the final part of the woods. He saw the Kurakin lines for the first time. They were smaller than he imagined. It was only a few rows of black-clad troops along a ridgeline opposite the Wahrian lines.

The rest must have already broken, or they were pressing Neipperg in the west. That could be the only explanation, Rapp thought to himself.

Another cannon volley erupted from the east and Rapp watched as the ground under a portion of the Kurakin exploded upwards and the line of that unit broke apart. The Horde was already fleeing. Already caught off guard by Rapp's decision to concentrate artillery from his right flank.

The king smiled to himself as his aides grouped behind his horse. This was a good day. This was a glorious day.

"Sir, a message from Neipperg." One of the aides nudged his horse forward and bowed his head at Rapp. "He's turned their western side, says they're breaking."

Rapp nodded. *Of course they're breaking, they're facing the Wahrian royal army today.*

The Kurakin were not an unbeatable foe at all. The legends about their race being the descendants from demons would be disproved with this war. All the nightmares of northern children would be proved false by the new King of the Wahrian Realm.

"Keep the artillery going. Move the cannons up parallel to our press."

Rapp kept his eyes forward as he talked. He heard the horses of aides galloping away to relay the first order to the artillery.

"Press the Fourth and Sixth forward. Turn their retreat to the east and use Neipperg's attack to envelop them."

More aides left. Another artillery barrage ripped through the ridgeline. The Kurakin now cowered behind it.

"I want cavalry to scout east. Follow their retreat and make sure we know where they cross the river. We'll attack them as they try to retreat south and capture as many as we can."

"Yes, Your Highness."

The last of the aides dispersed and King Rapp was left alone on the hilltop. He couldn't see Neipperg's attack in the far west, but he knew the general would be aggressive. Rapp knew that flank was forcing the entire left portion of the enemy to retreat.

The Wahrian division in front of Rapp now would break the enemy center. The eastern flank, on the left, didn't matter. They would break too once the rest of the Kurakin fled south back towards the crossings of the Vitha River.

This was Rapp's day. This was a day for the king. The southern Horde never stood a chance against him.

It had almost been too easy. Rapp shook his head and watched another round of cannon fire rip through a group of Kurakin cannons trying to find cover in the distant trees.

He could already imagine the feeling of leading the victorious army back into Citiva to cheers from his people.

Rapp looked up and closed his eyes and felt the midday sun beat down on his face. It was a warm contrast to the cold fall breeze that swept over the land.

Rapp didn't need a direct conversation with the god. The king may have failed the initial task, but he was now winning the war the god had called "unwinnable." He was free from his mother's peace summit. He was gaining glory through warfare and would bring victory back to Wahring in a way his father never could.

"Sir, the artillery is pressing forward to the tree line."

Rapp turned his horse to face the aide who brought the message. The king's mount snorted jealously as the aide's horse breathed heavily from his recent gallop.

"Good, have them keep the pressure on. Any word from Neipperg?"

"Nothing yet. I'll go see what I can find out."

"Thank you."

The aide bowed his head quickly and whipped his horse back around and returned east. Rapp's mount stamped a hoof in the mud, longing to run after the other horse.

Rapp patted the side of the beast's neck. "It's okay, we'll ride soon enough."

Rapp wanted to be at the front of the attack. He wanted to lead a column of men into the broken Kurakin lines, but a king had to protect himself. He had to lead and coordinate from the back.

Rapp pulled the horse around to face back towards the south and watched the last of the Kurakin retreat into the woods. The day was won.

Rapp had to smile at the images of Leberecht running with the Kurakin somewhere in those woods. The king hoped Leberecht would be captured alive. He'd like to see the look on his former mentor's face while rotting in a jail cell and waiting to be executed on the plateau's cliff.

Today was a good day. Rapp kicked his horse into a trot and followed the road down the other side of his hill. He would go and oversee the final push to ensure the Kurakin retreated south. The battle was over, this part of the war was a success.

Rapp took a final look south and the remains of the battlefield with the earth torn to pieces and the bodies of the enemy strewn about. Somewhere beyond the distant tree line was the traitor Leberecht. Rapp would get revenge for his country soon enough.

Leberecht

The sounds of the battle were distant and rumbled like a storm far out to sea that would never reach the coastline. Leberecht imagined if he could get high enough, he'd be able to see the flashes of the cannons like lightning illuminating the ocean's horizon from the coast of Morada.

He closed his eyes and imagined what each of the rumbles meant. It was a calming feeling somehow. The deep and distant sounds of war meant death and destruction.

But not to Leberecht's army.

King Rapp would think he'd won. He would assume he was attacking the main Kurakin force, but Leberecht and Mikhail and the Kurakin generals had never wanted to defeat Rapp's army in open combat at this stage in the war.

They had only ever wanted to outsmart it.

There was a larger goal for this campaign. The Wahrian army could be defeated in other ways besides direct confrontation.

The Kurakin were famous for prowess and ferocity on the battlefield, but they excelled at strategic warfare as well.

Leberecht smiled and climbed back up into his carriage. "Back to the headquarters," he called up to the driver.

The main Kurakin force now sat east of the Wahrian king's forces. They were north of the Vitha River and hunkered down in the dense woods that stretched over the land like a woolen blanket.

They had more men than Rapp and were between the king and his precious capital.

The land around Vith and the far western provinces of Wahring wouldn't support an army of Rapp's size. He would need the farmland on the other side of the western woods. Leberecht's carriage now traveled through that farmland. The Kurakin and Moradan armies now controlled the crops Rapp would need to survive.

Leberecht smiled and shook his head. His cheeks no longer cramped; his muscles had grown strong enough to handle the constant joy of this victory.

It'd been too easy. Leberecht wasn't a warrior, and yet he would bring down a warrior king and his realm with one simple campaign. All it had taken was a strong army with intelligent generals and Leberecht's reading of historic battles and his knowledge of how rash King Rapp would be in his first battle.

The carriage bumped down the road back towards the Kurakin headquarters in their new camp. The thunder of the far-off battle still grumbled behind Leberecht. Fields of wheat flickered by outside the window.

It wasn't glorious to win a war this way. But glory wasn't what Leberecht sought.

He strove for power and would take it any way he could.

Citiva was that power. Leberecht now stood on the doorstep of the city he coveted. He'd grown up with the plateau on his horizon and was told it was too distant and that he would never reach its height. He was about to prove everyone wrong.

The army would fend off the feeble attacks Rapp would launch once he realized where the real Kurakin army was. The Wahrian army would slowly drain its resources and become bogged down in the west.

Leberecht chuckled to himself in the carriage. It was a wonderful day. A wonderful time to be alive.

Once the Kurakin ensured Rapp was trapped with the army in Vith, Leberecht would turn and march east. They would besiege Citiva and take the palace on the plateau.

The Wahrian royals were done. They were the first of many royal families to fall. Leberecht shook his head and couldn't believe he was so close to the power he'd dreamed about for so long. In just a few short days he would march towards Citiva and besiege the plateau he'd wanted to rule from since he was a little boy.

Rapp

Rapp sat on a log and stared at the mud. His aides built up his tent around him. The camp was quiet as the soldiers nursed wounds and recovered from the day's fighting.

None of anything made sense. The Kurakin army they'd attacked had been a small force. There hadn't been more regiments waiting deeper in the woods. Leberecht or Mikhail or any Kurakin generals weren't leading the army they'd faced.

It had been a decoy. King Rapp had been fooled.

He'd called for his generals to give their report on what they'd found after the battle. They sent out scouts to the south and east to find the rest of the Kurakin. Rapp would demand answers tonight but knew that he wouldn't get any.

The next steps in the war would take days to parse out. In real war, there is no climax. There was no single great moment of victory.

Rapp knew deep down that he was learning something. He was being taught a lesson by the Kurakin. War was drawn out. It was long and one battle didn't always lead to glory.

It was months of planning. Weeks of marching and establishing supply lines. A battle occurred in a day, but it was won long before.

That first night staring at the mud was the worst for Rapp. The following days didn't bring relief. The army took control of the Vith region and sent out more scouts. The next evening, a column of cavalry found the main Kurakin force.

The Horde was east of Vith.

Between Rapp and Citiva.

Even as his officers told him the news, King Rapp could feel the war slipping away from him. They were trapped in the west. They would have to attack the Kurakin position in the forest from a weaker position.

The days passed by in a blur. The attack never came.

Rapp tried to move his army back east, but every time they tried to press up a road or through the forest, they were turned back by the Kurakin.

The Horde were experts at harassing. They sent units of Kurakin cavalry with short muskets who could fire on the Wahrian column and ride away without slowing down. They crouched in the underbrush and sprang up to ambush the king's supply lines.

Any pitched battle was small and never allowed the Wahrians to gain anything. Everything was a defeat, and Rapp blew through his army's supplies early.

The campaign was over. Rapp couldn't break through. He wanted another chance at battle, but Leberecht and the Kurakin weren't going to give it to him.

They had the upper hand. There was no big moment that swung the tide of this war. There was no opportunity for glory. There was only the slow, long slog towards defeat.

Rapp had failed.

He'd failed the Ascended One first and then his realm. He was now trapped in Vith, far from home, and powerless to stop Leberecht from attacking his mother and his capital city.

Chapter 24

A great general must have luck on his side.

Quote attributed to Marshal Lauriston
Year 1112 Post-Abandonment, during the Moradan Campaigns

Andrei

Andrei watched through a gap in the trees as the hawk circled over the valley. He closed his eyes and let them roll into the back of his head. His next view was high above the forest with the wind rushing past his head.

The Scythes moved around their prey. They stalked silently and kept the girl's group within view but never gave away the chase. They would cut the Erlonians off and would soon trap them in the hills.

The night before, Andrei had placed men throughout the forest at various places he thought the Erlonians could be hiding. But the waterfall had always stuck out the most in his mind. He'd chosen to stake that location out himself.

The Erlonians had proven fast and crafty. They were easy to track but harder to catch.

Today, Andrei wanted to stalk them slowly and lull the prey into a false sense of safety. They thought their waterfall ruse had worked and Andrei wanted them to keep thinking they were almost safe. He would wait to strike until the moment was perfect and his men could not fail.

It took patience from his men, but they could feel the attack coming. They would lay the trap soon and finally end the prolonged chase. Andrei nudged his wolverine forward down the hill.

"What are you thinking on, Commander?" Jerkal rode beside Andrei. Both men shifted back and forth as their wolverines moved beneath them. "You've been quiet today."

"The end of this, friend." Andrei kept his eyes forward on the trail ahead.

A message came back from the scouts. The Erlonians were moving where Andrei had predicted, along the valley's curve between two hills. They were traveling right into good land for a trap.

"Soon, Jerkal. We attack soon."

Lauriston

Lauriston ran a whetstone along the edge of his bayonet and listened to the steel and stone scraping against each other. He'd sleep little during the coming night. The silence of the approaching danger would be too much. Most of his men would be the same way.

Lauriston glanced around the campsite in front of him. Mon measured out powder for everyone's pouches. Lodi sharpened his two short swords, three daggers, and the tip of his spear. Quatre cleaned and loaded his pistols and stared off towards the west.

The Princess Elisa sat and cleaned her pistols next to Lauriston. He wondered what she was feeling. It had to be obvious that the camp was nervous.

The soldiers here were veterans. They would be nervous but ready. Lauriston couldn't imagine what a girl of only fourteen would be thinking, though.

Lauriston had to get her to safety. His promise to her father still echoed in his mind. He would keep it. He wouldn't fail Lannes.

"I hear we're not far from your army." Pitt joined Lauriston by the fire and placed his saber across his lap to use his own whetstone on it.

Lauriston only grunted in response.

Pitt began sharpening his cavalry sword. Long, smooth strokes along the length of the curved blade. "You think your army is still by the lake?" Pitt said.

"It's where we agreed to hide," Lauriston said. "But things may have changed for the general I left in charge. We can only hope this crazy war hasn't pushed them somewhere else."

Pitt didn't say anything. For a long while there were only the sounds of the fire and their whetstones sharpening their weapons.

"How many men does a Scythe party usually travel with?"

"Fifteen, give or take," Quatre said before Lauriston could answer. The general walked around them and dropped his pistol-cleaning pack next to his bag behind Lauriston.

Both men turned and looked at Quatre. "You do the math," he said as he marched back the way he came.

"He's right." Lauriston shrugged and went back to his sword. He didn't want to think about being outnumbered against enemies on wolverines right now.

"And you've fought them before?"

Lauriston paused before answering. He wasn't sure he wanted to relive these memories the night before a potential fight. "Yes. They plagued our cavalry during scouting on our campaigns in the south. They kept us blind and afraid."

"And they're in bands of fifteen?"

"Usually more with a large army like that." Lauriston shrugged again. "Fifteen is the standard scouting unit, though. I'd assume that's what's after us."

Pitt didn't ask more questions. Lauriston was thankful. The Brunian finished sharpening his sword and bid Lauriston good night.

The rest of the camp slowly retired as well. Elisa went to her tent early. Lauriston took first watch and stayed up as the soldiers rolled into their sleeping bags against the chill of late fall.

It would be a long night. Tomorrow would be a long and dangerous day.

* * *

Low clouds hung over the hills to start the next morning. Lauriston wanted the group to move efficiently and he kept scouting to a minimum in the rear.

"Only a half day's ride to Lake Brodeur, I'd say." Quatre helped Lauriston strap down a pack on the back of his horse.

"Let's hope so." Lauriston's throat was sore after a night of fitful sleep and the chill in the night. He looked up at the specks of sky visible through the trees.

Hope was all they had now. Lauriston wasn't naive enough to believe they'd escaped the Scythes completely. Their trick with the waterfall had maybe bought them some extra time. They hadn't seen the Scythes behind them in a while, but Lauriston knew they were there.

He fully expected another attack to come before they reached the lake and the army that hopefully waited for them there.

"We'll be ready if they come." Quatre slapped a hand on Lauriston's shoulder and went off to help some of the others load up.

The woods were quiet around the camp. Mon and Lodi helped Elisa pack up her tent. Desaix checked the muskets of his scouts one last time.

At last they were all ready and they set off as the sun appeared fully over the hills in front of them. The world glowed and the trees around them turned golden. Lauriston felt exposed in the bright and open air.

Lauriston spurred his horse and waved for the group to follow. He led them down into the valley and rode at the front with Quatre close behind. Elisa was in the center with two Jinetes stationed on either side of her. Mon and Desaix brought up the rear.

No attack came through the first part of the morning. Quatre even made a joke about all their preparation being for nothing.

But Lauriston knew better.

Something felt wrong. Things were too quiet.

The group came around a curve in the hills and the trees thinned slightly. He caught a glimpse of sky and finally saw the dark speck floating towards them that signaled the coming end to the quiet.

A hawk circled lazily on the wind.

"Hawk sighted," he called back to the group.

Quatre's joking stopped. The men checked weapons and readied muskets. A horse snorted.

"Where will they attack from?" Lauriston heard Lodi ask Elisa.

"The rear, hoping to make us fly forward into a trap," Elisa said in response.

Lauriston nodded to himself. That's where he expected the attack to come from as well.

The marshal saw the curve of the path and the narrowness of the space between two hills in front of them. A steep incline rose on their left. A rock terrace sat farther ahead on the right.

The hawk still circled above them.

Lauriston sensed the attack before it happened.

Lodi whistled a signal. The forest was still quiet, but Lauriston could feel the Scythes about to make their move.

He saw the ambush through the land in front of them. He also saw a way around it, but it would be tight. He flicked a hand signal behind him and drew his pistol. He spurred his horse faster and the group followed.

The first shot came from the Erlonian rear. A yell answered it. A wolverine roared.

The horses spooked immediately.

Lauriston snapped his reins and dug his spurs to send his horse into a full gallop. He hoped the others would be able to match the new speed.

Lauriston looked behind him and saw Lodi reloading while galloping onward. The princess kept up with him.

More shots echoed from the rear of the group. The black-coated enemies appeared as shadows behind them and answered with their own shots. Musket balls smacked against trees.

Lauriston gave another hand signal and broke off up the slope on the right. They'd be slower moving uphill, but he wasn't going to gallop directly into the Scythes' trap.

The ground shook under the horses' hooves. Lauriston saw the white and black fur of the wolverines charging through the trees on their right now.

He pushed towards the crest of the ridge. He broke off to the left slightly. "Stay with me!" he called behind him.

The whistle of a musket ball went past his head. He pulled out his pistol and fired back down the slope at a Scythe trying to cut them off.

The Erlonians crested the hill. Lauriston launched his horse down the opposite side. He saw more Scythes moving in the adjacent valley. His soldiers had the high ground now, though. He slowed slightly and thought through his next decision.

Quatre's musket erupted nearby. A Scythe soldier fell backwards off his mount on their flank. The wolverine kept coming.

Lauriston pulled out his own musket and fired a quick shot at the beast. The ball struck its mark, but the wolverine only roared and moved faster up the hill in response.

"Keep moving!" Lauriston's decision had been made for him. They couldn't fight the Scythes—they would have to outrun them.

He put his musket back into its straps and spurred his horse forward. Lauriston heard the distinctive pops of Elisa's silver pistols behind him among the booms of muskets.

The group flew along the top of a ridge and down a slight slope. He wanted to reach the flat forest floor below and put space between them and the wolverines. Then they could angle towards the lake ahead and hope to find the rest of the Erlonian army.

The trees thinned out and he could see farther ahead. To their left, the valley rose up to meet the end of the hill at a point. He saw two Scythes galloping on their beasts along a path. They were in front of the Erlonian horses and were about to close them off.

"East!" Lauriston turned down the last bit of slope on the eastern side of the hill.

He glanced behind him and saw the group still with him. The second he took his eyes off the path in front of him was almost his last.

A Scythe came out of the brush as they leveled off the slope. The wolverine was three bounds away, the enemy's sword pointed at Lauriston's chest.

Gunfire came from behind him and he watched the chest of the beast under the Kurakin explode in blood. The monster's roar gurgled and its head fell forward and smashed into the ground. The Scythe went down with the beast and his sword tumbled in the air as he smashed into a rock.

Lauriston's horse hurdled over the wolverine's body and kept going. Lauriston said a silent thank you for the accuracy of his soldiers behind him.

He shifted his focus back to the path. The land was flat now. Lauriston forced his mind to reorient itself. They were in the open. They needed to find the lake. They needed to find the Erlonian army.

The horses couldn't keep this galloping pace up. The thought nagged at the back of Lauriston's mind. But they had to outrun the Scythes.

And there was nowhere to hide this time around.

More roars came from behind them.

The Scythes could have them surrounded already. The wolverines behind them could still be funneling the group into a trap. Lauriston wondered if he should turn and make a stand. Something screamed at him to second-guess his current course.

No. Stick to the plan.

If they were going to fight, they should've done it from the high ground. Lauriston had made his choice. They had to keep galloping. They had to hope for a miracle.

Elisa

Elisa strained to ignore the cramps in her legs. She was surrounded by the heavy breathing and snorts of horses as they galloped. The trees thinned around her and the air changed. There was a faint smell of water. Not salty like the coast, but a lake or river.

It would've been a peaceful and happy smell had the roar of a wolverine not ripped through the forest behind her.

The group galloped through the edge of the trees and into an open field. Tall grass waved in the wind. The horses tore across it.

A group of Scythes came out of the woods on the left. Seven riders on wolverines and two extra beasts unburdened by soldiers. They matched the Erlonians' speed.

Even Elisa could see that the Scythes had an angle for the Erlonian flank. A hand signal came back from Lauriston and the group shifted around Elisa. The soldiers moved left, putting themselves in between her and the enemy wolverines. Elisa tried to move with them but Lodi kept her on a straight path.

They were protecting her. They were going to take the brunt of the wolverine charge in order for her to reach the far tree line.

Lodi made eye contact with her. His look urged her to keep galloping. His hand reached out for her reins.

No.

She wouldn't abandon the soldiers who protected her. She wouldn't run off while they died.

She snapped the reins away from Lodi's hand. Her horse slowed and drifted right. Lodi matched her but was late. Elisa came to almost a complete stop and whirled to the left and back to face the oncoming Kurakin.

She had a perfect view of the Erlonian line as it shifted again to charge the Kurakin attack. Smoke billowed from guns on both sides. A cloud obscured the scene. Elisa lost sight of most of the clash but saw the wolverine in front of Quatre go down and the Erlonian slash his sword at the Scythe falling with the beast.

Lauriston felled the Kurakin adjacent him as well, but a riderless wolverine smashed into his horse. Elisa watched Lauriston fly forward as she galloped towards the fight. The smoke flew into her face and she lost sight of the tumbling marshal.

She heard the roars of the monsters, the pops of guns and the screams of men.

The smoke cleared briefly. She pulled out both pistols and fired straight down into the wolverine on top of Lauriston's former horse. The beast roared and stood up on its hind legs to swipe at her. Elisa's horse reared and pulled away. A third bullet came in from behind her and struck the beast in the face. It fell over backwards and writhed on the ground.

Elisa turned back in front of her and saw a new wolverine charging. Marshal Lauriston was pulling himself to his feet between her and the beast. The wolverine was closing too fast. Elisa pulled her sword and charged her horse at the enemy. She wouldn't make it in time.

Lodi's spear cut through the smoke above her and bore into the side of the beast. The wolverine was pushed sideways by the force and rolled over and thrashed about.

Lodi galloped past her and swung his sword down and slashed the monster's throat. The thrashing stopped. Lodi pulled his spear free without leaving the saddle. Behind the Lakmian, Elisa saw more terror coming.

Four more Scythes and two more riderless wolverines came out of the forest. They were already at full speed and ripping towards the far side of the fight.

Elisa's mind picked up the wider world in her periphery. The smoke cleared and she caught a glimpse of the full fight to match the screaming and explosions.

A naptha blew the horse out from under Mon. A wolverine stood over another horse and tore into the flesh of its neck. Quatre fought sword to sword with a Scythe warrior. Pitt charged an enemy with his bayonet. Desaix fired a pistol from his horse at a downed Kurakin.

"Go!" Lauriston yelled from the ground.

Elisa's eyes snapped back to the new arrivals. None of the other soldiers could see the approaching enemy reinforcements.

Lodi kicked his horse forward. Elisa did as well, keeping right on the Lakmian's hip. Lauriston scrambled to his feet and ran after them. He shouted something else at Elisa but she couldn't hear it over the battle.

Elisa and Lodi rode around the fighting to face the newly arrived Scythes. Lodi launched his bloody spear across the opening between the two sides. It traveled the gap in an instant and pushed through the chest of the middle Kurakin. The man was flung backwards, but his wolverine kept charging.

Elisa and Lodi reined to a stop. There were too many enemies. They would be crushed.

For the first time during the battle, Elisa took notice of the fear running through her. She felt it sweep over body and her muscles froze. She took a breath and forced herself back to numbness. She had to focus.

Lauriston stood below her horse. She saw him calmly reloading his pistols. His movements were practiced and steady even in the face of approaching death.

Elisa tried to reload as well, but her fingers trembled. She fumbled and dropped a ball. She wouldn't make it in time. She took her eyes off the work and stared at the wolverine bearing down on her. It opened its mouth in a roar, bloodred eyes fixed on its next meal.

Elisa felt the freeze of fear grip her again.

The crack of Lauriston's pistol came from her left. She saw the bullet hit her wolverine's shoulder, but it didn't slow the beast down. Lauriston fired again, ignoring the Kurakin directly in front of him. The second bullet didn't stop Elisa's monster, either.

Elisa's pistol hung limply in her hands. There was only the wolverine and her fear left for her.

Lodi moved his horse in front of hers. Lauriston stepped forward as well. The wolverine was only a few bounds away.

Movement came from behind Elisa. She saw blurs on the edges of her vision and realized the ground was shaking. A cavalry charge engulfed her from behind and her mind continued to falter while trying to understand what was happening.

The riders were wearing blue.

The cavalry smashed into the smaller line of Kurakin and swept them backwards. The monsters disappeared from Elisa's view. Cavalrymen formed a circle around her and Lauriston and Lodi. The marshal said something, but Elisa couldn't hear over the crush of horses.

The Erlonian soldiers formed up around Elisa and the battered group of Lauriston's men pulled back to their feet.

This was the rest of the Erlonian army. More cavalry poured out of the trees and pursued the Scythes back into the forest.

It was a few more moments before Elisa finally understood. They were saved. They'd found the army. The Scythes' chase had been defeated.

Pitt

Pitt awoke and saw the treetops moving above him. He was on a stretcher. He rocked back and forth as soldiers carried him.

The memory of the battle came slowly back to him.

There was a pain in his leg.

A naptha had exploded near him?

He couldn't remember.

He'd taken down a wolverine at the very beginning, lost his horse, and charged a Kurakin. Then everything went dark.

"You're awake."

Pitt looked up and found Lauriston on a horse riding above him.

"We're with my army." Lauriston looked up ahead on the path. Pitt couldn't see around the man carrying the front of his stretcher. "They've made camp on the lake nearby."

"Did we get all the Scythes?" Pitt felt a cough coming and tried to hold it inside. He knew instinctively it would hurt to cough.

"Most of them fled, but we got some."

"Good."

"Get some rest, we'll be there soon. You have time to sleep now." Lauriston smiled down at him.

Pitt let his head fall back to the soft cloth of the stretcher. He felt a much-needed sleep take him once again.

Chapter 25

Rise again, noble warriors, the mighty voice said. *And join my hosts to fight for eternity.*

Tome of the Ascended One
Parable of Resurrection

Elisa

Elisa walked towards the smells of breakfast. Her stomach growled up at her.

She'd finally reached the Erlonian army. She walked down an aisle between rows of tents and heard soldiers waking up and preparing for the day. The cooks were clanging pots and stoking fires. Cavalrymen were feeding their horses and checking their shoes.

Lauriston and Mon and everyone had gotten her to the army. Her father's army. The last of Erlon's great warriors.

She was safe. She was finally safe.

Two of the sharpshooters who'd helped rescue her crossed the path in front of her on the way to breakfast. One had a splint on his leg and was helped along by the other.

Elisa sped up and ducked under the injured soldier's other arm to help speed the pair along.

"Good morning, Princess." The uninjured soldier nodded at her.

"Thank you, Princess. I can manage," the other said with a grunt of pain. "I don't think your father would approve of the princess having to help a common soldier."

Elisa didn't respond. She thought the exact opposite would be true of her father. He would smile on her helping the men who'd protected her and the empire and the people.

The group of three stumbled along the last few steps to their destination. There was a stump open next to where the cooks were handing out food and they eased the injured sharpshooter down into a sitting position with his broken leg straight out in front of him.

There was a station for the cooks in an open area that broke the rows of tents. Elisa could only see two pots being serviced by three cooks. There must be other cooking stations throughout the camp. This one was only big enough to serve a portion of the men.

Breakfast was a piece of white bread served with some kind of stew. Elisa walked closer and thought it smelled like venison. Her stomach growled again.

"Venison stew. Some vegetables in there. And some bread."

The voice startled Elisa. She looked up and finally noticed the man who was serving the stew out of a pot with a giant ladle.

Marshal Lauriston, the leader of this army, was serving bowls of breakfast stew to the men.

Lauriston smiled at her. Elisa stood in shock for a few seconds before regaining control of herself.

"Good morning, Lar. Thank you," Elisa said as she took the bowl of stew from him. "An extra slice of bread for your sharpshooter?"

Elisa pointed back towards the pair she'd helped to the stump. Lauriston smiled and nodded and filled another bowl with a little extra stew and put two slices of bread on top. He winked at Elisa when he handed it over.

She walked the bowls back to the sharpshooters.

"Thank you, Princess," the injured one said. He bit into the stew-soaked bread immediately. "Never thought I'd be served breakfast by a princess."

"Here," Elisa said to the other sharpshooter. She held out the other bowl to him. "Take this, I'll get back in line."

"No, Your Highness. You eat it, I'll wait in line."

He walked off before Elisa could protest.

"It's good stew," the injured soldier said through a mouthful of the meal.

Elisa took her first few bites and felt the warm broth spread across her stomach. She turned back to watch Lauriston while she ate.

More soldiers arrived for breakfast and a line had formed. Each man greeted the marshal and he smiled in return and talked to them while he served.

Elisa finished her bowl quickly. She offered her piece of bread to the injured sharpshooter and he took it gladly. She kept her eyes on Lauriston and the line of soldiers that now stretched down the far row of tents.

Elisa walked back over to Lauriston without really thinking her actions through. She walked around the table Lauriston was using to serve and took a place next to him.

It was the right thing to do. It seemed like something her father would do, something Lauriston and Mon and Lodi and all the soldiers would approve of.

She was a princess. She could lie around in her tent and let the officers run the army and fight the war for her country. But she'd seen the way Lauriston's soldiers fought for her and she'd seen how much stronger they were when they saw her fighting with them.

Her father always walked and talked among the men. He always tried to relate to everyone in his army, down to the cooks and the common line infantrymen. Elisa would do the same. Even if it meant literally serving the soldiers alongside Lauriston.

There was a knife and cutting board with a large loaf of bread and she started slicing off chunks for the soldiers after they'd received their stew from the marshal.

Lauriston didn't say anything. He only smiled with a sideways look at her. He ladled the stew into the soldiers' bowls while Elisa cut pieces of bread and set them on top of the bowls as the soldiers passed.

The men smiled and greeted Lauriston. Seeing the marshal serving them breakfast didn't seem out of the ordinary to them. They all took it in stride like it was a common occurrence.

But when they saw Elisa, it was a different story.

One of the first soldier's eyes went wide and he started stuttering as he stared at her. He took his slice of bread and stumbled away, continuing to mutter incoherent words.

The next only gaped at her.

The third recovered quickly enough to be the first to speak to her.

"Your Highness, it's an honor."

Elisa smiled and did a small curtsy as she handed him his bread.

The men continued to react in various ways all down the line. One soldier with bars on his shoulder to denote the rank of captain let out a high-pitched squeal.

Lauriston laughed and shook his head at every reaction and they kept serving until the line died down.

The very last soldier in line wore a general's jacket. He shook Lauriston's hand and welcomed the marshal back to the army.

"And you haven't had a chance to greet the princess yet, have you?" Lauriston said after handing the general his meal.

The general smiled at her and bowed. "No, I haven't. Good morning, Princess."

"Elisa, this is General Murat. He led the army while I was gone."

Elisa curtsied again and handed the man his bread.

"Glad you made it to us alive and unhurt, Princess."

"Thank you, General. I had good protectors. Thank you for saving us yesterday."

"That wasn't me," the general said with a smile. "I was way back here at camp doing nothing important. My cavalry is to thank for finding you and arriving right on time."

"They certainly were timely," Lauriston said. "We weren't going to make it without them, I'm afraid."

"Well, you made it, and that's all that matters now." The general smiled at both of them, but his eyes settled back on Elisa. "Thank you for serving the men, Elisa. It means a lot to them to see you out here."

"Of course, General."

Murat bowed again and left them to go eat with his men. Lauriston hefted his almost empty pot of stew up and hauled it back towards the cooks. Elisa made to follow him.

"We can clean, Elisa. You've helped enough."

"I'm happy to help," Elisa said. She didn't think it would be right to stop assisting before the pots were clean.

"Thank you, serving the food was enough for you. The cooks can handle the cleaning." The marshal set the pot down and the cooks bowed to Elisa. Lauriston turned and pointed over Elisa's shoulder. "You've earned some rest. Don't push yourself too hard, we've only just arrived. How about going and relaxing with Mon this morning?"

Elisa followed Lauriston's point and saw Mon talking with some soldiers in a circle. The soldiers looked to be in the process of saying goodbye to the older general.

"We'll have a meeting later on with the officers," Lauriston said. "You can join too, if you want. But enjoy the morning. Talk with the men. Talk with Mon."

Elisa nodded and walked towards Mon and saw the soldiers leaving him. Mon shook some of their hands and waved goodbye. By the time Elisa reached the general, there was only one soldier remaining next to him

Elisa had been relieved that Mon hadn't received any major injuries in the fight against the Scythes, but she hadn't had a chance to talk with him at all since they reached the army.

"Good morning, Princess," Mon said when she approached.

The remaining soldier bowed to Elisa. "Your Highness."

Elisa nodded her head respectfully in reply. The soldier bid goodbye to Mon and excused himself.

Mon took a seat on a log by a tent-side small fire and stretched out his legs. Elisa took the spot next to him. No one else sat with them.

"One of your old guardsmen?" She nodded after the soldier.

"He was close to my son. I hadn't seen him in years. Didn't know he was still in the army."

Elisa looked around her once again. The soldiers were finishing breakfast and moving off to their drills or preparations or whatever Lauriston and the officers would have them doing that day.

She half expected the scene to fade away like her Lakmian vision. The entire morning and the escape from the Scythes seemed too good to be more than a dream.

But the log she sat on was very real. The smells and sounds of the camp were real. Her father's soldiers protecting her were very real.

"I'm glad we made it here," she said.

Mon grunted and smiled as he brought out a bottle from around the log and uncorked it.

"I'm glad we can fight now. I'm glad the army is still fighting," Elisa said.

"Good," Mon said, taking a pull from his wine.

Elisa took in a breath and held it. She was ready to fight and lead and push Erlon forward, even if things were hopeless.

Though looking at the army now didn't make their situation seem hopeless at all. The men were in good spirits. They were hidden in the woods with no enemies closing in on them. Erlon may be falling around them, but these soldiers were going to fight on and fully believed they could still win this war.

"Thank you, Mon," Elisa said.

She was going to say more, but just the thank you part seemed to be enough for now. She looked at Mon and he met her eye and nodded. Elisa knew she didn't have to say anything more.

Mon took a large breath.

"I had three sons." He exhaled with the words.

Elisa stiffened.

She had completely forgotten about their conversation in the caves. About how Mon had promised to tell her his full story if they reached the army safely. All the excitement and fear and stress of the escape had caused Elisa to forget her questions surrounding Mon and his history with the army.

Mon looked at her over another drink of wine before continuing. "I feel you deserve a full explanation now, like I promised."

He set the bottle back on the dirt. "Victor was in the Imperial Guard with me. He'd shown himself to have valor at Riom. Noah was infantry and Paul an artillery officer; they joined in time for the Plains Campaign."

Elisa could already start to piece together what was going to happen. Mon had never mentioned children before. The farmhands back near Plancenoit had never mentioned any family for Mon at all.

She felt her heart drop down lower and lower with every word Mon spoke.

"Noah was wounded at Stetton, the middle one. He earned a Silver Cross for that. They all fought bravely and I was proud of them, both as a general and a father. Your father, newly crowned emperor at that point, pinned the cross on Noah's chest himself. Everything was grand, we were the perfect Continental family, warriors through and through."

Mon paused, as if gathering himself. Elisa remained quiet. His bottle lay untouched at his feet.

"Three Bridges changed all that. The campaign for Brun with your father would be my last. And the last for my sons as well." Mon's eyes stared down into the fire. "Victor died in my arms, on the southern bridge. That's the hardest of the three, because I was with him. Noah and Paul drowned when the sorcery came. They were on the central bridge. I watched the entire collapse from afar, powerless to stop the deaths of my boys."

The morning fire let out a pop. The sounds of the army camp faded away and Elisa's heart hit bottom. Tears welled up and blurred her vision.

"I'm..." She struggled to find words. "I'm sorry, Mon."

"Your father." Mon's voice came close to breaking, but he held it strong with a short pause. "Your father wanted to give me the Soult Medallion. He wanted my oldest to get it posthumously."

Mon looked at Elisa again and she saw a range of emotions. Sadness, of course. But also anger and regret and shame and fear. Somehow all of it and more in the old man's expression.

"I refused both." Mon's voice was low now. "I stormed out of the palace without a goodbye to anyone. I left the army. I returned to my family's farm to live out a slow death with the memories of my boys. I put down my musket and picked up the bottle."

Mon reached down to his wine and took a long pull. He held it out to Elisa after he was finished and she took it from his hands, mainly because she didn't know what else to do. She took a timid pull and passed it back.

"I think your father understood," Mon said after a long bout of silence. "But I don't think he was pleased with a general directly refusing the Soult."

"Why have you come back?" There were numerous questions in Elisa's mind, but that was the only one she could get out of her mouth.

Mon didn't answer for a few moments. The fire crackled.

"Duty, I guess. Guilt, possibly." Mon shook his head. "I don't know. It finally caught up to me. But mainly it was duty. Lauriston asked me to protect you, and that's what I did."

Elisa gave a nod to show she understood. She placed a hand on Mon's shoulder.

She saw now why Mon had never mentioned his time in the army. Why he hadn't told her he was an old general who knew her father. She understood his drinking and the darkness behind his expressions even in happier times.

Mon's eyes cleared and he looked up from the fire. "And now we're in a fight for the end of the empire. I won't walk away now, not again."

Mon took another long drink from the bottle. Elisa watched him and tried to keep the tears from escaping her eyes. Mon wiped his mouth on his sleeve. "There's a battle coming. Maybe it'll be my last, but I'm not going to turn my back on Lannes again and watch Erlon fall. I've got another chance at a last battle, I'll go out fighting this time. And if I fall, then I'll join the Ascended One's hosts and see my sons again."

Mon stood up and wiped his eyes. He looked down at her and nodded.

"Thanks for serving the men breakfast," he said. "It means a lot for them to see you. It'll remind them of Lannes."

Elisa nodded and couldn't say anything in response. Mon walked off into the commotion of the morning camp and left her sitting alone to stare into the fire.

She took in another breath and her thoughts raced.

Mon was right. He'd been right from the beginning.

Her father had inspired the men. Elisa was able to do the same simply by being present. She felt ashamed at her thoughts back on the trail about giving up or running away. Now she knew that she would never give up. She never wanted to quit and give herself over to the enemy.

If Mon could come back and fight again and keep striving for the empire, she would fight as well.

If Erlon was meant to fall, the army would go down protecting it until the end. If they could save the empire, the army would find a way. If there was a battle coming tomorrow, they would fight it.

And Elisa would fight with them.

Andrei

Andrei entered the tent and was relieved to find most of the other generals were already there. Heads turned and looked at him, disdain filling most of their eyes. General Duroc's were the worst.

The general stayed silent and let Andrei file in with the other men. The last of the army leadership arrived and the meeting began. Duroc ran through everything quickly.

Andrei was already nervous, but he became even more worried when Duroc started dismissing the other leaders one by one after their orders were given out. The Scythes would be left for last. And there would be no one else in the tent to hide behind.

"Commander Andrei." Duroc finally looked at him. The last of the other generals ducked out of the tent.

"General Duroc." Andrei nodded and stood at attention.

"Where is the Erlonian princess now?"

"Her group reached a holdout army of the Erlonians, sir."

"So we've lost her."

Andrei closed his eyes. "Yes. We ran into the army's scouting party and were flanked while attacking the girl's position. By the time my *sakk* saw the cavalry, it was too late."

"I see."

Andrei didn't have anything else to say. Duroc didn't look angry, but he stayed quiet and let Andrei squirm. Another voice broke the silence.

"She's slipped through his grasp once again."

The god walked forward from the tent's far corner and sat down on a chair behind Duroc. The Kurakin commander didn't say anything. He looked at the god and waited for him to continue.

"We'll have to get her with war. Your Scythes have failed us." The god spoke to Duroc but didn't look at him. He kept his eyes on Andrei.

"I know." Duroc turned to address Andrei. "You'll lead a division east, along the river they call the Branch. You need to secure a crossing. I've marked it within your orders."

"Yes, sir."

There was one remaining bundle of papers on the table in the center of the tent. Andrei walked over and grabbed it and made to leave.

Duroc stopped him before he reached the door. "Take the crossing and then the girl is trapped in the south. It won't matter how big of an army protects her."

"They'll harass us from the forest, sir. It'll be hard to snuff them all out." Andrei fully faced his general and tried to keep his knees from shaking.

"I know, but that won't matter. We have larger enemies to face now." Duroc had already returned to writing out letters.

"Don't fail this task." Both men looked back towards the god. The shadows of the tent seemed to move around the being. Andrei could only see his outline on the chair now.

"The girl is our priority," the god said. "But this war needs to be won. Duroc has assured me that we won't be slowed down by mistakes again."

Andrei didn't need to look at Duroc to feel the disappointment. His orders were a demotion. He'd been given a division, a sizable force, but the Scythes were taken away from him.

He looked back at Duroc and kept his chin up. "We'll take the crossing." Andrei saluted and turned to leave.

He exited the tent and hurried off. He wanted distance between himself and the shadowy vision of the god inside the tent. Duroc and the god could plan their grand war without him. Andrei had lost his Scythes, but at least he'd be far away from the schemes of leaders and gods much more powerful than him.

Chapter 26

It's a beautiful feeling, to march with a strong and confident army. A general should relish the boot falls and steady drums. For when the battle comes, he will send his men to die.

From Emperor Lannes's Personal Journal
Year 1114 Post-Abandonment, during the Southern Campaigns

Leberecht

Leberecht broke away from the main column on the road and trotted across a field of winter wheat. There was a tiny farmhouse nestled between groups of trees just to the north. Leberecht only had eyes for what was in front of him.

The eastern horizon held his prize. The reason for all his scheming.

The plateau of Citiva.

The royal seat of the Wahrian Realm.

Mikhail rode up behind him. "The officers are distributing orders for positions around the city. They don't expect any resistance outside the walls. The queen has already barred the gates."

"Good." Leberecht nodded and kept his eyes on the rock in the distance.

The train of the Moradan and Kurakin armies pushed forward down the road. Leberecht brought his horse to a stop and watched the column marching by.

"We'll have the Moradan regiments in the north. I want the plateau to have a clear view of who is besieging them." Leberecht felt his smile widening. His cheeks were cramping again from too much work over the last few days. But the twinge of pain was well worth it. "They'll know the Kurakin. But let them see their former allies pointing cannons at their main gate."

Leberecht went back to staring at the plateau and the spires of the palace on top. The queen of his birth nation would be sitting up there.

She would be in shambles.

Her son was defeated and trapped in the west with a slowly starving army. Her allies had betrayed her, her grand peace summit had failed. Now her city would fall and she'd lose her precious palace and plateau once again.

Leberecht spat down at the short green wheat grass at his horse's feet and spurred back into a trot parallel to the road.

Someone like Queen Caroline or anyone in her family wasn't fit to lead. None of the royals across the Continent were.

If anything, Leberecht had respected the Emperor of Erlon the most. He wasn't a royal. He'd risen to power through merit, not by birth.

Leberecht was doing the same.

He'd reached this point through schemes and cunning and with only his mind.

And his empire was going to be bigger than even Erlon's at its height. The entire Continent would be his.

Leberecht spurred his horse into a trot parallel to the army's march and basked in the perfect execution of his plans. Soon they would begin their siege. He would draw it out and make the royals suffer through a winter without supplies.

Leberecht was going to enjoy the next few months immensely.

"Still no news of the fleeing king." Mikhail matched Leberecht's trotting pace. They angled their path to cross an irrigation ditch in the field and continue along with their army.

"That's fine. He'll turn up eventually." Leberecht had barely thought about the little King Rapp since the battle. The boy didn't matter anymore. He was defeated.

Once Leberecht sat on the throne in the palace, nothing else would matter for Wahring. Everything would be his and his alone and the old ways would be over.

The Kurakin armies would continue their conquest in the west and defeat the remaining enemy armies there. Leberecht's new alliance would replace the weak Coalition and drive the Continent towards prosperity in ways the old royals never could.

It was almost too easy.

Leberecht spat into the crops again and shook his head.

"What is it, friend?" Mikhail looked over at Leberecht with a fang-toothed grin.

"Nothing, my friend. Nothing." Leberecht winked at his Kurakin companion. "I'm happy, that's all. Couldn't be more content. Come, let's pick up the pace. The vanguard should be reaching Citiva soon and we don't want to miss the show."

The pair of riders moved to a faster trot and returned to the road and sped along the lines of marching soldiers. They moved east and pressed closer and closer to Citiva and Leberecht's future throne.

Elisa

The army's officers assembled on the shore of the lake just outside the main portion of the Erlonian camp. Elisa chose a spot in the back next to Mon and Desaix. Marshal Lauriston stood in front.

"We'll need to march soon, tomorrow if possible." Lauriston looked at the officers. Heads nodded in agreement in front of Elisa as the marshal continued. "The army should be able to mobilize quickly. The injuries from the skirmish with the Scythes won't hold us back."

Elisa saw Mon and Desaix nod as well. She watched the other generals but saw no disagreement with the plan there, either.

Elisa's own emotions swirled. She had settled down enough since her talk with Mon. She knew finally escaping and being safe from the Scythes helped as well.

But some doubts and fear had returned in the bottom of her thoughts, only now they were more focused on the army and the empire as a whole. There were plenty of brave soldiers in this army, but what could they do against the entire might of the Kurakin?

Lauriston's plan was supposed to have that answer. She listened and waited to find out what the marshal had in mind.

"The Kurakin march north. They attack their former allies." Lauriston pointed to where General Pitt stood. The marshal had already explained what they'd learned from the Brunian general about the Kurakin betrayal to General Murat and the other officers. Elisa had been impressed with how they'd handled the news of the strange turn in the war.

"We're on their eastern flank. They have a clear path up the Broadwater and we don't know how the Wahrians and Brunians will respond to the main army."

Lauriston left the worst possible scenario unsaid. The armies of Brun and Wahring could be overrun already. They could already be broken and fleeing or worse.

"But the key to the north is through Vendome. We all know that." More head nodding from the generals, especially the older veterans like Mon. "The Branch is difficult to cross. The best crossing is the town of Neuse, directly north of our current position."

Elisa would have to look at a map if they had one back in the camp. She tried to remember the exact path of the Broadwater and Branch rivers. She knew they met west of here, just north of Ligny and continued on towards the far northwestern coast.

Before they combined, the smaller river, the Branch, would divide the northern portion of the Dune Forest from the Vendome hills in the north.

The Kurakin would need those hills if they wanted to conquer the north. They would push north along the Broadwater in the west but also needed the eastern bank.

Elisa saw that the other generals agreed with Lauriston's view of the overall strategy of the new war.

The marshal pointed to General Pitt at the side of the group to Elisa's left. The Brunian was recovering nicely from his injuries in the skirmish and stood leaning on a crutch. He straightened at the mention of his name from Lauriston.

"General Pitt informed us the Brunians should still hold the crossing at Neuse. Our army will march north and attempt to treat with them."

A few soft gasps escaped from the officers in front of Elisa. Lauriston continued as if he hadn't noticed.

"I plan to offer our help to the Brunians in holding the crossing in order to keep the Kurakin from flanking Vendome in the north."

Some of the officers shifted in their stances. Pitt looked around the group and Lauriston stared forward and waited for questions.

Elisa met Lauriston's eyes and he smiled at her before his eyes moved on to the others.

"What if the Brunians won't have us?" Mon said at last. His voice broke the long silence.

Elisa looked at the old general and wondered if Lauriston had asked him to voice this question in case no others came forward. She wouldn't put it past the two friends to plan this.

"Good question, Mon," Lauriston said. "Pitt here believes they will accept us. He, being a general, should outrank the officer in charge of holding the bridge either way."

"It should only be a major-general commanding there." Pitt shifted his weight over his crutch.

"Hopefully that's true. And Pitt has volunteered to ride forward with our cavalry scouts ahead of the army. He'll prepare the Brunian army for our arrival."

Lauriston paused. Elisa waited. The marshal hadn't answered Mon's specific question yet.

"As to what happens if that doesn't work and they still don't accept us?" Lauriston looked at the ground for a second before bringing his head back up to the men. He shrugged. "Then we still fight. We fight in these woods, we hinder the Kurakin advance as best as we can. They're on our territory, but Erlon isn't dead."

Lauriston met Elisa's eye again.

"Erlon isn't dead at all," he repeated. "We've got a Lannes with us. And the best soldiers in the world ready to fight. The Horde doesn't stand a chance."

One officer let out a cheer. Others clapped. Most everyone was grinning. Elisa joined them. Lauriston's smile was the biggest of all.

"Desaix has your orders, gentlemen. Get your men ready. We march at dawn. Onward."

* * *

The army marched north around the lake and back into the dense forest. Elisa had been told the march would take three days. It'd be quicker if it was still only her small group of soldiers on horseback. But an army of infantrymen moved much slower.

The soldiers packed up their tents and the rest of camp and formed up into their units. Elisa was given a horse and rode with Mon at the front of his new command. His column marched behind the Lakmian regiments with their tails curling and swishing about as they walked.

"You'll stay with me during the fight," Mon said at midday of the second day of marching.

"I'm sorry?" Elisa had been watching the Lakmians march in front of them and thinking on a fond memory from back when her family was together and would travel to Papelotte in Wavre for a winter retreat.

"When the Horde attacks, Lauriston wants you to stay with me. The Lakmians will stay close to us as well."

Elisa looked at Mon. The old general didn't have a bottle in his hand this morning. Now that she thought about it, she hadn't seen Mon drink the day before, either. His eyes were less bloodshot and more focused than she'd ever seen them.

"You're going to let me fight?"

Mon looked at her and raised his eyebrows. "Don't you want to?"

Of course she did. But that didn't mean Elisa had assumed Lauriston would allow it. Especially after all the trouble they just went through to keep her safe and alive.

Mon seemed to understand her thought process. "We had a long discussion about it. After all you've been through, you deserve to do what you want." Mon turned and looked behind them at the column stretching through the trees. "But if you'd rather sit in the back to be safe—"

"No. I'll fight." Elisa gripped the reins of her horse tighter in her gloved hands.

"I thought so." The old general smiled at her.

They marched along in silence for a long while. The men were quiet behind them. Only the marching of thousands of boots disrupted the peaceful forest they traveled through.

"Just stick with me during the battle, okay?" Mon said eventually.

Elisa nodded.

"Whether the Brunians let us cross or not and wherever Lauriston puts us, stay with me. Lodi will be nearby too."

Elisa nodded again. She wondered what a full battle would be like. It was hard to imagine after seeing the small fight against the Kurakin cavalry when they'd found the Brunian. That had been chaos. A full battle would be total devastation.

Her heart beat a little faster as she thought through what was coming for the army. She didn't feel fear, but there was some new feeling inside of her.

Was it excitement?

"We'll win, whatever kind of fight comes. Lar will make sure of that." Mon looked over at her and gave a quick grin before returning to his normal grimace.

Elisa knew his words to be true. Marshal Lauriston would put them in the best position to succeed. Outside of her father, he was the best man for the job of leading this army.

They marched onward. The boot falls of hundreds of soldiers behind and in front of them echoed through the trees. Elisa was ready to fight.

So was Mon. So was Lodi. And his Lakmians. And the entire Erlonian army.

The only question that remained was whether or not Pitt would succeed in getting the Brunian army in the town of Neuse to ally with Erlon and fight with them.

They would have their answer very soon.

Lauriston

Lauriston rode at the head of the column. There was a vanguard in front of him and Desaix's cavalry troop even farther beyond them, but Lauriston sat alone at the head of the main army.

No direct roads traveled through this portion of the forest. This caused the column's march to be more of a mass of men that shifted and moved with the terrain. They would form up into a presentable army when the forest fell away and they approached the river and the town.

The Brunian, Pitt, had ridden north on the first day of the march with Desaix. Pitt would already be with the Brunian army holding the town. That portion of the plan was out of Lauriston's hand now. He would have to trust Pitt to convince the Brunians to fight with the Erlonians.

The first two days of marching were spent trying not to think about all that could go wrong with his plan. Lauriston was only marginally successful at keeping his worries and doubts at bay.

It was now the morning of the third and final day of the march. The marshal said a silent prayer that Pitt had convinced the Brunians to fight the Horde together with their former enemies. If he hadn't, the Erlonians under Lauriston would be in trouble.

"Still half a day out, I'd say." Lodi rode next to Lauriston. His Lakmian regiments were a couple units back in the column and could march without their commander at the head.

Lauriston nodded. "We'll get there early afternoon. And then we'll see what Pitt's done for us."

"They'll take us," Lodi said. "Or if they won't have us now, they'll want us to help once they see the Horde coming."

"I agree."

They rode along without continuing the conversation. Lauriston let his mind wander off again.

He had too many things to think about. The organization of the men. The layout of the town and the bridge over the river and how the Horde would attack.

He turned to Lodi and was about to ask about his thoughts on a defensive plan for the bridge but was stopped by a sound in the distance.

It was a low rumble, barely perceptible. Lauriston looked at Lodi. The Lakmian's raised eyebrow showed that he'd heard it too.

Both men knew what the sound meant.

"Could be thunder." Lodi shrugged his shoulders.

But the sky above them was clear.

Another rumble in the distance came. Their horses continued to move forward at a walk. The men behind marched on, but Lauriston could hear the beginnings of murmuring.

A third rumble erupted.

"That's not thunder," Lauriston said.

"No. I don't think it is anymore."

Lauriston listened for a fourth rumble and ran through his options. They needed to speed up the march. They needed to get to the town as quickly as possible.

The sound of cannon fire could only mean bad things for Pitt and the Brunians in the town ahead.

"Rider!"

The call rang out in front of them from one of the vanguard outriders. A galloping horse soon followed.

Lauriston recognized the rider immediately and it only confirmed his suspicions of what was happening.

Desaix closed the last distance to the marshal quickly. He whipped his horse around and fell in next to Lauriston and Lodi.

"The Horde attacks." The cavalryman was out of breath but continued his report anyway. "They've reached Neuse and attacked the bridge. The Brunian cannons are harassing them, but I don't know if they can hold."

"General Pitt?" Lauriston said.

"Across the bridge with the Brunians."

Lauriston nodded. His mind started working.

"Your cavalry troop?" Lodi said.

"I've got them scouting the Kurakin numbers, but they remain hidden from view."

"Good," Lauriston said. His mind worked through the plan quickly and continued to weigh options as he relayed orders to the generals. "We march double time and hope to reach the town by midday. The vanguard should shift west and let the main column push up on their east flank. We'll finalize a plan of attack once we reach the town."

Lauriston knew the forest would cover his army's approach. He would decide on how to attack the Kurakin force before they reached the town. Maybe they could surprise the Horde and turn them away with a flank.

First, the priority was for Lauriston to get the army into position.

Desaix nodded at the orders and broke off to run the updates to the vanguard ahead. Lodi fell back to alert the other officers and distribute the orders along the column.

Lauriston hadn't planned for this. The Horde had marched east too fast. But he could adjust. He could adapt and still win this battle.

Pitt would have to hold out with the Brunians for a few hours. And Lauriston had to hope the Kurakin force wasn't too large for the defense to handle and that the Erlonians could arrive in time to save the day.

Chapter 27

War is chaos. Those who can make sense of it will be victorious.

Maxims of War, Entry Seven
Emperor Gerald Lannes

Nelson

The wind died during the second week of Nelson's long journey home. The sea swells ceased and the air hung heavy over the still water and Nelson's ship.

Emperor Lannes was happy. His stomach finally settled down.

Nelson couldn't have been more frustrated.

"Why worry?" Lannes leaned back in his chair across from the king. "We've nowhere to go."

"We're even more in the dark stuck here than back at the fortress." Nelson stood up and looked out the stern windows. The ship drifted as the sailors waited for the prevailing winds to return. The stern now faced west, towards the coast of Morada and Wahring.

Brun was to the north. Nelson's home was close but felt very far away at the moment. News of the developments in the war against the Kurakin felt even farther away.

"We should've sailed for Wahring. I could help the Wahrians plan against the Kurakin there," Lannes said.

Nelson turned his head to look back at the emperor. "You think the Wahrians would listen to you? You think they'd be happy with you as an ally?" He chuckled at the image of the Wahrian queen meeting a freed Lannes on her own country's soil. She would be too horrified to speak.

Lannes shrugged and took a sip of his tea. He swung his legs up onto the king's desk with a thud and leaned further back in his chair.

"I could convince the Lakmians to come down from their mountains and help, at least," he said. "Anything we try would be more productive than sitting back in Brun."

Nelson didn't answer. They'd had this argument before and it was always the same words from both men. They wouldn't get anywhere by going over things again.

Yet the questions still stuck in Nelson's mind. He looked back out over the still water stretching to the horizon and thought through the answers he couldn't yet give. He couldn't let the emperor loose with an army on the Continent. Not yet, at least.

The other Coalition powers would never go for it, even if Lannes was leading a group of Brunian soldiers with Nelson at his side. The sight of Emperor Lannes leading men into battle once again would be more frightening than even the Kurakin Horde was at the moment.

Nelson must wait. He had to use Lannes's mind to help plan a grand ally strategy from afar and then pick his spots to send more Brunians into the fray.

The king kept reminding himself why he'd chosen to break the emperor free from Taul in the first place. It was for his advice and knowledge of warfare, not to give Lannes back control of an army.

Nelson turned on his heels and walked back to the desk. He looked down at the map of the Continent sitting on the wood and clasped his hands behind his back.

"The Wahrians and the eastern Kurakin army clash in the east," he said.

"The Moradans will help there too." Lannes appeared to be focused on cleaning the underside of his fingernails, but Nelson knew the man well enough now to know he was listening.

"Yes, the Moradans are there too." Nelson nodded and kept his eyes down on the map. "We'll wait for news of how that campaign goes. Now, in the west, I have less news than I'd like."

Nelson's thoughts trailed off as his eyes shifted over the Antres Mountains to the west and settled on Erlon.

"Lauriston will take care of things there." Lannes was still focused on his own hands. He didn't glance at the map or Nelson once.

"How?" Nelson said. He'd thought on the situation in the west more than anything else on this journey and had no idea how that side of the campaign could hold together. The Kurakin were already past Plancenoit and had the larger force. Not to mention the Brunian army was shattered and would need to coordinate with their former enemies to have any chance to succeed.

"General Duroc will be aggressive."

Nelson thought that was stating the obvious and almost let an exacerbated sigh escape from his mouth but held it in check.

"But the end of fall approaches." Lannes dropped his legs from the desk and leaned forward. He looked up at Nelson across the map. "If Lauriston can use the Erlonians he has left to bog Duroc down in the south, below the Branch and well south of Vendome, our side has a chance."

Nelson's eyes followed across the locations on the map as Lannes talked.

"If they can keep the Kurakin in the south before the break in the campaign season and gives us time to plan out this war, it lets your Coalition take time to regroup and come to terms with my country as your ally."

Nelson nodded. All of that made sense. It was still a difficult task, but the armies in the west just needed to survive until winter.

The pair continued their discussion over various parts of the sprawling war and Nelson started to feel a little better about his side's chances. Even the sea chopped up a bit behind them and they could hear the sailors moving about and raising sails up top in preparation for the winds to return.

Nelson still had one large question that he didn't like his current answer for. The question wouldn't leave his mind and the king knew he would lose sleep contemplating it in the coming nights.

As Lannes talked through his thoughts for the western campaign, King Nelson sat and listened and tried to ignore the thought that threatened to overtake his entire mind.

What happens if Lauriston and whatever is left of the Brunian forces in the west fail? What happens if Duroc gets north of the Branch and all of Erlon is lost?

Everything Nelson had planned in response to the Kurakin betrayal would be for nothing. The west would fall and it would be hard to hold the east with Erlon's army gone. How could they defend the east if Duroc invaded from Erlon and up from the south at the same time? They'd be outnumbered and outflanked.

If the west fell, how could they possibly win the war?

Andrei

The rumbling shook the ground under Andrei's feet. His army charged east along the road towards the town. The Brunians answered the attack with cannon fire.

Andrei closed his eyes and rolled them back and let the world drift away below him. He flew high above the fight. The soldiers were only specks of black against the landscape below and the concussion of the artillery was barely felt on the light breeze.

General Duroc could take away his wolverine and the Scythes, but the connection with his hawk would always remain.

Andrei's hawk drifted on the wind just below the cloud cover. She focused on the northern bank of the river that wound its way through this land. The ribbon of blue cut the forest in half and divided the two sides of the battle for the town that was only just beginning.

Red coats of the Brunian enemies on the northern bank. Black coats streaming in from the west and into the town on the southern bank.

Andrei could see most of the Brunian position. Pockets of trees obscured the area just above the bridge. The enemy artillery was well placed to harass the Kurakin approach. But Andrei knew his men would be able to fight through it and once his own cannons were in place, they would pound the Brunian defenses until they crumbled and the Kurakin took the bridge.

Andrei opened his eyes and returned to the ground. He took in a deep breath. The chill morning breeze smelled of gunpowder. It was a good day for battle.

"Push into the town." Andrei mounted his horse and nodded for the aides to carry the orders to his officers. "Take the square and begin to push the bridge. Our artillery will cover the movement."

The aides scattered. The Kurakin units around Andrei continued down their path towards the end of the forest and the open field before the town.

It would be tough to cross that field, but the Kurakin would do it. They could withstand artillery fire from a weak Brunian battalion. Then they would attack the bridge and force their way across over the bloody red coats of the enemy.

General Duroc would have his crossing. Andrei would give him his gateway to the rest of Erlon. Then Andrei would get his wolverine back and command the Scythes once more.

"Forward," Andrei shouted over the din of the march.

The next infantry units of Kurakin lurched forward. The front group broke into a run as they reached the open field. They charged towards the town and the cover of the houses as the Brunian artillery shells erupted around them.

Lauriston

Lauriston called Quatre, Mon, Desaix, and Lodi to him as the Erlonian army drew close to the town. The army had marched double time to make it to the battle before midday. The soldiers would be tired, but they had no choice but to dive right into the fight.

"The artillery won't make it in time, Lar." Quatre shook his head.

"I know. We'll have to do without." Lauriston scratched at the stubble on his cheeks.

What a horrible feeling. An army was exposed without artillery. He could see the doubt on the faces of the generals before him.

"The Kurakin artillery will need to focus on the Brunian positions. If they turn to us, we're only freeing up the Brunian defense." Lauriston needed to instill confidence in his officers, no matter how nervous he felt himself.

He stepped forward to the edge of the forest for a view of the town of Neuse. The fields between Lauriston and the town were open and freshly planted and sloped downward towards the river. It would be difficult to attack across.

At least the Erlonians would have surprise on their side.

The Kurakin poured in from the west down the main road. Many of their men had made it into the town already and would be bunkered in the homes against the Brunian artillery. The stone bridge was already contested and the Brunians held the northern bank as more and more black-coated Kurakin pressed forward.

The Brunian command looked to be up on the hill just above the bridge. Lauriston briefly wondered what General Pitt was thinking with the Kurakin rushing in on his soldiers and taking the brunt of his artillery in stride.

He must feel very alone. Lauriston and the Erlonians needed to help him.

To the east of the town, the forest stretched around the fields and ran all the way to the river bank. That would be good cover.

A plan formed in Lauriston's mind immediately.

He scanned over the field of battle once more.

Kurakin in the west. Brunians holding the bridge in the north. His main force to attack across the southern fields directly in front of him. The tree cover sat in the east unused.

Lauriston turned back to his generals.

"Mon," he said.

"Sir." The old general stepped forward.

"You units will take the eastern flank. Use the trees as cover. Our main attack will distract them, you should be able to get into the town before they know you're coming."

"Yes, sir." Mon nodded and looked off towards the eastern section of trees.

"The Lakmians will go with you." Lauriston nodded at Lodi and got a confident smile in return. Lodi was always ready for a fight.

"Quatre and I will push the main force across the field here," Lauriston continued. "Desaix, you harass the Kurakin that are still marching in from the west."

Lauriston looked at the town again. There was a spire to the Ascended One that shot up from the town's square in the center and stood twice as tall as any surrounding building. It looked like a stone castle turret from the olden ages.

Lauriston nodded towards the tower. "Use the spire as your reference point. We'll be in different positions for the whole attack. But our goal is to meet at that spire and the main town square."

"My sword will nail the Horde commander to the front of the Ascended One's house," Quatre said.

"My spear will beat you to it." Lodi smiled and winked at Quatre.

"Any questions?" Lauriston looked around at his men.

None of the generals spoke up.

"Good. You have your orders. Ascension be with our soldiers. Onward."

"Onward!"

The men answered in unison to Lauriston's last word. They saluted and split off towards their units. Lauriston made to turn back and watch the battle in the town again but thought of something at the last moment.

"Mon," he said and took a step after the elder general.

Mon stopped and faced the marshal.

"Protect Elisa, keep her with you." Lauriston put a hand on his old friend's shoulder.

"Of course, Lar. She's safe with me," Mon said.

Lauriston nodded once. Mon's eyes were focused and stern, like they'd been all those years ago at the beginning of Emperor Lannes's rise to power. The old warrior was fully back now.

Lauriston smiled. Mon saluted again and walked off to where his men and the princess waited with the rest of his part of the army.

The marshal of the last Erlonian army was now alone. The chaos of the growing battle echoed behind him.

A heavy sigh escaped Lauriston's mouth and he felt his shoulders drop. He was tired. Weary from the long flight from the Scythes and the double-time march to get to the town in time.

But a marshal never had time to rest. There was always another fight.

Lauriston stood still and watched the town and the smoke billowing up from destroyed homes and the gunfire over the bridge and chaos on the river banks. This was quite a battle.

It was time Lauriston's Erlonians joined the fray.

Elisa

Mon came back and distributed the orders to his officers and soldiers. Elisa stood with Mon and the men formed up to move through the trees in the east.

Waiting for the orders had been an exercise in nervous patience. The rumbling of gunfire was no longer a distant and foreign noise like it had been all those weeks ago on Mon's farm.

Elisa was the closest to a battle that she'd ever been.

The booming of the artillery shook the trees around her. It echoed in her ears. It pounded relentlessly and she was still well away from the center of this battle.

Although that was about to change.

They would flank the city using the forest as cover. Mon seemed hopeful with the plan and the soldiers were confident as well, especially with the Lakmian regiments marching with them.

Lodi led the column of Lakmians just to Elisa's left. They looked like shadows flitting from tree to tree in their dark green coats. The only thing that gave away their movement was the gleam off their bayonets or the spearheads on their backs.

The normal Erlonian soldiers moved slightly less gracefully than their Lakmian counterparts but still stealthily enough. The men stepped quietly through the trees and the booming of the battle came closer and closer.

They stopped a hundred feet away from the edge of the forest. Elisa could just make out the top of the Ascended One's spire in the middle of the town through the treetops.

Elisa was ready.

Despite the ground shaking under her feet. Despite the nerves she felt. Despite her hands shaking slightly. She was ready for her first battle.

The soldiers stood steady behind her. The strength of the Erlonians welled around her and were ready to fight for their country.

"Stay with me when we reach the houses," Mon said.

He stood to her left and stared at the town through trees. No movement could be seen in or around the homes. It seemed the Kurakin were focused on the bridge and hadn't seen the Erlonian approach.

"Are you afraid?" Mon turned his head to look down at her.

"No."

Elisa wasn't lying. She didn't feel fear at the moment.

Mon nodded and turned back to the scene in front of them.

Elisa looked over her left shoulder. Over the heads of the Lakmian regiments were more trees hiding their approach. Beyond that stretch of forest would be the rest of the army preparing to attack across the open southern field. Once they attacked, Mon would order this group forward to execute the flank.

And then the fighting would begin.

Movement caught Elisa's eye. She had to focus on the spot where she'd seen it. Slowly, she saw the outline of a Lakmian perched on a high branch above Lodi's soldiers.

He wasn't dressed like the soldiers, but his tail was clearly curling back and forth below the branch he sat on.

It was Elisa's guide.

He smiled and waved at her. She nodded in return and he nodded back.

Elisa glanced at Mon and found the general hadn't noticed anything. None of the other soldiers seemed to have spotted the vision, as they were all focused forward.

Seeing the guide helped to fully ease the last bits of her nerves. She had her friends fighting with her and the strength of her father's army around her and the guide watching over her. They would win this fight and then continue on to fight the war.

It was time to join the battle. She glanced at the houses just through the trees once more and everything was still.

Elisa turned back and saw the guide had disappeared from his perch. Lodi led the Lakmians in their pre-fighting movements and the silence before the attack echoed around the soldiers.

As soon as Lauriston started his attack, the game would be on. Elisa fingered the silver pistols at her hips and looked forward. The imperial seal was cold against her skin and she traced the outlines of the symbol and thought on her father. He wouldn't be afraid at this moment and she wouldn't be either.

She was ready to fight with her friends for the last bits of his empire. She was ready to fight for Erlon.

Lauriston

Lauriston stood on the very edge of the trees and stared down at the town. The Kurakin were still marching men into the town. Their artillery had established a position on the river bank in the west and now answered the Brunian cannons.

Houses were on fire. Smoke billowed up to the sky. The towering spire to the Ascended One stood tall in the center of it all.

Lauriston turned his head to the east. He couldn't see Mon and Lodi's units. He had to trust they would be in position. Lauriston's own push up the center would draw the enemy's attention and ensure Mon could get into the Kurakin flank.

The plan was a sound one. It'd been thrown together quickly, but Lauriston trusted it to work for his men. He wouldn't second-guess himself this time.

There were bodies on the bridge on the far side of the town. Red and black coats alike were piled on the edge of the bridge. There was a line cut down the middle where the two sides cleared a path to continue fighting. The Brunians barely held on.

It was up to Lauriston and the Erlonians to relieve the pressure on the Brunians. They wouldn't be able to hold off this Kurakin attack forever.

"Form up," Lauriston said over his shoulder. He heard the order being echoed up and down the line of men behind him.

The din of the battle seemed to pause and hang over his head. It was a long moment, as if Lauriston was stuck in time.

The marshal drew his sword and raised it above his head.

"Forward!"

The lines of Erlonians marched forward. Lauriston stepped out of the cover of the forest and into the afternoon sunlight. His boots sank into the recently tilled dirt.

Drums beat the time for the men to march to. Lauriston briefly wondered if the Kurakin would hear the drums over the roar of their battle.

It didn't matter. If they didn't see Lauriston's attack coming, they would soon feel it.

The Erlonian lines straightened once they emerged out of the trees. Quatre controlled the flank on Lauriston's right.

"Onward!" came the cheer from a unit directly behind the marshal.

Lauriston waved his sword in the air to praise the spirit of the men and more cheers came. The time for stealth was over. It was time to attack.

"Onward, Erlon! Onward, Emperor!"

The cheers grew even louder. Lauriston let the light gleam off his sword in the air. There was no time for a speech, but he didn't need to rally the men. They were already roaring.

The marshal of Erlon dropped his sword down and pressed forward. The soldiers followed him. They picked up speed slowly and were soon at a run.

Lauriston let out a yell of his own as they charged towards the houses and the Kurakin beyond. He was drowned out by the cheers and the thundering charge of his men.

"Onward, Erlon!"

The Erlonians flung themselves into the battle.

Chapter 28

Battle is easy to make glorious until you're in the middle of one.

Select Sermons
Baptist VII, 21st Tribune to the Ascended One

Pitt

It was a disaster.

The Brunians held the bridge, but only by the last few bits left in their strength. Pitt knew the Horde would break his defenses soon.

The enemy had too many men. There weren't enough Brunians to stop them.

Pitt paced on the hilltop overlooking the bank of the river. The town and the bridge and the swarming Horde army sat below him.

The Brunian line held against the latest Kurakin attack on the crossing. Pitt's artillery pounded the houses on the western side of town and the adjacent field. The Kurakin cannons answered. Their volleys were an octave deeper and came with less space between.

Pitt shook his head.

"Send the Fourth down to the bridge," he said to an aide. "How's the First recovering?"

"They're fairly beat up, sir." An officer stepped up beside him.

"They'll need to reinforce the bridge again soon. They won't have time to keep resting."

The officer nodded and didn't argue back. Everyone on the command hill knew how dire the situation was.

Pitt had reached the town and been dropped off by Desaix less than a day before the Kurakin army appeared. Pitt had ridden into the town and found the Brunian soldiers on the bridge. He'd set out to prepare for the arrival of the Erlonians, not the Horde.

The town hadn't changed much in the weeks since Pitt was last here. No citizens were around. The houses still sat deserted. The market square around the Ascended One's spire was empty and silent.

The quiet was a far cry from the chaos that now engulfed the little town.

Pitt had set up the defenses and taken control of the Brunian units present on the northern bank. He'd explained the approach of Lauriston's army and the need to treat with the Erlonians. There'd been trouble getting the Brunian officers to understand the need for the alliance.

Not that it mattered anymore.

Now everything was done for. All of Pitt's efforts, all the luck he'd needed to survive the Kurakin betrayal and the flight from the Scythes in the woods. All of it was for nothing.

Pitt had failed again. He had always been a failure.

He would die right here trying to hold this little bridge. The Horde would break the defenses and then overwhelm the Brunian hill before Lauriston and the Erlonians could march north.

It was all but over.

"Keep the artillery on the western houses." Pitt looked at an aide and the boy nodded and ran off.

The orders felt useless, but Pitt continued. The action of saying the words made things feel less hopeless.

Pitt shook his head. He shouldn't think like that. A general needed to be positive no matter what the situation. He'd seen that firsthand from watching Marshal Lauriston lead his group of Erlonians away from the Scythes chasing them in the previous weeks.

Pitt nodded to himself as he watched more Kurakin enemies swarm into the town. He needed to somehow stay positive.

The Brunians still had the high ground. Pitt maybe couldn't win this battle, but he could make the Horde pay dearly for taking the bridge.

"Sir!"

More shouts followed this first outburst. Pitt looked around for the source and saw multiple aides and officers pointing south.

Pitt followed their outstretched arms and looked south. Many homes sat smoldering. Black-uniformed Kurakin swarmed up and down the streets.

But the shouts weren't directed at the town. The men pointed beyond, to the fields south of the town and the tree line in the distance.

An army was forming up to attack.

An army clad in blue coats.

"It's him." Pitt said the words too quietly to be heard over the battle and the shouts of the men. "It's the Erlonians. They've come to help us."

The aides quieted down. Some exchanged confused glances. Pitt had informed his officers of the Erlonians' desire to help Brun hold the bridge and the town, but he hadn't explained things to the full army.

"Erlonians, sir?" one of the aides said.

Pitt found himself smiling wildly. He felt like jumping up and down and cheering.

"Marshal Lauriston and his army."

None of the confused looks from the boys went away. A few of the aides were watching the rows of blue coats with wide eyes, thinking another enemy had come to attack the bridge.

"We're really done for now," one of them said.

"No." Pitt's smile dropped and he looked at the aides. He pointed to the black army in the west. "The Horde is the enemy. The Erlonians fight them too. They are here to help us hold the town."

Nothing changed about the boys' expressions. Pitt could understand how difficult of a situation this was to grasp, especially for the common soldier, but the battle raging right in front of them should make the shifting allegiances slightly easier to swallow.

The Brunians had been doomed. And now they were saved by their former enemies.

"Shift the artillery." Pitt nodded to the second artillery aide. "Have them focus on the Horde guns. Keep them from focusing on the Erlonian advance."

Pitt also didn't want to be firing into the town as the Erlonians attacked. He didn't want to hit Lauriston's men.

The aide stared at Lauriston for a second before regaining his composure and running off.

"We can win this fight now. This bridge won't fall." Pitt looked at the others and his smile returned. Most men still looked too confused to move. Orders would help with that.

Pitt started in on his new commands. He'd reinforce the bridge and attack the Kurakin cannons with his own artillery. That would give time for Lauriston's attack to hit. Then the battle could be flipped and the new allies could push back on the Kurakin and run the Horde out of town.

Pitt yelled out his orders and the aides and officers dispersed to relay them to his soldiers. The sun shone a little brighter as Pitt turned back and watched Lauriston's army start their charge across the open field towards the Kurakin.

Lauriston

Fear was present even for the greatest of warriors. Marshals were supposed to be the best of the best. The strongest of the empire.

But Lauriston still felt fear in every fight.

The ground exploded in front of him as he ran for the town. Dirt rained down around him and he came out the other side of a wall of smoke from the exploding shells.

His men followed him. Quatre charged on his flank with the rest of the army. The Erlonians approached the first houses of the town at full speed before the Kurakin could fully focus on them.

The Kurakin responded quickly to the flank, far quicker than expected. They'd already gotten off a few artillery volleys. More were to come, but it wouldn't be enough. Lauriston would reach the houses with minimal casualties.

This will be a true fight, Lauriston found himself thinking as another cannonball exploded nearby.

He yelled and waved the men forward. Quatre did the same, leading the men on the right and the Erlonians swarmed farther down the field.

Lauriston couldn't see beyond Quatre's men to their far-right flank. He hoped Mon was protecting Elisa. He hoped that those units were already in the cover of the houses and pressing the Horde flank. If they were, and if Lauriston could smash through the Kurakin force in front of him, his plan could work.

A cannon ball landed between the regiments, directly in line with his view of Quatre. Lauriston's stomach dropped. Quatre was gone from his view. It had looked like a direct hit.

But the dirt fell back down and the smoke cleared and Quatre still ran even with the marshal. The general was unscathed and charging at the Kurakin still.

More cannon shot fell on the line of attack and blew holes in the Erlonian lines and Lauriston pushed the men farther. They had to reach the houses and the cover they offered.

The Kurakin infantry had formed a quick line with a small group of soldiers on the edge of town. It wouldn't be enough. Lauriston could envelop them; his men were moving too fast for the enemy and the Kurakin couldn't protect their exposed flanks.

Lauriston slowed and sheathed the sword he'd used to start the charge. He threw a hand up in the air and fell to one knee and brought his pistol up. The men behind stopped and raised muskets in one motion.

The volley tore into the Horde line. Black-coated bodies tumbled forward to the ground.

"Onward!" Lauriston yelled, diving into the smoke between the two sides.

The Erlonians echoed the cheer and closed the final gap on the run. The fight erupted with the clang of steel.

Lauriston drew his sword again and crashed his shoulder into a Kurakin soldier and swung his blade at the head of another. The rest of his men hit right after him and the entire battle fell away from his vision. The view in his mind of the entire attack plan disappeared and there was only the crush of men directly around him. It was only Lauriston and his sword and the Kurakin soldiers unfortunate enough to be in his way.

Lauriston's blade came up just in time as a Kurakin ax swung at him. He parried the swing and stepped aside to drag his blade along the side of the enemy.

"Onward!" Lauriston yelled over the din of battle, pressing farther into the fight.

He cut down two more Kurakin before the enemy formation broke. A cannon ball careened through the battle and threw bodies into the air.

The full battle came back to Lauriston as his men ran after the retreating Kurakin. He urged his formation forward. Quatre would do the same on the right. They had to reach the houses and gain cover. They had to get away from the open field and the deadly cannons. They had to press their advantage from the surprise attack and disrupt the Horde pressure on the bridge.

Elisa

The trees hid their approach until the last minute. Elisa heard the attack against the Brunians holding the bridge booming in front of them. Explosions began to sound on their left as well.

"Their artillery reacted quickly," Mon said behind Elisa in a low voice. They crept closer to the edge of the forest and the first houses. "Let's get into the town and flank any defense the Horde sets up."

The formation moved quickly. Lodi's regiment of Lakmians were out in front on their left. The Lakmian soldiers moved smoothly and silently between the trees.

The first outlines of houses appeared as the edge of the forest approached.

The sudden eruption of gunfire from the houses took Elisa by surprise. Musket shot crashed into the trees. Men fell all around. Her heart ramped up to full speed and fear finally gripped her.

Mon yelled and waved the men forward. Elisa could see Lodi's group charging the row of houses. Mon moved the rest of the attack towards the right flank.

A second volley hit them. Elisa heard screams of dying men. The smoke obscured her vision. Mon ordered a volley of their own and Elisa dropped to one knee.

The Erlonian shots went over her head. Elisa added one pistol shot. She aimed at the window of the closest house. The glass exploded.

A body slumped out of the broken window. Black coats fell dead in an alleyway between houses. Other Kurakin jumped over the bodies and fled back into the town.

"Onward!"

Mon yelled for the Erlonians to press forward.

Elisa stuck with the old general like she'd been told. Through the smoke on her left, she saw Lodi take down a Kurakin soldier with a running thrust of his spear.

The Lakmians were surrounding the first house. Mon had his unit perform a similar maneuver around the neighbor. Soldiers pushed their way inside but found the house was empty.

Elisa watched the street from the outside corner. She saw movement on the roof of a house farther into the town. A black hat shifted up and a Kurakin soldier raised a musket to fire. Elisa proved faster and fired her other pistol at the man's head.

Her aim was true.

The bullet entered the soldier's forehead and blood spurted and the dead body tumbled off the roof.

Mon emerged out of the house behind her and yelled for her to keep moving.

"Onward!" He waved for all his men to press into the houses and grabbed Elisa's arm. She was pulled away from the sight of her first kill of the battle.

They pushed up to the next house and found less resistance. Elisa saw some black coats running away from them down the streets. The Lakmians were still in front and moved after the fleeing enemy on the adjacent line of houses.

"We've got to keep moving." Mon pointed men forward. He sent lines of men to either side of the next house. "Keep taking buildings. Keep pushing forward."

Elisa could barely hear him over the sounds of the battle. She leaned against the next house and reloaded her pistols and felt the wall vibrating with the rumbles of explosions. The cannons, even on the far side of the town, were deafening.

Pitt

The artillery raged from the hill to Pitt's right. His long guns pounded the enemy position.

The Kurakin didn't answer. They were now fully focused on the Erlonian attack.

They had to be.

Lauriston had reached the town. Pitt lost sight of the battle through the smoke. The battles lines were hidden in the houses anyway.

"Push up two batteries on the far right, on that bank there." Pitt pointed to the west for his artillery officer's benefit. "See if you can draw some of the fire away and rake the side of the town."

If the Kurakin weren't going to attack his artillery, he could push them to a more forward position. The Brunians needed to weaken the Horde guns to ease the barrages on Lauriston's men.

The Erlonians would take the pressure off the bridge and give the Brunians a much-needed rest. But Pitt would have to do all he could from this bank to help Lauriston break the Kurakin in the town.

Movement caught his eye on the opposite side of town. The eastern houses were engulfed in a battle too.

"What's that there?" The aides had spotted it too.

Pitt smiled as he realized the marshal's full plan.

Lauriston was a genius.

"An Erlonian flank," he said over his shoulder.

They were flanking the town from the east. They used the cover of the trees to get in close and now the Horde retreated from the buildings and Pitt could see the Erlonians moving from house to house.

That flank would help Lauriston's main push.

"Make sure the Fourth holds the bridge. We still have a role to play in this battle, don't forget it." Pitt pointed to get the aides and officers to focus again.

The bridge had to hold or all this was for nothing.

Pitt would support Lauriston's attack as best as he could. But the Brunians still had to keep the bridge from breaking as well.

Elisa

Elisa helped take three more houses. The Kurakin continued to fall back in front of them. There hadn't been much resistance since the initial exchange of volleys and she'd only fired one more pistol shot since the beginning.

Mon's voice was already hoarse from the strain of shouting orders.

"We'll choose a line to hold soon," he said to her as they crouched and looked out the windows of the latest house.

"Sir!" A messenger came through a doorway.

"Yes, soldier?"

"From General Lodi, sir. No contact with Quatre's group yet, but he and Lauriston should be in the town pushing forward."

"Good, thank you, sir. Tell Lodi we'll push up a little farther."

Mon called for the other soldiers in the house to move forward. The first out the door was struck in the leg by a Kurakin musket ball and fell over screaming. Mon was next out and stepped over the man and fired down the street.

The rest of the soldiers filed out and took cover under a half stone wall. Elisa joined them and fired off a shot at the black hats crouched behind various cover points in the street beyond. The injured soldier continued to scream as he was dragged back into the house.

The street was filled with smoke and scattered bodies. More musket smoke poured from the houses and walls that the Kurakin used as a defense. Elisa saw the outline of the Ascended One's spire through the smoke over the far homes. It was directly in line with their attack path.

Movement caught the corner of her eye over her left shoulder. She turned and watched a figure sprinting along the roof of the row of houses across the street.

It was Lodi.

The Lakmian's tail trailed behind him as his light feet approached the edge of the roof. He hurled himself off the house and cocked his spear arm back. As he descended towards the street, he hurled the weapon down into a group of Kurakin. They scattered as if a cannonball had hit them.

More Lakmian infantry filed out of the houses and down the street. Lodi pulled his spear out of a dead enemy and pressed forward with his men.

Elisa saw the next Kurakin line falter. They wanted no part of the Lakmians warriors. They gave up ground to avoid fighting against the spears that chased them.

"Volley, boys! Up and fire!" Mon yelled.

Elisa rose up with the rest of the men and fired her pistol down the street after the retreating Kurakin. Many of the enemy fell.

"Onward!"

The men obeyed.

They ran down the street and reached the next line of buildings. Elisa knelt against the wall of a house and kept her eyes forward, waiting for a Kurakin to poke his head around one of the buildings.

She saw Lodi, standing in the open street, motioning something to Mon.

"He thinks we should hold this line," Mon said from behind Elisa. The general shrugged. "I guess we'll do that, then."

Mon pointed the men into positions. The soldiers shifted and moved up to be even with Lodi and the Lakmians.

The continuous pounding of the cannon fire had turned into background noise for Elisa. She'd grown used to it. But as she reloaded her pistol and Mon finished his latest orders, the rumble changed.

She wouldn't be ignoring the noise for much longer.

The rolling concussion from the cannons now sounded different. It was louder and more clear now. Elisa actually heard the whistle of the balls as they traveled.

An explosion near Lodi in the street confirmed what Elisa's mind had only just realized. Dirt was flung up into the air and the force of the explosion ripped down the street.

The Kurakin artillery was now focused on their part of the town.

Elisa saw a cannonball clearly, as if in slow motion, bounce down the street and pass by Lodi's legs. The Lakmian barely flinched as the ball exploded into a wall behind him.

"Cover!" Mon yelled.

Elisa ducked. Lodi walked calmly towards his side of the street. The Erlonians pressed up against the walls of the homes and ducked their heads.

More cannon fire. More whistling and explosions. The volleys came faster and faster and the Erlonian position was engulfed in explosions.

Lauriston

Lauriston's troops had gained the first row of houses on the southern side of town. He could feel the momentum of his army. As if they were attacking downhill. He had to press and keep moving forward.

Lauriston grabbed a messenger. "Send word to Quatre. See if he's made contact with Mon's left. But tell him to keep moving forward no matter what. We must envelop them."

The messenger moved off and kept behind cover along the right flank.

"Let's push up." Lauriston waved the rest of the men forward.

He watched his men file around the house and push on to the next structure.

"Marshal, sir! Messenger!" a voice came through the din of battle.

Lauriston turned and saw a horse coming across the field at full gallop. The man dismounted before the horse fully stopped and began the message immediately.

"Still more Kurakin, sir." The messenger was completely out of breath. "Coming up the road."

"Catch your breath, soldier." Lauriston kept his voice calm. A cannonball exploded on the other side of the house they hid behind and made everyone flinch.

The messenger took two deep breaths before continuing. "More Kurakin, sir. Desaix is confirming, but there are more troops moving down the road."

"Reinforcements? How many?" Lauriston couldn't see the road in the west anymore. The houses blocked his view.

"We don't know yet, sir."

"Okay, thank you, soldier. Tell Desaix to alert me when he confirms."

The messenger remounted and rode back out of the town and up the slope of the field towards the forest.

Lauriston's mind went to work. His strategy was working, everything had moved along as planned, but if Desaix thought that the Kurakin had sizable reinforcements in the west, there would be trouble.

That could be a big issue.

Lauriston trusted Desaix's instincts. Emperor Lannes had always said to trust the cavalry. They were a general's eyes in the thick of battle.

Now the explosions and screams of the battle faded away from the marshal's mind. His thoughts were fully back on the strategy of the attacks. He had to think on the larger picture and how he could win the fight for his side.

The Erlonians could still break the Kurakin that were already in the town. That much was clear. But if the enemy reinforcements on the road were big enough, his line could be counter-attacked and surrounded. They'd be outflanked and trapped on this side of the river.

Lauriston stood up. He looked east along his lines in the town. Quatre was still pushing up. Mon's flank would be just beyond. The attack was working.

They could keep pressing and hope for the best. Or they could alter the strategy and make a bold move to change the battle.

Lauriston ran through the risks in his head. Doubts filled his mind as they always did. He shook them away and focused.

Another cannonball exploded close by. The sounds of a volley echoed off the walls of the homes. Musket pops and screams carried on the wind with the battle smoke. The ground shook from the fighting as the Erlonians pressed farther into the town.

Lauriston watched the men closest to him. They looked to him for direction. For their next orders.

The battle would hinge on his next decision.

His head cleared. He made his choice. Lauriston knew what he had to do.

Chapter 29

In the midst of battle, a shift in plan is the hardest to execute and should be avoided at all costs.

Maxims of War, Entry Twenty-Four
Emperor Gerald Lannes

Lauriston

"We've made contact with Mon and Lodi." Quatre had soot caked on the right side of his face but was otherwise unharmed.

Lauriston and the general met inside a house between their two sections of the attack. He could see the top of the spire to the Ascended One through the northern facing window. The din of the fighting shook the ground under their feet as they talked.

Lauriston stared at the broken furniture strewn on the floor of the house. Smoke drifted through a cannonball-sized hole in the western-facing wall.

Quatre looked at the gray sky through the hole. "They're being shelled pretty good, but they're holding a line. We're on their flank."

"Good." Lauriston nodded. "Look, I've got news from Desaix. He says there are more Kurakin coming up the road."

"Shit." Quatre's eyes left the cannonball hole. He spat on the floor.

A particularly close artillery explosion rumbled the house, but Lauriston didn't flinch. "Yeah. We can envelop the Kurakin here."

"But then we'll be flanked by the reserves."

"Exactly." Lauriston twisted up his mouth in thought.

"What do we do, then?" Quatre met Lauriston's eyes.

The marshal chose to stick with his plan. He hoped it was the right choice.

"You push up and hold Mon's flank." Lauriston pointed east through the broken rooms of the home. "I'm going to attack up the middle and turn the Kurakin. I won't push on their right. If their middle breaks, the whole group will retreat west. We'll push them up the road back and never give their reinforcements a chance to fight."

Quatre nodded his understanding.

"We take the central square. That spire." Lauriston pointed out the northern-facing window to the tower in the center of town. "We meet Mon and Lodi there and then push the Kurakin away from the bridge."

Quatre nodded again. Lauriston saluted and bid Quatre good luck and the general marched through the hole in the wall and back off to his side of the battle.

Lauriston stepped out through the main door and moved in the opposite direction. He reached his men and found them both in good cover and spirits.

Expectant eyes looked up at Lauriston. He met them with confidence and spoke clearly.

"All right, let's push onward. Towards that spire."

Pitt

Bodies piled up. Both black and red coats combined to recolor the stones of the bridge. Men fought in a knee-deep pool of blood and pieces of their dead friends.

"Send the Third down to relieve the Fourth." Pitt kept his eyes forward and focused on the carnage. He had to yell the orders over the rumbling artillery.

"Yes, sir."

A messenger was sent off and Pitt watched his orders carried out. The Third moved down to fill in the spaces needed around the bridge. The remains of the Fourth shifted back in a ragged-looking group.

The Horde attack never relented. Pitt was numb to it all.

They fought Lauriston's men in the town beyond and pushed against the Brunians on the bridge at the same time. Their artillery had been beaten back but still lobbed shot into the southernmost houses of the town. The enemy had also started hurling shot back across the river towards Pitt's own men.

The spire to the Ascended One jutted up above the smoke on the other side of the bridge. The Horde formed under it for another bridge attack. Beyond would be Lauriston's attack, but Pitt couldn't see the Erlonians anymore. For all he knew they were bogged down in the houses and wouldn't make it to help the Brunians on the bridge.

"Sir, an ammo update from artillery."

The aide's words pulled Pitt's eyes away from the carnage in the town. He turned and was prepared to receive the report, but a horrible sound interrupted the exchange.

A Kurakin cannonball overshot the main Brunian defense and bounded up the hill. It bounced twice and sent black dirt into the air as it shot towards the command horses.

The ball took an aide directly in the chest.

In one instant, the man sat straight-backed on his horse. In another, the body of a dying horse flailed on the ground. Only the legs of the aide were still strapped in the stirrups.

There was no scream. There were only pieces of the man's body thrown like shrapnel among the officers.

Blood splattered on the surrounding group and the men struggled to control their mounts. Pitt's own horse swung around and wanted to run up the hill.

"Sir, we should get out of range." The suggestion was eerily calm. Pitt knew the man's steadiness was more from shock at the gruesome scene than anything.

"We'll move back. Hold the ammo report until we relocate." Pitt nodded and took a final glance at the dying horse as an officer fired a pistol into the animal's head to relieve the suffering.

Pitt took another look at the hazy outline of the town beyond and the bridge with the pile of bodies and the tall spike of the spire. The Brunian Third Brigade fired a volley at an approaching Kurakin infantry column. Another unit formed a bayonet wall for the next enemy charge.

Pitt turned away and moved up the hill out of range of the enemy guns. All he could do now was pray they could find a way to hold out. And hope Marshal Lauriston's Erlonians would succeed in surrounding the Kurakin before the bridge defenses broke.

Elisa

The cannon fire came in quick succession. One minute the din of battle would be low, only a buzzing in Elisa's ears, and the next it became a cacophony of explosions. Metal and wood flew at them and Elisa and the soldiers cowered behind walls they hoped were thick enough.

Elisa crouched behind a wall running between two houses. It was half the height of a man and plenty thick. Most of the unit used it for cover, with the remaining soldiers spread out between the two houses. The Lakmians surrounded the next block over.

"They're going to push us soon." Mon passed by her section of wall in a crouch. He shouted orders to the men in the far house and circled back to her position. Muskets poked out of windows and over walls towards the Kurakin side of the fight.

"Hold here, then?" Talking made Elisa's fear seem farther away, as did reloading and checking her pistols.

"Yeah." Mon looked at her.

Elisa didn't answer. She kept her eyes on the silver of her pistol as she rammed the next ball down the barrel.

Mon seemed to think this meant she was okay. He nodded and moved off. His prediction of a push proved true almost immediately.

There was a yell from over the wall and the Erlonians around Elisa started firing. She poked her head up and saw a group of Kurakin running up the street. Four of the enemy fell from the Erlonian volley, but there were plenty more.

Elisa fired both her pistols at the group and saw two men stumble to the ground. One looked dead and the other screamed and writhed about, holding his thigh.

She ducked back down and focused on reloading as the crack of enemy musket balls hitting the other side of the wall returned. To her right there was a commotion and she looked up before she could finish with the first pistol. Three Kurakin came over the wall and fell on two Erlonian soldiers.

Elisa called for help and ran towards the struggle. Other soldiers reacted, but she was the closest.

Two enemies were already locked in a struggle with the unfortunate Erlonian soldiers. The third turned to meet Elisa.

He had a long beard down to the second button of his coat and his eyes were dark black pools. His sword was longer than her own height. It looked sharp and deadly.

She drew her own cutlass and attacked. The motions and steps came back easily to her. She felt quick and smooth. Fear fell away to the bottom of her mind and there was only the sword in front of her as she fought to stay alive.

The Kurakin underestimated her. That was his downfall.

He swung down with his sword using two hands in an attempt to end things quickly. Elisa sidestepped and brought her cutlass up. She spun and used her turn as force to rake the enemy's side with the blade.

She executed the move Lodi had taught her on the trail to perfection.

The Kurakin stumbled forward and almost fell over his own blade. He regained his balance and clutched at his side. Elisa quickly pressed her advantage.

Her practice in the palace and in the woods around Mon's farm and on the trail with Lodi flooded her body. All the work paid off in a natural and deadly motion.

She slashed at the man's back and ripped open the black coat. The Kurakin turned and brought his sword up again. But before it could be fully raised, there was a gash across his throat. He gurgled and fell over.

His eyes were full of shock. He hadn't even seen the killing swipe from her sword.

The rest of the Erlonian soldiers streamed past her and finished the other two Kurakin off. Elisa stood still and watched the life fade from the black pools of her enemy's eyes. His hand tried to keep the blood inside his throat, but he was already finished.

Mon's yells brought her out of her stupor. He called for the men to rally back to the wall. More Kurakin had reached the defensive line.

A new group of enemies came over the barrier back where Elisa was positioned before. Her half-reloaded pistol sat in the grass at their feet.

Musket shot erupted from behind Elisa. Acrid smoke filled her nose. Mon stepped in front of her. He dropped his pistol and drew his sword.

An enemy faced them and fired his musket from the hip. More shots came from around Elisa as the Erlonians responded to the attack. Some Kurakin fell and others charged. Elisa and Mon ran forward to meet them.

A bayonet thrust came for Elisa's stomach. She turned it away with a swipe of her sword. Mon's weapon came over the top of her parry and sliced the enemy's face open. Mon stepped in front of her and fought the next enemy sword to sword.

Two more Kurakin came over the wall behind Mon. They stood on the top over the battle and made to leap into the fray. A Lakmian spear took one in the chest and sent him back the way he'd come.

But the second had his eyes on Mon's back as the general fought another enemy.

Elisa brought her sword up as the enemy jumped with his ax raised. He didn't see her. The tip of her blade slid easily into his stomach. His momentum did the rest of the work for her.

Elisa crumpled under the dead enemy. His weight pressed down on her arm and dragged her downward into the mud.

Rough hands grabbed her shoulders. She was pulled upward and found Mon holding her. Kurakin lay bleeding on the ground everywhere and the other Erlonian soldiers finished off the last of the Horde attack.

"Okay, Princess?" Mon's hands turned her head from side to side, looking for injuries.

"I'm fine." Elisa's voice was a croak. She coughed and repeated herself more clearly. "I'm fine."

Mon hugged her. It was a quick but strong motion and gave energy back to Elisa's limbs. The sounds of the battle still raged in the distance, but for a brief moment everything fell away and Elisa felt safe.

Then Mon let go and bent down to retrieve her sword from the dead Kurakin. Elisa's hand went to the front of her jacket and she felt something warm covering her.

Was it mud from the ground? She looked down and found her hand red. Blood.

Had she been injured?

Elisa couldn't feel any wound. There wasn't a hole in her jacket.

She realized where the blood had come from when Mon stood back up with her sword. The front of his uniform was soaked.

She had a brief hope it was from the enemies he'd killed. But even as she thought it she knew it wasn't true.

The world broke. The battle was lost around her. Mon's expression froze in her mind as his hand found the patch of blood spreading across his shirt.

The memory of one of the first enemies firing a musket from the hip struck her. It'd been right after Mon had stepped in front of her. Before they'd charged the second Kurakin wave.

Mon looked down at his hand as if it was someone else's. He winced and staggered slightly to his left. Elisa was frozen in place.

"Mon!"

Lodi swept by Elisa and caught Mon as he went to one knee. Elisa's sword fell back to the mud and she finally moved. She lunged forward to help Lodi.

They leaned Mon back in the mud. Lodi rolled a Kurakin body out of the way.

"Back to the wall. Defensive positions!" Lodi called to the men around them.

The soldiers stared at Mon as they moved back to defend their position. Lodi looked back down and pressed on Mon's stomach.

"Damn." Mon's voice was hollow. Spittle of blood gurgled up from his throat.

"Quiet now," Lodi said. "Keep your breath."

The Lakmian ripped open the general's coat. The undershirt was already drenched with dark blood.

Elisa felt tears on her cheeks. Mon smiled up at her and raised his hand off the ground. She gripped it in her own.

"You'll be fine, Mon. Just breathe." Lodi pulled medical tools from his bundle and inspected the wound. "Elisa, I've got this, we need you on the wall. Keep the men focused."

Elisa didn't want to leave. She wanted to help save Mon. She wanted to stay holding his trembling hand.

But Lodi's look told her to go.

There were more yells of charging Kurakin coming. "I can handle this, Elisa. We need you back there," Lodi said. Mon looked her in the eyes and nodded his agreement. She squeezed his hand a last time and forced herself to her feet.

She ran back to the wall and grabbed her pistols. She reloaded with numb hands.

It took all her energy to not look back to where Mon lay in the mud. She finished with the pistols and fired at a group of enemies over the wall. She bent back down to reload as more of the Horde poured up the street towards their position.

Soldiers yelled. Smoke billowed around her. She glanced back to where the Lakmian knelt over the old general and more tears came to her eyes before smoke and soldiers obscured her view of the sad scene.

Lauriston

Lauriston pushed forward with his regiments but met a wall of Kurakin hunkered down in houses on the outskirts of the town's square and at the base of the spire.

He turned down a street and found two cannons pointing down the alley at him. They fired, but Lauriston ducked his men around to cover. The explosions shattered a neighboring building.

"We won't go that way, then." Lauriston shrugged to his men.

He looked around. They would have to flank the gun position. He could go back and try a different street, but that would be a long way around. His eyes fell on the windows of the house they hid behind.

"Through there." He nodded the soldiers towards the closest window.

He gave a hand signal to the men across the street. They would do the same maneuver parallel with Lauriston's own group.

The soldiers helped each other through the windows and through the house to the other side. Lauriston found a path that led through a garden.

Another idea came to him.

He reached into his pack and pulled out two of the napthas they'd taken off the Scythe dead during their journey north. He looked at the men and got grins of understanding back.

Lauriston crept up to the edge of the road. A soldier lit both fuses for him. The sparks danced around his hands. He took a quick look around the corner to sight the guns and threw both bombs one after the other.

When the explosions went off, he flung himself out into the streets. The enemy was surrounded by smoke. Kurakin were sprawled on the ground. One officer was still standing and Lauriston's pistol shot took him in the forehead.

Lauriston charged into the smoke and heard the Erlonian yells around him. He stabbed down into the stomach of a Kurakin on the ground. The enemy position was overrun.

Beyond the smoke of the exploded cannons, Lauriston saw an open square. The entire Kurakin regiment was falling back. His Erlonians were pressing in on all sides. The spire to the Ascended One rose above them.

"All right, we'll move up now," Lauriston said to himself.

He yelled out the orders and they were passed back through the part of the town they'd just taken. His army fell in behind him.

"Pursue them." Lauriston pointed towards the square and the fleeing Kurakin. "Force them out of the city, make them run back west."

"Onward!"

The soldiers flew forward with battle cries. Lauriston stayed in place and thought through the rest of the battle. He wanted to make sure he kept the momentum on his side. There couldn't be a mistake with the approaching enemy reinforcements. The Kurakin in the town had to break completely to make the reinforcements useless.

Lauriston's mind could see the positions as if he was a Scythe hawk in the sky. They'd turned this portion of the town, they needed the rest to break and run now. The enemy center was breaking, but the bridge beyond the square was still under heavy assault. Lauriston needed the entire Kurakin attack to break. He needed General Pitt and the Brunians to push across the bridge and finish the rout.

The marshal's aides reached him. One held the flag of the Erlonian army on a pole. Lauriston took it without a word and sprinted off across the square and left his confused-looking aides in his wake.

The large door to the spire of the Ascended One stood open. The stairwell inside wound up around the walls and Lauriston took the steps two at a time. The flag streamed behind him.

He was out of breath when he burst through the top door and out onto the platform that stood high above the battle in the town below.

The Kurakin cannons had ceased and the last of their smoke blew away to the west. He could see the fighting on the bridge. He could see the eastern part of town still engulfed in fighting from Mon's flank. And he could see his own men chasing the Kurakin and turning them west out of the town.

Lauriston waved the flag above his head in big sweeping motions. His aides started to cheer from the square below and the soldiers echoed them across the square as more and more men noticed the marshal high above them.

"Onward!"

"Onward, Erlon! Onward, Marshal! Onward, Emperor!"

"Onward, soldiers of Erlon!"

The cheering passed through the town and carried over the gunfire and the fighting. Lauriston kept waving the flag and yelled with his troops. They needed to push on. They needed the entire allied army to turn the Kurakin attack before more enemies arrived.

Pitt

Pitt saw the shift in the battle. Kurakin began to flow out the western side of town and back up the road. The Brunian cannons were positioned perfectly to rake the retreat.

He almost felt bad ordering the artillery to fire. The Horde was fleeing. They were helpless. Many didn't even have their muskets anymore.

But he remembered the night he'd spent tied to a tree. He remembered the look in the Kurakin captain's eye when they turned Pitt loose after letting the dog catch his scent. He remembered the cold terror they'd caused him and the brutality Kura was bringing to the Continent.

"Fire at will." Pitt didn't hide the anger behind his words.

The aide carried the message off and the cannons opened up on the uncovered Kurakin retreat.

It was a massacre.

Pitt's eyes returned to the town and the bridge in front of his position. There were still plenty of Kurakin fighting. Explosions and smoke still came from the eastern houses.

Movement caught Pitt's eye. High above the battle, he saw a flag waving.

"It's Lauriston," he said under his breath.

Pitt stared at the figure. He couldn't believe it. The marshal stood atop the spire in the center of town and waved a large Erlonian flag.

The marshal's army pushed forward through the square. They pursued the Kurakin west. The blue threads waving back and forth rallied them to pursue with vigor. But Lauriston was also signaling something else.

Pitt brought a hand up to call for an aide. His mind was still thinking on the order.

"Sir?" one of his aides said behind him.

"We must push forward." Pitt brought the hand down. He nodded his head as his mind confirmed the move.

"Sir?" A couple of other aides exchanged confused glances.

Pitt glanced again at the bridge and the town and the flag on top of the spire. The Kurakin on the banks of the river still pressed against the bridge, unaware of the fate of the battle behind them. Pitt needed to press back and complete the push against the enemy. They needed to push all the Kurakin back against Lauriston's army and crush them.

"All forward. Relieve the Third and move in the First and Fifth," Pitt said. "We'll push the Kurakin off the bridge and to the west."

The messengers ran down the lines with the orders and the army formed up. Pitt led the push himself. They stepped over the dead bodies of the fallen Brunians and pushed up against the Kurakin soldiers still fighting.

The Third, exhausted from the fighting on the bridge, filed back and let themselves be replaced. Even before Pitt fired his first round, the Kurakin were retreating off the bridge to join the rest of the army in a full flight away from the town.

Andrei

Andrei had been part of a defeat before. He'd felt the turn in the momentum of soldiers and the fear crashing through regiments like a cold wave onto a rocky coast.

Instinct for survival took over. Every Kurakin wanted to run for safety. No one, not even the mightiest warriors, wanted to keep fighting.

Andrei knew it was no use trying to rally. All was lost when the troops began moving off the bridge and the Brunian push came.

An open gap swelled behind them as other regiments pulled out of the city. The square was taken by the Erlonians. The Kurakin cannons faltered.

Andrei's army was done.

Even with the rearguard reinforcements, the army wouldn't hold together. Andrei didn't even need to order a retreat. The army ran on its own.

He went to his horse but found his command area deserted. Foot soldiers streamed past him towards the western road. His aides were gone. His horse had fled with the army, something his old wolverine never would've done.

Kurakin soldiers ran through the streets. Musket and cannon smoke pushed after them. Through the haze, Andrei could make out the shadows of the Erlonians coming for him.

Andrei ran.

He ducked off the main road and moved between the houses. He jumped a fence and ran straight into a surprised Erlonian soldier.

The pair tumbled to the ground. Andrei landed an elbow across the enemy's jaw and rolled away. By the time the Erlonian recovered, Andrei was on his feet and running for the next alley.

A yell went out. More Erlonians were on the next street over. Andrei heard the crack of a pistol and the snap of a ball hitting the side of the house as he dove across the street.

He found more of the enemy down the next alley.

It was hopeless.

The thought screamed in Andrei's mind, but he kept running. He made a turn into a house. An Erlonian uniform met him and gave him the butt of his musket.

Andrei flipped backwards and felt his head hit the ground before everything went black. The smoke and the explosions and the screams of the lost battle filled his head one last time before the darkness took him.

Lauriston

Lauriston came down from the spire and handed the flag back to the original carrier. From the top of the tower, he'd been able to see the full Kurakin retreat. The Brunian cannons raked them as they fled and allied cavalry chased enemies into the trees.

Lauriston moved across the square. The Kurakin were gone from the row of houses and their muskets were strewn across the cobblestones, thrown away in their haste to get away.

When the marshal reached the houses neighboring the bridge road, he was greeted with a column of Brunian soldiers.

Pitt marched at the head.

"Well held, General." Lauriston saluted Pitt with a smile.

"Brilliant attack, Marshal." Pitt saluted as well. "You have quite a sense of timing. Thank you."

The Brunian column spread out through the square. Some of the Brunian soldiers eyed the Erlonians cautiously.

"How was the bridge?" Lauriston shook Pitt's hand. This friendly gesture got even more confused looks from the aides around Pitt.

"Tight, but the men fought bravely. How was your side?"

"A near-run thing. Their cannons raked us harder than I wanted."

"I think we're paying that back in kind." Pitt turned to look towards the sounds of the Brunian cannons and the explosions throughout the Kurakin westward retreat.

"That you are." Lauriston listened to the beautiful sound of the artillery. He was thankful to be on this side of the battle and not engulfed in those volleys. "We'll round up prisoners and regroup. The eastern flank still has some fighting."

Pitt nodded. "My men will be fully across the bridge soon."

Lauriston took a deep breath and sighed. "Quite a day." He shook Pitt's hand before the Brunian walked back towards his men. "Quite a day."

"Yes," Pitt said as he left. "That it was, Marshal. That it was."

Elisa

Elisa didn't feel the fear anymore.

Not because the Kurakin were falling back in front of them. Not because the fight was already won.

It was because she was numb.

She couldn't even find her sadness and worry for Mon anymore. There was only the next row of houses to take. Only the fleeing Kurakin in the alley to attack and pursue.

She stopped firing at the enemy. She let them run. It didn't seem right to shoot someone in the back.

The rest of the Erlonian soldiers didn't have the same mindset.

After the last volley, Elisa hadn't even reloaded her pistols. She entered the next house with only her cutlass out and found it empty. The Erlonians ran farther down the street and Elisa was left behind. Through the far door of the building, she found an alley. She realized her mistake with her pistols only after it was too late.

One last Kurakin waited for her in the next house.

But this one lacked a beard.

Sensation returned to Elisa in time for her to feel a cool breeze blow eerily across her neck. It was the same feeling as when her guide appeared, but this figure in front of her was a Kurakin.

The filed teeth of his smile proved that.

The sounds of the far-off cannons receded. Gunshots were muffled from the adjacent houses. Fear gripped Elisa once again.

Movement came from the left. A different cool breeze passed from the other direction and Elisa's fear lessened.

Her guide stepped through a doorway. His face was stern and angry and terrifying. He stood between Elisa and the evil being. Sounds came back and the pops of muskets were clear again.

"Away with you." The guide's voice was deep and powerful.

"I only seek the mother." The evil god's smile had only faltered for a second when the guide appeared.

"I know what you seek."

"Our goal is the same." The evil god held his hands out wide.

"But the means are very different, *Chaos*." The guide shook his head.

Elisa had no idea what their words meant. Her heart hammered in her chest from how serious her guide was taking this Kurakin god. The enemy's smile was too confident. Elisa wanted to run, but her legs wouldn't move. They would only shake.

The evil god took a last look at Elisa before turning his back to leave. He stopped in the doorway for only a second, as if contemplating spinning back to attack. Instead, he stepped out into the alley and faded away like gun smoke.

Elisa fell to her knees and wanted to cry. The guide turned and smiled at her.

"You'll be okay, Princess. You fought well, you're safe now." The guide faded away too as Erlonian soldiers came through the house and into the alley.

They pulled Elisa to her feet and sent her back towards the rear lines.

The battle was over.

Elisa was finished with fighting. She retraced the path they'd made through the houses and trudged to the wall where Mon had been shot.

The memories came back to her in waves. She remembered him falling. Lodi crouched over his chest.

The images overwhelmed Elisa and she ran the final few steps and hurdled over the wall.

She found two figures alone on the ground. One with his head on the other's chest.

The sounds around Elisa went away again, as if the evil Kurakin god was back in front of her. She stumbled and collapsed next to Lodi.

Mon's eyes were closed. His face looked peaceful. His undershirt soaked pink. The dirt around his torso dark and muddy.

"I'm sorry." Lodi's voice was broken.

Elisa wasn't sure if the words were directed at her or Mon's body, but it didn't matter.

Elisa was sorry too. She was sad. She was exhausted. And she couldn't muster tears for her friend and protector.

The sounds of the end of the battle came back to her ears. They were far off now. Elisa wanted to collapse into the dirt and let it all fade away. She wanted to turn back time somehow and protect Mon. To somehow stop the musket balls from striking him.

But she was powerless. The Erlonians were victors. The battle was won and Elisa still felt like she'd lost everything.

Chapter 30

Lannes believed that even in victory, a general should feel loss.

Tome of the Emperor
Nelson Wellesley

Elisa

Elisa walked through the battle's aftermath as if in a dream. She worked with the soldiers and helped organized things. She did as she was told and tried not to think on the memories of the battle.

The full Brunian army marched over the bridge and into the southern forest hills during the evening after the battle. Artillery was placed in defensive positions throughout the town and the surrounding fields.

The Kurakin reinforcements didn't attack. The enemy army was broken and needed to regroup.

The victors sent out scouts and pressed the advantage they'd won in the town. Houses were turned into headquarters and the alliance between Brun and Erlon continued, with the common soldiers still overly cautious about working so close to their former enemies.

Regiments were reformed and men were accounted for and losses tallied. Multiple medical areas were established and served both sides of the new alliance together.

Soldiers helped bury the dead. The cleanup continued through the evening of the following day. Work was stopped as night fell.

The army finally paused and allowed a time of reflection. The Erlonians gathered and held the vigil for the lost and gave General Montholon the soldier's farewell that he deserved.

Lodi came and got Elisa from her tent in the center of camp. "Come, Princess," he said.

Elisa had worked all day with the soldiers. Her body ached, but she barely felt it. The monotony of battle cleanup helped keep her feelings contained deep within her.

"Grief is good after a fight such as this." Lodi helped her to her feet. "We must pay our respects to the fallen. The Ascended One is already greeting Mon with open arms."

The funeral pyre was set up in a clearing to the east of the battlefield. There were three platforms. Mon lay on the highest of them in the middle. Two other soldiers deemed to have died bravely were included on either side. One Brunian. One Lakmian.

The entire Erlonian and Brunian armies had gathered in the clearing. They cleared a path for Lodi and Elisa to get to the front.

As she approached the center of the gathering, Elisa heard the cries of "Onward!" from the Erlonians. They were weaker than normal, given the setting, but they rang out nonetheless. A determination and pride shone through in the cheers.

Lauriston and the others already stood at the front by the pyre. Quatre put a hand on Elisa's shoulder, but no other words were spoken until Lauriston addressed the crowd.

"These men died bravely, defending our country and its alliances. They died defending the Continent." He swept a hand behind him to indicate the pyre. "This fire is to honor them, to send off their mortal remains on the wind. May they be carried to the Ascended One's feet, as a memory of their sacrifice and bravery on this ground."

The fire was lit and the platforms burned quickly. The flames climbed up the wood to the bodies. Elisa had to take a step back from the heat.

She watched Mon's body disappear in the orange and red and her vision went dark from the brightness of it all. Sparks were flung up into the starry sky.

Quatre produced a bottle of wine and passed it down the line. Every one of the officers drank, even Marshal Lauriston. Elisa took a pull and found the liquid burned her throat on the way down, just as it had when she'd stolen a sip on Mon's farm so long ago.

The sting reminded her of the old general. She saw him sitting on his horse, swaying back and forth and holding a bottle by the neck. She saw him sitting by the fire in the dark in the deep forest, telling stories of old battles.

It made her smile and she took another swig before passing the wine back down the line of officers.

The group stayed by the fire for a long time. The other soldiers filtered out after the ritual and went back to the camp. Elisa's group stood and stared at the flames as the platforms were reduced to a pile of smoldering wood.

No one said anything. The wine was finished. The stars came out fully in the cloudless sky and the smoke of the dying fire was carried off towards the north.

"So long, Mon," Lauriston said after a long time.

Quatre nodded from beside Elisa. She wiped a tear from her cheek. The group turned away from the pyre and walked back to the tents.

Lauriston walked with Elisa to her tent. "How are you feeling?" His voice sounded strained from overuse and fatigue.

"Fine."

That was all Elisa could think to say.

"Fine is okay. Battle is a hard thing, even for someone much older than you." Lauriston's face was hidden by shadows, so she couldn't see the expression behind his words.

"I'll be fine, Lar." They passed by a fire among the tents and Elisa knew the flames cast light on the tears staining her cheeks.

"I know you will be. If you had only one part of Lannes in you, you'd be more than fine. And we both know you've got plenty of the emperor in your blood."

The comment made Elisa smile. It felt strange. Her mouth was out of practice with the expression. But it felt right in the moment.

They reached her tent and she sat down on a log just outside the door flap. Lauriston knelt down as well.

"There's more to come." Lauriston looked her in the eye. She could see his face in the low light now. There was a determined set to his mouth and his eyes were steady. "This war is far from over."

Elisa knew what Lauriston was asking her.

Did she want to leave the army? Go to the safety of Vendome in the north behind the new front? Leave her friends? Her protectors?

Elisa hadn't thought about her next steps, but she wasn't shocked by the answer she gave.

"I know," Elisa said in a confident tone. She knew Lauriston would understand the full answer.

She wouldn't leave the army. Not yet. Not with a fight still in front of them and Mon's memory to honor. Not with Erlon still in danger.

Lauriston's eyes searched hers. He nodded.

"Sleep soundly, Elisa."

"You too, Lar."

Lauriston stood and left her and Elisa spent a few moments looking up at the stars. The night grew cold around her and she pulled her jacket in close against the chill. She looked off to the northern horizon one last time.

"Goodbye, Mon," she said and turned in for a long night's rest.

Leberecht

The roasting pigs smelled sweet to Leberecht as he approached the pits. He walked with long strides and head held high. The confidence of leading a victorious army made him feel both taller and stronger.

Citiva lay across the field before the main army. The sun shone brightly on the houses and walls and gleamed off the windows of the palace spires atop the great plateau.

"The wind is out of the north today," one of the chefs said without looking up when Leberecht arrived at the cooking pit.

Three large pigs hung on a spit over the fire. They were split open and spread wide for the heat to slowly lick at the meat that would make an incredible meal.

Leberecht felt the wind pick up and he followed its direction with his eyes. "Right towards our foe."

He saw the northern gate of Citiva. The main entrance to the city. Beyond were the wealthiest homes in the realm. And further beyond was the stone of the plateau shooting upward from the city's center.

"They won't be out of food yet, but we can at least let them know our soldiers are having a feast."

Leberecht smiled along with the chef. The man was smart and clearly had the same sense of justice as Leberecht.

An idea struck Leberecht when looking at the chef's smile.

"Let's dig more pits."

The chef looked at him with one eyebrow raised. "You want to cook more hogs?"

"Potentially. But let's dig the pits around each gate." Leberecht pointed southeast around the curve of the city's wall. "If the wind shifts, we'll want our cooking to be upwind from our friends inside the walls."

The chef's smile grew again and he nodded. "Yes, sir. I'll pass along the plan to the engineers."

"Thank you."

Leberecht left the pit. His stomach was beginning to growl from the smell and there was still a long time until dinner.

He hoped the royals atop the plateau were having the same reaction. He hoped they were stuck eating a bland meal tonight because of siege rations.

Leberecht's cheeks had grown stronger and no longer cramped from his smiling. It was almost his permanent expression now. And he felt he had an entire winter siege's worth of smiling still to go.

There was so much joy to be had in the army.

Winter was approaching. There was a long time to wait until they took the city walls, but this was still enjoyable.

The camp was happy around him. The Continent was in a good place. General Duroc would take the western half of the Continent. The east belonged to Leberecht and this army. The Coalition had crumbled and the Wahrian royals would soon fall.

Their king was defeated and in despair. The queen sat trapped and under siege in the capital.

Everything was right on the Continent.

His long and patient waiting was almost over. He'd sat through the summit and toyed with the royals and then struck when they were most vulnerable.

Leberecht smiled and looked at the spires of the palace up on the plateau once again. He felt like laughing out loud. A farmer's boy from Grose now held power over the mighty queen of Wahring.

King Charles was dead. The prince, now king himself, was defeated. And next to fall would be the glorious palace plateau and then the people of this country would belong to Leberecht. He could shape the government and policies of the Continent to his will. He would finally have the power he'd long sought and the remaining monarchies of the Continent would fall to his power one by one.

Leberecht turned back to look at the cooking area and the fire pit under the hogs. The wind picked up and carried the dark smoke towards the city. Wafting smells to the enemy over the northern gate.

Leberecht looked up at the sky and smiled and thanked the Ascended One for glorious and sweet victory. He'd have all winter to savor the siege. Leberecht knew he would enjoy every minute.

Pitt

Pitt left his headquarters tent and walked to the outskirts of the Brunian camp. Screams and coughs still came from the medical areas on the edge of the clearing. Mist hung between the trees of the forest beyond.

Pitt walked around a medical tent and followed a path into the woods. He needed to move his legs and clear his head.

He reached the Erlonian camp in the adjacent field and found more tents in organized rows. Pitt followed a path straight to Lauriston's command tent.

"Pitt, come in," the Erlonian marshal said when Pitt poked his head in the door flap.

"Marshal Lauriston." Pitt stepped inside. Lauriston sat behind his writing desk. "How's the army?"

"Fine. Resting now, but getting restless." Lauriston set his pen down.

"And how's the princess?"

"She's holding up. She'll be okay. How's your side?"

"Good, same as yours. Still waiting on word from our other generals throughout the north. I'm ready to move whenever, though."

"Good."

Pitt looked around the tent and his eyes stopped on a table by the door. It held various bottles of wine and liquor.

"Don't tell me you're drinking now?" Pitt walked towards the booze.

"No, no. That's for the men." Lauriston shook his head with a smile. He stood up and walked over to the table to join Pitt. "They found some of the Kurakin liquor after the battle. This was combined with the stash we had for Mon, but there wasn't a good way to split it up. The compromise was for me to hold it and the generals drink it during meetings."

"Fair enough." Pitt picked up one of the clear Kurakin bottles. He'd never had southern liquor before.

"Made from potatoes, apparently." Lauriston examined the contents of another bottle.

Pitt took the stopper off his own and smelled the liquid. It singed his nostrils.

"Supposed to be strong." Lauriston gave him a warning look.

Pitt shrugged and took a swig and regretted it immediately.

Lauriston laughed as Pitt coughed and sputtered. The drink burned his throat the whole way down.

"I've been told it's pretty terrible." Lauriston took the bottle from Pitt and replaced the stopper.

"It is. You're not missing anything." Pitt coughed again and picked out some wine to wash the sting from his mouth.

The two friends laughed and Lauriston motioned for Pitt to follow him over to the campaign map on the far side of the tent.

"We'll press Duroc's flank." Lauriston ran a finger along the path of the Branch River west to the Broadwater. "They'll be pushing somewhere north on the western bank but will fall back when they get news of our victory here."

"And then we press our advantage." Pitt nodded.

"Hopefully. But I fear winter will stop any plans soon."

"True." Pitt hadn't thought about how late it already was in the campaign season.

"There may not even be another battle this season." Lauriston pulled his arm back from the map and paced a slow lap around the table. "Actually, that's what I would predict. Duroc will fall back and choose to wait out winter and resupply his army. He's been aggressive getting this far north. He'll need to regroup."

Pitt looked at the center of Erlon and the position of their army currently. "I wish we could move faster."

"If we had more men, we would." Lauriston completed his lap and stopped on the other side from Pitt. "But the winter will give us time to coordinate with the other parts of the army. If we can get the Erlonian prisoners free from Vendome, that adds men."

Pitt nodded along with the marshal's points. It was a large campaign and was only going to get larger next spring. Their focus now should be coordinating with the Brunian armies spread across northern Erlon and what was left of the Wahrians.

This new alliance would be tricky to coordinate, but Pitt trusted Lauriston to be able to handle it. They just had to make sure the Brunians cooperated properly.

The marshal crossed his arms and continued. "For now, we press west and use our advantage gained here. We'll see how Duroc reacts and fight from there."

"Agreed." Pitt nodded.

There was more conversation on the coming campaign, mainly mundane specifics on supply and order of march. They discussed some of the news from the western Brunian armies and how they'd fared against the Kurakin on the coast.

Pitt poured himself another cup of the wine and was surprised to see Lauriston take one for himself this time. It was a small pour, but still more than what he'd seen the marshal drink before.

"For Mon." Lauriston held up his cup.

"For Mon." Pitt raised his cup too before taking a drink. The liquid was sweet and smooth and warmed Pitt's chest. It made him think on the journey through the forest and the short time he'd known General Montholon.

They finished their cups and talked of their memories from their long trek north and the recent battle. Mon was mentioned with smiles of fondness and the stories were all happy.

Pitt would've stayed and talked through the entire night if both men didn't need their rest for the coming march.

"Thank you, Marshal," Pitt said as he was leaving.

"Thank you, General." Lauriston set his empty cup on a table and saw Pitt to the door.

"No, I mean it." Pitt gave a slight bow towards Lauriston. "Thank you for everything."

Pitt saluted the marshal and Lauriston returned it and they shook hands.

"I think we've got this alliance off to a good start," Lauriston said.

"I agree, Marshal. I agree."

Pitt left the tent and walked back through the Erlonian camp. There was hope in the army on both sides of the alliance now. They had a long way to go in this war, but they'd won a battle and turned back the Kurakin aggression. There was plenty of confidence to go around.

Nelson

The stairs creaked under Nelson's boots as he walked up to the main deck. He wore his naval dress uniform, the royal red riding jacket with crisp white pants and brown boots. The salt air hit his face as he reached the ship's deck and he inhaled the sweet air of his home.

Brun.

The island stood off the starboard and the sailors worked to anchor the ship and prepared for going ashore. The water was calm and a bright blue below the open sky and afternoon sun.

Emperor Lannes stood facing the island as the crew moved around him. Nelson nodded to the men and smiled and thanked and encouraged them as he walked towards the emperor.

Lannes had nearly broken his empire trying to conquer Nelson's island. He'd fought Nelson's father for a decade and come close to successfully invading the island numerous times. The Battle of Three Bridges had been the last and most deadly attempt.

Nelson and Brun were lucky the Erlonians had failed. They were lucky to have Thirona and her sorcery on their side. The world would be in a different position right now if not for that great battle.

"Great sight, isn't it." Nelson stepped up next to Lannes.

The emperor didn't turn but stayed staring off at the island's shore. "It is. It's a beautiful home."

Nelson nodded. "We'll go ashore immediately."

The sailors were scrambling about below them as the ship's main tender was lowered down towards the water.

"I wish I were visiting under different circumstances," Lannes said.

Nelson looked at the emperor and found him smiling the kind of smile a man uses when lost in a deep memory. It surprised the king to see genuine sorrow and regret behind his eyes.

"Me too, Lannes. Me too." Nelson looked back out over the bay of Trafal and the green forests of his home rising up in hills behind the port on the horizon.

The pair boarded the main tender and were rowed to shore. The crew worked and the sea was calm and quiet, but Lannes and Nelson didn't talk anymore during the trip. Nelson's mind had time to wander and he pondered the most recent news from the Continent.

Wahring was in trouble. Their army had been defeated in multiple battles in the west near their border with Vith. Now Citiva was under siege from the Kurakin and Moradan armies.

News from farther west was more promising. Duroc and the Kurakin were pushing up through the western states of Erlon now but had been slowed in the center at the Branch. News was slowly coming in of a defense of the crossings of the Branch that would keep the Kurakin out of the north at least through winter.

There was no official word from Lauriston or the Erlonians yet, but Lannes was adamant in his belief that the marshal had helped with the defense of the north. Either way, Nelson now slept a little easier knowing the western portion of the war wasn't going to collapse altogether.

At least they would last until spring, it looked like.

The tender was rowed into the port and a royal honor guard awaited them on the dock. Twelve muskets were fired in unison to announce the king's arrival. The smoke blew across the water into their faces.

"Why twelve muskets, again?" Lannes turned to look at Nelson behind him in the stern of the boat.

"Twelve provinces of Brun."

Lannes's eyes flashed with recognition and he nodded his head.

The boat was tied to the dock and the rowers and other sailors stayed seated to allow Nelson to disembark first. The king stepped off onto the solid planks of the pier and turned as Lannes made to do the same.

The former emperor stood and looked across the small space of water at the king. "You sure you want your greatest enemy back on the Continent?" Lannes smiled behind his words.

Nelson's thoughts froze for a second. Every doubt and question he'd been dwelling on for months came back all at once. Was setting Lannes free the right move? Or was it just another step towards the destruction of his island and people?

Nelson pushed the doubts away. He would stick to his plan. There was no going back now.

Nelson matched Lannes's smile and offered a hand to help the emperor over to the dock. "You're not on the Continent. You're on Brun, *my* island."

The former Emperor of Erlon took the king's hand and stepped across onto the dock.

"I guess that's right." Lannes took in the port around them.

Another twelve muskets fired off to complete the arrival ceremony and the pair of leaders walked down the dock. Lannes stepped on Brunian soil for the first time. A guard led them to a red carriage adorned with patterns of gold around the frame.

Nelson stepped in first and Lannes came behind. The carriage started moving immediately.

Lannes sat facing Nelson. "Hopefully we'll have more news from the fronts waiting for you at the palace," he said.

Nelson nodded.

"How long of a ride?"

"About an hour." Nelson watched the port recede away and the neighboring town whisked by the carriage window.

Lannes leaned forward and Nelson recognized the now familiar focus behind the emperor's eyes. "Then we have time to start planning."

Nelson turned and raised his eyebrows at Lannes.

The emperor grinned with only the right side of his mouth and an excitement glinted behind his eyes. "Let's get to work planning the next campaigns for our armies. Let's get to work on winning the Continent's next great war."

Elisa

Elisa walked alone in the woods on the outskirts of the Erlonian camp. She felt fine. She was rested and recovered from the battle.

She still saw glimpses of Mon among the army, laughing and talking with his soldiers. The flashes only highlighted his absence more. They only made things infinitely worse inside of Elisa and kept her from moving on.

She walked now to get away from the army. She'd helped with the wounded and to bury the dead and repair parts of the town destroyed by the fighting. She'd set up tents in the camp and served meals and cleaned pots and pans. The continuous work kept her mind off the losses of the battle and the many fights still to come.

But when the work ended or the men wouldn't allow their princess to help them anymore, she had to find other things to occupy her mind.

She could only clean her pistols and sharpen her cutlass so much.

Elisa's hand dropped and touched the silver engraving of her weapons. Thoughts on her father and mother came to her. Happy memories appeared from the time before the empire's fall.

Elisa was a small girl running and squealing through the hedge maze on the upper terrace of the palace back in Plancenoit. Her father growled like a bear and ran after her as her mother laughed and looked on. All three had big smiles on their faces and the sun above them was bright and happy too.

Elisa kept walking and tried to focus on these positive thoughts and images. She rounded a large oak tree and climbed over a boulder protruding from the ground and continued along a deer path until she ran into a now familiar face.

"Good morning, Princess," the guide said.

Elisa had expected the vision might appear if she wandered off alone.

"Good morning." She stopped on the trail a few feet in front of the guide. "Thank you for protecting me during the fight."

The memories of her mother's laughing face faded away. They were replaced by the image of the evil Kurakin god staring her down in the house at the end of the battle a few days before.

The guide waved off her thanks. "It was nothing, you weren't in any danger. Although I was surprised he appeared to you in the middle of all that."

The memories and sadness from Mon had outweighed the questions surrounding the Kurakin god's appearance during the fight. But now Elisa started to sift through those questions some more.

"Who was he?" she said. "He was like you but Kurakin."

"He is like me, you're correct there." The guide shifted his weight and leaned a shoulder against an elm tree. The forest was quiet all around them. "We're still very different, but he's like a relative of sorts."

"Like your brother?" Elisa stayed standing in the middle of the path.

"More like a cousin."

The guide didn't say anything more. Elisa thought through the encounter at the very end of the battle and the largest question jumped to the front of her mind.

"He said he sought my mother. What does he want with her?"

"Ah, that is a good question." The vision stood straight from the tree and motioned for Elisa to follow him as he turned up the path in front of them. "He is guiding General Duroc, similar to how I'm guiding you."

"You mean how you just told me to run north and had me figure the rest out on my own?" Elisa walked slightly behind the guide as they made their way through the trees.

"Exactly."

The guide didn't appear to understand the sarcasm behind Elisa's words.

"This new war," the guide continued. He paused after the first words and seemed to weigh what to say next. "There are a lot of moving pieces on the Continent right now. Lots of forces at work that haven't been active in a long time."

The guide paused again and Elisa allowed the silence to sit between them as they walked along the edge of the forest. The distant sounds of soldiers chopping firewood in the camp drifted over their heads.

"You don't know where your mother has gone, right?" the guide said eventually.

"No."

Until the recent memory from her childhood in the palace, Elisa hadn't thought much on her mother at all. She used to dwell on her absence while on Mon's farm, but the flight north had pushed those thoughts from her mind for the last few weeks.

"Did you ever wonder about her? What she's doing?"

"Yes. Of course. But it wasn't the happiest subject to think of. Especially with my father..."

Elisa's voice trailed off. She didn't need these thoughts right now. It was sad enough dealing with the loss of Mon. She didn't need to be reminded that her mother had abandoned the empire and her father was in exile.

The guide ducked under a low branch and then sat on a log at the side of the trail. Elisa stayed standing and crossed her arms across her chest.

"That Kurakin you saw is looking for Epona because he believes she's is searching out something," the guide said. He looked up at Elisa. "A long-dormant power. He believes it'll change the war. It'll change the whole Continent."

Elisa wasn't sure what to make of the information. It was vague and ominous, like most things the guide told her.

"Do you know where she is then? Or how to find her?" Elisa shifted her weight and stared back at the guide. Of course she wanted to see her mother again, but that didn't do much to dampen the feelings of betrayal that still boiled within her.

"No."

That was all that was offered. Elisa felt like she was back on Mon's farm and the guide was telling her only part of the story again.

"Maybe she's gone for good." Elisa couldn't keep the bite out of the words. "Maybe that Kurakin god is searching for nothing."

"I doubt that," the guide said with a thin smile. "But the important thing right now is that you're safe and with the army."

"Why do I matter?" Elisa's said the words loudly and they echoed through the trees beyond their trail.

The guide was talking in circles. Half the time Elisa wished he wouldn't appear at all and just leave her in peace.

"You lead Erlon. It's important to keep the alliance against the Kurakin strong. It's important to keep the Continent alive."

The guide stood up and a breeze passed along Elisa's neck. Their conversation was almost over. The guide was already beginning to fade away. He still wasn't telling her everything.

"So I'm to just keep fighting then?" Elisa said. She didn't expect to get much more information.

"And leading." The guide nodded and smiled at her. "I'll be in touch over the winter. Stay with the army and help to lead. Things will change in this war yet. But for now, the key is to keep fighting."

The breeze picked up and the last outline of the guide shifted and blew away. Elisa was left alone in the forest with more questions than answers running through her head again.

* * *

That night, Elisa dreamed about her mother. In the morning, she couldn't remember the details, but her mind didn't dwell on it. There was too much distraction in the real world, as the day had finally come for the army to break camp and march.

She hoisted herself up on her horse at the front of the army. Quatre sat beside her. Lauriston and Lodi rode in front of her.

The sun was just poking its head out over the forest in the east and the southwestern horizon was open in front of them.

It was finally time to move again. The guide and his vague instructions and her swirling thoughts on her family and the problems on the Continent would soon fade away. The action of the march would keep Elisa focused on the tasks at hand.

Lauriston and the other generals had told her the campaign plan. Elisa knew where they were heading, but she didn't know what would happen through winter and beyond.

That was fine with her. She was with her friends and protectors and the great Erlonian army. It didn't matter who the foe was. They could be gods or men or Kurakin. She would fight on with the soldiers around her.

Elisa looked behind her as they started marching. The Erlonian soldiers had cleaned their uniforms and stood in neat and organized rows. The tents were packed and the camp cleared. Feet kicked up dust and they set off on the next portion of the campaign.

There was hope in all of them after the victory at Neuse. There was a buzz of energy over the whole army and Elisa felt that she may be the most hopeful of them all.

"This is the way to march," Quatre said from beside her. "Much better than sneaking through a forest."

"Seems like it." Elisa returned Quatre's smile.

"I'll take the men at our back against anyone."

"I agree." Elisa looked behind her and made eye contact with a guardsman in the front rank. He raised his musket in a salute. Elisa gave a wave back.

"Onward, Emperor!"

It was a single voice that rang out over the march. One soldier called out and started it all.

More cheers drifted forward from farther back in the ranks. Elisa waved again at all the men and more chants started. They were soon roaring up in waves from the marching soldiers.

"Onward, Emperor!"

"Onward!"

"Onward, Princess!"

"Onward, Erlon!"

The roars wouldn't stop.

"Boy, do I enjoy hearing that again." Lauriston turned around in his saddle and smiled at Elisa.

Elisa enjoyed it too. It took her back to Plancenoit and the parades of soldiers that her father would observe on the palace grounds before a campaign. She remembered the adoration of the people during his Ascension Day speeches. There'd been hope and happiness everywhere. The memories made her smile as the roars kept coming from the Erlonian soldiers.

They were marching off to war and death. But this would be a war on equal footing. Erlon had hope again.

Whatever games her guide and the Kurakin god and her sorceress mother were playing didn't matter. The only important things were Elisa's friends around her.

"Onward, Emperor! Onward!"

Elisa smiled wide enough to make her cheeks hurt. The Kurakin Horde had pushed too far north. Now they would pay the price for sacking Erlonian cities. They would have to face an army of allies that would only grow stronger.

"Onward, Erlon!"

Elisa would fight the Horde, as would every man who cheered behind her. The spirit of the emperor was back once again.

And Erlon's enemies didn't stand a chance.

Onward.

Epilogue

The sorceress's footprints stretched behind her across the sand of the desert. No relief from the heat came from the wind as it kicked up waves of biting specks into her face.

Dunes rose on the path in front of her. The top of the great basilica was visible beyond them.

"Not much farther to walk," Epona told herself. The city would be just over a few more of the dunes. Her long journey north was almost over.

Epona wrapped her headscarf tighter around her face and forced her legs to move up the next giant dune.

"Almost there," she said to herself. "Almost there."

The peak came quickly and she started down the other side. She didn't stop and stare at the view of the ruined city in front of her.

Momentum carried her down the hill and she reached level ground and found a path between the last dunes to the entrance of the city. There were no streets visible and all the structures were half buried. Some structures were completely consumed by the drifts of sand.

The stone edges of meeting halls and cathedrals and military barracks were worn away and rounded. Toppled columns and collapsed roofs jutted out of the mounds and the windswept sand up and down the streets.

The great city was empty. It was only her and the sand and the howling wind.

She'd had a small hope that the place would be different. That someone else would've come back to where things ended. Or that the Ascended One would still be sitting atop the basilica waiting to greet her.

"No, you're far away somewhere," she said as she walked past the collapsed facade of a tiny house in the middle of an open square. "You're not here."

Maybe she'd been wrong to make this journey. To leave everything behind. To abandon those she loved to call on a god.

But there was a higher purpose. She had to keep reminding herself that. She left to protect her family. To protect everyone on the Continent.

Epona moved across the square. She passed toppled statues and mounds of broken brick. Collapsed structures lined the main street until she reached the city center and the great basilica of the Ascended One towered above her.

There was no wear on this building. The columns still stood strong. The corners of the facade were still pointed and crisp and the engravings as clear as if they'd been carved yesterday. The basilica's front doors stood open.

Sand covered the steps up completely and she crawled up the slope and passed through the giant opening.

At first glance she thought the Ascended One was on his throne waiting for her.

Her eyes adjusted to the light and saw it was only a statue in place of the old throne. With a closer look, Epona saw the figure was larger than life. The depth of the room and the height of the throne platform skewed the normal aspects of proportion.

She walked across the open throne room and knelt down at the foot of the platform steps.

The figure was reclined in his throne with both hands gripping the armrests. The god's face showed no emotion and he had short, curly hair and no crown atop his head. He was adorned in a simple cloth toga instead of armor.

Epona looked into the god's marble eyes. They were the same color as the rest of the face. There was no power behind this statue. It was only decoration.

"No matter," she said as she got up and looked around her. There was a doorway to the right of the statue platform.

She moved towards it and found a dark stairwell. She conjured a flame in front of her and started her ascent.

The stairs went on forever. They curved around the outer wall of the basilica's dome. The curve got smaller and smaller until she reached a stone door at the very top.

Epona pushed it with her mind but it wouldn't budge. She tried again with more force but found the same result. She looked down at the door handle. A golden ring.

She grabbed it and turned, and the door snapped free and swung outward.

"Strange," Epona said.

Sunlight poured into the stairwell. She extinguished her flame and stepped into the open air that overlooked the broken and buried city below.

There was another statue here. This one smaller and made of black marble. It was the Ascended One again in full battle dress. His shield was down at his side and his sword was up and pointed towards the north.

Epona followed the direction of the blade but could only see the desert and the sea beyond stretching to the horizon. She walked around the statue without touching it.

"Yes." She nodded to herself. "This is it."

She found an engraving on the floor. The symbol of the Ascended One's Holy Guard. A round shield with two lines crossed across the middle.

She knelt and touched it and was about to pray when the noises came.

The wind shifted with a howl. The basilica shuddered.

Epona jumped up and steadied herself on a column, but the shaking was over just as quickly as it began.

The wind continued to howl.

She watched the gusts change direction and begin to whip in from the south and throw sand off the towering dunes. The sea in the distance turned to whitecaps and swirls of sand began to be carried down the streets of the ruined city.

The prevailing winds pointed north. The dunes all sloped to the north. But now the balance of the desert and the sea beyond were changed. The top of the sea churned up for as far as she could see.

Epona felt something else. It was on the wind and moved through the stones of the ancient basilica. It was an unmistakable power. She looked out over the ocean to the horizon in the north and smiled.

He was coming.

Book Two: GODS OF GUNPOWDER

Available Now!

Continue the fight against the Kurakin Horde with book two in the series, available now:

Amazon US - https://www.amazon.com/dp/B084NV6CD3

Amazon UK - https://www.amazon.co.uk/dp/B084NV6CD3

War Rages Onward.

Erlon won an epic victory at the Battle of Neuse and turned the tide of the war for the falling empire. But as winter gives way to spring, the fierce Kurakin Horde marches once again. Elisa Lannes is thrust into the heart of another sprawling campaign with Marshal Lauriston and the last Erlonian generals fighting at her side. She steps bravely into the next battle, but unknown powers and devious enemies scheme against her and Erlon's brave soldiers.

General Duroc and the Horde army approaches. The allies are ready. But will old conflicts and ancient evils prove too strong to overcome as the Continent's last great war explodes into chaos?

Pick up book two and continue the story HERE -

https://www.amazon.com/dp/B084NV6CD3

About the Author

Robert is a writer of fantasy stories who lives in Charlotte, North Carolina with his wife and their Staffordshire Terrier puppy. He grew up in Raleigh, North Carolina before attending UNC-Chapel Hill to study Economics and Creative Writing.

Robert has always been drawn to fantasy authors and the worlds they create—from Harry Potter and Middle Earth as a child to discovering Westeros as a teenager. He has since fallen in love with the worlds of Sanderson, Erikson, and Sapkowski (as well as many more).

Robert's enjoyment of real-life military history has combined with his enthusiasm for creating fantasy worlds in the *Falling Empires Saga*.

When not reading and writing fantasy, Robert enjoys cheering on his beloved Tar Heel and Carolina Panthers teams, exploring the exquisite North Carolina craft beer scene, and feasting on his wife's fine southern cooking.

To get in touch with Robert, please visit his website and join his reader community!

roberthfleming.com

THE FALL OF ERLON